BOOK OF THE ANOINTED

SAGA OF THE SONS

J. MOON

(Seventh Sense Publishing LLC)

J. MOON

Book of the Anointed by J. Moon Published by Seventh Sense publishing LLC

© 2018 Seventh Sense Publishing LLC

All rights reserved. No portion of this book may be reproduced in any form without permission from the publisher, except as permitted by U.S. copyright law. For permissions contact: jmoonwrites@gmail.com

This is a work of fiction. Names, characters, businesses, places, events, locales, and incidents are either the products of the author's imagination or used in a fictitious manner. Any resemblance to actual persons, living or dead, or actual events is purely coincidental.

Designed By: Jeremy Dixon

Cover by Jake Clark

WARNING TO THE READER

Warning to the readers of this story. The magic, miracles, and mystery hidden within this book is real. Please read with caution for the pages sizzle like catfish hitting a cast iron skillet. The words crackle like fireworks on a midsummer's night. And the characters are prone to live long in your mind. Book of the Anointed will seize you, haunt you, and keep you thrilled until the last page. Dark terrors roam within this tome. And the monsters themselves were born out of nightmares. But do not be afraid, for the magic in this book is the essence of light. A light that can be used to combat the harsh darkness we face in the world every day.

Continue at your own discretion. You have been warned.

J. MOON

For the boy who waited,

CHAPTER ONE

Boy Meets Evil

Jaden stood on the porch, with as much fear as looking over the edge of a five-hundred-foot drop. Uncertainty choked him like hands cold as marble as he wondered what he was doing in this upper-class neighborhood. It was all strange to him. The day started with a trip to the mall and then he heard a voice, speaking into his head, as clear as day. The first words of the voice came as a whisper, delicate as a gentle breeze, but powerful as rolling thunder.

"So is this the house?" Jaden asked aloud.

Yes, the ominous voice answered in his head.

Jaden looked upward. "What do you want me to do?"

Save the child

Jaden smirked at himself, laughter begged to escape from his lips. At first, he didn't want to believe, but the voice knew many things, intimate things, things he would never tell his closest friends, well.... if he had any friends.

You still don't believe, the voice continued. Its timbre rolling around like a leaf caught in the breeze.

"It's pretty hard to believe," he replied.

I have already made miracles to show you my magnificence.

Jaden nodded in agreement. "I'll give you that, driving sixty miles on an empty tank of gas that is a miracle. But I can–"

Do we need to talk about how you're sixteen, and you still need a night light?

"Hey c'mon, I use it dispense essential oils. If you are so powerful and all knowing, then why are you trying to diss me?"

I'm not dissing you, that's something only your mind can conceive. You're stalling because you are afraid. The words echo in his head as if he was thinking them himself, but he wasn't.

The voice knew about Marquis the boy who had bullied him all throughout middle school. It knew about the time he stole from that convenience store in Compton with his cousin Day-Day. It knew he was afraid of the dark. And it knew he could hear the secret thoughts of others. An ability his grandfather called gleaning.

Jaden's breath froze in his chest. He raked his gaze around the neighborhood while the California sun casts a blood orange color across the sky. Nothing about the house seemed special to Jaden. It was in a suburban neighborhood, modern architecture, perfectly trimmed green lawns, and blooming flowers teeming in every yard. Kids played just across the street where he parked his dented black Mustang, and there were a handful of neighbors jogging around the corner.

Normal.

So many questions poured into him like water. Why this neighborhood? Why this house? And why him?

"I am," he admitted.

Do not be afraid. I am the Creator. You are my Anointed, and I have called your name. You should be happy because I will use you to do a new thing. Now save the child.

Then there was silence in his head like a radio turned off.

Jaden looked up. "Hello?" he beckoned to which there was no answer. "So you're just going to leave me like that huh?"

There he stood at the door, scared out of his mind, but still curious. With a deep sigh, he raised his hand to knock, but the door inched open by itself.

"Hello?" he called. He waited a moment for an answer but no one spoke up. "Would anyone like to buy a box of chocolates?"

Silence strangled the opening and curiosity drew him in further.

"Did you know you left your door open? I can just close it for you," He said out loud.

Then the thought crossed his mind that he was a young black male in a suburban neighborhood. An easy way for him to get locked up for breaking and entering, he had two cousins in Compton who got locked up for the same thing, but they actually were trying to break into the house.

"Hello," Jaden repeated as he opened the door further.

As much as he was afraid, he still walked in. A cold sweat coated his palms, and he trembled with every step.

Jaden took only two steps into the house before his legs flew up into the air and his back came crashing to the floor. He fell with a hard thump, and the pain was like a whole house fell on top of him. Jaden moved his legs to get up, but they merely slid across the floor. A dense liquid drenched his back. He sat in a warm puddle. A metallic smell went into his nose, and he tasted it at the back of his throat. Jaden peered down at his hands and once he saw the red, he shouted in horror.

Jaden looked to his left and saw the body. He screamed again, and it was so sudden that it felt like something jumped out of him. An old lady slit from ear to ear and pinned to the wall like she was hanging from a cross. Sour liquid rushed from the back of his mouth and made Jaden rolled over to his knees. A foul smell assaulted his nose, a stench so foul he couldn't recognize it. He thought for sure it was the blood and that made the metallic taste in his mouth, then he also figured it could be the decay of the body. But between the two, there was also a strong smell of rotten eggs, and he couldn't make sense of why that smell would be present. Without a second thought he turned to go back out the door, but as soon as he turned, the door slammed shut.

"Stay away from me!" A voice shouted from up the stairs.

A gust of wind blew against the door and held it shut. Everything in his body screamed at him to get out of the house, by any means necessary. But he remembered the words of the Creator.

Save the child.

Slowly he trekked up the stairs. The door to the main bedroom was wide open, and he saw two people standing inside. A man stalked a woman pinned against the wall while a baby cried on the right. Jaden took one step into the room and the man whipped his head at the inkling of Jaden's presence. There was total darkness in the man's icy blue eyes. His eyes looked like a tundra, frozen and bitter to the core. A sinister grin swept across his face, and without warning, an unstoppable force lifted Jaden then pinned him against the wall. The weight of it felt like a bus crushed him.

"I can smell you from a mile away, Anointed."

"Put me down," Jaden shouted.

"No. I'd rather feed on you once I'm finished," he said in a voice as cold as a winter's night.

Jaden's head throbbed, ears rang, and his eyes struggled to focus on the baby. It sat on top of the bed, swaddled in blankets, and crying in a fit. The man flicked his wrist, and Jaden leaped through the air again, like trash swept by the wind, as he slammed into the opposite wall with a thunderous crash.

"Your fear is delicious," the man said as he pointed a

talon towards Jaden.

A searing pain ran through the side of Jaden's neck. It was if a needle-like blade tore him apart. Survival instincts slammed into his head. "Put me down!" he shouted again.

"Why have you come here," the man bellowed. His voice carried the menace of pure darkness.

"My baby!" the lady cried as she levitated on the opposite side of the wall.

The unbearable pain spread across Jaden like a California wildfire. He grinded his teeth, as he tried to endure the pain. Then he noticed he could wiggle his fingers. He concentrated, tried to fight the force pining him down. "Put me down!" he shouted again. His palm burned and stung as blood flowed at the center.

Jaden's hand came free. With a guttural shout, he threw his fist out at the man, wanting to destroy him. Almost instantly, and at a speed too quick to see, he pummeled the man out of the window. Glass shattered and the frame of the window splintered into many small wooden pieces as if a train ran through it.

Jaden collapsed to the floor and an overwhelming fatigue fell over his body.

The women fell as well, and crawled over to the bed to grab the baby. "It's all right," she declared as she bounced the child in her arms. She went to the window and looked over. "He's dead," she said.

Jaden leaned back against the wall, with the stunning realization that he just killed somebody. "Are you for real?" he asked.

She nodded. "Yes." Then she took two shaking steps towards him. "Thank you. You saved me and my baby. I don't know what happened to him. It was as if he was someone else." She took a deep aching breath, trying to wrap her mind around the horror. "What's your name?"

Jaden's feet struggled to find grip as he rose and turned towards the door.

"What's your name?" she demanded again.

Jaden ran as fast as he could. In two long leaps, he flew down the stairs, jumped over the pile of blood, and slammed the door behind him. He ran straight to his Mustang, over the debris of the broken window. Jaden cranked his car and peeled from the neighborhood.

CHAPTER TWO

Evil Strikes Back

The screeching roars of Jaden's Mustang echoed throughout the quiet Pinedale gated community, located just north of Baldwin Hills. By the time he got back home, the sun had set and a moonless night loomed around. He pulled up in the driveway, just a little past midnight. The old engine of his car made a loud rumble before shutting off, as he parked in the garage.

He sat in the car for a moment, even after the engine quieted, just to collect his thoughts and pull himself out of the nightmare he had just witnessed. So many images ran through his head at once, and it seemed like the more he tried to wish them away, the more they came back to the forefront of his mind. Jaden looked down at his hands. Blood still covered them and crusted his fingers. A funk wafted from his body, a mixture of blood, sweat, and fear. When it hit his nose, it made him claw at his shirt and pull it over his head. In one hand he held his dirty shirt and opened the car door with the other.

Before he went in the house, he thought of his parents. If luck was on his side, then his father is still researching at his lab downtown and his mother is fast asleep.

Jaden made his way into the house through the garage door. He walked from the garage to the kitchen, trying not to make a peep. Looking behind himself, he noticed a trail of crimson footprints in the kitchen. He thought to himself that he would just clean it up later. The most important thing he wanted to do was to get out of these clothes, so he continued to strip.

Jaden ran up the stairs to the bathroom across from his room. He locked the door behind him. Immediately he went to the sink to purge himself of the filth covering his hands and smeared across his body. The hot water felt so good across his body as it cleansed him. With both hands anchored at the side of the sink, he looked into the mirror with his stomach in knots. A door opened from down the hall, and footsteps marched down the stairs. His mom was awake. He will be dead next.

"Jaden!" a loud voice shrieked from downstairs.

He opened the door and called down. "What's up?"

"Bring your butt down here," her voice was sharp as nails.

Jaden cursed to himself under his breath as he

splashed more water and soap across his body. He looked down and saw that the sink was also a crimson stained mess.

"Jaden!"

He reached for a towel. "Coming!"

Quickly he dried himself as best as he could and gathered the dirty clothing in a heap. When he came out of the bathroom, he dashed across the hall to his room.

"Boy, what is this mess you made down here? And where have you been?"

"I was just hanging out," he said as he tossed the dirty clothes in the hamper

His mother stood at the foot of the stairs so she could hear him. "Out where?"

Jaden didn't respond. He searched the pile of clothes on his bead for a clean shirt and a pair of shorts.

When he didn't respond, she strolled back into the kitchen. "Come downstairs and talk me," she shouted again.

Jaden stepped into a pair of basketball shorts. "Hold on I'm coming."

Downstairs his mother grumbled as she stared at the mess of prints left on the floor. She went to the broom closet to fetch a mop. The back door inched open behind her.

Jaden could tell from her tone of voice she was

getting angrier by the minute. "I'm coming down!" he shouted as he trekked down the stairs. Every step increased the growing dread he felt, expecting the wrath of his mother.

Jaden arrived downstairs to a ghost-quiet kitchen. No sign of his mom. "Mom?" he called.

He raked his gaze across the kitchen trying to figure out where she could've gone, but he couldn't understand why she would call him downstairs and leave. "Mom?" he asked again as the silence tightened the fear he felt. It was a child's fear, the loneliness, and feebleness of being left to fend against the darkness by yourself.

Dead air sucked all of the oxygen out of the room, and he flinched as a droplet fell on the top of his head. Then another fell on his shoulder. Another fell by his lips. Jaden ran his hand across the wetness and looked at his fingers. He shuddered at the red. Jaden peered up and inwardly it felt as if all the stars plummeted to the Earth. She dropped to the floor on top of him, in a heap.

He called her name again as he shook her. Out of the corner of his eyes, he saw a dark figure stand by the door. It was him. The man with the blue eyes. Jaden thought he killed him.

The man looked around. "Nice place you got here."

Jaden scurried back on the ground, pulling his mother along with him.

"Now let me ask you something, kid. What were you doing back there? I thought we got rid of your kind a long time ago," he asked with a snarky grin.

Jaden bucked at the man as if he would attack. "Get out of here."

"Nice try, kid, but you can't kill a demon by throwing him out the window," the man rasped as his cold eyes widened, and he broke out into a fit of laughter.

Jaden looked over at the body slumped on the floor. Everything inside him felt hot and black. The man continued laughing. Anger filled him and again he felt some massive force possessed him. This time his head burned with a righteous fury like a living flame ignited between his ears.

A cloud of pure crimson energy pummeled the man. The man screamed with rage as he flew across the kitchen counter, slammed into the wall, and landed with a thud. Beating in his head, Jaden heard a pulse that raced almost as fast as his heartbeat. It was throbbing. He reached out and pulled. The man fell to his knees as something resembling a bat came thrashing out. Clawing and scratching it came out of the man, surrounded by a billowing black cloud. Jaden got up and stomped on it. Suddenly the demon's voice slammed into Jaden's head, burning itself into every cell, every synapse of his being. *You've crossed the wrong demon. I am the King of demons. The defiler. A son of chaos. There is nowhere to run where I won't find you.*

As the voice faded away, like waking from a nightmare, the creature burned into ashes.

Tears stung the back of Jaden's eyes as he saw the look of mingled fear on his mother's face. Jaden stayed there, crying in disbelief, begging his mother to get up. Anger filled him like a cup. He sat there helpless to make this all go away. This was his fault, he thought.

A throbbing pain slammed into the right side of his head. Voices moved and bustled through his head, like a radio switched on, searching from station to station. Everything in the kitchen lurched to life and soared through the air. The refrigerator trembled as a toaster, microwave, blender, knives, and all the items near the stove levitated. Cabinet doors opened and closed, while forks, spoons, butter knives, and other items shot out drawers, soared into the air and stuck to the ceiling. To Jaden it was meaningless noise, the things flying by him did not matter, nothing mattered except the body lying on the floor.

From behind him, the stove erupted into fire, glass shattered, and the temperature in the room soared. A large black plume of smoke billowed into the air, and darkness surrounded Jaden as he sat on the floor.

Swirling into one muddled mixture, this overload of

mental pain went through Jaden like a bullet and soon all he could see was darkness as the flames spread. Just as he was reaching the edge of absolute agony, the pain faded, and he was lying face down on the floor, shivering as though he was buried in a tomb of ice. It all soon will be over, he thought to himself. Out of the corner of his eyes, he saw someone. Someone who stepped through the fire reached down and grabbed him.

Chapter Three

Rebirth

John looked over at his son with a smile spread thin across his face. "We're almost there."

His father drove them to their new home with the windows in the jeep rolled down, and the wind blowing in their faces. It was seventy-five degrees in Atlanta, the sky a perfect, cloudless blue. To Jaden, the warm weather down south did not feel the same as California. He missed the breeze from the ocean and the way the sun reflected from the water, casting a golden glow against the city. He was wearing his favorite hat, a faded blue L.A Dodgers cap, because he didn't want to get caught not repping his hometown in this new city.

Jaden looked over at his father and remained silent as he stared back at the wide open field. They were driving further out from the city, and the stark contrast from L.A made him feel like dark clouds hung in the sky. Jaden turned to his father and said, "So we will definitely be living in the middle of nowhere."

John chuckled. "Don't say that. We're only twenty minutes away from Atlanta and there is plenty to do in Alpharetta. You know the locals call it Awesome Alpharetta."

Jaden smiled sarcastically. "I'm sure they do."

John continued, "There is a movie theatre fifteen minutes away, a mall, and a skating rink."

Jaden roll his eyes. "Dad, I haven't gone skating since I was a kid."

"True, but it's still something to do." John reached his hand over to pat his son on the top of his head. He only toppled the hat that covered it.

Jaden pulled away. "Stop." He adjusted the cap and starred back out of the window.

The smile vanished from John's face. To have a child and not know what makes him tick tortured him, as a scientist. The space between them always felt a million light-years away.

John's face became tense as he took a breath. "Look I know these last few months have been tough, on the both of us. But I know we can get through this. The doctors said a change in environment would be good for you—"

Jaden's face curled into ugliness. "Please don't mention doctors anymore," he interrupted.

John's jaw tightened. "Okay. But either way, this move will be good for the both of us. I always wanted to work at the CDC, plus I hear North Central is an amazing school. You will do wonderful there, you were always an amazing student." A smile came across John's face as he thought about his next words. "This is going to be good. You will see. How do the kids say it these days? It's lit!"

Jaden cringed. "Please stop. Don't say no more."

John laughed. "Just make sure you don't follow a crowd. Be a leader. Make your own decisions. And make wise ones at that."

Jaden was so tired of this conversation. "I wasn't following a crowd, dad. I have no friends."

John's voice became tense. "Well, whatever you were doing then." Then he stopped and waited for a beat, and remembered what the doctors told him, that such confrontation would make him run away again and could trigger the night terrors. "Jaden, you're not a bad kid. I know you're not. We just went through a tough time. I miss your mother. God knows I do and I'm still working through this myself. But we have to do this together."

21

As the words left his lips, another thought came to his mind and went into Jaden's head. *I don't think two months was enough. He might need to go back to Whatley Reid.*

Jaden turned his head to look over at his father incredulously.

"I'm sorry. I don't mean that," John said as he faced the road.

Jaden faced forward. "Sure."

Twenty minutes later they drove past several fast food restaurants, and a strip mall to pull up to their home. Moderate sized houses of all colors, lined up together with overgrown lawns, blooming flowers, white pavement, and garages. John brought his car to a stop at a burgundy craftsman. "We're here."

They got out the car and walked inside. With four bedrooms and two and a half bathrooms, the house was an upgrade from their previous home, in size and space.

"What do you think?" John asked.

Jaden nodded in approval. "You did good doc."

"Let's get moving then," John said as he went back to the car.

It took Jaden only about three trips to get most of his stuff upstairs. He was lucky enough to have his pick amongst three rooms to choose from. He decided upon the east bedroom that faced over the backyard. Lush trees brimming with wildlife, filled the back of the house. The scene looked like something out of children's book.

He had one box remaining, and it was his coveted hat collection. Jaden went back outside to get it when a sudden sensation came to him. The usual small static of voices in his head fell silent, and a perfect peace replaced it. Jaden paused, almost dropping the box, and looked over.

"Are you new here?" She asked.

Jaden turned to the soft voice and his heart stopped for a moment. He traced long slender almond legs, up to hazel eyes, and bone straight black hair that fell across a red sweatshirt with 'Dope' written on the front. She sat on a high rise bike, wearing bright pink sneakers and denim booty shorts.

Jaden froze, he couldn't believe that such a beauty was talking to him. Here he stood in sweats and a low fitted hat, while she looked as if she'd just finished shooting a music video or a campaign for Mac.

She slapped her chest as she laughed. "Are you okay there?"

Jaden shook off the trance. "Oh, my bad. What did you say?"

The girl smiled and cleared her throat. "All of these boxes makes it seems like you moving in."

Jaden laughed nervously. "Yes, I am"

She cocked her head to the side, and through the glaring sunlight, he could see dime size dimples and the hazel in her eyes. "Where are you from?"

Jaden's bottom lip fell and he had to blink twice to stammer an answer. "L.A"

"L.A," she repeated. "That's Hollywood… cool."

"Yes, it is."

The girl stood from the bike and she was about the same size as Jaden, with long slender model like legs that said she probably ran track or played on the basketball team. She folded her hair behind her ear and held out a hand. "Hi. My name is Imani."

His heart slammed into his chest. "Jaden. It's nice to meet you." He took her hand and the strangest thing happened as he touched her. A beautiful tranquility swept over him. It was peaceful, almost as peaceful as when he heard the voice of the Creator.

She smirked, and his heart thundered. "Jaden … you seem more like a Hollywood. That's what I'm going to call you." Then she tugged his fitted, and pulled it to his nose.

Jaden lifted his fitted. "I'm cool with that. Do you go

to North Central?"

Imani nodded. "I'm a sophomore. How about you?"

"Same. How is it?"

Imani sighed. "Hell. But what high school isn't?"

"True."

Imani looked at him from the side. "You don't talk much do ya, Hollywood?"

"Not really." He shook. Then he peered down at her lowrider bicycle that had a black frame, accented by pink handlebar grips, and a pink leather seat. It reminded him of the bikes he used to ride on Venice beach. "Dope ass bike," he murmured as he walked alongside.

Imani strode over to the bike and mounted. "Do you ride?"

"No, but I skateboard."

Imani smiled. "Nice." She looked over at him and his breath caught. "Maybe after school we can go riding together or something. There is a park not too far from here called Union Hill."

Jaden lifted his head, just slightly to cast his smoldering gaze under the brim of his hat. "That'd be dope."

Imani placed feet on pedals and backed out of the driveway. "I'll hit you up." She reversed out of the driveway and looked over her shoulder. "See you later, Hollywood!"

Jaden nodded his head bye as he watched the most beautiful girl he had ever seen ride away, hair glistening, and shining in the sun, his heart trailing after her. Then a sudden realization came to him. "Wait, you don't have my number."

He ran behind her, but she had already turned the corner, hair blowing in the wind.

Chapter Four

Fatal Temptations

The line wrapped around Safari lounge, from the entrance to the corner of the building and all the way back into the adjacent lot. Teens from all over the city waited with determination to get in for free. There were only fifteen minutes left before twelve, and the crowd grew with agitation. One bouncer clipped the velvet rope behind him, as he backed them from the door.

"No one is getting in here, if yawl don't back the hell up!" He shouted. His arms were the size of tree trunks, and his eyes bulged in rage as he regulated his authority.

Twenty or more of the teenagers, stood at the door in a large cluster. Some already had i.ds out and were eager to get in, after waiting over thirty minutes in line.

One boy wearing a silky shirt that was too small for his hefty frame spoke up. "Man stop playing and let us in. It's almost twelve and nobody is trying to drop twenty dollars to get in there."

A collective yeah rang out through the cluster as the other teens agreed with him.

"Nobody is getting in, if yawl don't get in a line. So get in line." The bouncer barked, as a vein snaked across his bald head.

Another bouncer, this one slimmer but still toned, crept from by the doorway. "Keep em back Tiny." He examined the boy's outfit. "I hate to say it, but you won't be getting in for free anyway. Just looking at your outfit. We expect you to dress your best when you come to Safari."

The boy frowned at him. "What chu' talking about? This shirt I got on is Versace," he said as he pointed.

"Stop lying. That looks like its H&M," Tiny quipped.

The boy's face soured as the bouncers erupted into a fit of laughter, as well as everyone else in the crowd.

He wasn't going to take the joke in stride.

"Man shut your muscle milk looking ass up," he returned.

Laughter swept over the crowd again. Sprinkled throughout the line were guys who wore blazers, fitted caps, and button-ups, along with girls who wore stilettos, tight dresses, skinny jeans, and fur lined boots. Some laughed and talked while they waited to get in while others were already grinding to the throbbing beat coming from inside. The bass from the hip-hop music thumped so loud, it rattled the building. Tyler came outside with a green eyed, sun kissed skin, exotic beauty on his shoulder.

"Look Marv, there she goes?" Tiny said as he elbowed the other bouncer.

Marvin licked his lips. "Is she leaving with Tyler?" He leaned over to catch a better glimpse of the couple walking out hand in hand. "Tyler!" Marvin called.

Tyler looked over his shoulder and smiled.

Marvin gave him a thumbs up. "I wish I was bagging them like that in high school."

"Tell me about it," Tiny agreed.

"Can you let us in!" Someone in the back shouted.

Tiny snorted like a bull and flexed his muscles. "Get in a line."

She nestled her head against Tyler's shoulder, and smiled up at him seductively. "Are you sure you're eighteen?"

Tyler grinned. "Trust me. Not only am I eighteen, I'm a full grown man."

She bit her bottom lip, as her alluring green eyes

pulled him back to her spell. "Oh, I bet you are."

Tyler stood back and looked her over again. Once or twice he'd been fooled by what looked good in the dark corners of Safari, but the girl in front of him was still a sight to see on the outside. Her body was ample and voluptuous, and those green eyes made her irresistible. Tyler thought for a moment, and he couldn't recall ever seeing a better looking woman on his Instagram timeline or Tumblr feed. "You never told me your name?"

She smiled. "Just call me Eva."

"Eva," he repeated in a moan. "I like that. It's sexy." He pulled her to his side as they stepped across the broken parking lot. "Follow me."

Tyler escorted her back to his car. The whole time they were talking inside, he could already imagine the two of them driving off somewhere they can get into something heavy. As soon as she slammed the door, Tyler sped off in his dark blue BMW. Tires screeched as he pulled out of the parking lot, one hand on the wheel as and the other on her thigh.

Tyler drove two miles out on the interstate and hopped off an exit leading to Bufford. He was taking her to what everyone at North Central knew as Freaky Fields. A field in a private section of a nearby farm. The road to Freaky field was a long, shaded and snaking road. Ten minutes down the road and the street lights disappeared. Instead large towering oak trees formed a tunnel on the long winding road.

Eva shuddered. "Where are we going again?"

"A nice little spot. You'll like it, just chill out." Tyler said.

Twenty minutes down the road and the trees opened to a large, stretching field. Dull brown wheat, large patches of grass, and trees surrounded them as Tyler brought the car up to a wooden gate. A symphony of crickets and cicadas played all around them. Tyler turned off the engine, then he turned to her. "Now that we're all alone. What do you want to do?" He leaned in to kiss her but she pulled away, opened the door, and ran out into the field.

A childlike smile spread across her face. "Catch me!" She took off running through the field, wild and free like a roaming stallion.

Tyler huffed. "Hold up, girl!"

They chased each other, with wild thoughts running through their minds, as they ran the vast open field full of brown wheat. Tyler chased her until they came to a small bush of trees. She smiled coyly as her alluring eyes held Tyler in a trance. He pushed her against the body of a small oak, "I've got you," he said.

She giggled. "I guess I have to give you a prize."

Tyler leaned in closer. "Give it to me then." He murmured as he ran his hands around her waist and buried his lips on her neck. Suddenly they heard a strange rustle coming from the trees behind them.

Eva gasped at the sound and pushed Tyler off. "Did you hear something?" She breathed in a hiss. Fear drained the color from her face.

Tyler shrugged it off. "Hear what?"

"Nothing, I guess," she said returning back to Tyler's embrace.

They kissed again. Tyler pressed his body against hers on the tree as they aggressively kissed, then just as his hands found their way up her thigh, sounds of sudden movement made her pull away. "I definitely heard something," she squealed.

Tyler looked over and heard nothing but the rustle of weeds, and call of Georgia cicadas. "I don't hear a thing," Tyler said frustrated. His brow wrinkled as he looked totally annoyed and confused. "Stop being so scared."

An icy breeze streamed by and made the leaves of the trees crackle. Eva wrapped her arms around her chest, trying to warm herself. The more she rubbed the more she could feel goosebumps prickle all over. She pushed

Tyler off and shot him a serious look. "No, I definitely think something is out here. I'm scared.... we should go."

Tyler laughed obnoxiously and waited until he could stop before he spoke. "Why are you scared? There is nobody out there. It's just us baby. It's probably a deer or something."

Eva frowned, the look on her face said she was not amused. "I don't think so."

Tyler sucked his teeth. "You can't be serious."

Her green eyes narrowed. "Yes, I am. Can you just walk around and see?" she pleaded with her arms still folded as her legs shook.

Tyler's jaw tightened. "Are you being for real right now?"

"Yes," Eva blurted as she buttoned up her blouse.

Tyler strode a few steps further into the field with her following behind him. He saw nothing but trees and tall strands of untamed wheat stretching another five miles.

"See there is nothing out here," Tyler shouted to the distance as he turned his back to face the empty field.

"Except me," a menacing voice declared.

Every hair on Tyler's body stood up, as fear stabbed him in the spine.

Panic made him turn around, and horror crippled him as he watched the beautiful girl, staring back at him with malevolent green eyes. Eva grinned like a hungry shark. Scales as dark as the night's sky covered her body, small black horns twisted from the top of her skull, and a tail uncoiled from her backside. Her delicate fingernails turned into vicious black claws. She opened her mouth and her tongue flicked like a snake, before stretching to caress Tyler's cheek. He twisted his face in disgust.

Eva pouted. "What's wrong baby? Have you never met a horny little she-devil?"

Eva pulled at thin air, and before he could even let out a scream, the vines of a nearby tree yanked him by the neck. Tyler swirled in the air, like a yo-yo spinning. The vines pulled him to the base of the tree and continued to wrap themselves until they held him captive. He twisted and squirmed from the firm grip of vines that held him.

"What are you doing?" Tyler asked.

"Baby, don't be scared," Eva declared as she slashed his shirt open with her razor-like claws. A scream tore out of his throat.

She stepped closer and caressed Tyler's body. "You're young and strong. He will enjoy wearing your flesh." She looked down at his well-sculpted chest and smiled. "I couldn't have picked a better one."

"What the hell. Who?" Tyler screamed

Eva cackled. "Don't worry, honey. You'll still be in there. It will be like watching a movie. So sit back, relax, and enjoy the show."

With her claws, she carved a pentagram in his chest, and Tyler wailed as she ripped into his flesh. Latin chants came from her mouth as her dark sinister voice matched his agonizing wails of pain. The ground quaked underneath them, and nearby trees swayed. Swarming from the soil beneath came two pythons with fiery red eyes.

Eva's lips twisted into a smile, and her remorseless cold eyes widened as her chants grew louder. Slithering up the tree, the pythons intertwined as they wrapped their bodies around Tyler incredibly tight. The sheer mass and muscle of these demonic creatures crushed Tyler's body. Bones crunched as the snakes hissed, snapped, and coiled around his torso. His eyes turned bloodshot red from the pressure.

Tyler tried to scream as loud as he could but the snakes muffled him, by applying more pressure. Both pythons stretched jaws to reveal large white fang. Tyler summoned all his strength for one last shriek of terror.

Just as his last cry echoed in the woods against the symphony of the crickets, the pythons sunk their fangs into his neck.

Eva sighed. "I thought he would never shut up."

His head lulled over and his eyes became an icy tundra. Eva waved her hands and the vines fell away along with the pythons. Tyler collapsed to the ground and Eva stood over him. "Arise son of chaos."

Tyler stood but he was no longer in control. He huffed, stretched, and looked all around. He turned to her, and his pupils glimmered blue.

Eva studied him. "Identify yourself."

"Devil number two. Asmodeus."

Chapter Five

Traces of the Past

Jaden ransacked all of the boxes in his room, and he still couldn't find any more hangers. He opened one box and came across a newspaper clipping with the headline *Crucifier now dead.* Along with that newspaper clipping were many others buried at the bottom of the box, along with printouts from blog entries. He recognized them as the remnants of his search for the demon. Brian Lamont was the name of the man who the demon possessed. But who the demon was, he had no clue. The only thing his victims had in common was that they all had newborn babies. Jaden never understood why, and till this day it still bothered him.

Local news called Brian the Crucifier because he left many of his victims suspended along the wall, and slit from ear to ear. How these victims stayed pinned to the wall with no rope, and no nails made no logical sense. But it only added more proof to the ghost hunter blogs and forums, of the growing presence of monsters in the world.

The Crucifer became the latest supernatural trending topic, just after the music video with rapping vampires that went viral. Jaden rolled his eyes just thinking about the number of memes, YouTube videos, and gifs that followed. It was like the ninety's again where gangs were cool, except everyone wanted to be a part of the #Vamplife movement. Most of the adults thought it was a joke, but it didn't stop kids from flocking to the streets and joining the vampire broods that operated like gangs. Most of media regarded them as vampire fanboys who were simply troubled, and misguided. Jaden knew the truth and that fueled his brief stint as a hunter.

Hidden under the clippings and blog printouts laid a worn, black bible. The cover dangled off the seams, and the edges of the page crinkled brown. Jaden picked it up. Sam gave it to him, and the thought of that crazy Texan was enough to make him smile. He would've died in that fire, had not Sam pulled him out.

While holding the Bible, his arm vibrated, and he checked his smartwatch. It was time for his medicine. He went to the floor and checked a red duffle bag, where he found the small vial of medicine. It helped with not hearing the thoughts. If his mind was a radio shifting from station to station, it kept it off for most of the day and turned low when it wasn't. Jaden popped open the bottle and took one of the oblong green pills. He was about to throw down his throat when he stopped and remembered he had nothing to eat. The thought of food made his belly rumble.

Jaden walked downstairs. He would get more hangers and remind the doctor he had to feed him. As soon as he walked into the living room, he dug through more boxes looking for hangers. The room was barren except for one couch and the dozens of boxes laying around.

"Jaden," his father called from around the corner in his office

Jaden found the hangers he wanted and made his way to his father's office. "Yes sir," he responded.

"Could you bring me something to drink?" John asked. His eyes didn't leave the laptop screen as he typed.

With a sigh and moan, Jaden dragged his feet to the kitchen. He opened the door to the fridge and saw nothing but a box of baking soda. "There's nothing in here, remember!" He shouted from the kitchen.

"Come get some money and go to the store then."

Jaden cursed under his breath as he strode back to the office. John's eyes don't move as he reaches into his wallet to pull out a crisp twenty and slide it over.

Jaden folded the money into his wallet. "Is that it? You know I'm a growing boy who needs a full meal with vegetables and stuff."

John grinned. "Here," he moaned as he unrolled another ten. "Go ahead and get yourself a sweet tea and honey bun like I know you will."

Jaden cracked a wry smile. "Thanks." He started for the door and turned around. "Can I get the car?"

John peered back down to his laptop. "No. I'm not letting you drive this late. It's deer country around here, and they like to cross roads at night. There is a local market still open that's less than a mile. Go play with your skates."

Jaden frowned. "Skateboard. It's a board that comes with skates, and you don't play with it. Men make whole careers behind learning how to master the board. It's not a toy. It's a whole sport now."

John laughed at the word sport. "Whatever." He took off his olive speckled horn-rimmed glasses and wiped the lens with his handkerchief. "Be safe and be back by midnight," he said as his eyes returned to the screen.

"Alright,"

As Jaden went back to his room he could hear his father's thoughts trail into his head.

Dear God, just bring him back safe. He is the only thing I have left.

He paused for a moment then went back upstairs, to grab his favorite hoody, a pair of chucks, and a cap which he always kept pulled down way low. Most people thought the hoodie and cap made him look suspicious, but in actuality they were his go-to gear because of his acne. And even when he had clear skin, he still wore the other two. Jaden plucked his keys from the mass of clothes on the floor, picked up his skateboard, and headed out

Chapter Six

Swarm

It was colder outside than he expected. A chilling breeze swept across his face as he threw his board to the ground. For a moment he thought about going back in for a jacket, but he figured he'd warm up once he started moving. Jaden put in his earbuds before stepping on the board. Once the music played, he hopped on and soared down the driveway to the streets. Wind bristled through his woolly hair as he rolled down the hill, the sound of his board rolling across pavement echoed through the empty night. At this time most houses in the neighbourhood were dark. In mere seconds he peeled past his community gate, the Windsor Hills sign illuminated his back, and he cascaded down a curving lane.

As he rode down the street, he peered up for a moment to notice just how bright the stars shined in Georgia. It brought awe and wonder to his eyes because it seemed like he had never noticed them in L.A. Even the call of the night insects seemed like a new wonder he'd never knew before.

Ten minutes down the road, his mouth became dry as cotton. Inside he prayed there was store on the way to the market that was open this late. Jaden pivoted around the curb, and he spotted the lights of a Young market gas station. He smiled in relief and slowed the board down. In one long sweeping roll he swerved up to the curb and jumped off.

Jaden walked in and a girl not much older than him, sat at the cash register. She was arguing with someone on the phone. The doorbell rang and she whipped her head over, "Welcome to Young's."

The first aisle he strolled down he found Doritos, amidst a modest selection of chips. In his head, he went back and forth between Cool Ranch and Thai Chili. He decided on sticking with his favorite, Cool Ranch. Chips in hand he headed to the back of the store for an Arizona tea. He walked past at least a few freezer doors before he found the section for teas and juices. Cold dew from the freezer misted his shorts as he held the door trying to decide which flavor to choose. An arm reached across his head, and he shuddered as it picked up a fruit punch.

"Hurry up, Hollywood. The drinks are getting warm," Imani said.

Jaden stiffened. "It's you again," he mumbled. Not taking his eyes off her, Jaden reached for an Arizona. He paid no attention to the flavor.

Imani grinned. "Yeah, it's me again." She cracked the top of the fruit punch and took a long savoring sip. "This is my hood you know."

Jaden laughed nervously as he tugged at his cap. "True."

Imani looked him over. "Tomorrow is your first day, right?"

Jaden choked. He coughed to clear his throat and smiled again before looking down at his shoes. He waited to hear her thoughts. But surprisingly no inner voices came to him. He looked back at her, with the smile missing from his face, and replaced by curiosity. This time he purposely tried to read her mind. Still nothing but silence came to him. Something about her made him tingle.

Imani stared back at him, waiting for him to respond. Judging from the wrinkling of her brow, Jaden realized he had spent too much time in his head. "True. I mean, Yes. It is my first day."

"Ayo, Imani. Are ya trying to buy me these Hot Cheetos?" a southern heavy voice called from behind her.

A tall boy about their age with braids sweeping his face walked up to them with a handful of snacks. The tattoos written across his arms reminded Jaden of the gangsters he left behind in Compton.

"Go put all of that back," Imani snapped.

The boy got in her face. "Oh come on, they have em' on sale." He opened a honey bun and bit in half.

Imani blew out hard. "You eat them every day."

His eyes narrowed as he swallowed. "Because they are good, and good for you."

"How?"

"They cure the munchies," the boy said.

"Get out of my face," Imani said as she thumped him on the forehead. He stumbled back into the aisle, causing multiple bags of candy to topple to the ground. Jaden shook his head in embarrassment.

The boy tries to pick the candy up, but he only makes more items fall. "Oh, come on shawty. See what you just made me do?"

Imani laughed and looked back to Jaden. "Don't mind him," she said shaking her head. "This is my boy, Deshawn. Deshawn this is Jaden, he just moved to the A from L.A. He's going to North Central with us."

Jaden sighed. *Great, she has a boyfriend*, he thought to himself.

Deshawn placed all of his snacks on the shelf to the side. Jaden offered his hand for a handshake but Deshawn took him in for a hug, a shake, and a dap.

"What's up, homeboy. You good?" Deshawn asked as he continued to make Jaden feel more uncomfortable.

Jaden shook his head, "Yeah,"

"Are you sure?" Deshawn asked again.

"Yes, I'm fine," Jaden said, this time loudly. "Okay, I guess I'll see the two of you later." Jaden turned to walk away and two other boys blocked his path, one tall and light-skinned, the other a slim Asian. "What is this a gang?" Jaden asked out loud.

"Woah, slow down Flash," the tall one said. He stood a few inches taller than Jaden, exceptionally handsome, with a large nose, light brown eyes, and other features that made it hard to pinpoint his ethnicity.

He looked past Jaden towards Imani. "Do you want to introduce us to your friend?" he said in slight rasp.

"Real low key," Imani murmured as she face palmed herself. "Jaden, this is Romeo and Lay."

Romeo crossed his arms as he nodded at Jaden, his slender muscles bulged as they crossed. "Sup."

Jaden sized the boy up and down with his eyes. Everything about Romeo said basketball player, from his tall slender build, his demeanor, and steely gaze. Jaden nodded back. "Sup," he repeated.

Lay reached across Romeo with his hand outstretched and a smile plastered on his face. "Hi buddy. My name is Lay. How's it going?"

Jaden shook Lay's hand. "Good, just chilling."

Lay was shorter than the two, his hair a crown of well sculpted black mass, and round spectacles framed his face. He looked the youngest amongst them to Jaden, with high cheekbones, a bright face, and broad shoulders despite his lithe frame.

"Chilling, that's us too," he said with a jitter as he looked over to Romeo, who's face remained stone cold.

"Lay is a cool name," Jaden commented.

Lay smiled. "Thanks. My real name is Jin-Soo Lee. I'm Korean. But my friends call me Lay, so feel free to call me Lay."

"Cool," Jaden said. He turned back to Imani. "This was hella weird, but it was nice seeing you again and meeting all of you." He cast an awkward gaze around the group.

"This is my crew," Imani said.

"Yes, our lovely crew. We are like a family," Lay said as he wrapped an arm around Romeo, who looked over, and made him remove the arm with his scowl. "Do you want to hang out with us?"

Jaden remained silent as he tried to wrestle with the question. "No thanks. I think I'm going to bail."

Imani smiled. Her hazel eyes made his heart flutter. "Okay. See ya around Hollywood."

Deshawn waved, "Bye Johnathan."

Jaden made his way to the front and Lay raced to his side. "Where are you going? If you're not busy, we can tag along with you."

"No thanks," Jaden interrupted.

He tossed his items on the counter. The clerk rung him up, and he paid for it with the ten-dollar bill.

"But wait, are you sure you want to be out there by yourself?" Romeo asked. Then he looked up as if he was searching for words. "It's pretty late and you might get robbed. So it's better to walk with a group."

"I'll be fine." Jaden spat. He grabbed his bag and dashed out of the gas station.

Imani threw up her hands.

"Are you sure that's him?" Lay asked

Romeo reached into his pocket and pulled out a folded picture. "That's him alright." On the picture was a vivid scene of Jaden being chased by green insect looking monsters.

"Well, we tried. What do you want us to do?" Deshawn cried out.

"Let's go after him," Imani ordered.

While they talked, the girl at the counter clutched her phone tightly as she exchanged glances with Romeo. "Oh my god he's in my store," she whispered. She dropped her phone and leaned over. "Hey Romeo. Is there anything I can get for you?"

"No mami, I'm good." He said with a cocky smirk.

She clutched her chest and crumbled to the floor.

Imani pushed him forward. "C'mon let's go."

****

Jaden turned the music to full blast as he stepped on his board, and sped down the road. Trap music made him come alive. It thumped in his ear as he shifted his weight on the board, nodding his head and pivoting his body to the beat. His right leg vibrated with life. Jaden looked down at his wrist. It was a text from his father.

Dad: *Where are you? Hurry up and come home*

While reading the text, he fails to see the shoe laying in the road. His board rolls over the shoe and Jaden topples over, wind smacking his face as he's flung from the board. The pavement felt cold and wet as he fell to the ground. A throbbing pain shot above his elbow and across his knee. His elbow began bleeding, and he groaned as he lifted his head. Flashing lights flickered in his face, drowning him in a sea of orange. They shined just a few feet ahead.

Jaden raised his hands against the blinding lights. He

stood up and saw a black jeep with the driver's side open, headlights beaming on the road, blinkers flashing in the back. A sudden growling noise made the hairs on his forearm stand upright like soldiers. It sounded like hungry dogs eating. He took a step further.

Jaden crept towards the middle of the road. When he saw them, his breath caught, and he almost screamed out loud. Three creatures devoured the innards of a man who laid outstretched in the middle of the road. He covered his mouth to hold back the sour liquid rising in his throat. They were shaped like men, with faint green insect like skin. It reminded him of grasshoppers.

One of them stopped eating and stuck its nose into the air. A high pitched wail came out its mouth which stretched out into four corners, each corner containing rows of red glowing teeth. "Something smells good," it said.

"What is it?" the others asked.

Jaden's mouth fell wide open, as he stumbled backwards, he couldn't believe the monsters were talking.

"Do you smell that," one asked the others as it rose off the pavement, sniffing the air to catch the scent. Jaden reached for his board, and three heads turned to his direction.

Jaden became a statue. He dared not take another footstep. Dark eyes sized him up. He took one step backwards, and they rose to their feet revealing long pointy spines along their frail bodies.

"His scent is tasty," the first one said. It shoved a

piece of bone and flesh into its mouth and then licked its fingers.

Jaden bent down for his board. His chest rose and fell with such a heaviness that he thought he would almost fall out from freight. "No I don't. You guys don't want me. I'm hella skinny and all bones."

Another creature leapt from the right, it crept over, still crouched, an insatiable look of hunger on its face. "Bones and tender meat. Succulent. Warm blood. Blood that is blessed."

"Anointed," they all said in unison. All of their jaws stretched and high pitched screams sounded in the night.

One crept closer. "Locust want anointed flesh."

"It will make us strong, so we can fly." Another said, crouching near.

Suddenly one of them rubbed its hands against its face, and a high pitched rattling noise emitted in the air. To Jaden the rattling sounded like cicadas, but with a growl. Soon the others joined, and his dread magnified. They drew close to each other like a pack of Hyenas. And just when Jaden thought things couldn't get worse, the woods surrounding him erupted into rattling. Jaden whirled around in disbelief. There were more of them. A lot more.

One of the locusts inched closer to Jaden. "I want to taste the Anointed. Let me at him."

Another bumped it out of the way. "I smelled him first. He's mine."

Jaden beckoned for the board with his hand outstretched. And It sprang toward him, leaping several inches.

Another Locust leapt out of the woods, and knocked the board out of his hands.

"Where are you going?" It asked.

Jaden sidestepped it and ran closer to the car. Another one came leaping from the right, and landing on the roof. He could hear the other creatures come hopping out of the woods. Claws swiped at his chest, and Jaden threw up his hands. At his whim the creature stopped mid-air. It floated before him in a cloud of crimson, with its jaws outstretched and hissing. Jaden could feel the creature within his grasp. It writhed like a cockroach, snapping and clawing towards him.

With his palm flat, he pushed outward and sent the monster cascading back into the woods. Another grabbed him from behind and threw him into a ditch. His body crumbled to the ground, like an egg thrown against the wall. Before Jaden could react, the locust climbed on top of him. All four corners of its mouth stretched, and it dove at his neck. Jaden held it back, but the creature pressed back against his hands harder. Summoning all the strength he could, Jaden pushed the creature off of him with an incredible force. He glanced over, searching for his skateboard. It laid wheels up on the side of the road.

Jaden beckoned for the board with his hand, and it rocketed towards him. It flew across the road over to him, but it didn't land on the ground. It hovered in the air, floating in a misty crimson cloud. Jaden's eyes widened. "Well that's new." An epic thought came to mind.

The Locusts scrambled off the ground and lurched towards him. He heard one word in his head that made his hands tremble.

Swarm

Swarm

Swarm

All the trees in the woods to his right shook. He could hear more of the rattling noise closing in on him, and he swallowed hard as a hot sweat formed underneath his arm pits. Jaden placed both feet on the board and balanced himself with his hands outstretched. He placed his hand in the center of the board, pushed, and the skateboard lifted off the ground. "Woah!" he shouted as the board took off.

Five feet

Ten feet

Twenty

The board continued to rise higher and higher into the air. Jaden held his hand forward, and the skateboard held steady. He sucked a deep breath in, exhaled out, and the weightlessness he felt reminded him of being on a motorized scooter. He always wanted one of those, but his father forbid it after his cousin Eugene's blew up. And there he stood a few feet off the ground, with the Locusts rattling below.

"Come on crickets, try to catch me now." Jaden taunted.

One raised its head towards him and leapt into the air, several feet off the ground. Then another did the same, crossing over the other in the opposite direction.

One by one the creatures continued to spring up into the air, coming dangerously close to Jaden each time.

Jaden gasped. "Bad idea….bad idea." With his hand outstretched to the front of the board, he commanded the board to move, and it rocketed down the road with a mighty jerk. Jaden pivoted with the board, wind whipped his face, and blew through his hoody like a cape. He soared off the road and blew across the woods. The locusts followed behind, leaping and hopping over each other as if they were grasshoppers caught in a cup. Looking below, Jaden spotted more of the Locusts shuddering and lurching upright, joining the swarm, and following him.

Jaden grinned. "I can't believe this," he said as the board inched ahead. He soared higher from the monsters below. "Eat my dust suckers," He shouted to the ground.

Suddenly the board went limp. Jaden looked down and he no longer floated in a crimson cloud. "Oh no," he murmured as gravity pulled at him.

He fell to the ground cart-wheeling in air, his back smacked by branches, his head scratched by sharp twigs, and his face eating dirt.

"Grab him!"

A sharp pain stabbed Jaden's back and ran down his whole left side. All at once the Locust came leaping and rattling. Jaden climbed up to his feet and ran.

Branches snapped behind him and the rattling sound filled the woods. He could sense them closing in on him. His back ached terribly, and he struggled to hold on to his breath. The Georgia air was so humid and thick it felt like wading through a swamp. Still he ran wild and blind, hands outstretched, pushing against branches, and feeling his direction forward. Ear piercing rattles sounded from his left, he looked over, and saw four of them on branches.

Swarm

Swarm

Swarm

Jaden jumped over a log, ducked under branches, and criss crossed past an occasional Locust that tried to hop on top of him. Wind screeched through the neighboring trees, which shook as the Locusts leapt from them.

A locust came down upon him, and made his head smack against a rock. The chasing halted, and the locust held its position in the trees as Jaden laid there panting by the rock. It glared down at Jaden with lust and hunger in its eyes.

"We've got him."

The Locust dug its claws into his chest, and he hiccupped a cry as the sharp pain hit him. Jaden felt like a gazelle caught between the paws of a lion. A desperate cry for help came out of his mouth as the monster's jaw stretched out to four corners again. His heart dropped to his stomach and he prepared for the worst.

Claws sank deeper into his chest as the monster's head lowered, but this happened unnaturally slow, almost as if some force slowed the creature down. Sonic blasts heralded the arrival of four dark shapes alighting the woods, hurling streams of light that gleamed like fireworks during the Fourth of July. A crashing noise clattered like gunfire as shades of golden yellow, and blazing fire streaked across a star studied sky. A loud bang erupted beside him, and a brilliant stream of golden light smacked the side of the locust. It dissolved to dust like wheat burned by fire. Jaden popped up, and a fierce stream of raging fire soared past him, scorching four other Locusts.

Jaden's mouth fell open as he watched the ashes of the creatures blow through the wind in a funnel. Then a blaring explosion erupted from the left as more jet streams of golden light cut through the darkness of the woods. Jaden shielded his eyes from the blinding light.

Imani tugged at him. "Are you alright?"

"What are you doing here?" He asked.

"Saving your butt, now get up!"

Imani helped him to his feet as the others pushed back the horde of Locusts. Romeo shot bright beams of light from his fingers like a laser gun and Deshawn hacked and slashed left to right with a long battle axe.

Jaden looked in Imani's hands, and she held a huge gun made of a bright orange and green plastic. It reminded him of a super soaker.

"Don't worry. We'll get you out of here," Imani shouted as she shifted his weight onto her and helped him up to walk.

Out of the shadows, two Locusts came at them, hissing, and rattling. Lay flipped in front, and knocked both of them out with a backhand swing of a staff made of pulsing blue light. "Go Imani! Get him out of here."

Imani tugged on Jaden's hands. "Come on, we have to run! Let's go."

She pulled Jaden away. He followed her as she jumped over fallen trees. "Where did these monsters come from? I've never seen anything like them before."

Imani glanced back. There was another one arm's length away from Jaden. She lifted her gun and shot. A fluid stream of blazing fire came out, and licked up the monster, causing it to stumble back. The ashes blew away before the creature could topple to the ground.

She shot a concerned look to Jaden. "I don't know. They're called Locusts, and they hunt in swarms. We are as good as dead if we don't get out of here. Now move!"

Together they ran. Rattling sounded all around the woods and pierced his ears like shattering glass as the Locusts pursued. Imani lead the way with Jaden, Lay, Deshawn and Romeo close behind.

Two locust charged at Deshawn, but with a simple gesture from his hand Deshawn threw a pulsing orb into the air, and it billowed into a cloud of fireworks, spiraling like an out-of-control Roman candle. It unleashed a small explosion that sent the two creatures flying. Another came flying down from the tree, and Lay cut it into half, with a strike of his light staff.

"Imani we got problems," Romeo stated as he flung one creature gnawing at his neck over his shoulder.

"Handle it," Imani said.

Lay cried out, and Romeo ducked and spun just as

the locust sprung at him, teeth bared, quick as a viper.

Romeo pummeled it with a blast of light. "Deshawn, where is the crowd control?"

Deshawn spun and took the head off a Locust. "Jesus Christ, it's too many of em'." He said huffing, almost of breath. "I'm draining. We need to come up with another plan quick."

Lay's body was like water pouring into a glass as he flipped past him, spun his light staff around his neck, then struck the Locust in front of him, and the other to his left. "Just keep fighting. Don't stop."

Imani clutched the gun under her right shoulder as she aimed and shot with the streaming fire. "This way!" She commanded as she turned to go down a winding path on her right.

Before she could lead them down the path, four dark figures descended from the air in front of them, blocking their escape. Jaden looked behind them and another group encircled them.

Imani drew up her gun, then turned to Jaden. "Get back!" She pulled the trigger but nothing came out. "Yikes."

Before she could utter another word, a Locust sank its teeth in her right shoulder, yanked her backwards, and dragged her away.

"Imani!" Jaden called, reaching out his hand to grab her.

"Just run, Jaden," she cried as the creature dragged her away.

The locusts out maneuvered them, by flanking them on all sides. The swarm pushed the group tighter, by surrounding them. Jaden could hear the terrible thoughts of the creatures, but their thoughts didn't make him worry, the deep sense of fear that came from the others did.

Lay shivered so much that his light staff trembled in his grip. He held it out-stretched to defend any oncoming attackers. Deshawn tightened the grip on his axe, as Romeo also drew closer, the light coming from his fingers dimming. Fear, adrenaline, and snarling teeth, slammed Jaden's chest like a heavy weight.

"Get back! Get back," Jaden screamed. He rubbed the temples of his head, knocking over his hat, and raking every grain of his wooly hair. A sharp sudden pain exploded through the right side of his brain and Jaden staggered back, falling down to his knees.

He let out a guttural scream, as the adrenaline inside of him spread like wildfire, and went off like an atomic bomb. A shockwave emitted from his head and swept through the whole pack of vicious creatures, knocking them off their feet. It illuminated the woods in a sea of white lights, as the locusts floated in the air, and the surrounding trees bent like powerful gusts from a hurricane pushed them. A thunderclap deafened the air, and every locust burned into ashes that scattered into the wind.

"Oh snap!" Deshawn exclaimed.

Everything all around Jaden became a blur, as life itself seemed to drain from his body.

Lay noticed this and shook him. "Jaden are you alright?"

Jaden tried to focus on Lay, and stand up right, but darkness and silence surrounded him as he fell backwards. It was like he was falling deep under water. Blackness followed and the group circled him as he passed out.

Chapter Seven

Sanctuary

Jaden relived the same nightmare ever since he faced the demon. Images slammed into his head, like he was drowning in a river of horrible memories, which dragged, pulled and tossed him about. He walked down the stairs of his old house, knowing what awaited him around the corner. This frightened him and made the weight of each step ten times heavier. Jaden sucked in a breath as he walked down the last step, and turned the corner.

The demon stood in the kitchen, staring back at him with cold blue eyes. He had a name to attach to the host, Brian Lamont, but none for the evil controlling him. Jaden stared at him in terror. He looked the same as before, tall, pale, an uneven stubble on his face, short buzz cut, and wearing red flannel with blue jeans. Brian clutched his mother's throat and displayed her like she was some prize. With his hands clenched around her throat, he squeezed so hard that she couldn't even let a single sound escape her lips. "Nice try kid but you can't kill a demon by throwing him out the window," the demon said with a wicked grin.

Jaden's heart banged against his chest. Before he could take one footstep closer to save his mother, the demon ran his knife along her neck as smooth as butter. Jaden's heart sank. A ghostly looking bat creature came out of the man. It began howling as it flapped its wings frantically about. Jaden jumped back as the creature snapped and gnashed at his face.

Jaden shielded his face and closed his eyes. The cries of the bat subsided. He opened his eyes and saw a brilliant white light, along with soft padded walls everywhere. He ran to a dark corner in the room with his arms restrained, and there was no way out. The lid closed the door's peephole. He was back at Whatley Reid. Jaden screamed as he flung himself against the soft padded walls. Blue eyes stalked him, like a panther in the bush. Echoes filled his head, the thoughts of the people in the city. Bright lights flooded the area. Everywhere he saw blue lights, swirling, dashing and filling his room.

Jaden opened his eyes for real this time, and thank God, he was only dreaming. He looked up to match beautiful almond eyes covered by pink bedazzled spectacles.

A beautiful woman ran her hands across his forehead. "Come here dear, he's awake." She said.

Her voice was Memphis honey poured into a cold glass of iced tea. She had skin the color of Café au lait, and bountiful black hair that fell in voluminous curls across her chest. Jaden guessed her age to be somewhere around late twenties and early-thirties.

Imani leaned over him. "Jaden, can you hear me?" She asked as she caressed the other side of his head, her warm touch soothed him. "Are you alright," she asked.

This must be heaven, he thought to himself as the two beautiful women stared down at him. "My head hurts a little, but I'm fine."

"Oh you pour thing. Bless your heart." The woman ran a light across his eyes. Then she pried each eye open. "How is your vision? Can you see hun?"

"Yes," he responded, wanting to put his hand up against the harsh light.

"How many fingers am I holding up?" She asked.

Jaden looked, one eye open and the other closed. "Three."

She smiled, "Okay dear. I think he is fine."

"Back up. Give the boy some space and stop babying him. He will be alright," a rumbling baritone called from the back of the room.

"Sit up," Imani said as she pulled at him.

Jaden sat up gingerly in a foggy haze. He stared at Imani for a moment, then dabbed at the side of his head. Strangely no blood. "I'm fine." He scanned around the room, grey walls, three other beds surrounded him, and bare halogens buzzed overhead. "Where am I?"

The woman rubbed his back. "Calm down sugar. It's okay. Don't be afraid because you are safe here. You are in the Sanctuary, and no one will harm you."

"The Sanctuary," Jaden repeated. He looked over to

Imani, searching for answers. "What happened? How did we get here?"

Imani smiled. "You did. Glory to the Creator. You neutralized the Locust swarm. It was awesome. Not many can take out a whole pack of demons like that. Let alone ones that haven't been topside in decades."

"I remember, just before I blacked out. They took you." He ran his hand across her shoulder, the same spot the demons sunk their teeth into. Her sweatshirt was slanted over that shoulder. He ran his hand across her skin, searching for bite marks or wounds of any kind and surprisingly finding none. "Are you alright? I thought they killed you."

Imani grabbed his shoulder. "They tried, but it doesn't matter since I'm already dead."

Jaden gulped. "I beg your pardon."

"I'm already dead," she said.

Jaden glanced over to the lady, the look on his face that of a lost child. "Did you hear what she just said?"

The woman nodded. "Yes, of course. She was only being sassy. What she should've told you, is that she is an angel and they can't kill her again." Then she thought about it a moment. "Well not like that anyway."

"You're an angel?" He asked Imani.

"I am," she responded with a stone face.

Jaden took a deep breath. "I think I need to lie back down," he said as he slammed his head back to the pillow.

"No, son. Get on up. We need to talk to you." A man

said as he stood at the foot of the bed. He was a tall, bald, black man somewhere mid-forties, with a look of intensity on his face. "My name is William J. Franklin, but the kids around here call me Coach Franklin. How are you doing Mr. Davis?"

Jaden rose back up. "Not too good Coach. It's a lot going on right now."

Coach Franklin cracked a wry smile. "I can understand that. But don't worry we are here to help you out, and get chu' straight." He paused for a moment. "What do you know about the Order of the Anointed?"

"They are—"

"Soldiers in the army of the Lord," Coach Franklin finished. "The Anointed are sensitive to the move of the holy spirit. They can bend it, use it, and discern truth from it."

"Okay?" Jaden said.

Coach Franklin pointed with his eyes. "Let me introduce to our resident Shepherd Ms. Day, she represents the Shepherd's Guild, and helps me keep missy over there and the boys in line."

Imani shot him a sassy look. "Really Coach."

Ms. Day put up her hand to say Hi, and Jaden acknowledged her with a nod of his head.

"And I know you already got a chance to meet Imani. She's a guardian angel and representative for SMITE."

Jaden nodded. "I have." He raked his gaze around the room.

Large silver doors parted open. Brilliant halogens

reflected off of poly-material flooring, which made no sound as the boys walked in.

"Has sleeping beauty woken up?" Romeo asked.

Imani's eyes tore into Romeo. "Don't start. Jaden is fine. He just needed rest after I healed him."

Jaden scratched his hair. "You what?"

Deshawn answered, "She healed you, big dog. You should be happy. We really thought you were dead. You know it looked like you had a stroke with the whole eyes rolling to the back of your head." Then he smacked Jaden on his leg.

Lay stepped in between the two. "Don't let these guys fool you. We were all worried."

Jaden looked over. "Thanks man."

"No, thank you. You were the one that saved our butts out there. I feel like I owe you a burrito bowl or bubble tea."

Jaden could tell he liked Lay. The other two he didn't care for so much. "I'm from L.A and I'll eat anything as long as it's in a taco."

Romeo sucked his teeth. "Big deal. He got lucky and almost killed himself. I wasn't sweating it anyway because I definitely had a plan to get us out." He said, with his voice a rumbling rasp

Deshawn turned to him. "Oh yeah? What was your plan big dog?"

Romeo looked up to the ceiling for an answer. "I can't remember, but I'm sure it would've been good."

Imani nodded sarcastically. "Right."

Lay snickered. "Don't be a hater Romeo. Jaden saved our lives."

"Okay, that's enough," Coach Franklin stated in a firm, commanding tone. "Jaden we have a couple of questions for you."

Jaden slid to the edge of the bed. "Well, you know what. I don't know what's going on. Thanks for the bed, but I'm finna bail," he said.

"I'm sorry Jaden, but we can't allow you to leave just yet," Ms. Day said as she grabbed his arm. "We have to talk about what just happened."

Imani pulled him back. "I know this must be all scary to you. But there is something important we have to tell you. Jaden, you're special and I'm sure you don't know what you are or how you could stop them."

Jaden peeled back the covers and whirled his feet over the bed. "I know, but I wish I didn't. You don't have to explain a thing, a crazy man from Texas already told me." Jaden shifted his gaze over to Ms. Day. "He was a shepherd too."

Imani twisted her head to the side. "What do you know?"

"I'm one of the anointed. I met a shepherd just after a demon killed my mom. He said he was going to train me so I can hunt and finish off the demon. Finish him off for good."

Ms. Day leaned in further. "You said he is from Texas. What's his name?"

"Sam," Jaden said with a stammer. "Sam Matthews," he completed.

"I know Sam," Ms. Day said with a jolt in her voice as she elbowed Coach Franklin. "We learned about Catholic exorcisms together in New York." Then she turned back to Jaden, and he could see the wheels spinning in her eyes. "Why did he not tell the rest of Guild that he was going to guide you? There is only a few anointed left, and we are always searching for more at headquarters."

"I was hidden from everyone. Sam only knew about me because an angel came to him."

Ms. Day tensed as she asked her next question. "What happened to Sam? Where is he now?"

Jaden drew in an aching breath. "Dead."

She peered down at the floor, almost as if the news stabbed her in the chest. "Oh no, bless his heart. Very well, you are here with us now. We shall carry on the work Sam started and complete your training."

Jaden shook his head as he sprung off the bed. "No we will not. I'm not ready to jump back into this whole Anointed thing." The floor felt cold as he stood on it with his bare feet. His shoes and socks were nestled at the foot of the bed. Jaden started putting them on. "I actually spent my whole life thinking I was a mutant and my ability to hear thoughts was just a mutation or something. I was fine with that. My father is a scientist, and it could've been possible that some experiment happened that I didn't know about, or maybe I got bit by a spider. Either one would make more sense than this."

Lay spoke up. "I know how you feel, and trust me

the best thing you can do is join our team and fellowship with like-minded individuals."

Deshawn raked his dreads. "Easy there, partner. You don't want to make him think this is a cult."

Imani sat back on the cot and motioned for Jaden to do the same. "First of all, an Anointed one is not a freak. The anointed are mortal individuals chosen to be warriors in the Heavenly host. Blessed by the Creator to harness the living Spirit, to save innocent souls and hunt the sons of the darkness. Each Anointed is special. Each one can manipulate the spirit in their own way. You should be happy that you are chosen to do his bidding, and to bring him glory."

Jaden curled his eyebrow. "Happy?" The word came off his lips as if it was a joke. "My life has been everything but happy. I'm sorry but this doesn't sound like good news. You're asking me to risk my life. And at first I was okay with that, because I was so angry, and helpless. I didn't want to be helpless anymore. But I also don't want to be dead either."

"Son, quit your whining. We have all lost someone in this war against the Sons of Chaos. And we will lose more if we just weep over our losses, instead of helping those who we can." He inched closer to Jaden and held out his hands as if molding clay. "Right now, you have the opportunity to be a part of something so much bigger than yourself. Bigger than all of us."

"Sam said something along the same lines, and he died trying to make me something I not. From where I see it, an Anointed is nothing more than a foot soldier.

You know what happens in wars?" He waited a beat before he answered the question. "People die."

Coach Franklin's jaw tightened, as he leaned further towards Jaden. "I tell you what? Keep running from your destiny. You see what happened to Emanuel, if you don't get aboard this train, then you might get left behind."

Romeo's thoughts trickled into Jaden's mind. *He's tripping now. Dude is really going to flip when she mentions the Book of the Anointed.*

Jaden turned to Ms. Day. "What is the Book of the Anointed?"

Ms. Day's face lit up in shock as she turned to Coach Franklin searching for approval. "It's pretty complicated and I hope we would've covered some easier topics before we tackled that. But since you asked, we can discuss it. And I can even give you a tour while we are at it," she said with enthusiasm.

Imani tugged Jaden's arm. "Come on."

With a sigh he followed them past the silver doors, and further into the Sanctuary.

CHAPTER EIGHT

Book of the Anointed

Water dripped on top of Jaden's head as he stepped over rats scurrying past. It fell in dotted spots along the hall and made a rhythm with the soft mechanical buzz that hummed in the air. Jaden figured they were underground. The walls crumbled and the florescent lights flickered dimly, making their path difficult to see. While he strained his eyes to follow along the path, the others navigated the path instinctively.

Deshawn sighed out from the back. "Can we hurry this up? I'm so freaking hungry and I've been thinking about an all-star breakfast from the Waffle House since forever."

"When are you ever not hungry?" Imani asked sarcastically

Deshawn thought about it for a moment. "That's a good question."

"Here is the War room" Imani said as they walked through a pair of large silver double doors.

Jade noticed every door was silver and slid open with such ease, and swiftness that they made a soft coo as they parted. Everything in the room was all white and state of the art, with polished walls that gleamed like new enamel, and stretched high to a crystal ceiling. The stars glittered like sparkling jewels as they reflected into the room and casted a heavenly glow over them. They entered from the left and there were two other doors on opposite sides, leading to other rooms, and another set of large double doors straight ahead.

In the middle of the room was a circular table, with three large holographic screens towering above. Lights from the screen flickered along their faces, etching them in shades of red and blue.

"This is hella dope," Jaden said as he took in the room. "It makes me want to be a Power Ranger again. I feel like I'm seven." A fleeting thought made his eyes light up like diamonds. "If there are costumes, armor, or any type of suit...Then I just might join. Just as long as I get the red one."

Coach Franklin walked by with his hands clasped behind his back. "No suits."

Imani pulled Jaden further along. "Let's continue the tour. To the left you have the armory. On the right is a training room we call the Ring."

"My favorite place," Romeo added

"Let me guess…. you love to fight huh?" Jaden said.

Romeo flexed his biceps. "What can I say? I'm like a Spartan warrior through and through."

Jaden rolled his eyes. *More like a dickhead*, he thought. He quickened his pace behind Imani. Etched across the double doors were the repeated sigils of a hammer, shield, and cross fashioned into a sword." What do these symbols stand for?"

Coach Franklin turned shoulder. "The cross is the symbol for the Anointed, The Creator's chosen."

Ms. Day pointed. "The shield is the symbol for the Shepherds. We are the keepers of knowledge, we protect, and prepare the Anointed to combat evil forces. For as long as there have been Anointed, there have been Shepherds."

Coach Franklin pointed. "And the last sigil, the hammer is the symbol for SMITE, the pantheon of archangels who gather intelligence for war and protect mankind from high priority attacks."

Imani touched Jaden's shoulder. "I'm training to join SMITE." She beamed with delight. " Hopefully I will be an Archangel someday."

"What are you now?" Jaden asked.

"Just a guardian. I only heal and guide." Imani shrugged, sounding so displeased. "It's like babysitting. I want to kick some ass."

Jaden had only known her for a day, but he could tell she was tough. There was something about Imani that reminded him of the girls he grew up with. They were the ones first and last on the basketball court, eager to prove themselves so they would never be chosen last for teams. "So why do you go to school if you're an angel?"

"I got special permission to keep an eye on these

knuckleheads at all times."

Jaden laughed. "That's cool I guess."

Imani smacked her fist. "When I become an archangel I'll get my armored wings and blazing sword.

"Come along, let me show you the study," Ms. Day said.

Together they walked past the second set of double doors into a wonderfully spacious library. The Marble floor clattered as they walked into the room, each one spreading out. It reminded Jaden more of a museum with the various artifacts displayed across the floor in glass cases.

"This is the study," Ms. Day said. There was a hint of enthusiasm in her voice.

Modern sculptural chandeliers hung high from the vaulted ceiling, and shined a soft white light that gave everything a luminous shimmer below. The study was shaped like an octagon, with walls that towered three levels above, and were all lined with books encased in glass shelves that sled from the wall upon entrance.

Stained glass windows with moving portraits of warrior angels lined the upper levels, all around the room. Each of them struck down the demon immortalized with them. They all turned eyes towards Jaden, casting a threatening look at this outsider. A long table was placed at the center of the room, with round emerald leather chairs fashioned about it. Even though the library was vast, there was still an intimate feel in the room. Tiny lamps decorated the table, and every other table in all the nooks and crannies of the space, their lights like small flickering torches.

Coach Franklin silently climbed the polished oak staircase. Romeo, Lay and Deshawn each took a seat at the long table while Jaden continued to follow behind the two ladies.

Jaden sighed. "Let me take a guess to what's in this book. It's going to say the apocalypse is near. The world is ending. We have to stop the four horsemen from riding, find the antichrist, and a lamb at the zoo, for a sacrifice?"

Romeo propped his feet on the table. "Hate to break it to you, but we're past all of that. The world is going to hell as we speak. We've seen some strange things these past few months."

Ms. Day sashayed over, and snatched Romeo's legs down. "What is this? Do not come here and damage the furniture." She said through tight teeth. Her accent more pronounced than before.

Deshawn leaned back. "And bro, we have fought some even crazier monsters. Do yawl remember the possessed octopus?"

A collective yeah echoed around the room.

Romeo stood up. "And let's not forget," he said before pausing.

"EVIL ELROY," they all said in unison.

Ms. Day pulled off her glasses and wiped them clear. "Even though I think it's childish to delight in demonic activity, I must admit we have seen some good times on this side of glory."

"Evil Elroy?" Jaden repeated.

Lay's chair screeched when he slid back. "Yes. Come on it's over here," he said as he walked to the far side of the room.

Jaden followed behind him. Hidden in a small corner of the room was a furry red doll, concealed in a glass case. Jaden noticed the case was positioned in the center of a strange drawing on the floor.

"What is that?" Jaden asked as he pointed.

"It's how we keep him jailed. We weren't able to vanquish the demon or break his attachment to the doll, so we brought him back for safekeeping." Lay bent down and smiled at the doll. "Isn't he cute?"

Jaden grinned. "He kind of is with his bow tie." Then he reached out to touch the glass case.

"No!" Ms. Day shouted as she sprinted across the room in heels. "Do not touch the case." She stood in front of Jaden and Lay, then pushed them back. "It took us weeks at the Shepherd's Guild to find spells to bind this thing." She pointed a warning finger at them. "If you tickle him, he will stab you. So do not touch the case."

Romeo died in a fit of laughter behind them. "Do yawl remember how he chased after Deshawn with an axe?"

Imani buried her mouth in her hands. "I don't think I ever saw something so funny." She sat on the side of the table near Deshawn. "Do you have anything to say about your old friend?"

Deshawn shook his head. "Hell no." He turned his head, glaring at the doll from across the room. "Elroy," he said with a shudder.

Ms. Day clasped her hands. "In all seriousness Jaden, this is why we need you now more than ever. The evil in this town has grown strong. And you need to be here to complete your training and protect yourself. Evil is drawn to you as one of the anointed. Your soul is like a light that pulls them like a moth to a flame."

Jaden hung his head low. "I hear you, but I just don't think I'm cut out to be anybody's hero. I'm good."

"I know how you feel. Trust me I do," Lay added. "Like you I can say I have had my gift since birth."

"And that gift is?" Jaden asked.

Lay adjusted his glasses. "I can talk to computers, it's like I can see speak code." He paused for a moment and then said. "I can also do this," he pulled out the light staff and it made a brilliant noise as it flickered against the marble. "And we all have our struggles with these gifts given to us through the spirit." Lay beckoned Romeo with his eyes.

Romeo pointed to himself. "My turn? I can see into the future and channel light energy. I can bend light around me or shoot it through my fingers like a laser. And my boy Deshawn can control molecular acceleration, either making a time field slowing something down or speeding it up until it detonates and explode."

"Almost like time control?" Jaden added

"It helped me to run away from the cops back when I was a little hustler," Deshawn admitted.

"See? I would even take the visions over the

headaches and nosebleeds that come with reading minds and bending spoons."

"I don't think so... I went blind once," Romeo added.

Jaden shook his head. "Oh never mind then."

"Anyway like I said I've had my gifts since birth too. Back then the visions used to be dreams and the whole light bending thing didn't start until I met Imani."

Jaden turned to Deshawn, "How about you? Had yours since birth too?"

Deshawn typed furiously on his phone.

"Deshawn!" Imani shouted.

"Hold on," Deshawn said as he typed. He dropped his phone on the table with a loud clatter. "Like I said I didn't do anything until one night when I was a little hustler, the police chased me. I slowed down time and ran away."

Coach Franklin cleared his throat as he descended the staircase. "I don't know if your new buddies have told you, but our town sits right on top of a Hell gate." He carried a large black leather book in his hands, like it was a baby.

Jaden raised an eyebrow. "What is that?"

Coach Franklin frowned, "You've got to be kidding me. Are you sure you've been trained by a shepherd?" He slammed the book on the table. "A Hell gate is literally a portal between our world and the Hell dimension. As long as there have been Anointed, there have been Hell gates for us to take down. It's ridiculous how this thing goes. We take one down. They build another up. We take that one down, then they move to another city to dig another one up."

Coach Franklin boots clamored across the floor. "They are currently four active Hell gates in the world, and you better believe they will do whatever they can to get another one up and running. Even in its dormant state, like the one near our town, they still draw monsters to the city like a magnet," he said pointing. "Now you see why you're here and we are all here, it's part of the Creator's plan."

He paged through the book with an anxious finger, turning to the page with Hell Gate written in bold letters. "This is the Book of the Anointed. At its core it is Bible, but really it's so much more than that. It can be considered a code of arms for the Order of the Anointed, a guide to demon hunting, or even a book of magic for the rituals listed in capturing and summoning demons. But for the most part it is a codex with over a thousand demons, monsters, angels, and deities." Coach Franklin slid the book across the table to Jaden.

Jaden ran his hand across the hallowed pages of the tome, the parchment was brown and so thick that it felt like the cover of the paperback book. "How did you get this?"

"The Book has been passed down over the centuries to Anointed warriors. It's a direct link to the good folks' upstairs, and continues to write itself from the words of angels. Others may have copies, but I have the original. I found it myself over thirty years ago in Jerusalem," Coach Franklin said

Ms. Day lowered her glasses. "Legends say that the Archangels crafted it from the tree of knowledge, and gave it to King David. He was the first Anointed. He filled the book with the information about the demons he crossed, and the knowledge he got from the warrior angels in SMITE."

Jaden flipped through the pages of the book, and his face curled in horror at the true visages of the demons. All of the depictions were wonderfully illustrated in lush vivid colors, making them appear as grisly dark art. In their true form outside the shell of humans, the demons appeared as twisted hodgepodges of random human and animal parts.

Jaden pushed the book away in disgust. "Coach, what happens when one of these Hell Gates are open?"

Coach Franklin face became rigid. "It opens. And trust me, son, you better hope you're not there when it happens. I've only deactivated one Hell gate before in my life." Coach Franklin lifted his shirt, turned his back, black claw marks stretched from his back to the right of his chest. "I got the souvenir that signified I survived, and I give glory to the Creator, because I was the only one on my team who did."

"What did you see?" Jaden asked, his lips trembling. blood pounding in his ears.

Coach Franklin's lips curled. "Horrors you can only imagine. Hell gates are buried underground and surrounded by a space that can only described as an abyss. This book covers over one thousand demons, and

I'm sure each of them was down there. Human centipedes, cyclops, gargoyles, and angry spirits. We saw a lot of horrors down there, but nothing like the Locusts. I got this scar from their queen. That's why I'm worried about you boys finding Locusts hatchlings."

"Coach, the Locusts haven't been seen for over three decades." Lay said.

"I know. Somehow they must've came through the gate."

"But how?" Imani asked.

Ms. Day rubbed at her neck. "Someone or something must be powering it."

Coach Franklin slapped Jaden on the back and stood. "I think we have enough action tonight. The best we can do is get some rest, and work on it tomorrow." When Jaden stood, Coach Franklin clasped his hand on his shoulder. "I know this is a lot we are asking of you. But I think you should PRAY about this, and let us know if you will be joining us or not."

"Deal," Jaden said.

Ms. Day opened her arms to direct him. "Please let me see you out."

Jaden followed her and Imani stood in his path. "Are you going to be alright?"

"I'll be fine," he said on shallow breath.

Imani wrapped her arms around him. The hug was so sudden, that he didn't have time to think. She buried his nose in her silky smooth hair, and the scent of coconut danced into his nostrils.

"Do not be afraid. I will always find you." She

whispered, before letting go.

Jaden stood there stunned. In only one day, this girl, this angel had managed to touch him in places he didn't know existed.

"Goodnight," he said as he followed Ms. Day

"Good bye!" Lay said as he waved.

Ms. Day led him over to a regular wooden door, concealed underneath a spiraling staircase. There they entered a small anteroom that was dim, dry and smelled of old dust. At the center of the room was a glass elevator, framed by glistening oak, and another portrait of an Archangel displayed on top. Ms. Day summoned the elevator with the push of a button.

Ms. Day rubbed her hands across her bare arms. "Darling, are you okay?"

Jaden grinned, "Yes mam."

"Get home and get some sleep sugar." She said with a grin as she patted his shoulder.

A bell dinged and the elevator doors parted open. They both stepped in, standing shoulder to shoulder. By Jaden's guess the elevator could hold no more than four people inside. Ms. Day waved her hand over a marble panel and blue light scanned her wrist. She pressed the L for the top floor, and the elevator jerked as they ascended.

Ms. Day spoke to him softly, as the elevator gears cranked. "We are aware of the trauma you have endured. Bless your heart. The guild does know that an upper level demon murdered your mom."

She said the word murder, and the word itself hung

in the air, making sadness choke his heart. Jaden said nothing.

"Just know this dear child" Ms. Day started as she leaned in closer, almost as if she was telling him a secret. "Whether or not you use your abilities, they will come for you. Especially in this town."

"Let em' come," Jaden said with fire in his eyes.

A loud ting broke the silence that followed Jaden's words. The doors opened to the elevator, they got off and walked into an empty gym. It was dark and all of the lights were turned off. There was a small boxing ring at the center, punching bags and heavy weights scattered along the sides. Jaden only had a brief look around as they headed straight to the door.

"Come I will take you home myself," Ms. Day said in a high merry voice.

They walked across the gym and outside to a parking lot. He got in the car and remained silent all the way home.

Chapter Nine

King of the South

The only thing vampires craved more than blood was power. And from where Fangz stood he was pretty powerful. Fangz slinked off the elevator like a panther, swathed in a magnificent black fur, his personal guards strolled beside him. Below them stood glistening gold decorated bars, serving champagne glasses of blood and hors d'oeuvres of human flesh. Italian rugs covered a polished marble floor packed with bodies dancing to the music from his new mixtape, Blood & Gold.

"Nice turn out boss," his guard, a bulging hulk said.

"Just make sure they are recording this," he replied.

The scene that laid out before him looked like a perfect background for a music video, better yet a movie. He gave strict order to take care of his VIP human guests. There would be no tasting without consent. For them he had endless bottles of champagne, vodka, and cognac flowing everywhere, as well as blood drawn from willing vampire hosts who laughed as the humans drank in an erotic frenzy.

Every guest dressed in designer black silk, and adorned themselves with thousands of dollars in jewelry. Fangz made his way over to the balcony, tossing the fur on the floor like it was nothing. He had rock sized diamonds in his ear, half a million in canary diamonds on his neck, a quarter million on his wrist, and one million for each diamond crusted fang. They were an upgrade from the gold. Fangz stood average height, medium size build, dark skin, and shoulder-length dreads. Steampunk sunglasses covered his eyes, tattoos ran all over his body, including his face, a blood covered crown by his right ear.

Fangz raised his hand. All at once the music lowered and the crowd quieted.

He lifted a blood filled champagne glass. "Tonight I raise a glass to all yawl, my squad, my fam, my True Bloods. On this night we go live with our newest product, B13 aka Becky. After tonight we will find Becky in every club, every lounge, on every corner and every major city all over the south."

Fangz pulled out the small purple pill. "And not only that, thanks to my new homies in the back." He pointed his glass to the table of executives who sat in the corner. "Blood & Gold will conquer the airwaves this summer." Fangz hardened his jaw. "If you not down with this Vamp life, then you'd be better off dead. I'm telling you now that ain't no old blood suckers about to stop me, nor any juice boxes bout to stand in my way." There was cackling in the room, followed by hand claps. Fangz rose his glass higher. "Now let's turn up one good time for the True Bloods."

"To the True Bloods." The crowd said in unison.

Hundreds of glasses raised towards him and once Fangz drunk his down, so did the others, and the music came back on in full force. Fangz felt a powerful presence in the room. He descended the stairs and met the gaze of the southern King, Marcus. His skin was the shade of a frosted cinnamon bun, and his hair was the color of night, slicked and styled up into a pompadour do.

"Can I help you playboy?"

"I've come to deliver the punishment for your crimes." Marcus raked his gaze across the room with his nose frowned. "You new bloods sicken me with your need for attention. It is like that of a spoiled child." He touched Fangz on the shoulder. "Didn't Midnight teach you anything? We are the Lords of darkness. Our power lies in our omnipotence. We command from the shadows."

Fangz moved his shoulder. "Us new bloods are tired of those rules. We don't want to lurk in the shadows. We want to shine like diamonds in the moonlight." He said as he lifted his chain.

Marcus laughed in a pompous manner. "You don't think you're the first one to try something like this? There have been others who have tried drag our nation out of the shadows before. Only difference between them and you, is that you have a powerful maker that has petitioned for mercy on your behalf."

"But look around," Fangz said. "The mortals are so happy to be here. They love this lifestyle. We don't have to hunt for them, they come to us, flocking like cattle to the slaughter. They all want to be a part of this movement. To dance in a new night."

Marcus spat on Fangz sneakers. "That's what I think about you and your new night. Out of my close relationship with Midnight, I Marcus, King of the Southern ward have come to deliver your punishment myself."

"Punishment for what? I did nothing except make a music video and put out some songs."

"You almost exposed us to the world. Do you know how much damage you could've caused? The only reason your head hasn't been ripped from your shoulders is because of Midnight. You should praise him at his feet once this is all over." Marcus circled Fangz, "How did you do it? Get your reflection recorded."

Fangz unbuttoned his shirt. "It's the ink man."

Marcus ran his hand along the tribal tattoos written across Fangz ashen brown chest. "Impressive. What is it?"

"Magic," Fangz answered with a cocky grin. "When you got the green and the knowhow, you can make things happen."

Marcus swirled his cloak. "You're smart for a young arrogant bastard."

"And you're foolish for coming here," Fangz bellowed. Then he raked his claws across Marcus' face. His fangs dropped as he battle bulked. His face shifted into a contortion that resembled a hungry lion, completed with golden eyes, and wrinkles around the mouth that stretched to unveil glittering fangs.

"You fool!" Marcus touched the wound slashed across his face. "I came to show you mercy and you dare defy me. You dare defy the will of the Vampire council."

"Did you really think you was about to roll up in my crib and disrespect me in front of my own? That's not about to happen." Fangz shouted.

All at once fangs around the room clicked as they dropped, and talons elongated.

"I'll destroy you all." Marcus hurdled a ball of shadows to the penthouse floor, and black smoke billowed around him. There was a roar and a hiss as something grew in the billowing darkness that became a consuming cloud.

A bear the size of a Hummer truck emerged from the smoke. It anchored itself on the ground by slashing through the marble, then it leaned back, and roared in Fangz face. "You will pay for such insolence."

Fangz didn't move an inch as the hot breath of the beast, blew his dreads off his shoulders. "Now," he ordered.

Two vampires leapt from the balcony and unloaded silver bullets. Marcus roared, reared, and cocked his head back as the two overwhelmed him with rapid fire. By the time they both landed on their knees, right behind Fangz, the elder vampire had transformed back.

Fangz stood over him. "Never underestimate a young

blood. Ain't no mercy in the new night. Only savages."

Marcus coughed as silver seeped out of his eyes, mouth, and ears. He choked as he laughed. "Not even Midnight will get you out of this one."

Fangz turned him over with his foot. "He won't need to. We needed you out of the way to take over the council."

Garrett dropped the gun to his side as he approached Fangz. His complexion was even paler in the moonlight that spilled from the floor to ceiling window. "Now, before the silver spreads to his heart."

"Lights out old man," Fangz bellowed. In one quick motion, he reached into Marcus chest, and retrieved his heart.

"Eat it," Priyanka said as she came closer.

Fangz sunk his teeth into the heart and trembled at the power. He released a guttural roar that shook the penthouse and made the human guest search for exits.

"How does it feel?" Priyanka asked.

"Magnificent," Fangz declared with his eyes turning a dark crimson red. He faced the crowd. "I apologize yawl for the interruption. It was just a little razzle dazzle, but we shall continue the party. Now turn up the music and bring out more bottles."

The music cranked up and the partied resumed like normal. Garrett offered Fangz a handkerchief to clean his hands, as a server offered him a glass of blood to sate his thirst.

"Report," Fangz declared.

"We got some news we need to discuss in private."

Garrett said.

Fangz sipped at the blood. "What is it?"

Priyanka stepped forward. "I got the word that demons are about to move in on our territory."

A scowl curled on Fangz' face. "Let's talk about this in my office." He strutted across the crowd, and they followed close behind.

Fangz was a few steps from his office, when a woman blocked his path. She had olive skin with blazing red hair, and made his fangs lengthen at the sight of her thigh which stuck out of the long split of her flowing black gown.

"Fangz, I've been waiting to thank you personally for all your help with my campaign,"

Fangz grinned at her. "No problem Mayor Fenty. The pleasure was all mine. Believe me baby. Let me look at ya," He spun her around, admiring her shape. Then he slapped her bottom. "You look mad fat back there. Did you get your tattoo?"

Mayor Fenty curled her hair to the right, to show the sigil tattooed on the back of her neck. The mark of a familiar.

"It looks beautiful baby." Fangz said.

Her lips pursed sensuously. "Thank you."

"I'm going to talk a little bit of business, with my people but I'll be back out talk to you later."

A waiter handed the mayor a glass of champagne. "Okay. I have big plans for this city. Plans that involve your generosity. Do not keep me waiting."

"No doubt," he said as he put on his shades. He walked into his office, and Priyanka closed the doors behind them once they entered.

"Tell me what's going on?" Fangz said as he sat on the edge of his desk.

Priyanka stood on his right, "One of my sources has told me that an upper level demon has made his way topside."

"You're kidding me," Fangz commented.

Priyanka shook her head, "No. And that's not it. This demon is one of the Sons of Chaos, and most likely a devil."

"Devils are powerful." Garrett commented.

Fangz walked around his desk and lit up a cigar. He took a slow pull of the cigar and blew out smoke. "Okay one devil in the city is something to be concerned about. Nothing to make me lose my cool, but definitely something to watch."

"Sir, that's not it." Garrett interjected. "One of our boys came across locust ash outside the city in Alpharetta."

Fangz snarled. "Locusts? I don't remember ever even hearing about a locust demon topside."

"I know sir, we think they crawled out of the pit." Priyanka added.

A revelation hit Fangz and as fear swept through him, and covered his face. "That means whoever came topside, is here to open that Hell gate. And if they do that, then it's bad for business. Too many demons in one small city. Hell with a devil and a whole horde of locusts they can wipe out everything." Fangz snapped his fingers.

"Priyanka find out everything there is to know about this demon. I want to know who came topside, what do they want, and how to kill them."

Fangz took a puff from his cigar, before he spoke again. "Is there anything else?"

Garrett relaxed his jaw, "What about the Anointed? With the launch of the new product tonight, I'm sure they've heard and they will be out hunting our boys."

Fangz nodded in agreement as he tried to piece together a plan in his head. One of the rare times he wished Midnight had been near. Midnight had killed over a dozen Anointed himself. Fangz took another puff, blew out, and outed the cigar on the corner of his desk. "This is what I want you to do," he started as he walked over to his desk and took a seat behind.

"Garrett I want you to go out to Safari tomorrow night and round up some fresh meat."

Garrett rubbed his hands greedily, as his fingers lowered, then he licked his lips. "No problem boss."

"Get a large group. Mostly girls and take them to one of the trap houses nearby. I'll be there waiting for them."

"You will handle them yourself?" Priyanka asked

"Yes, with all this going on I have rage to get off my chest." Fangz turned to the window, "Now go you two, and don't mess this up. The streets are mine. This city is mine. I run the south." He declared.

Chapter Ten

High school is hell

Jaden rose the next morning, from the most restless sleep of his life. He felt a familiar sense of dread he had long forgotten, coupled with a roaring hunger pain from not eating last night. Today is his first day of school and if it was anything like his first night, then he would be doomed. He walked downstairs to find his father drinking coffee and reading the news on his tablet. For some reason Jaden expected breakfast to be on the table, but then he remembered they had no food, plus his father was no cook anyway.

"You came home late last night." His father said without looking in his direction.

"I got lost." Jaden replied as threw his book bag over the shoulder.

"Uh huh," John said before taking a sip of coffee. "Did you get something to eat?"

Jaden grabbed at his stomach. "No and I'm starving."

"We can get something on the way to your school." John settled the mug on the counter. "Did you take your medicine?"

Jaden shook his head.

John's face became stone. "That's not very responsible Mr. Davis. What do I tell you about responsibilities?"

"Yeah, I know. Can we just get something to eat because I'm hungry?"

John set his jaw hard before getting up to grab his keys. They got in the car and their first stop before jumping on the highway, was to a fast food joint to pick up breakfast sandwiches before making their way to Jaden's school. The ride over to his school was mostly silent, and that was fine with him because he only wanted to eat. Jaden inhaled his sandwich in three bites.

From a quick Google search, he discovered that North Central High had a total of three hundred and twenty-nine students, which wasn't even half his freshman class at Crenshaw High. Jaden imagined most of the kids grew up together or were related to one another.

His status as the new kid on the block, scared him more than the monsters he faced last night. That anxiety alone was enough to make him want to scheme his way out of going.

Surprisingly North Central wasn't too far from his home. When he clicked directions on the app, it estimated a fifteen-minute ride using an exit right off the highway.

He stared out of the window watching nothing but trees and fields of brown grass roll past. His father pulled up to the curb and the school looked better than the online pictures. The school had only been seven years old, the Google search showed some tragic accident happened at the old school, prompting them to build another. Jaden bookmarked the article to read later. A plain brown field surrounded North Central, with hardly any trees or greenery at all on the lawn. The building wasn't too shabby. It was a medium size complex made of maroon bricks with a faded green roofing.

His father finally spoke as the car slowed. "I don't want you to stress about anything today. Just be yourself and do your best."

"Sounds good doc," Jaden said as he made his escape out of the car. He unbuckled his seat belt, grabbed his bag and hopped out.

"Son," John called back. His face stiffened. "Don't get into any trouble."

Jaden curled his lip. "I'll try not," he said with a sarcastic grin.

"Also don't forget to go up to the Principal office. I think she wants to give you a tour or something."

"Got it. See you later." Jaden said. He watched his father drive off before he turned to the entrance.

A crowd moved across the stone steps towards the school entrance like sheep. There was an occasional bunch of stragglers who stood aside, each talking in different groups. Jaden took a deep breath and made his way into the crowd. He reached the top of the stairs, and a strange odor of manure made him cover his nose. The smell hit him like a punch in the face. Other students walked past him with no sign of the same disgust, and Jaden wondered how anyone could be used to such a foul stench.

"Hollywood," Imani called.

She spotted him as soon as he climbed the steps. He stood out of the crowd like a sore thumb. He carried the sun and the breeze of California from the way he dressed to the way he walked. In the full light of day, she could see again how handsome he was with his curly brown and blonde hair. The fact he acted like he had no clue to this made him seem even more adorable in her eyes.

Jaden turned and smile. "What's up. It's nice to see a friendly face." The smell hit him again and he wrinkled his nose. "What's that smell?"

"Oh that's just the field or some farms nearby." Imani said.

"How do you stand it? Jaden asked.

"I don't know. Guess everyone here is just used to it," Imani said. She waited a beat before she spoke again. "About last night-" she started.

Jaden held out his hand. "Let's not talk about it. I have enough to deal with, like not trying to be a complete outcast like I was at my old school."

Imani tried to hide the smile on her face. "Why do you say that?"

"They called me a creep because I would sometime stare at people."

Imani chuckled, "Why were you starring?" "If you heard what some of these kids think you would look at them crazy too. I don't hear everyone's thoughts all the time, but I swear it's only the deep, inner most thoughts they wouldn't dare say out loud that come to me."

Imani rolled her eyes. "I can only imagine."

Jaden's shoulder slumped as he held the door for Imani. "Tell me about it. I don't understand why I can't hear your thoughts though. It's so strange. Normally I'm doing my best to tune people out, but with you, I do my best to listen, and I can't hear anything."

Imani considered it for a moment. "I'm sure there is some science behind it. I'm technically dead so there is nothing to hear. It's the same way with vampires. Brain waves and synapses and stuff. Take AP neuroscience and you'll figure it."

"Ha ha true."

Side by side they strode down the hall and came to an atrium, where three other halls laid in front of him. North Central was a large stretch of a school with no upper or lower floors. Chatter surrounded them, along with the clamors from footsteps of students as they walked the halls.

Jaden stood on the corner, near the tinsel trophy case. "Do you think you can point me to the principal's office."

Imani pointed. "It's down the hall and to the right. All of the admin offices are down there, the principal's office, guidance counselors, and career coaches."

"Where are you going?"

"I have Spanish the other way."

"Alright. I will catch you later." Jaden said.

Imani backed away. "Have a nice day," she said with a lingering smile.

Grinning from ear to ear he turned, and headed down the hall. Jaden found the principal's office with no problem. It was a lot nicer than he anticipated, the outside was an all glass modern design, with the word admin written over the top. Inside it was brightly lit, warm, and spacious. He stood near the door in the waiting area, black padded chairs lined the wall to his left and a long counter that slashed the room in half. A woman sat on the other side, with a short pixie cut that made her look half her age in a good way.

"Good morning. How may I help you?" she asked in a cheery tone.

Jaden cleared his throat. "I'm here to meet the principle. My name is—"

"Jaden Davis," a voice completed from the back. A tall heavy set, black woman with large curly hair came around the corner. She held out her hand. "Well good morning young man. My name is Dr. Ball."

"Jaden," he said as he took her hand.

"Mr. Davis, it's nice to meet you. Why don't you follow me." Dr. Ball said as she led him around the corner. Jaden walked into the office behind her, and she pointed towards the chair in front of her desk. "Have a seat."

Jaden felt hot air blew at him, walking in. There was

a hum of a machine in the background and he figured she had the heat on full blast. An intoxicating smell of dandelions and sage danced into Jaden's nose. "It smells good in here."

Dr. Ball's glossy lips twisted into a smile, "Well thank you. That's Eucalyptus oil, If I'm not mistaken."

She rested her hands on her desk. "It's not every day that we get new students all the way from California. On behalf of the faculty and staff I want to welcome you to North Central High."

"Thanks," Jaden said

Dr. Ball took a quick glance at a folder that was laid on her desk. It sat on top of memos, flyers, and budget printouts. "Now our records show that during your first year at Crenshaw High, you had high grades and high aptitude. That's the Jaden we want at North Central. Now, let me be completely honest with you, all that other stuff that happened in your past semester." She stood and leaned over the table. "We aren't having none of that over here."

Jaden leaned back in the chair, as if she spewed fire. "Ms. Ball, just let me explain. I'm not sure what is says in that file over there, but I can tell you that it was all just a misunderstanding."

"Doctor Ball," She corrected as she picked up his folder, and adjusted her glasses. "Let me tell you what it says. I see fighting, tardiness, skipping classes, and FIVE-THOUSAND-dollar damage to school property." She slapped the folder back on the desk and bit her tongue. "Son why did you turn on the sprinklers in a computer lab?"

Jaden choked. "It was filled with a bunch of demo-" He coughed. "Bugs. It was a lot of bugs in the room and I couldn't kill them all. So I thought I'd drowned him."

"Bugs?" She repeated with her eyebrows raised.

Dr. Ball walked behind Jaden's chair. "Young man, I also read about what happened to your mother. Such a tragedy. Trust and believe we are all thankful that the days of terror from the Crucifer are long gone."

Jaden hung his head low.

Dr. Ball tapped him on the shoulder. "No sir Mr. Davis. Don't ever put your head down. Here at North Central we always want our students to reach for the stars and be optimistic. I too have lost a parent, and I can empathize with the pain you must feel. But dear you have to ask yourself if your mother was here, would this be the life she wants for you?"

Jaden remained silent. Dr. Ball's thoughts came swirling into his head. *Look at this poor baby, he sure looks pitiful and don't know what to do with himself.*

Dr. Ball rubbed his shoulders. "Don't worry Jaden. As you go through the grieving process we will be right here with you. Anything you need. The North Central staff is a family and for that very reason I am recommending two things."

"What is that?" Jaden asked.

Dr. Ball walked back behind her desk and smiled over to him, "I want you to meet two very special people," she said. Then she lowered her lips to the speaker. "Tish, can you please send them in."

"Right away Dr. Ball," a voice responded back.

"Jaden I'm sure you are going to appreciate this, because we are going to set you on the right path at North Central."

The door cracked open and in walked Ms. Day and Lay. Jaden's jaw fell open. "This must be a set up. What are you doing here?"

Dr. Ball frowned. "Excuse me, am I missing something."

"No," Everyone said in unison.

Dr. Ball walked over to Ms. Day. "First Jaden I would like you to meet Dr. Melissa Day. She is our newest guidance counselor, hailing from Jackson, Mississippi."

Ms. Day wore an extravagant red wrap over a black dress. She pulled the wrap closer before extending her hand. "Hello Jaden, it's nice to meet you."

Jaden shook her hand, "Likewise."

"Like I said Jaden I know you've been going through a rough patch as all high school students do, plus moving to a new school can be difficult. That's why I'm advising you to do a weekly visit with Dr. Day."

"For what? I'm fine." Jaden shouted.

"I understand that son, but like I said I'm expecting good things from you. I want you to have all the emotion support you need at this time." Then she stepped over to Lay. "With that in mind I want to introduce you to the incredibly smart Jin-Soo Lee."

Lay waved his hand and beamed. "Hi. Jaden."

Dr. Ball continued, "Jin-Soo is number one in the sophomore class. He along with a few other students such as Makayla Lawson, Amy Cho, Lori Gunther and Dorian Blackwell have some of the highest GPAs in not just their class, but history of North Central High. I spoke to your father before you came in today and he informed me that after the tragedy of your mother, you fell into the wrong crowd."

Jaden wanted to shoot himself as Dr. Ball rubbed his back.

"That's why I want to make sure to introduce you to the right crowd. Most of your classes are with Jin-Soo Lee and he has agreed to be your tour guide."

"Don't worry Jaden I'm sure we are going to be great buddies, or should I say great homies."

Jaden cringed at the word homies and forced a fake smile. "I'm sure we will."

A digital bell sounded and made Dr. Ball pause before starting her next sentence. "Well I should let you boys get on the way."

Jaden silently followed Lay out of the office, and into the hallway. He wasn't sure if destiny was trying to thrust him back into the folds of the Anointed, or if these people just wanted to harass him. Either way he will be seeing them consistently for the school year.

"Tell me about your old high school in California." Lay asked, breaking the silence between them.

Jaden adjusted his book bag strap. "It was a lot bigger than this. Crenshaw is about the size of a college campus. Every classroom had smart boards and we used tablets for everything."

"Neat," Lay exclaimed. "I'm sorry to say we don't have any of that here, but we do have a very good AP program and many dedicated teachers for it." Lay waited a beat. "How were the kids back there?"

"What do you mean?" Jaden asked.

"You know, are there any mean kids? Is everyone nice and do they get along?"

"No, that's what I miss about Cali, my dude. Everybody is just super chill, except the ones that like to do the most." He cleared his throat, "Don't get me wrong you did have your occasional douchebags and stuck up pretty girls."

Lay adjusted his glasses. "Same thing here. There are a few people that are just mean, like that girl over there Erica King. And—"

"Gang gang, the night calls my name. True Bloods is the squad and I got the fangs that drive these girls insane." A boy raps as he and his friend stomp down the hall.

A burly dreaded boy next to the one rapping, brushes Lay by the shoulders. "Move out of the way juice box."

Lay snatched his glasses off. "Hey, that was not nice."

The boy whirled on his right foot, and the guy he was walking with a much slender dude, with a maroon fro-hawk said, "We got a problem, Hello Kitty?" He squared off against Lay.

"Yeah do we have a problem? Meow. Meow" His

friend quipped.

Both of their voices were muffled. Jaden noticed they wore gold fronts in their mouth with elongated incisors. *Vamp life fanboys*, he thought to himself.

Jaden dropped his bag to his legs, in his hands it became a weapon. "Just keep it moving bro. Unless you are trying to catch a fade."

Lay brushed him back. "There is no problem. Just a mistake. We don't want any trouble."

Dread head groaned. "That's what I thought. I know you were not trying to see me with the hands."

"Come on," Lay murmured to Jaden as they turned and walked the opposite direction.

The boys continued walking down the hallway. "You better watch who you hang with cuz. You're going to mess around and become a dead man. Vamp life suckers!"

Anger rolled off Jaden like billowing steam.

"Why didn't you destroy those guys just now? I saw you fight in the woods. You're a low-key killing machine and if anything would've happened, I would've had your back."

Lay grinned. "Thanks Jaden, for the warm words and sentiment. But I couldn't because it's not the way of the Anointed. As soldiers in the army of the Creator we are here to keep the peace, protect the people, and smite the enemy."

Jaden arched his brow. "The way of the anointed. You guys sound more like a cult every day."

"It's not," he said as his jaw slacked. "It's a calling and way of life. Don't worry, once you start your training you will get used to it. That is if you will join us?"

Jaden rubbed the back of his head. "I still have to think about it. I just got kicked out of school and moved across the country to start over."

"I see," Lay said sounding deflated.

"Who were those guys by the way?"

"Quentin and Daquan." Lay said.

Jaden shook his head. "Don't tell me there is a big Vamp life following down here too."

Lay forced a smile. "There is. Fangz is from Atlanta."

"Who?" Jaden asked.

"You know the rapper that sings Dead and Boogie. Gold fangs?"

"Oh yeah...him."

"Yes." Lay chuckled. "He has been our biggest enemy for the longest."

"I can imagine," Jaden said nonchalantly. He thought for a moment. "You know I've never been able to talk about this stuff before. Anyone I tried to warn about vamps and demons, just thought I was crazy. I'll think about joining. No promises though."

Lay nodded. "Please do." Then he searched his bag. "Jaden what is your first class?"
Jaden reached into his pocket and unfolded the crumpled up paper. "It says English Literature with Mr. Smalls."

"Sweet, that's with me. Come on."

BOOK OF THE ANOINTED

Chapter Eleven

Stir of Echoes

The classroom was small, plain and had only one window near the back. Everyone walked in and sat in dirty brown top desks that were scattered throughout the class. Lay walked Jaden over to a short balding man who sat on the edge of his desk.

"Mr. Smalls this our new student Jaden."

Mr. Smalls hopped up off the desk, and held out his hand. "Finally a new student. It's been awhile since we had one of those. These days all we hear about are the ones who died."

"Nice to meet you too," Jaden said sarcastically.

"I'll go grab us some seats." Lay walked away.

Mr. Smalls pulled Jaden to the front. "Class we have a new student all the way from the west coast. Can you tell us a little something about yourself?"

A burning fever swept through Jaden's veins. Public speaking was one of his greatest fear, along with darkness. Give him a demon to face any day and he'll take them on. Hell, give him a whole army. He'd do anything other than speaking in front of the class.

Mr. Smalls shot a nod of encouragement his way. "Go ahead."

Jaden cleared his throat. "My name is Jaden and I'm from California," he said in a voice just above a whisper. Over a dozen heads strained forward.

"Speak up! We can't hear you from the back." Quentin shouted from the right side of the classroom, with his hand cuffed around his lips.

Laughter swept around the classroom like a whirlwind, and Jaden died inside.

Mr. Smalls leaned over. "Speak a little louder," he murmured.

Jaden cleared his throat again. "For those of you in the back. I said my name is Jaden and I'm from California." He walked over to Lay who literally held on to a desk.

"And what part of California are you from?"

Jaden whirled over his shoulder "Los Angeles."

"La La land. Do you have any hobbies?"

Jaden sighed. "Skateboarding, playing video games and—" he paused to turn his head towards Que and Dre. "Hunting."

"Nice, that's all, for now, Mr. Davis."

Lay let go of the desk so Jaden could take a seat. They were sitting by the only window and for that Jaden, couldn't be happier. He went in his bag and pulled out a three subject notebook and pen.

Mr. Smalls paced the front of the class. "Today we

will be continuing our discussion of Kindred by Octavia Butler." He went to the edge of his desk and sat down again. "Jaden have you had the opportunity to read Kindred yet?"

"No I haven't," Jaden said, forcing himself to speak loudly.

"Don't worry because your new, I'll grant you past. Everyone else open up your books and turn to page 101."

All through the room students reached for the books, while Jaden just sat there tapping his pen. Lay pulled out his book and scooted his desk over to Jaden's. "Don't worry we can share."

"Thanks Lay." Jaden said.

"No problem."

Book in hand, Mr. Smalls paced the front of the class. "The ease. Us, the children.... I never realized how easily people could be trained to accept slavery. We are now back in the present time and Dana says this to Kevin. Let me ask to what extent, if any at all, do you believe racial oppression exists today."

One girl sitting at the front, raised her hand before Mr. Smalls could finish the question. She was very round, marble skin with blushing red chipmunk cheeks, and long flowing brown hair that went down to the pink sweater she wore.

"Go ahead Ms. Gunther."

Lori Gunther clasped her hands as if she was preparing to make a speech. "It's obvious that with all the stories in the news concerning police brutality against men and women of color, that racial oppression exists today. And I believe the author was trying to parallel the conditions of racial oppression today to the acceptance of slavery by the slaves."

"Very good Ms. Gunther. Anyone else?" Mr. Smalls asks.

Lori claps her hands and smiles giddily. Then she turns shoulder and scowls at Lay.

"What is all that for?" Jaden whispered to Lay.

"Lori is number two in the class. She has always been behind me, since I moved here in the third grade."

"Looks like you have a nemesis." Jaden quipped.

Lay chuckled as he straightened his glasses.

Jaden was peering down into the book when he heard a voice trail into his head. *Mr. Smalls just looks like a huge slice of devil's food cake.* He matched the voice in his head to Lori, who sat at the front completely enthralled by Mr. Smalls. She was resting her head on her right hand and drinking in his features, as if she was dying of thirst. *And that milk dud of a head. I could just take my tongue and lick all around it.*

Jaden shuddered, and strained over to the right to bury his head in the book.

"Are you alright?" Lay asked.

"I'm good, just trying to read." Jaden responded.

Another voice entered, the source came from in front of them. *My balls are so itchy and red. I wonder if I have an STD. Can you get an STD if you're a virgin? I should probably Google that.*

Jaden rubbed the right side of his head. He could feel more voices fighting to be heard and it sent a sharp pain across his forehead.

No one sees me here. It's like I'm invisible. I swear to God I'm drowning and no one gives a damn. Another voice said and Jaden could feel her desperation in the tone of her thought.

Jaden looked across the room and stared at her in the eyes. She was pale with dark hair, green eyes, and sulking in her desk.

She stared back at him, her gaze like a deer caught in the headlights.

He smiled.

Someone saw me, she thought.

Jaden turned back around and beamed. That was his good deed for the day. He tries to focus back to the teacher but the voices increase, he hears the thoughts of someone in the hall. Then the thoughts of someone walking by. And as more thoughts pour in, it dawns upon him that he forgot to take his medicine.

Jaden shuddered as a sharp pain stabbed his right side. He closed his eyes and drew in a deep breath, summoning calm to the storm. Sam taught him to imagine the thoughts as raging water, and to mentally picture a boat being tossed about as the voices and thoughts increased in his head.

Sweat formed near his temple lobe and wildfire ran through his blood. He was becoming hot and his head faint. Then he caught a glimpse of Imani walking past the door, her dark hair covering the right side of her face, and her hazel eyes connecting with his for just a fraction of a second. *Does she know what is happening to me*, he thought. Just like that he felt the waters ease, the voices in his head fell away, and all he could feel was her. The peace that came with being in the midst of an angel.

The electronic bell sounded and everyone bolted towards the door. Jaden followed behind Lay as they both funneled to the front of the class.

Jaden walked past Mr. Smalls and heard, *I'm going to need stronger chains.*

The chilling thought made Jaden stop dead in his tracks.

"Is there a problem," Mr. Smalls asked.

Jaden faced forward. "No there is no problem." He pulled up his backpack and slung it over the shoulder, and high-tailed it out of the class.

Chapter Twelve

Dead Meat

Lunchtime came and Jaden stood in the cafeteria line debating whether to choose the meatloaf and potatoes, or sloppy joe with fries. Red meat swam in a tomato-sauced swamp. "Ugh," Jaden said to himself as he grabbed the Sloppy joe.

North Central's cafeteria was pretty standard as school cafeterias go, with a black and white tile floor and old lady's that looked like your grandma serving the food. It was definitely smaller than Crenshaw's and to Jaden's estimation it could only hold a little over two hundred students. The tables were all round and scattered across the floor randomly.

Somewhere deep down Jaden hoped that this new school would be his chance to be someone different, exciting, someone interesting. Jaden walked away from the register and Lay sauntered up to him.

"Sloppy joe, that is a good decision. I know five people who got sick from the meatloaf."

Jaden laughed. "Where do you want to sit?"

Lay walked over to a table in the right corner by the window. "How about over here," he said as he pointed with his eyebrows.

They sat down with Jaden on the right side and Lay across from him. He chose this way because he liked how warm the sun felt as it shined from his right side. With his food tray in front of him, he placed his Arizona on his left and chocolate pudding on the right side. Jaden reached over to pop the top of his Arizona when suddenly it was yanked off the table.

"Yoink," Quentin said as he snatched the drink and continued walking towards the other side of the cafe, leaving Jaden with a dubious look on his face.

"I can't believe he just did that," Jaden murmured.

Daquan chuckled as Quentin turned shoulder, "Welcome to Atlanta hoe," he barked. Then he snapped open the Arizona and downed it.

"Well, there goes all of my hopes for finally having the juice at school." Jaden huffed. He picked up his sloppy Joe and tore into it.

Lay cocked his head. "But there is juice over there." He pointed to the drink refrigerators at the end of the line.

Jaden grinned. "It's a saying. You know if you have the juice, then you got power. It means you're popular."

Lay laughed, his cheeks became round balls protruding out the side of his face. "I see. Please don't let Quentin and Daquan get to you. They have nothing going on for themselves so that's why they take their frustrations out on others." Lay said and then he reached into his bag. "I don't have juice but I do have an extra water?" He offered.

"Good looking out," Jaden said as he took the water.

Lay pulled several items out of his bag as he unpacked his lunch. There was a small soup, fishcakes, kimchi coleslaw, pork dumplings, and a gigantic bowl of rice.

"Is that your lunch for the week or just today?" Jaden asked

Lay grabbed his other bottle of water and twisted the cap. "Just today."

Jaden gasped. "So you mean you're going to eat all that rice?"

"Yes," he said.

"All that rice?" Jaden repeated again, only this time louder.

Lay shrugged. "My family eats a lot of rice."

Jaden tossed his sloppy joe back on the tray. "You must love rice like I love tacos," he said.

"What's up Hollywood?" Imani slammed her tray on the table, and made Jaden scoot over.

Jaden straightened once she heard Imani's voice. Her long dark hair swooped over her right eye, and her dimples poked out on her left. "What's up?".

Imani smiled back. "Nothing. How are you?"

"Just got my tea stolen but I'm hanging in there. What ever happened to Southern hospitality?" He said.

A light sandwich and chips sat on Imani's plate. She popped open her soda "Questions that need answers."

Radiant light from the window stroke Imani's hazel eyes so perfectly that it almost had Jaden in a trance. "Yea I guess so, huh?"

Lay scooped bowls of rice as an awkward silence rolled over the table like a tumbleweed. "You know I am sitting here too"

Imani waved her hand. "Hey boo. I could never forget about you."

"Hello Imani," He said before slurping his soup.

Jaden ran his hands over his knuckles and licked his lips. The silence made him so uncomfortable and his lips burned to say something. "So angels eat lunch too?"

Imani placed a finger over her lips. "I need you to be a little more low key. And yes we are supposed to be a part of your everyday life, just in the background protecting you. Most people don't know who we are or that we are even around."

Jaden thought about it for a moment. Random strangers including people we work with, go to school with, or even party with, people that are rarely noticed could be our biggest protectors. "Well why do I know?" He asked with his raspy voice dropping down almost to a whisper. "Why did you reveal yourself to me and to the others?"

Imani smiled. "Because your special...Anointed."

Romeo made his way out of the lunch line greeting every guy and girl, at almost every table in his path as he maneuvered through the cafe. Romeo proudly sported his black and gold North Central letterman jacket. He was a part of everything in North Central high, from basketball team, track, student government, and he still had time to paint.

Imani waved him over as he walked across the room.

Romeo gave Imani a slight hug as he sat at the table. This made Jaden feel a small sting of jealousy. Why he didn't know.

Romeo sat down and leaned in so only they could hear, "Did you hear about what happened to Tyler? He didn't come home last night. His parents think he's missing."

Jaden picked up his sloppy joe. "What's so weird about that? Maybe he stayed out all night or something."

Imani turned to him and took a break. "Missing means dead around here."

"It's more than that," Romeo started. "I definitely had a crazy dream last night with Tyler in it, then I woke up and started drawing. At first I thought you know I was having another one of my nightmares I usually have after a red bull crash but now I think—"

"It was a vision," Imani completed.

Romeo reached into his pocket and pulled out a picture. "Look at it."

"Oh," the collective gasp went around the table.

A colored pencil drawing showed a guy in Tyler's likeness being bitten by snakes.

Lay sat up and leaned across the table, his chest practically rested on Jaden's sloppy joe bun. "Looks like a ritual to me," he said as he adjusted his round his spectacles.

"Where is Deshawn? Romeo have you seen him?" Imani asked.

Deshawn's thoughts revealed to Jaden his location, "Over there," Jaden said pointing to a corner that lead to a back exit.

Deshawn leaned against the wall outside trying to hide the fact he was smoking.

"Are you serious," Imani murmured, annoyed as she waved Deshawn over to the table.

Deshawn outed the cigarette and reluctantly he made his way over to the table. Another lunch tray slammed on the table. This time it belonged to an incredibly beautiful girl with very fair yellow skin and wild free flowing brown hair.

She smiled at Jaden as she seductively crossed her legs. "Sup, you must be the new kid. My name is Tamiyah and these are my girls Lawanda, Amy, Brittany, and Jessica," she said pointing to the four girls hovering behind her.

"I'm Jaden," he said

Tamiyah turned around closer to Jaden. "I hear you're from L.A, the city with all the movie stars and everyone who's anyone. You must know some rappers too, huh?" Tamiyah asked.

Jaden felt awkward, "Something like that."

Tamiyah caressed her neck line with her glittering pink nails. And even though her lips said nothing, her thoughts revealed her true intentions. *I bet this loser knows somebody who can help me finally get a record deal so I can get the hell out of Georgia.*

Jaden frowned. Romeo coughed loudly. "Tamiyah, it's like that now? You're just not going to speak," he asked in loud irate tone.

Tamiyah folded her arms. "Go home roger!" She blurted with a frown. Tamiyah touched Jaden's arm. "I know your new so allow me to tell you what's up. You won't get anywhere in this school being around these lames."

Imani leaned over. "Excuse me?"

Tamiyah continued. "Romeo might think he's on ten right now because he's an athlete, but he's still late. And he ain't all that fine. Trust me. I know."

The girls behind her laughed, and Imani prayed for strength inwardly "Oh, and this girl right here is just a hot mess. By all means just look at that horrible weave!"

"My hair is natural," Imani snapped back.

Tamiyah cackled. "It still looks horrible." She whipped her hair as if to brush Imani off. "Anyway Jaden, I just wanted to be a good Georgia peach and welcome you to North Central. If you need anything just hit me up." A sudden thought made her beam. "Oh, and also tonight we are going to be kicking it Safari, which is always popping. Me and my girls will be there looking gorgeous and we will be dancing all night. How about you?"

Jaden nodded his head. "Yeah, I might come."

"Great. Welcome to Atlanta boo," Tamiyah said as she made her way from the table.

Romeo set his jaw hard. "Trick," he murmured under

his breath.

"Yo mama," Tamiyah returned as she walked away with her group towards another table.

Imani turned to Romeo. "You need to come handle your ex."

Romeo laughed. "I did. That's why she is my ex,"

"Sup, fools!" Deshawn shouted as he sat on the table top and immediately helped himself at Jaden's fries.

Jaden jerked his plate away. "Stop it! Buy your own,"

"Why can't I have none of your fries Jacob? We are supposed to be boys." Deshawn asked.

"Man, it's Jaden!" He corrected as he swatted at Deshawn's hand.

"Bro, you look more like a Jacob. I'm just saying." Deshawn quipped as he quickly grabbed more fries off of Jaden's plate.

"Okay chill," Imani interrupted. "Romeo might've had an important vision," she said with her face stone cold, and Deshawn knew this face. It meant she was serious.

Deshawn spun around the top of the table and dropped down into a seat. "About what?"

Imani raked her hair out of her face. "Tyler Brooks. He has gone missing recently and we believe that might've been sacrificed in some sort of ritual."

Deshawn nodded along as if she was repeating his order at Burger King. "Cool story, bro. Too bad I don't really care," Deshawn said as he laughed.

Imani shook her head. "Deshawn, be serious. Hey Jaden, do you think you can come to the boxing gym downtown tonight?"

Jaden sighed deeply. "I don't know. I'm still trying to wrap my head around what happened last night. I really don't want to be mixed in with this angel demon stuff anymore."

"I'm sorry Jaden but this is still your purpose. Your destiny." Imani said, her tone sweet as honey and soft as a pillow.

He thought of his mother, and that mental image of her on the ceiling. "Yeah, it's just too much for me. All I want to do is go back to pretending to be as normal as possible," Jaden said as he walked away from the table.

"Wait Jaden!" Lay called.

"That's it though. You're not normal, you're special," Imani whispered.

Jaden burst through the doors of the bathroom. A rank smell welcomed him from the stalls and stayed far away from it. He went to the sink to splash water on his face. The sink was already wet with so many students he was alone. Perfect, he thought to himself.

Silence yawned all around and a still voice spoke to him. *Don't you want to make friends.?*

Jaden examined the mirror, almost expecting a familiar face to greet him. There was no one there. "Nice of you to show up. I haven't heard from you in a while."

I was around as I said I would be, the Creator replied in a snarky tone.

"Where were you when I called?"

The Creator paused. *Listening. Never mind that. I thought you wanted friends more than anything.*

Jaden was at a loss. "Yes, I do."

Then you should go then. Have fun

Jaden nodded. "Maybe I will."

Just remember free will, but it's a suggestion.

An electronic bell sounded. Jaden snatched a paper towel from the dispenser and ran it across his face. "Whatever."

Before Jaden could leave he had to stop by Ms. Day's office to start his therapy session. Her office was in the same suite as Dr. Ball's so he had no problem finding it. He knocked on her door and she seemed happy to see him as she opened it.

"Have a seat," Ms. Day stated and Jaden so happily obliged.

Ms. Day pulled her red shawl closer. "So how is your first day so far?"

Jaden sighed. "I don't know." Then he leaned back in the chair, trying to search for the right words. "I am tempted to give a mixed review."

"Well how did you want it to go?"

"I don't know.... different."

Ms. Day loosened in her chair. "Different how?"

"Today seemed like everything I wanted to leave behind on the west coast. Vampires, missing kids, and just a lot of strange things going on."

"Hmm really," she asked with the slightest of head nods. After reading so many people's minds, Jaden developed a knack for discerning out people's personality. He could tell she was trying to get a take on him.

Jaden took a breath before he began his next sentence. The thought came out of his mouth like a bullet. "Look I just want you to know that I'm here to go to school and that's all. Demons, vampires, and monsters I don't have time for it."

She picked up a mug that sat before her. "That's the point isn't?" she blew at steam. "You come to school to learn. One of the most important things you can learn about is yourself. What have you learned about yourself?"

"That I'm a magnet for the strange and it seems like evil won't be giving me a break."

"Do you know what that sounds like to me?" Ms. Day raised her brow.

"What?" Jaden asked.

"It sounds like light. Everything is attracted to light. It's honest and pure. Maybe that's why all of this is attracted to you."

Jaden cocked his head. "I never thought about it that way. These sessions might not be bad after all."

Chapter Thirteen

Number Two

"We've been preparing for your arrival a few weeks now," Eva said as she escorted Asmodeus down the tunnel, her torch flickering and providing light as she stood down the cavern. Pitch black darkness surrounded the landscape.

"How many upper level demons do we have amongst our ranks?" Asmodeus asked

Eva swallowed hard. "Only a few."

Asmodeus cocked an eyebrow. "Why only a few?"

Eva hung the torch on the cabin and her lips curled in a smile to mask her own disappointment. "Sir, we have been having some difficulties in re-activating the Hell gate in this area. That's why I believe the chairman sent someone of your rank topside."

Asmodeus leaned in further, his interest piqued. "What kind of difficulties?"

Eva's face lined with worry and the faint glow of the torch made her appear even grimmer. "Anointed," she said in a hiss of a breath. "And not just one, it's three of them." Asmodeus huffed. "I thought they were extinct."

"I thought so too," she added. "I believe these boys are the only ones chosen from this generation."

The demon's lips twitched. "Boys you say?"

"Yes," she answered as she continued to lead him to the seal. "They are teenagers but they are strong. I think they are stronger than any of the Anointed we ever faced before, because there are so few of them."

The tunnel opened up to a much larger cavern, and together they strolled over to the seal. Locusts stirred overhead as the torch brought light to the darkness they had become accustomed to.

"It doesn't matter. We shall bathe in their blood soon enough," he said as he ran his hand across the seal. At his touch it quivered like a heartbeat lurching for life. "Once we activate the Hell gate we will have more than enough ranks to overthrow the Anointed. The chairman's Locusts have already been seeping out and my own personal legions have been put into position." He turned back over to Eva, "What have you discovered about Solomon's ring."

Eva smiled again, and this time genuine. "We are working on it. My human pets have located it in Canada and it should be delivered shortly."

"Perfect. I will need to be at my full strength before the reaping." The locusts flittered all around them, their wings hung down their backs like trench coats. "Until the time comes, let's take care of these babies." He looked over his shoulder. "Any other complications."

"Vampires."

Asmodeus spat on the ground. "I can't believe you've allowed children and half demons halt progress in this area. What's with the vampires?"

"A master by the name of Fangz controls this area. He and his True blood brood have accumulated quite an amount of power along the south."

The demon kept his gaze on the seal, which warmed up at his touch. "Vampires are no concern to the Sons of Chaos. The seal needs to be fed with blood."

Eva tossed the torch over to Asmodeus. "Allow me to go find a victim."

Asmodeus threw the torch back. "I'll go myself. I need to test out this body.

"Very well, follow me." Eva said as she disappeared in a thunderclap of smoke

*****

"I'll be home in twenty minutes. Just let me get to my car," Alloura said as she walked into the garage. She could barely keep her phone to her ear as she balanced her briefcase, gym bag, coat, and lunchbox. "I'll call you back once I pick up dinner. Bye I love you too."

This was third time this week she stayed behind to work an extra three hours, to work on the Brady account. Alloura was poised to be a senior consultant at ITN and knew that if she wanted that position, she will have to blow this project out of the water. The position would add another 20k to her salary. She smiled just thinking about that money. It would help her and Mark pay for the dream wedding in Hawaii she had been planning since she was a six-year-old girl in Tampa.

Alloura scurried along the underground parking garage in search of her car. She was no older than twenty-six, very short, long dark hair. She had just gotten off of work, tired, in need of a shower, and exhausted to the point where she was becoming paranoid. Every other step she paused because she felt like something or someone was following her. The clack of her heels echoed loudly in the parking garage, making her heartbeat increase with every step she made. Coming to a halt, she suddenly paused mid step.

Asmodeus clung to the shadows like a lion waiting in the bush. The smell of her fear was faint but still sweet and delicious. Her sweat coated the air and wafted into the demon's nose, enticing his hunger even more and strengthening him. Vampires need blood to survive and demons needed fear to give them power.

An eerie feeling made Alloura shudder. She scanned across the garage and spotted her dust covered royal blue Toyota Camry parked by a maroon Mazda 6. She searched through her pocketbook for keys. In one swift move Asmodeus spun out of the shadows, and had her up in his arms with a deadly grip over her mouth. She squirmed, squealed, and tried to fight back against this deadly invader, but was helpless as a lamb in the demon's arms.

With Alloura in his arms, he spun back to the Abyss, twisting out of a whirlwind of dark shadows. He tossed her on the seal. Alloura cried out in pain as she fell back on the cold steel, which felt like a bed of ice. Eva sashayed out of the shadows with a torch in her hand. A menacing smile swept across her face as she watched.

"Please.... Please stop," Alloura begged.

Asmodeus dropped to his knees and climbed on top of her. She shivered underneath his towering presence. He ran his nose from her navel to her neck, making sure not to miss one drop of sweat, or one ounce of pheromones that released into the air. Fear makes a soul so delicious to a demon. The new vessel he possessed could barely contain his dark splendor. He needed to kill. Blood needed to be shed to give life to the soul. The more souls he devours the more time he has here. With his right hand he lifted the girl to her feet.

Locusts swarmed in the air above them, fluttering like flies in the light of the flickering flame. Currents surged from the demon's hand and into the girl as she remained helplessly trapped. The wave of energy surged further and further into her body and made her violently shake. Her skin began to smoke and her shrieks rung loudly throughout the echoing darkness. The seal glowed a brilliant light in the darkness, as it drank down the crimson pool.

"More. We need more." He said as he stood over the seal. "There is much work to be done."

Chapter Fourteen

Safari

Jaden laid sprawled across his bed, scrolling through his timeline, and yearning for the fun everyone else was having at Safari. As Jaden continued to scroll, his phone came to life in his hands, with a message from Lay.

Lay: Just finished meeting at the sanctuary. We are thinking about going to Safari. Want to come?

Jaden mulled it over again in his head a thousand times. The house was pin drop silent, so there was a part of him that figured why not. Once he came to that conclusion, he texted Lay back.

Jaden: *I'm down. I'll meet you there in half an hour.*

Lay responded with a silly face emoji. Jaden tossed his phone over the bed, hopped up and strolled over to his closet.

It didn't take long for Jaden to get stuck sorting through his closet trying to decide what he would wear. His first time at an actual club and the first time in a long time he went to a party. Those old awkward birthday parties his parents made him go to didn't count. As Jaden rummaged through his closet, his father knocked on the door.

John poked his head around the door. "Are you going somewhere?"

Jaden grabbed a dark pair of blue jeans and tossed it on the bed, "Yes, just some local restaurant everyone is hanging out at called Safari."

John rubbed his chin. "Safari…. ain't that place more like a club after six?"

Jaden snatched a red and black flannel, then tossed it over his jeans. "Yeah," he said nonchalantly.

"I hear some of my coworkers talk about that place. Isn't that a bit adult for a bunch of teenagers?"

Jaden paused. "I think it's the other way around. A lot of teenagers hang out there since there is not many under eighteen clubs. If your co-workers hang out there, then they must be pervs."

A smug look came across John's face, and then he chuckled. "I suppose so huh." He took off his glasses, cleaned them with a cloth out of his pocket. "So basically you're going to a party. That's good, just you know make sure your careful. Go be young, adventurous, and have fun." He thought about his choice of words. "Wait...not too much fun." Then he corrected himself. "Just tell me do we have to talk about doing the right thing?"

Jaden moaned as he searched his closet to find a pair of sneakers to match the jeans he had laid out. "Trust me you don't. I'm sure it will be hella lame anyway, and I won't stay too long."

John sat down on Jaden's bed next to his blue jeans. "No you're a young man you can stay out a little late." He paused mid-sentence.

Jaden didn't need to read his mind, to guess what he was trying to say. "Look I'll be fine. I'm cool. As matter of fact I'm like better than cool.... I'm chill...I'm chilling. Atlanta is okay for now, and I'm glad we moved."

John placed a hand on Jaden's shoulder. "Are you sure you okay? You've been through a lot Jaden, and I still don't know if going to school is such a good idea after you know"

Jaden shook his head, "No it's fine. I can't stay home all day watching Dragon Ball Z and SpongeBob anyway."

John smiled, "Hey, there is nothing wrong with a little SpongeBob."

"I'll be fine," Jaden reassured

"All right if you say so. Just remember you're my number one boy. You're my only boy." John said as he exited.

Jaden threw on his outfit, brushed his wooly medium length hair, threw a cap on, and dashed out the door.

*****

Both floors of Safari overflowed with teenagers dancing and grinding their bodies to the booming thump of music. Strobe lights flashed all around and they added to the thick heat on the dancefloor. The only relief to this unbearable heat was a breeze coming from the left on the open terrace that was adorned with swaying palm trees and various other greenery.

Jaden found a corner with a nice view of the dance floor, and he posted up there. He searched for any sign of Lay and the others. He pulled out his phone, to check if anyone responded to any of his messages, and of course they didn't. His battery had only two percent of power left and blinked red. "Great," Jaden murmured out loud.

He'd been standing in the spot for close to an hour, when he decided to go to the bathroom. Jaden took two steps towards the bathroom before someone brushed into him.

"Watch it," she said.

"My bad," Jaden apologized. Then he recognized the girl as Lori. She wore a knee length plaid skirt that looked straight out of fifties. "Nice fit," He complimented.

"Thank you," Lori said as she straightened her pearls. Her hair was French braided to the back, and she wore a white shirt underneath a yellow canary sweater. "You're the new kid right?" She paused for a moment to recall his name. "Jaden?"

"Yes,"

"Are you friends with Jin-Soo?" She asked.

"Lay? I am, as matter of fact I'm looking–"

"Let me just warn you–" Lori interrupted as she pointed a finger to Jaden's chest. "Jin-Soo is a lying snake that is ruthless and evil to the corner."

"Lay?" Jaden asked, with his eyebrow cocked. "Lay

is an innocent as a lamb."

"I thought so too," Lori said as her voice cracked. "But that's how he gets you. I'm telling you now, he uses people to get to number one, and then he tosses them away like trash." She backed away. "You might not see it today or anytime soon, but trust me Lay is a snake waiting in the grass."

Lori disappeared back into the crowd, leaving Jaden stupefied at her personal attack against Lay. There was a pungent odor assaulting him in the area he stood, and it smelled illegal. Somebody reeked in it. Tamiyah walked over from across the room.

She grabbed Jaden's shoulder, "Hey Jaden?"

Jaden's jaw dropped at Tamiyah's edgy ensemble with her hair wild and free flowing. Jaden gulped hard, "Hi." He replied in a weak voice. Then tugged at his hat. "You look amazing."

Tamiyah flipped her long curly mane, "I know. I always do." Her lips curled into a smile and her nude lip gloss shimmered under the neon strobe lights. She stood back. "And you do too. Is that shirt Gucci?"

Jaden timidly grabbed his collar, "This....um yeah." Really it was something ordered from an online store, but he didn't want to tell her that.

Tamiyah smiled again and she raised her brows. Jaden read her thoughts, *I know he had to be rich. I will definitely make him spend money on me.* Tamiyah grabbed his hand and pulled him to the dance floor. "Ooh this is my song. I love Fangz," she shouted as she dragged Jaden through the crowd and to the middle of the dance floor.

Seductively she wrapped Jaden's hand around her waist as she pushed her hips against his. Sweet almond oil drifted into his nose as she buried her head on his shoulder and slowly bent over. He was so lost. Turned on yet lost and confused. Tamiyah with her hands on her knees continued to whine her body to the hard thump of the beat.

Romeo spotted the two dancing, and jealousy hit him like a gut punch, as he along with Deshawn came down stairs from the top floor. With a presumptuous grin, he maneuvered through the crowd of dancing bodies to Jaden and Tamiyah. "I got this." He pushed Jaden to the side and he replaced his position dancing behind Tamiyah.

"What's your problem man," Jaden asked as he bumped into another dancing couple who pushed him back, as they fell off step.

Romeo grabbed Tamiyah by her side and turned to Jaden, "You don't know what you're doing, so let me handle this."

Tamiyah stopped dancing and folded her arms. "What are you doing? If I wanted to dance with you, I would've acknowledged you the first hundred times you kept staring at me from across the room." She jabbed him in the chest with her pink stiletto nail. "What don't you understand? You are late and I'm over you."

"Come on ma, stop playing." He said with a sneer. "I know you still want me. You still like all my pictures and

I see you're the first to watch anything I post online. When are you going to stop acting up?"

"Acting up?" Tamiyah repeated with a frown. She shot daggers from her eyes. "I hope you know that I'm about to start talking to Corey Jackson. He's a senior and a quarterback playing on varsity. So when you see us all over campus, just remember what you lost because YOU were acting up."

Romeo waved his hands, "I don't care. You don't like me then get out of here. Just remember you can't reclaim your spot when you get out of line."

Tamiyah snatched a drink out someone's hands and tossed it into Romeo's face. "Screw you. I don't have time for this." She pushed her way through the crowd of dancing bodies.

Deshawn jumped from behind Romeo, "Ooh dog she slayed you."

Romeo wiped his eyes. "Whatever."

Lay walked over to Jaden. "There you are. We've been looking for you all over."

Jaden showed him his phone. "I've been texting you but my phone is dead."

Lay held out his finger, "Hold on." He pulled out a battery bank, and handed over to Jaden.

Jaden smiled as he took it and charged his phone. "Thanks Lay, you're so clutch."

"No problem."

Jaden tucked both phone and charger in his back pocket and asked, "Where is Imani?"

"She didn't want to come, so she stayed behind at

Sanctuary." Romeo answered as his face still dripped.

"Oh!" Jaden shouted over the loud music, feeling bummed out.

Deshawn turned to Jaden, "I can't believe Johnathan actually came. What are you doing here?" He leaned in Jaden's ear. "You trying to get some tonight too?"

"It's Jaden thank you, and why wouldn't I be here. Don't I look like I usually go to clubs and have fun?" Jaden snapped.

Deshawn turned to Romeo, "No," they said in Unison. As the two laughed hysterically, a revelation slammed into Romeo's skull. Flashing in his head were images of Tamiyah being dragged down an alley and across a railroad. Then he saw Tamiyah's neck being ripped into by a vampire with long dreads.

Romeo gasped for air, as the terrible images disappeared from his sight.

Deshawn recognized this reaction from him. "What did you see?"

"Bloodsuckers feeding on Tamiyah," Romeo said as he panted.

"Where?" Jaden asked.

"That's what she gets for trying to play me," Romeo shouted, trying to talk over the music. "Well they can have her."

"Are you crazy?" Jaden spat. "We can't just let them take her. Where did they go?"

"Let me search surveillance cameras," Lay uttered as he ran his fingers across his arm, and a LED screen of numbers and code displayed in front of him. "There. Over there heading out," he yelled as he pointed towards the door.

Tamiyah held hands with a tall pale man with short brown hair. Together they exited at the back of Safari. After spotting Tamiyah, Jaden dashed behind her with the others in tow. Jaden pushed open the door, and a frosty breeze blew in his face.

"There!" Deshawn said as he pointed.

Tamiyah clung on to the guy, and followed a group down the alley into a back parking lot.

"Are you dumbasses going to stand there all night, or are we going to go after her?" Romeo asked.

"Let's go," Jaden stated before taking off.

Together they sprinted after the group. When they came outside Jaden spotted the shadow of a man holding a girl, in the faint light of the alley.

Jaden pulled him off of her. She stumbled back and he could see it was the wrong girl. "My bad," he apologized.

A low snarl from behind made his pulse quickened. Slowly Jaden turned. The man who obviously wasn't a teenager, wearing a royal blue blazer straight out of the nineties, shifted to a predator appearance. His fangs dropped to an attack length, his claws extended, and his mouth wrinkled.

Romeo struck the vampire with the back of his elbow. "Come on! Come get some." He barked with his raspy voice.

More snarls sounded from around the corner.

Footsteps moved in the darkness towards them at a deadly pace. Four other vampires hung back in the dark waiting for the perfect time to strike.

"What the hell is wrong with your face?" Tamiyah screamed as she tried to pull her arm away from Garrett. He tugged her across the parking lot.

Garrett fangs extended further, "Don't be afraid. I just want a taste." He ran his tongue across her face and she hollered in disgust. "And I'm sure Fangz will enjoy you too." He yelled as he leaped up to the ledge of a nearby building and continued the trek back to the trap house.

Romeo lurched further towards the cries that rung out into the night. He took one step toward them, and a mighty grip pulled him back into a fight. Brilliant light formed at his fingertips, casting an illustrious glow that turned into sunlight. Romeo pointed his fingers, and the light emitting from the tips formed into a narrow beam. He shot towards the vampire, light jetted across the lot, but like a cheetah on the move, the vamp dodges out the way. In a motion that was almost too quick, he jabbed at Romeo's chin, and Romeo spins out of the way. Romeo grabbed the vampire's forearm, and tossed him over the shoulder.

"Stake!" Romeo beckoned with his hand out.

A piece of wood dangled out of a dumpster. Jaden reaches out with his hand, it snaps off like a twig, spins through the air, and impales the vampire.

Primal rumblings drew Jaden's attention to the left.

Something malevolent moved silently as a thief that slips through shadows. It seemed to grow stronger the more Jaden's heart slammed into his chest. Four golden eyes stalked them and slinked out like a pack of lions enclosing in on a cantaloupe. Jaden backed away. "Don't just stand there guys. Get ready to fight"

Before Jaden could lift a finger, the female that lead pack pounced on him, knocking him to the ground.

The three others that followed her encircled Dashawn and Lay. Deshawn blew in his hands, and prepared a goblet of explosive energy. Like wild dogs they growled before attacking, fangs out and hissing. The vampires lurched towards them, and Deshawn dropped the goblet. Smoke billowed up in one huge waft as it detonated, and sent the vampires reeling through the air, spinning in different directions.

"Look at you. So young and tasty. And those pretty doe eyes are to die for. You remind me of Bambi." She ran a talon on the right side of Jaden's face. She was tall, exotic, burnt toffee skin, with the body of an amazon warrior and bearing eight inches of battle fang. With impressive strength she pinned Jaden to the concrete and dove in for a bite.

"Jaden!" Lay shouted as he sprang into action. He raised the metal center of his light-staff, clicked, and two beams of blue light came out with a sharp crackle.

There was a male who stood in his path towards Jaden, he looked no older than the anointed, with blonde spiky hair. With a rumble in his belly, the vampire swung at Lay, he dodged, and cut him half with the light staff.

Lay ran over to strike the vampire on top of Jaden. He brought one end of the staff down to pierce her shoulder, but he impales the ground when she rolls out of the way. Like a cat, she sprung to her feet

Heart hammering in his chest, Jaden flattened his palm, and she lifted off the ground. With a backhand swing she spun in the air, like a rag doll being tossed, and smashed into the wall of the building. She collapsed to the ground and Jaden was on her in a second, rolling on the ground, to close the distance.

Romeo tossed the splintered wood. "Here!"

Jaden reaches for the wood and it slides out of his hands. A rumble sounds in her belly, and he knew she was about to attack. He juggles the wood in his hand, trying to get a firm grip. She stands to her feet and Jaden impales the stake into her chest. Fire and dust spurt into his eyes as she crumbles to dust.

Blinded by the ash, Jaden uses the bottom half of his shirt to clean his eyes. He wiped his eyes to the best of his ability but they feel sore and red with all the dry dust in them. He opens them and he can barely see in the faint light.

"Are there any more?" Romeo asks as Deshawn and Lay dust the other two.

Lay holds his staff to the side. "That is a negative. We are free to proceed."

"Are you alright Jacob?" Deshawn asked.

"It's Jaden and I'm fine no thanks to you," Jaden snapped. A pulse of energy made him stagger back. He ran his fingers along his neck and felt the puncture wound healed by itself. "I'm better than fine. I feel stronger."

"It's the spirit, it feeds our power. The more of them we take out, the stronger we get."

"I've never felt that before." Jaden declared.

Lay folded his glasses and stuffed them into his pocket. "It's stronger when we are together."

"Ready to move?" Romeo asked.

"Hold on," Jaden responded. He dug into his back pocket and pulled out a black scarf. He tied it around his neck, and adjusted it on his face.

Romeo shook his head. "Okay Batman. What's with the cowl?"

Jaden wrapped another in his right hand and picked up the stake again. "Trust me you don't want them to know your identity."

"Where did they go?" Deshawn asked.

"Follow me I know," Romeo ordered as he lead the way out of the lot. They ran down another alley and across a large untamed field. Thick overgrown grass came up way past their ankles and made the trek difficult.

"I don't know if I can keep up with this running," Jaden said out of breath.

Deshawn shook his head, "Same here. Romeo slow down, this is not track practice big dog."

Jaden paused in the middle of the field, "Wait... if Deshawn can slow down time.... why are we running behind them? Deshawn just use your power and we'll find them."

"They are too far away man and I can only

manipulate what's around me," Deshawn said between breaths.

"You're useless," Jaden said.

Lay placed his hand on his knees. "Now would be a good time for that drone I was working on."

"Tell me about it," Deshawn commented.

Just across the field were railroad tracks, where the vampires dragged Tamiyah and others along. "There they go. Come on. Keep up," he commanded as he high stepped across overgrown grass and tall fields of wheat.

Lay blinked Owl-like as he recognized one of the other girls in the group. "Is that Lori Gunther?"

"I think so," Jaden replied.

Lori pulled away from her captor. "Get your hands off of me. I'll have you know my father is the chief of police. If you eat me, he will kick your ass, his ass, and everybody's ass that has something to do with this."

Tamiyah shouted as the Garrett shook her by her neck. Garrett clenched her jaws, "Go to sleep," he commanded. Tamiyah stopped struggling and collapsed. He threw her over his shoulder. "Take care of the kids behind us."

A pale redhead bore fangs, "Ooh goodie." Her stride was swift as a lioness out on the hunt. "Who wants a taste of big red?"

Deshawn charged a particle, and then threw it at her, detonating a small explosion across her chest. "You're not my type shawty."

Unyielding she rose back to her feet despite the

gaping hole in her chest. While running at full speed, Romeo channeled light at his fingertips, and sliced her head clean off with a thin precise beam of light. Ashes blew into Jaden's face as he and Lay continued to follow behind.

"Come on we almost have them," Romeo shouted again as they hopped across the tracks and continued onward.

Peebles crunched beneath their feet as they then ran onto the grounds of an abandoned Tasty Bread factory, and hoped over a tall gate to get to the other side.

They followed Romeo past the factory and into a small patch of woods, to which they came out to a small neighborhood on the other side. He led them to the vampires by use of the spirit. They continued along until they came to an isolated two-story house that was dull with color, had an overgrown lawn, broken tiled porch, and boarded windows.

"There," Romeo said. "I saw it in my vision. Let's go."

Jaden stopped him as the others came to a halt. "We need a plan. I have slayed enough vamp nests to know you don't walk into an abandoned house all Willy nilly. At least let me, I don't know maybe scan the place and see how many are in there."

"That won't work. You can't read vampire's minds. Their dead. It's like a reflection that doesn't cast in the mirror," Lay added.

Romeo pushed him aside, "How about you pipe down. We've been slaying the True Bloods for months now. So do we know what we're doing."

Jaden threw his hands in the air. "I'm just saying, that we should be smart about this."

Deshawn added, "Bruh he's right. I'm not about to walk straight into a vampire nest to get eaten up, with no plan and no weapons and running on E in spirit."

"Slay some more vampires and get your strength back," Romeo retorted in Deshawn's face.

"Stop," Jaden interrupted. "Since you are so pumped up, how about you go through the front and distract them. Lay and Lay will sneak in through the side, and Deshawn you pop in through the back. That's the plan.

"Good enough let's go," Romeo said as he leads the way to the abandoned house.

Lay pulled him back. "Are you really going to go through with his?"

"Yes," Romeo said as he pulled his shoulder back. "Let's go."

Chapter Fifteen

The Trap

To get to the house required them trek down a hill. Jaden didn't let his focus drop for one second, he scanned around the house with a keen eye. The group split up with each one making their way to their designated area. Romeo walked onto the porch, the worn wooden boards cracked underneath his footsteps, and his heart pounded like a drum as he reached for the door handle. Deshawn crept around the corner. Lay followed Jaden to the side door.

Bullets of sweat rolled from Jaden's temple, as his chest rose and fell at an unnerving pace. "I have a bad feeling about this," Jaden told Lay.

Lay grabbed his hand, and pulled it across his chest. "Don't be afraid. The creator is with us."

"It's not that." Jaden thought hard for a moment and tried to pin down this feeling in his gut. "This doesn't feel random at all. I don't think they were just out for a hunt."

Lay removed his round specs. "We have tracked

vampires back to their nests all the time. I think you're just rusty on your hunting."

"I hope so," Jaden murmured.

A loud crash erupted inside. Roars sounded from within the house. "That's our cue," Jaden said. He blasted down the door with a telekinetic push. Jaden stepped into the house, and a firm grip around his neck welcomed him. Quicker than a hand clap, he was thrown into a wall over stairs.

"It's not delivery nor Digiorno. Food waiting at the door." the vampire said in a heavy Jamaican accent. Three others in the room sat around a table counting stacks of money.

Lay activated his light staff. He stepped into the house and a massive vampire grabbed him by the throat, and threw him into the wall.

A female vampire stopped measuring the pills on the kitchen table and sashayed to the front of the house. "Raheem, take them to Fangz."

Raheem curled his lip, "Aww man but they already brought him some girls from the club."

She snarled, "Do it! You know he wants everything first and untouched.

Romeo laid underneath the stairs, not too far from Jaden.

"What took you so long?" He said before his eyes blinked shut.

Jaden sat up. The pain felt sharp and blunt on his back.

A sonic boom hurdled Deshawn's entrance. He blew the backdoor open and stepped across a curtain of smoke.

Raheem covered his face. "What was that?"

"Don't nobody move and nobody will get hurt." Deshawn shouted as he rolled into the house.

"Get him!" Raheem shouted.

An idle vampire attacked Deshawn with a swift kick to the chin. The kick was so swift that he touched his face just to register that he got kicked. And once it dawned on him, he fell backwards.

Another yanked Jaden and Romeo from behind. The vampires dragged them all upstairs to the master bedroom. Over in the corner, two girls laid out who were already drained at the neck. Tamiyah and Lori laid on top of a couch, knocked out. "Tamiyah wake up," Romeo shouted.

Garret tossed Jaden into the wall. "Here Fangz....we find these boys sneaking around. They don't look like anything other than small juice boxes. You know like the ones you buy for lunch or a picnic."

Fangz rose to his feet and tossed Tamiyah across to the other side. "No these are more than juice boxes. These are the Anointed. Top of the line juice boxes." Fangz chuckled as he came from behind the desk, chain swinging. "Have you been watching too many movies kid? Vampire hunting is a quick way to get killed." Fangz bellowed in his heavy southern accent.

Romeo stood from his knees, spat blood on the floor, and wiped his mouth. "We are the Anointed. That's what we do."

Fangz laughed as he sat on the corner of his desk. Garrett laughed along with him. "What are you crazy or something? I run these streets. This is my territory! You can never kill all of us. We are eternal and everywhere just like the night. There are plenty of us and so few of you."

"There is more of us than you think," Jaden spat back.

Two more vampires entered the room with Deshawn and Lay in hand. They threw them next to the wall beside Jaden.

Fangz laughed harder, "That's it?" He jumped up from off the corner of the desk. "You're just a bunch of scrawny kids." He turned to Garrett. "You're telling me these punks have been taking out my crew, and messing up my money?" He waved a dismissive hand at them.

"A vampire named Fangz doesn't sound intimidating to me. Sounds dumb," Jaden said between his teeth.

Fangz came down on him like thunder with a backhand. "Talking out ya neck like that will get your throat ripped out!" He bellowed. Then he turned to Garrett and laughed.

"I could've whoop their asses when I was still human. I don't need to be a vampire." He walked over to his desk and poured himself a glass of blood out of a crystal decanter. "Contrary to popular belief. I'm not a bad guy here."

"Really though?"

"Just hear me out," Fangz protested. "All I want to

147

do is get this bread. I don't want to open no portals to hell and I'm not trying to start an apocalypse. I'm just trying to stack paper and feed from an occasional baddie or two. As a matter of fact, I'm just like you guys. I remember what it was like being a young buster, running the streets. I grew up not too far from here in Bankhead. Now I run the night." He strolled in front of them and sat back down.

"If only you know what I know. There are other vampires that have been around for centuries. Old, pale, and stinking rich. They use their money to control governments, people, and countries. They use their influence to make life harder for people that look like us. All I want to do is the same. But I'm going to use that power to help the neighborhoods."

Lay put on his specs, "How is unleashing drugs more devastating than crack, helping the community?"

Fangz sipped from the glass. "You got a point. But I gotta get the money somehow right?" And he waited for them to approve.

Fangz paced around them, rubbing his chin, and contemplating the situation. "But you know what....I like you boys. You have balls to stand up to me. That takes courage. And since you do, I won't kill you. Instead I'll turn you and make you one of my own. Or since you want to be Karate kids, I'll let you guard my trap houses." Fangz said. Then he lowered himself to Romeo's level.

"Don't be fooled this is just one trap house out of money. I could easily kill you all now. Rip out your hearts and eat it before your eyes." He stopped and turned around. "But instead I'm offering you a seat at my table. Don't you want to be a part of the True bloods, and dance in the new night? I'm talking about decade's worth of wealth and power. I mean real power. Nothing or no one could ever harm you. What do you say boys?"

Romeo curled his lip. "How stupid can you be? I mean did you believe anything that just came out of your mouth?"

"What about you short timer?" Fangz asked Deshawn. "Do you want back in?"

"I'm with him plus.... I don't work for nobody but myself." Deshawn chimed in.

Jaden shuddered a thought. *Atlanta would be the city to have drug dealing vampires. I need to move again.*

I know right, Lay thought

Jaden caught Lay's gaze. *You can hear me*, he thought.

Lay nodded silently.

Deshawn Can you hear me? Jaden asked telepathically.

"Yeah," Deshawn responded out loud.

Fangz frowned. "Yeah what?"

Deshawn shook his head. "Oh nothing."

Romeo can you hear me? Jaden called telepathically.

Romeo peered at him with his lips silent, Jaden continued, *now that everyone can hear me. Listen up. I have a plan, just follow my lead when I strike. We are going to take them out or distract them. When we do we need to grab Lori and Tamiyah then bail.*

All three boys nodded beside him.

Fangz turned to Jaden, "What about you tall and slim. Do you want the blood?"

I have a plan, just follow my lead when I strike.

Jaden turned to him, "Now!" He shouted as he brought down the cabinet with a whisk of his hand. Deshawn did his part by blowing it up. An explosion erupted and the flames consumed three vampires, while Garrett threw himself out of the way and Fangz collapsed into a swarm of screeching bats. Ashes and smoke filled the room. Romeo summoned all the energy he had left to hurl a ball of light into the swarm of bats, which screamed as they shattered through the window.

Romeo grabbed Tamiyah, while Lay grabbed the Lori. Deshawn blew out the wall behind them. They all jumped out in one quick leap. Glass, wooden boards, and debris rained behind as they fell down from the top floor of the abandon two story house. Just before hitting the ground they all floated, levitated almost nose length from the grass. Then after a brief second, of being suspended in air, they crashed to the ground.

Jaden was the first to his feet, "Let's get out of here."

Romeo snatched Tamiyah into his arms, "Imani we need you."

Imani appeared before them in a billowing dust of lights. "What are you guys doing I can sense your adrenaline spiking.

"We don't got time for too much explaining," Deshawn said. "We need to do a memory wipe on these girls and quick.

Two vampires searched for the group.

"Like now," Deshawn shouted as he threw a charged particle up towards the vampires.

Imani opened the balm of her hands and blew dust into the girls faces.

"What was that?" Jaden asked.

"I wiped their memories. They won't remember anything that happened." She folded her arms. "I let you boys go out by yourself for one night and look what you get into? I swear I can't let you out of my sight.

"We should get out of here" Lay cried.

"Let's go," Romeo declared as he carried Tamiyah in his arms.

All together they hurried into the night.

Chapter Sixteen

A great Calling

Jaden laid in bed with both hands propped up behind his head, wide awake, and unable to sleep. He felt good saving those girls, but there was a part of him that wondered would this lead him to more trouble. Trouble and sadness seemed to be the only thing constant in his life. They were like two relatives he couldn't get rid of for nothing. Life seemed to be one sad song, that he wanted desperately to be over. Every night he thought of his mom and wondered if her soul was at peace, and if it was truly possible to be with her somehow. Being with her would be a lot better than being here, he thought.

"Creator are you there?" he said out loud.

A perfect stillness came to his mind, as the creator answered. *I am here.*

"Don't take this the wrong way, but is there any way you can take this all back?"

The Creator laughed and the sound rolled around

Jaden's head, as if a friend laid there beside him, caught in a giggling fit.

Jaden didn't like that at all. "It's not funny. I am being serious."

I have forgotten how small you are for such a great calling that has been bestowed upon you. Your gift has been given to you for a reason. The thorn will keep you humble as well as give you great strength.

Jaden sighed. "When I am weak, you are strong."

Well look at that, somebody has been doing some reading.

Jaden sat up. "A little bit." He said pleased with himself, even though he knew he couldn't fool the Creator. "The others want me to join them and continue fighting the cause. I know you probably want me to join them too. Should I?"

The choice is yours. But you're wrong I don't want you to join them. I want you to lead them. Lead all of my people.

Jaden shook his head. "What?"

Descendant of David you are the once and future king who will bring peace across the land. But you will face many threats from friend and foe, flesh and spirit.

Jaden hunched his shoulders. "But there are no Kings in America."

Didn't I say I will use you to do a new thing. You still don't believe

"Well help a brother out," he said. "What if I don't join the others. They can handle it right?"

They will fail.

"I've only been here a few days and I've seen vampires, and demonic grasshoppers. So I know everything wants to kill us. Would it be bad to admit that if they want to kill Romeo, then I will give them a hand"?

The choice is yours. If you choose to deny the call, there will always come another, but the you will must be prepared to live with the consequences.

He laid there trying to absorb the Creator's words as the voice faded from his head.

Chapter Seventeen

Mama

After wrestling with the idea all night, Jaden was moved to visit Sanctuary just one more time. The gym looked entirely different in the light of day. It was packed with kids and adults of both genders. There was a trainer in the ring showing a group of middle schoolers how to throw a jab. A group of girls threw punches on the punching bag in the right corner. A few guys lifted weights in the middle floor. The equipment appeared to have a decent age with no sign of rust. Jaden found Coach nestled in the corner, talking to some lady.

Jaden went over and lurked nearby. His demeanor seemed like he was looking for an exit plan. He carried a cake in his hand, and every time he tried to end the conversation she just continued.

Coach Franklin smiled. "Thank you again Ms. Parker for this cake."

Ms. Parker fanned herself. "No problem Coach. I

think what you are doing for these kids is such a blessing." She laid her hand on Coach's forearm. "We need more strong men of faith like you in this community." Her voice was a true slice of sweet potato pie, southern and decadent. It seemed like everything on her shimmered, from the bangles on her wrist, to long golden necklace she wore, and the dangling ear rings. From her demeanor to her accent, she reminded Jaden of a pastor's wife, sans a hat and judging from her body language, a wedding ring too.

Coach Franklin pulled his arm away. "I remember what kind of knucklehead I was at that age. And I just want to give the kids a place where they can be safe, release the stress of today's world, and learn life lessons that will serve them well."

Ms. Parker waved her hand like a tambourine. "Amen to that. I rather them be in here then on the street. Have ya' heard about all the foolishness that has been on the news lately? Children joining gangs and thinking they're vampires. It's all over the Facebooks too, my niece showed it to me just the other day."

Coach Franklin rubbed his head and sighed. The sunlight made his mahogany scalp glisten. "I've heard about it, and it's sad. Kids at this age are misguided and easily persuaded."

Ms. Parker slapped her thigh with the fan. "Tell me about it. And it's just getting even more ridiculous. Now this whole vamp life thing is turning into a challenge. Did you hear about the fourteen-year-old boy from Florida?" She asked, leaning in.

"No I didn't," he said as he dropped jaw to her ear.

"This little boy jumped fifteen feet out of the window, talking about he wanted to fly."

Coach Franklin twisted his mouth. "Some of these kids are idiots."

Ms. Parker slapped his chest, "They said he was high off some new drug named Becky." She shook her head. "And don't forget about all of the mass killings going on around here. Twelve people killed at the high school near Stone Mountain, men eating off each other's face, and the increased drug activity. Seems like we have to stay prayed up."

Jaden waited as long as he could for the conversation to break. He cleared his throat

Coach Franklin patted Ms. Parker, "Excuse me, I have to go talk to one of my boys."

"Go ahead, I'll talk to you later Coach." Ms. Parker fanned herself and shuddered as she watched Coach Franklin walk away.

"Coach what's up?" Jaden greeted.

"I knew you would come." Coach Franklin said as he wrapped an arm around him.

"How did you know that?"

"This spirit told me," He answered. Then he ushered him to the back office. "Come follow me, the others are downstairs training."

Together they strolled into the back office and Coach Franklin flipped the switch to the secret elevator. Coach Franklin waved his wrist on the scanner and the elevator descended down with a jerk.

Coach Franklin leaned against the left side of the elevator. "Don't tell the others this. But I can see that you are very powerful in the spirit. Your cup runneth over."

Jaden pointed his brows. "Thanks I guess."

"Not many have what you have. But be careful. Although I see power, the spirit also reveals to me rage. A rage that will consume you like a devouring fire, turning everything in your life a living hell."

"I would say that's the sum of my life right now. A living hell. That's why I figure why fight it? Trouble somehow always finds its way to me."

The elevator hit the bottom floor, a chime went off, and the doors parted.

"That's life son. It's a journey filled with valleys, peaks, and rough seas." Coach Franklin said as he strolled. "But the true believer will have the strength to endure it all."

Jaden followed behind Coach Franklin, walking back into the study and off into another area of Sanctuary. He struggled to keep up with the older gentleman, who walked with the pace of a doctor about to go in surgery. Every so often he checked over his shoulder to make sure Jaden kept up.

"Today we are focusing on hand to hand combat. The Anointed cannot survive on the abilities the spirit grants us alone. I'm going to take you to the armory to pick out a weapon."

"Sounds good to me," Jaden said.

The hall opened up to a large corridor, and they

veered off to the left, and past silver doors. Inside the armory, smelled of gun powder, metal, and dust. But the layout was as impressive and polished like the rest of Sanctuary. Four shelves stood in the middle of the floor holding guns, with blue light gleaming off of them. Displayed on the walls were various swords, daggers, axes, throwing knives, uv bombs, silver bullets, beads of protection and crucifixes.

Imani sat on a long metal table top while she polished a steel sword.

"Jaden!" She said as she hopped off the table and pulled him into a hug. She was dressed in her usual casual glam, white t-shirt, tight fitting jeans, boots, and her long dark hair effortlessly flowing across her shoulders. "Finally joining the squad?" She asked.

"Something like that," he answered in a sarcastic tone.

Coach Franklin stood in the middle of the armory. "Okay Mr. Davis pick a weapon."

Jaden took a moment to examine along the walls. The only weapon he had experience with was a sword. And they were about two dozen of them alone in the armory, with different makes, design, and cultural significance. There were Spanish swords, medieval long swords, Katana swords, swords with various shapes. One sword in particular stood out to him, it had a golden hilt, long and glinting, with a black handle, words etched to the tip.

Jaden reached out with his hand. The sword jittered

in the holder, shaking side to side. Jaden tightened his grip and the sword whirled through the air and landed inside his palm.

"Nice choice. It's a classic warrior sword."

Jaden held the sword up to the brilliant light of the armory, and the golden hilt gleamed.

Imani went over to the table and picked up the sword she'd just finished polishing. "Coach do you want me to train him?"

"Sure, Ms. Warrior Angel."

Jaden shot her a sidelong glance. "Do you even know what you're doing with that?"

She spun with the sword aimed at his neck, and he brought his up for the two to clash. The sound of the metal echoed in the Amory. Imani's eyes were pure diamonds as she inched closer.

"Of course I do. How I else would you expect to become an agent of SMITE." She said with a smile.

"Alright, that's enough cup caking. Let's take it to the ring." Coach Franklin said.

Imani tugged at Jaden's hand. "Come on you are going to love this?"

"I'm coming," Jaden said.

Jaden had a feeling that whatever was in the Ring, it had to be great. Imani kept looking back at him with her eyes alight with glittering excitement. When they reached the apex of Sanctuary, the War room, they veered off to the right, and went down two flight of stairs. Silver doors opened into an enormous gymnasium with towering white padded walls, and black grids on the floor.

"Here it is," Coach Franklin said as he led them into the room.

Jaden gasped. "I've never seen nothing like this. Not even in my dreams."

Coach Franklin slapped his shoulder. "Yea I know son. Get used to it, because it's time to put in some work."

The others were already inside training and the walls of the Ring thundered with clashes and grunts. Three holographic monsters with bat like faces surrounded Deshawn. He fended them off with wide arc strikes from his battle axe, which had a large curvy blade, and sleek handle. It whistled like a hawk as he swung it about. Ms. Day stood a few paces behind him, taking notes diligently.

Lay and Romeo practiced with each other. Romeo shot darts of light from his fingers. Lay deflected them with the opposing ends of his staff. The back and forth between the two looked like dancing lights.

Coach Franklin raised his hand. "Bring it in."

Everyone stopped what they did, and came over.

"Listen up," He started. "Jaden is going to be joining our hand to hand training session. "Coach patted Jaden's shoulder. "Today and only today we are going to take it easy on you. Every day afterwards is going to be a long walk through hell, covered in gasoline. You are going to hate me from this point on out."

Ms. Day dropped her clipboard. "How about everyone grab some water and catch your breath. Then our training session will reconvene in a minute."

Lay wiped sweat from his forehead. "Coach is really tough. But we have good practice during our sessions. Why didn't you tell me you were coming?"

"I wanted to surprise you," Jaden said.

Lay strolled behind Jaden to grab a towel. He wrapped it around his neck, and dabbed it against his face, as well as his bird's nest of hair. "Consider me surprised then."

Romeo leaned in Deshawn's ear. "Watch this." With his two fingers by his side, he shot a jolt of light towards Lay's bottom.

"Ouch!" Lay shouted as it hit him in the butt. "Anyway, would you like to go for some bubble–"

Romeo shot him again and started cackling with Deshawn as Lay almost jumped to hit the roof.

Lay frowned. "Okay guys quit playing, I need a minute."

Romeo and Deshawn continued their fit of laughter, and Jaden's blood became hot lava. When Romeo shot a jolt of light this time, Jaden flicked his wrist, and it whizzed back into Romeo's shoulder.

Romeo winced as the pain seared across his shoulder.

"I think you need to chill out," Jaden said with an edge in his voice, and fire in his eyes.

Romeo smiled at his aggression. "Well look who's letting their balls hang out." His Latin rasp making the words come out like a growl.

The cockiness in Romeo's smile made Jaden's hand

tremble as he held the sword. "Who the hell do you think you are?"

Romeo set his jaw hard. "I'm the leader of this crew."

Jaden raised his brow. "And?"

"And, the sooner you realize this the quicker you can fall in line." Romeo dropped his hands to the side. His fingers itched to pull out the golden ninja sai concealed by his legs.

Jaden rested the sword along his shoulder. "I hate to break it to you buddy, but there is a new sheriff town."

Romeo laughed sarcastically. "Put your sword where your mouth is cowboy, and come see me in the ring."

"Now boys that's enough of this," Ms. Day protested.

Coach Franklin pulled her out of the way. "No let em' fight. This could be good." He reached into his pocket, pulled out a whistle and blew. "Now listen up, if we are going to do this, then we are going to do it right. I want both of you in the center, and in between the black circle. No biting, no scratching and no cheap shots below the belt."

"Coach," Ms. Day reprimanded.

"Can we use the spirit?" Romeo asked.

"I don't see why not," Coach responded.

Deshawn clapped his hands. "I wished I had some popcorn."

Jaden dragged his foot across the padded Ring floor until he came at the center of a giant black circle that enclosed them. Jaden's eyes narrowed at Romeo's from across the room. There was still a smug look on his face. A look that Jaden was eager to erase. Romeo reminded Jaden so much of the guys who tortured him since middle grade. He never wanted to use his abilities on anyone until one kid Reggie pulled down his pants in front of the whole class. So stunned by what happened, Jaden froze before picking up his pants. What matters worst was he was ashy that day, his skin was so dry that it was grey.

Romeo twirled two golden Sai around him, the pencil thin blades whistled, as they whirled through the air. "It's okay if you don't want to go through this. You can leave now and never come back."

Jaden brought his sword up and took a battle stance.

"Are you ready?" Coach Franklin shouted as he lowered his head to his knees. "We are going to do this on my word, understand?"

"Bet," Romeo muttered.

"I'm ready," Jaden said, his gaze not wavering.

Coach Franklin holds his lowered position, studying both boys. He stretches the start forever, making them both wait and run battle strategy through their head. It seems like the entire room hinges on one breath.

"Don't be afraid to battle at your own pace," Ms. Day advises.

"Shh!" Coach snaps. He lowered himself back down to the position.

Ms. Day holds the clipboard to the side. "Don't shh me. I have a voice and opinion. You will respect that."

"I do. Now can we continue?" Coach Franklin asked.

BOOK OF THE ANOINTED

Ms. Day nodded with a smile. Coach Franklin faces the boys again, and slices air with his right hand.

"Battle!"

Romeo closes the distance between them quickly. Romeo lifts from the ground as if his sneakers had wings on the side, and his feet kick at Jaden's face. Jaden dodged out of the way. The attack was so quick and sudden that Jaden thought for a moment, just maybe he might have bitten off more than he can chew.

With both hands on his sword, Jaden swung over his head and struck at Romeo's neck. Romeo leaned back, as Jaden spun to strike again. When Jaden brings his sword down for a third attempt, Romeo brings both sai up to block. Holy metal clash and the sound quaked along the walls of the Ring. The kinetic energy pushes the heels of both of their feet back.

Jaden clenches his teeth and grunts as he forces his sword down upon Romeo. Romeo takes the weight and uses it to push Jaden out of the lock. With the swiftness of a cheetah, he drops to one knee and rolls to the other side of the circle. A sharp pain slices across Jaden's back.

"Ow!"

Jaden caresses the lower left side of his back. There was no blood but the cut still stung something terrible.

"Did you catch that?" Romeo asks sarcastically.

Anger fills Jaden's veins. With sword in hand he charges like a bull.

Romeo steps back and points two fingers. Jet streams of golden light zap towards Jaden.

Pew! Pew!

Both bolts of light dart at Jaden, and he backhands them with his sword like hitting a tennis ball with a racquet. Romeo ducks, and the walls of the Ring absorb them as they land.

Jaden was going to win this fight. He felt it in his bones. In his spirit. Jaden backhanded the air, and a cloud of crimson energy pummeled Romeo. Romeo crumbled to the ground, but he didn't stay there. Romeo rolled himself into a ball, to creep behind Jaden.

Before Jaden could even whirl over his shoulder, he felt the hot beam of light shoot across his neck, blistering his skin.

"Ugh!"

"Slow it down!" Ms. Day shouts from the sidelines. Her hand resting against her shoulder as she paced. Her heart thumping in her chest.

Once Romeo saw an opening, he leapt into the air like a gazelle, and sliced across Jaden's back before hitting the ground. It was so fast that Jaden only saw a blur of black when Romeo went by.

Romeo held up a slice of Jaden's red t-shirt like it's a trophy. "Are you even trying?"

Hot tears swelled in Jaden's brown eyes. A sharp icy pain slashed across his back and shoulder. Jaden ran towards him with his sword raise, and shouting a guttural battle cry. His sword struck at Romeo's neck one moment, and slashed across his chest the next. Romeo countered each strike, and as he did his arrogant sneer seemed to spread further.

"You're a dick. You know that?" Jaden shouted as he kept the pressure on Romeo. He strikes with his sword as if it was as blunt as baseball bat.

Romeo sidesteps him until he is at the edge of the inner ring. "I bet your mama likes it though," he says as he grabs himself.

Rage flooded through Jaden, like a sweltering tide stampeding through his veins. He could hear his blood pounding in his ears, and all that he saw became red. Jaden lifted his left hand, flattened his palms, and Romeo's body went rigid. Both daggers fell out of his hands and clattered to the floor.

Jaden thrust his palm and Romeo went soaring, cartwheeling, and flying into the wall. Fissures radiated at the sight of impact. Everyone behind them gasped.

Coach Franklin blew his whistle. "That's enough."

Jaden ignored him. He strode in front of Romeo who struggled to pull himself off of the floor. Jaden clenched his fingers and a knot formed in Romeo's throat.

"Okay that's enough," Coach repeated. His voice now a tumultuous scream.

Romeo's skin turned bright red as he clawed at his neck, unable to breath. Jaden bought his fist up, and Romeo slowly lifted from the ground.

"I can't hear you," Jaden murmured. "What did you say about my mama?"

"I said that's enough," Coach Franklin thundered. He flattened his palm and pummeled Jaden from the right, sending him sliding across the floor.

Jaden stood up looking as if he was ready to retaliate. Eyes bloodshot red, one long throbbing vein by his right temple, and fists balled.

Coach Franklin pointed towards the door. "You are out of here."

"Fine," Jaden spat as he stomped across the floor. In a fit of anger, Jaden tossed the sword and blasted out of the doors.

For a moment everyone stood still. They were shocked at what just happened. Romeo struggled to pull himself off the floor, coughing for his life.

Imani went over to Romeo. "Are you okay?"

Romeo had hands on both knees, as he struggled to breathe. "Yeah,"

She held her hands up around his neck. Bright lights came from them, and the red marks on his neck faded away. "Better?"

Romeo sighed out in relief. "Much better."

"Good," Imani said before punching him in the shoulder.

"Ouch!" Romeo shouted.

"What were you thinking?" She asked. "You know what happened to his mother. Why would you bring her up like that?"

Romeo smacked his forehead. "My bad, I forgot."

"Yeah dog, that was pretty cold. I wouldn't even make no joke like that." Deshawn muttered as he put his hands in his pockets.

Lay folded his arms. "Sometimes Romeo you can be too cruel."

Coach Franklin thought he missed something. "I don't care what you all say. That boy is out of line. He needs to check himself."

"Coach just give him a break," Ms. Day hissed.

Imani started after Jaden, but Romeo pulled her back. "I got this. Trust me."

Romeo walked outside the silver doors and found Jaden sitting on the floor. Once Jaden was alerted to Romeo's presence, he clenched his fist. Romeo held his hands up. "Hold up there cowboy. I come in peace."

"What do you want?" Jaden asked.

"I just–" Romeo started. He rolled his eyes to the ceiling as if the perfect worlds would fall out. "Can I sit down?"

Jaden slid over.

Romeo sat on the side of the wall beside him. "Look man, I just wanted to say I'm sorry. I'm sure you know by now, but I can be a bit of an asshole sometimes."

Jaden arched his brow. "Sometimes?"

Romeo smirked. "Don't make this harder for me. But the biggest reason I wanted to apologize, is because I know what it's like to lose a parent."

"What do you mean?" Jaden asked.

Romeo swallowed hard. "My father was one of the Anointed also. And a demon killed him when I was seven years old."

"That's messed up," Jaden commented.

"So I know how that is. My father is a sour topic for me, and if anyone were to talk crap about him, I would want to beat their ass as well. So I'm not mad atcha." Romeo raised his fist. "Are we cool?"

"Sure," Jaiden said as he bumped Romeo's fist.

"Aww guys, this is what I like to see." Lay said. He, Deshawn, and Imani poked their heads out of the door.

"How long have you been there?" Jaden asked.

"We heard everything," Deshawn answered.

Lay ran over to the boys. "I think this calls for a group hug. Bring it in guys." He wrapped his arms around the both of them.

"Hell no," Romeo said as he pulled away.

Deshawn came from the other side. "Nah big dog, you have to do it for the crew."

Collectively they formed a circle with Imani in the middle. All together they took one deep breath in and exhaled out. "Aww guys this is beautiful. I love us for real," Imani cried.

Ms. Day and Coach stood by the corner. "Look at our precious kids. These are the Creator's chosen. So much love between them all."

Coach Franklin's face tightened. "It sickens me. I prefer them at each other's throats." Then he glanced over to Ms. Day. "It will make them better warriors."

When the group hug was over, Jaden felt a glimmer of regret for his disrespectful tone and behavior. But he wasn't about to apologize for her truly felt. "Coach I'm sorry for–"

Coach Franklin held up his hand. "You don't have to say nothing." He shifted his gaze towards the group. "How about we just call it a night for today. Let's continue sometime next week."

Deshawn's eyes grew large. "Really coach?"

"Yes. We'll give Jaiden some time to settle in and let you all rest a moment."

Ms. Day rubbed his shoulder. "That's a good call Coach. And that will give some time to talk with the guild on how we want to incorporate Jaiden with the hunting and training."

Jaden didn't need to be told twice, especially after all that drama in the ring. A part of him didn't know if he could move forward with the group with Romeo there. But he did feel that Romeo was sincere with his apology. Thinking about it all, he left with the same unease he came with.

CHAPTER EIGHTEEN

Shedding of Fears

"*Oh you think you got me huh?* Watch and see what my Cavaliers are about to do to you." Romeo shouted. He pressed buttons on the game controller like a wild man, eyes glued to the screen, dry from not blinking in the last hour and half. Icy hot pads covered him while his chemistry book laid beside him, untouched.

Jaden reclined back leisurely in a nearby rocker. A game controller levitated in front of him and the buttons pressed by themselves and matched Romeo's aggression, "The game is almost over Romeo. Just give up." Jaden obnoxiously boasted.

Romeo stood with his eyes keen on the screen. He was hell bent on winning. "Shut up dumbass. We're about to make a comeback. Come on!" Romeo roared, at the screen with a fierce intensity. "Nobody knows basketball like me. I do this. Do you understand? There is no way,

I'm going to let you beat me.

"And that's the game folks. Golden gate Warriors beat the Cleveland Cavaliers fifty-three to forty," the announcer on the screen shouted as a loud buzzer rang out. Both controllers vibrating steadily.

Romeo threw his controller behind his bed as Jaden laughed.

Jaden sat up in the chair proudly, "I told you man. I might can't play basketball for real. But I know games. I got skills."

Romeo groaned, "I guess,"

Lay stood up from the desk. "Now that the game is over. Can we get back to studying? Correct me if I'm wrong, but wasn't you Romeo that begged us to come here? It's been over an hour now and we've gotten nowhere. You're going to fail this exam."

Romeo threw his head back against the bed. "I hate chemistry, it's stupid."

Lay pointed a finger. "But you need to pass if you want to remain on the basketball team. The season just started."

Romeo curled a pillow around his head. "I know."

Deshawn strutted into the room, juggling handfuls of hot empanadas on a paper towel. "Thank you Ms. Rodriguez. You stay putting your foot in these empanadas," Deshawn yelled down the hall. His voice was muffled by the bits of food in his mouth. He stood halfway in the room, but he leaned his head out, and watched as Romeo's mom strutted down the hall.

Deshawn kicked the door shut behind him. "Aye big dog, your mom is so fine. If her empanadas are this good, I can only imagine her pupusa."

Romeo lodged a pillow at Deshawn's head. "Don't ever let me hear you mention my mom's pupusa."

Jaden erupted in a fit of laughter as Lay blinked owl like behind his glasses.

"I don't get it," Lay said.

Deshawn plopped down on Romeo's bed. "I'm for real though. And she is single too. I would definitely marry your mom." A glorious thought made his eyes light up in excitement. "Hey, you can be son."

Romeo chucked a basketball at Deshawn's head. Deshawn quickly tossed the bag of chips to the side, as he slowed down the basketball that was inches away from knocking him out.

Deshawn smacked away the ball "Ha. You missed me," he said with a sneer.

With a flick of his fingers Jaden tossed a game controller at the back of Deshawn's head, who cried out at impact. "I think I'm bleeding," Deshawn winced as he held his hand on his head.

Jaden laughed. He went over to Lay who was typed away fiercely at his laptop. "Lay, are your writing an angry e-mail?"

Lay scrolled further down on the screen, "Huh, oh no I'm just taking a look at these news reports. My mind is programmed to detect any crimes reported that might be related to the supernatural."

"How did you do that?" Deshawn asked.

"Keywords," Lay responded.

Romeo sat up and faced the desk from his bed. "What are the reports saying?

"Random people have been going missing for the past few days. The numbers are up to twelve now." Lay answered.

Deshawn scarfed down another empanada. "Doesn't sound too weird to me?"

"Twelve?" Jaden repeated. "That's a lot of people in such a short time. It definitely sounds like paranormal activity to me."

Lay scrolls down the screen and Romeo recognizes a face that makes him jump up from the bed. "Lay wait."

"What is it?" Lay asks.

"Scroll back up," Romeo commanded as went over to his drawer, searching through his drawings.

Lay scrolled up to the missing picture he was looking at. "To this?"

"Yes," Romeo said. He brought his drawing over to the group. Lately I've been having dreams for the last week or so that I just can't explain. So I have just been drawing whatever I can remember, like I always do. One thing I kept seeing was this girl, and now I think I'm starting to see a connection. In one of the dreams I saw a demon stalking this girl in a parking garage. That's her," Romeo shouted as he pointed to the laptop screen.

Jaiden read the name out loud. "Alloura McPherson. She has been missing for over three weeks."

Deshawn wiped crumbs from off his lap. "This

sounds like something we need to tell Ms. Day and Coach about. Let's mosey on over to Sanctuary," he suggested.

Lay snickered at Deshawn's word choice, "Mosey?" He repeated sarcastically. "I totally agree with you, by the way."

"I'm going anyway," Jaden said. "Tonight is my first time doing a simulation in the Ring."

"The shedding of fears," Romeo muttered.

Deshawn stood, "I can't wait to see this. This is going to be good. I'm telling you right now Coach Franklin is going to kill you!"

Jaden stiffened, "What do you mean? It's just a simulation. And what is the shedding of fears?"

Lay rolled from the desk. "The shedding fears is what we call the first simulation. It's on the first simulation, that the matrix of the Ring determines your worst fear and puts you against it. That's the easiest way to explain it."

Jaiden stood up and paced, "Why would it do that?"

"Because fear has no place in the heart of the Anointed." Romeo answered.

"It weakens us," Lay continued. "Our power comes from the spirit, which we wield, and the spirit is powered faith."

"Along with smiting," Romeo added.

Deshawn grabbed Jaden by the shoulders and shook him. "Don't sleep! He is going to kill you Jacob. Going into the Ring is like being dropped into hell. Everything moves, bites, and gushes blood all over. If I were you, I wouldn't go" Deshawn argued with a sneer.

Romeo rolled his eyes, "Pipe down dummy. Don't listen to this fool Jaden. You will be fine."

"Fine and dead. Coach is going to go ham on you for the first time," Deshawn insisted as he laughed.

"Romeo, how many times have you completed a simulation in the ring?"

"A few solo, maybe seven at the most. "Romeo threw up his hands nonchalantly.

"What about you Lay?" Jaden asked.

"Ten. They were not that difficult once you understand the controls, algorithm, and purpose of the training."

Jaden sighed. "Alright no need to delay the inevitable. I can do this."

Romeo jumped up from his chair, "Just let me get my shoes."

Deshawn jumped up also, "Alright let me just get some more of these empanadas and maybe a plate to go," he said

****

Jaden lead the way to the manager's office. Together they maneuvered by the few people who worked out along the sidelines. The overhead light fixture blinked on and off while they trickled into the main office. Romeo went straight to the junk covered mahogany desk. He pushed the red button underneath the desk, and the trophy case sled left to reveal an old fashioned elevator. They walked in and Lay pushed the button to descend down to

Sanctuary.

Slow rusty squeaks echoed in the elevator shaft as they descended. The elevator doors revealed Coach Franklin who looked highly pissed.

"You're late," Coach Franklin said. He took a long sip from a soda can.

Jaden spoke up, "But I was at Romeo's and—"

Coach Franklin cut him off, "Save it sir. I don't want to hear it. Head to the ring now." Coach Franklin ordered and he downed the rest of the soda.

Jaden's face dropped, and he slouched his way down the hall.

Romeo followed Coach Franklin's footsteps. "Wait Coach I got to tell you about these dreams I've been having. Might be a demon related."

Coach Franklin stopped and turned. "Did you see a face in these dreams son?" He folded his arms and leaned in. "Do we have a specific location or an innocent to save?" Coach Franklin asked.

"No, I just saw weird symbols but I think I know how he or it is killing."

Coach Franklin waved his hands, "Go tell Ms. Day and Imani. They're in the study. I'll be there when I'm done with Jaden."

Deshawn scratched his nose, "Hey Coach what do you want me to do?"

"Go with him!" Coach Franklin huffed as he headed back down the hallway. "The both of you," he directed towards Lay.

Jaden struggled to hold his breath as he sat in the

middle of the Ring surrounded by white. He felt so small in the room by himself. This time it would be just him in there, while Coach stood in the brown control office right beside the exit.

The fear almost made him want to wet his pants. But just as he ran through all his fears, he also remembered that nothing more terrifying than that night he faced the demon. After that everything should be a cakewalk. He lost his mother but he kept his life. Her memory gave him a bit of courage.

Suddenly a loud boom exploded through the air, and Jaden cowered to his knees. It was if a bomb exploded outside of the pristine white walls. Bright lights flooded the Ring and assaulted his eyes. A horrible mechanical clicking followed. Each tile along the walls lifted up and readjusted. It was if the whole world around him was moving. Jaden looked around in a frantic panic.

There was an ear splitting thunderclap and Coach Franklin's voice boomed over speakers. "Don't be afraid. The room is readjusting, and this will only take a few seconds."

The walls expanded a dirty brown plastic material over the white. And the walls closed in on him. When the transformation was over, Jaden found himself in a small locked room inside a warehouse. An onrushing sense of fear stifled him, and robbed him of whatever confidence he had before going into this experience.

Out in the distance Coach Franklin's voice called out to him. "Remember son the danger reflected in the ring is very real, and reflective of what you will face out on the field. This simulation is designed to train you on how to channel the spirit, sharpen your thinking skills, and develop your survival instincts. In this simulation your spirit is full so you won't drain. In the real battlefield, the spirit which is the source of our power, drains as we use our godly gifts. The consequences of draining your spirit is death. You should know that because, you have come close to that a few times now." Coach Franklin chuckled sarcastically. "But we want to keep you around a little bit longer. That's why we train to fight and replenish our spirit by smiting evil. How are you so far?"

"I'm good," Jaden lied.

"Good. Now let's begin. The spirit is a force. It is invisible like the wind, because it can be felt or experienced, but not seen. It is the breath of The Creator which disperses life, energy and wisdom. It is in every living being, but only we Anointed have the ability to manipulate it in different ways."

Jaden paced the room and a wooden kitchen chair materialized in front of him. "First we'll start off with something easy. By channeling your telekinesis through your hands I want you to pick up this chair in the middle of this room."

Jaden rubbed his hands together, he lifted his right hand and the chair levitated along with the level of height he raised his up-right palm.

"Okay good. Next challenge," Coach Franklin commented, his tone a little more pleasant than usual.

A boom thundered the air, followed by metallic

clicking, and the landscape of the room shifted again. Moonlight swept over him and cool air misted his skin. Moss covered trees grew from the ground and graves surrounded him. Fog rolled around him and the air carried the scent of swamp waters.

"Let's try this. I want you to use your telekinesis by throwing objects at this vampire. Ultimately the goal is to stake him by using your power."

Soil crumbled from the grave in front of him, and a man climbed his way out, stretching as if waking for the first time. He bore fangs when he steps onto solid ground, and brushes mud off his dingy black suit.

"I'm so hungry," the vampire growled.

Place directly beneath Jaden's feet was a shovel. Using his powers, he hurled it directly towards the vampire neck. The spinning shovel decapitated the vampire and covered the grave in ashes.

Thunder tore through the air, and the room shifted again.

Jaden stood at some secret army facility behind a locked door. This time there was a huge glass window where a security guard watched surveillance cameras and stuffing his face with donuts.

"All right Jaden, that was better. Now this is the final test. We will focus on your telepathic abilities, which refer to as scanning. You are stranded in this facility and you need to use a combination of scanning, telekinesis, and hand to hand combat to escape."

Jaden pressed his face to the cold glass, he could see

a few more rooms in the distance of the facility.

"There are three basic abilities that scanners use, which are compel, confuse, and psychic blast. Compel allows a scanner to control a target by mental suggestion. Confuse makes a target defend the scanner or attack anyone he/she chooses. Psychic blast is the most powerful method utilized. A psychic blast comes out as a mental projectile that targets the nervous system of a foe and knocks them out unconscious. First I want you to compel that security guard in the room to open the door for you."

Jaden pressed his face further to the glass, a security guard ate chips and faced the monitor opposite Jaden's direction. The man looked to Jaden to be in his forties or fifties, out of shape, and balding with a spot in the middle of his head, followed by long black strands on the side. "How? I can't look at him in the eye. He can't see me?"

"He doesn't need to. Suggest it mentally. Listen to his thoughts and as you are in his mind, mentally suggest it. Or when face to face just tell them what to do."

Jaden pressed his fingers against his temple. *Open the door*, Jaden suggested mentally. The words seemed to roll around his head like a leaf caught in the breeze, and then they faded as they rolled into the guard's head. Compelled, the guard rose up out of his seat very stiff and zombie like. He slugged over the monitor and pressed the button to unlock the door.

Jaden clapped his hands, and laughed. "That actually worked." He walked into the next room with the security guard, "What now?"

"Put him to sleep," Coach Franklin answered back.

Jaden caressed his own temple. *Sleep,* he suggested

The eyes of the security guard rolled and he fell to the floor. "This is so cool," Jaden exclaimed as he walked into the next room.

Two soldiers with assault rifles paced the room. Jaden ducked under a nearby stack of crates. One of the soldiers hoovered over his shoulder. Jaden cowered further behind the crates.

"Now Jaden here comes the real tricky part. Just like you mentally suggested the previous guard to let out of the room. I need you to confuse one of these soldiers and make him attack the other. Then afterwards disarm him and disable him by slamming him against the wall.

"Oh I'm screwed," Jaden cursed.

"And you might want to confuse one of them now," Coach Franklin commanded.

An assault rifle poked his face. "Move!" The soldier barked. Jaden got up from his hiding position below the crate with his hands in the air.

He trembled, "Okay man I'm moving. I'm unarmed."

"What are you doing here? No one is authorized to be here. My orders are to shoot intruders on sight."

Jaden stepped backwards, "I'm not intruding."

With a thudding click, the soldier armed the gun.

Jaden closed his eyes. *Shoot him, not me.*

The soldier's chest lurched, and his arms became rigid like a puppet. He turned around very slowly and aimed at the other soldier across the room and opened fire. Gunfire deafened the room as bullets littered the ground. His body disappeared into thin air as it slid down the wall full of bullet holes. The soldier turned back around towards Jaden. He flicked his right hand and the soldier's assault rifle flew out of his arms. Jaden extended his hand fully in the air and soldier lifted. With his fingers curled into a fist he slammed the soldier harshly into the wall. A crimson stain was left on the corner of the wall as the soldier's body fell and disappeared.

Thunderclap and metal clicking, as the room shifted and Jaden fell into a puddle. Darkness surrounded him and he scanned around trying to take in this new environment. Water dripped on his forehead and the hard rock concealed him in a narrow cave.

"Coach what is this?" Jaden asked as his fears kicked in. He didn't like sleeping in the dark and the cave felt like a gloomy pit. One ray of light spilled from a crack overhead. He stood near it.

"Finally it's time for the psychic blast. Besides knocking a human enemy unconscious, the great thing is that this attack can also expel demons out of their human vessels. This is very powerful since most Anointed can only do this through exorcism. I know you've done it before but now I want you to learn how to control your psychic blasts. Take out this demon before he takes you out. The primary objective is to expel the demon and save the man."

A man dressed in all black materialized in front of him. The demon's had cold blue eyes, just like his mother's killer. Jaden's breath caught in his chest.

Mentally he flashed back to that awful night. An image of his mother pinned to the ceiling snapped between his eyes. Jaden stepped backwards.

"Blast him now," Coach Franklin commanded.

Jaden stepped backward into another puddle and stumbled. His heart slammed into his chest as his hands trembled. He'd been waiting for this moment for so long, but he never imagined it would go like this. Jaden saw another image of his mother, dropping to the floor on top of him. The demon in front of him whisked his hand and Jaden flew back into the wall. He couldn't move his hands or his legs, the pressure felt like a car crashed into him. The demon stepped closer. A powerful gust of wind blew Jaden against the rock and out of the light. He could see nothing, only the blue eyes of the demon.

"Do it now Jaden! Blast him now! You blast him and the demon is exorcised."

The Demon retrieved a large ritual knife from his pocket. Jaden gulped at the glisten of the large blade in the light of the fire. With a smirk, the demon pressed Jaden against the wall harder with his elbow and drew back the blade. Jaden closed his eyes.

Thunder tore the air, metal clicked, and the room shifted.

"Jaden! What the hell was that kid?" Coach Franklin yelled as he stepped from behind the control room.

Jaden opened his eyes. He was back in the white room. The Ring was reset. Coach Franklin walked out of the ring shaking his head.

"That wasn't good at all, but that's okay because you're going to get it together. Get you some rest and meet me here EARLY tomorrow. Sixteen hundred hours." Coach Franklin spoke without facing him.

Sadden and disappointed in himself Jaden followed.

******

Fangz marched into his bedroom, and in the faint light of the moon's shadow he glimpsed the face of a man. The man stood six foot two, with a lithe dancer's body, and wild wooly hair. Moonlight etched his wondrous cheekbones, and made his skin glisten like the coat of a black panther.

"Midnight." Fangz gasped as he stepped forward.

Midnight faced him. "We need to talk." His baritone was smooth yet airy, like an extinguished flame.

Fangz strolled over to the bed. "Sit down. Can I get you a drink?

Midnight waved his hand, "That won't be necessary. I've only come to tell you one thing." He unbuttoned his blazer, and his bare chest spilled out like mountains.

"What's that?"

Midnight's eyes hardened. "Do not start war with the demons."

Fangz went over to the night stand and poured himself a drink. "They are moving in on my territory and that's bad for business. I have this city in my pocket and I want to keep it that way." He sauntered over to Midnight until they were arm's length apart. "You made me warden over the south, and I plan to govern this area the best of my ability."

Midnight nodded. "I know, but this is much bigger than us," he said, his voice trembled with thousand-year-old wisdom. "The angels and demons are about to wage war and I don't want me or mine a part of it." He pulled Fangz in by the back of his head. "Do you know there have already been sightings of two archangels topside?"

Fangz shrugged. "So what? We can deal with a few archangels. If the anointed can't stop us, then I'm sure they won't either."

Midnight twitched just a fraction, so slightly that Fangz hadn't seen him move at all. Mid-sentence Fangz screamed then clutched at his throat, while a wall of fire swept over his body. "Fool. The anointed are no comparison to an archangel, let alone an agent of SMITE." He bellowed with his fangs glaring. Midnight waved his hand and the fire cooled. "You can reason with a man, or find out their weakness. A SMITE agent will stop at nothing until their mission is completed. You'd be risking not only your meaningless existence, but that of the whole brood. I will not allow you to bring my kingdom to crumble. I already had to save your ass once, and I don't plan on doing it again."

Midnight walked across the room. The rage he felt almost billowed off of him like steam. He came back and pointed his finger. "I don't want to lose you," he said with a velvet tone.

Priyanka and Garrett stormed into the room. Midnight turned head and howled at them. Both cowered to his authority.

Midnight pulled Fangz closer, until they were breaths apart. "Just listen to what I say. Don't get involved. Stay out of this and hopefully they will destroy each other, like they always do. You saw how the demons took out the anointed. Let them handle this too." Fangz thudded against the ground. Midnight turned towards the moonlight spilling into the room.

"I hear you sire," Fangz said in between gasps.

Midnight whirled over his shoulder. "Heed my warning child. Stay clear from the demons. The worst they could do is get you involved. And you would be a foot stool for the Sons of Chaos."

Midnight closed his eyes and became one with the night. His body collapsed into wisps of smoke and swarms of bats that flew out of the window and across the star lit sky.

Priyanka knelt down to the aid of Fangz as he coughed and choked. "Are you alright."

"Yes," he said. "It's been weeks now. Have you learned anything about the demon?"

Priyanka collected her thoughts. "I only know that he is a high ranking devil amongst the sons of Chaos, and he's here to open the Hell gate. That's all I know for now, my contact told me he would find out where they are soon."

Fangz stroked his goatee as he processed all of the information quickly. "Soon is not good enough. I need you to find out tonight, then take a few young bloods and hit em up."

Priyanka's eyes lit with fire. "My pleasure." She

wasted no time in moving out.

"Wait—" Garrett interjected. "Didn't Midnight just warn you about this. If he flew here all the way from Trinidad than he must be privy of some information we aren't."

"Forget all that," Fangz bellowed. "We need to handle this ASAP. We take out that demon and the archangels have no reason to come here. You understand me playboy?"

"Yes," Garrett said.

Fangz punched a hole in the wall. "I'm the king of these streets, and I don't care how high of a rank he is. If you want to come to Atlanta, you have to come see me period. And since he didn't then he's got to go."

"But-"

"But NOTHING." Fangz stated with his hunting face on. Priyanka had her helmet in hand. "You find him and you kill him."

"I will not be challenged in my neighborhood. I run this city and no one can come for me!" His voice rolled like thunder along the walls. He snatched his cup and downed the last of the blood.

Chapter Nineteen

Rest Haven

Hidden in the backwoods of Decatur, is a small cemetery where the geese roam, the plots are well kept, and the grass is brown and brittle. Many of the plots were un-named and dated as far back as the 1860's. Amongst locals, Rest Haven became known as the hallowed garden. At night the land seemed peaceful and ghost-quiet. But for those in the know, and had information they wanted to seek, they knew one creature who lived deep within the cemetery, in a plain grey crypt by a creek.

Two matching black Ducati's disrupted all of the peace in the graveyard, as they rumbled along the dirt road that snaked to the lake.

"What are we doing here?" Garrett asked as they slowed their bikes down to a soft purr.

"Going to find a bone from the resident bone carrier." She said as she kicked both feet out. "Gilbert is known as the underworld snitch. Delighting in secrets and tea."

"Snitch huh?" Garrett asked as he followed Priyanka's lead. She brought her bike to a stop and parked it by a nearby gate. He did the same and hopped off. "His source?"

Priyanka pulled off her helmet, and whipped her long black tresses. "He has the dimensional keys to smuggle demons in and out past the Hell gate. And he also has many friends on all sides."

A rolling fog swept over the cemetery as they walked down to the lake. Three large white geese peacefully swam across the brown muddy waters. Side by side they entered the fog and walked pass the veil of magic. The closer they came to the crypt by the lake, they could hear joyous laughter cut through the stillness of night.

"There you are," Priyanka said as she waved.

Gilbert pulled three cigarettes out of his mouth. "How you doing doll face?"

Garrett grimaced. He leaned over into Priyanka's ear. "What the hell is that thing?"

"He's a ghoul," she said through tight teeth.

Gilbert was no more than four and a half feet tall, with decaying forest green skin, eyes that smoldered like a lantern, and wounds all over his body. Priyanka thought he was dressed down today with his brown rags, and paper boy cap, his pointed ears sticking out on both sides.

Gilbert flicked a cigarette bud at Garrett. "If you stare any longer, I'd have to ask for a tip." The ghoul's tone of voice was very muddled and gritty. He sounded like he was one or two coughs away from clearing phlegm out his throat.

"Watch it!" Garrett shouted as he stepped to the side.

Priyanka nudged Garrett back. "It's cool. He's with me." She pointed with her brows behind Gilbert. "Who are they?"

"These schmoes?" Gilbert said as he pointed. "Let me introduce you to my buddies Larry and Mo. They just got here."

Larry appeared very gaunt and frail, due to him being one of the living dead. He wore ripped jeans, flannel and brown boots. Like Gilbert most of his flesh was gone, and his jaw was barely attached by one or two pieces of flesh. Larry moved his mouth to say hi, but all that came out were muddled moans and hisses.

On Gilbert's right side was Mo, a towering six foot seven green goblin, with tusks sticking out of his mouth. "Evening," his dark voice boomed. They were all refugees from the Hell dimension.

"So how can I help you?" Gilbert asked, in his wheezy tone.

Priyanka dropped the bag in front of him. "Last time we talked, you said you will have the demon's name."

"Asmodeus," Gilbert finished.

"Good. Now I need to know where he's hiding."

Gilbert took a puff from two remaining cigarettes, and blew smoke at them. "What's in it for me?"

Priyanka picked up the bag and pulled out a grey streaked Persian cat. Immediately the ghoul's eyes grew large in excitement.

Gilbert held out his hands. "Doll face, you know my heart's desire."

"Not so fast," Priyanka said as she dangled the cat in front of him. "Tell me about the demon or no pussy for you."

Larry rose his rotten trembling hand. "mmm kitty."

"Hands off Larry," Gilbert spat as he smacked Larry's hand away. "His name is Asmodeus and he's ranked number two amongst the Sons of Chaos."

Priyanka stroked the cat. The ghoul salivated as her blood red stiletto nails, raked the cat's lustrous grey strands. "He has help, doesn't he?"

Gilbert threw his hands up. "Who knows why he is here. It's really not my business to say."

Priyanka's temper flared up and she dropped fang. "Answer me," she bellowed.

Both Larry and Gilbert jumped back. Mo unfolded his arms and Garrett dropped fang.

"Cool it doll. It's no need for the fangs and claws." Gilbert said. "Yes, he has help. He and few other demons are hold up underground, right above the seal."

Priyanka handed the cat over to Gilbert to pet. "How do I get there?"

Gilbert clicked his fingers together as his lips twisted into a diabolical sneer. "Do you have a little time for tea and a terrifying tale?"

Garett set his jaw hard, "No we don't have time for tea."

"Yes," Priyanka corrected

"Follow me," Gilbert said

Priyanka and Garrett followed behind the ghoul as he trekked over to his crypt. Gilbert led them alongside the lake, and past the rickety black gate into a more shaded side of the cemetery. Cool air cleared the fog and the night insects stirred. No sooner that the fog cleared, they came to a simple grey crypt.

"Can we all fit in there?" Garrett asked as he examined the crypt. "It looks like it can barely fit a casket." He said with a laugh.

Mo peeled open the doors, to reveal an immense cavern apartment inside. Dust and stale air spilled out as the goblin waited for Priyanka and Garret to enter. Garrett stood at the threshold dumbstruck. He took a gander on the inside and back to the out, and he was completely confused. "It's bigger on the inside."

"I get that a lot." Gilbert said sarcastically. Now

come on in before you let all of the good flies out." Gilbert said.

Mo shut the door behind him and folded his arms, like a diligent bouncer. On the inside the crypt was a decorated to like an apartment. There was a dusty hole ridden couch, flat screen tv, a long stone table, cobwebs, and posters of Rihanna.

Gilbert sat at one side of the stone table top while Priyanka and Garrett took seats on the other. Larry came with trembling hands holding tea, the pot shuddered in his grasp as he struggled to ease it down.

Gilbert took off his cap and scratched his head in frustration. "Just put it down Larry before you spill it all over the place."

"Tea," Larry moaned as he sat the tray down and went to the back of the cavern.

Gilbert took one sip and slammed the cup down. "Dammit Larry you had one job and that was to get the tea bubbling hot. This is lukewarm tea. Nobody wants their tea lukewarm."

Larry came back shuffling and moaning. He reaches to take the tea back, but Gilbert swats his hand. "Just go away and leave us to talk."

Priyanka took a sip of the lukewarm tea. "So what's going on?"

"Everything my dear. The underworld is abuzz with gossip as the big players have landed topside and the archangels have come along with them."

Garrett sat forward. "Wait, so an archangel is coming here to Atlanta?"

Gilbert smiled gleefully. "Yes good sport, that is the word on the street. But I believe coming is the wrong word to use. I would say here. No one believes me but I think he's here, watching and waiting."

"Who?" Priyanka asked, her face etched in concern.

"Michael." Gilbert said deliciously. "The other ghouls don't believe me, but I know SMITE will send their golden warrior after Asmodeus. And I say golden because he's not the best. Everyone knows Michael is just a show piece and Gabriel is the best agent at SMITE. But hey, that's none of my business." He took a sip of his tea.

Priyanka leaned over to Garrett. "We should probably tell this to Fangz. It's like Midnight says just let the angels and demons duke it out.

"Yeah but you heard him," Garrett responded. "He is going to want to put the hurting on the demon himself, to let him know not to disrespect our turf.

Gilbert clutched the teacup within his fingers. "So how is Fangz doing my dear? I heard he got a visit from Midnight?"

Priyanka arched her brow. "How did you know that?"

Gilbert circled his bony finger in the tea cup. "Oh I have friends who lurk in the shadows." He smiled and took another sip. "If you ask me there is something definitely more than a sire bond between the two of them. But hey what do I know?" He took another sip. "This tea is not that hot but it's still good."

Garrett pushed the tea cup in front him aside. "Let's get back to the archangel. How do we kill him?"

"There are several ways to harm an archangel. But I'm afraid that information would require you to cough up several more kitties." Gilbert said.

Garrett stood up in his chair and Mo moved along with him.

Gilbert held up a finger. "But what I can do for free is tell you the tale of Asmodeus the demon king." The ghoul snapped his fingers. "Larry bring me the Ars

195

Goetia."

Larry shuffled from the back, struggling to carry the massive book in his string bean arms. When he tosses the book on the table, his right arm breaks off with a snapping crack.

"Here take this," Gilbert says as he tosses the arm. He opens the dust covered brown book and traces his finger down the middle. "Gather around my blood sucking buddies and let uncle Gilly tell you a story. This story is told in the Testament of Solomon. When his Temple was being built, a demon plagued a young boy by making him terribly sick. This poor young chap was a favorite of Solomon. When the king heard about the boy's condition, he went into the temple to pray all night and day so that he might gain power over the demon. Solomon was one of the Anointed and protected by Michael. Michael heard him and appeared to Solomon and gave him a magic ring which was inscribed with a powerful pentacle. This enabled the owner to command all spirits. With the help of this formidable weapon, the King freed the boy from the demon, and then proceeded to use the ring to call other demons to help complete the building of his Temple. One day the King asked Asmodeus_"

"Listen pal, hurry up and get to the point of this story," Garrett interrupted. "What do you want us to know about this demon and how can we get rid of Michael?"

Gilbert lifted his head and frowned. "Priyanka please get your friend before I have Mo toss him out of my crypt."

"He is right. We don't have much time. Fangz wants us to strike at the demon tonight."

Gilbert sighed. "Very well then. Asmodeus tricked

Solomon out of the ring, kicks him out of Jerusalem and set himself up as king. Asmodeus was thus ruling the nation. Solomon wandered the desert until he was able to battle the demon, reclaim the ring and expel the demon back to hell."

"Back up so let me get this straight," Priyanka said. "Whoever possess this ring will have power over demons."

Gilbert nodded, "Correct."

Priyanka tapped Garrett's hand. "Wait until Fangz hears this."

Gilbert picked up his tea cup. "Yes, Fangz could use that ring. He has enemies all around him. Demons, the vampire council, Sons of Chaos, and now even the Anointed."

"Pff Anointed, give me a break. They are a joke" Garrett murmured.

"If they are such a joke, then why you haven't you killed them yet?" The ghoul said before erupting into a bit of high maniacal laughter, slapping the table. "Again none of my business. Just carry on."

Garrett snarled at the ghoul.

"Would you like the recipe for my tea?" Gilbert asked as he pointed. "It's a little bit of honey and a lot bit of poison. I find that the poison gets rid of the wrinkles, because it burns the skin." He slapped the table again as he erupted in laughter.

"That's enough tea. We need to get out of here and get back to Fangz," Garrett said.

Priyanka hissed. "Where is the map?"

"Come hither my dear and I'll show you.""

She got up from the table and waltz over to the ghoul. Priyanka bent over and the ghoul tapped her with his right index finger. An emerald light at the tip of his finger swept over her body.

"Until next time." She said as she strolled away.

"Wait that's it?" Garrett asked.

"He gave me a psychic map. Let's gather the others."

"Give Fangz my best doll face. He's running with the legends now. Let's hope he doesn't get killed. And if he does, then it's none of my business," Gilbert said. Then he sipped on his tea.

Chapter Twenty

Sons of Chaos

The chairman stood before them as a hollow frame made of swirling green embers. His presence brought calm to the Locust who usually stirred the air. He towered above them several hundred feet, like a cloud of fire, bringing light to the dark abyss.

Asmodeus knelt, "Mr. Chairman."

The chairman clutched his cloak. "Rise number two and give me the status of the reaping for Hell gate six."

Asmodeus rose and brought Eva to his side. "Plans to proceed with the reaping of Hell gate number six are fully operational. We have a few weeks until the reaping. Right now we are focusing on strengthening our number of brother's topside, and reclaiming Solomon's ring."

"That is marvelous news to hear number two," The chairman said with a thin sliver of a smile. "Everything is unfolding as I saw it in the light of the flame. Every mission shall proceed with excellent splendor. Agent number three, is right on pace to open Hell gate five in

Berlin, and number twelve is making strides to secure the weapon that shall bring the demise of SMITE. In one foul blow we shall cripple our oppressors, bring freedom to our brothers, and be one step closer to fulfilling the new dawn. A return to endless night."

Asmodeus shook his head, "Yes indeed."

The chairman strode among the cavern floor, his flames flickered off the black like fireflies in the night. "Tell me number two.... have you experienced any stumbling blocks?"

Asmodeus cleared his throat, "Not as of yet. I have chosen to keep movements hidden in the shadows until the time Solomon's ring can be recovered. But I have become aware of several threats that may pose problems to the reaping of Hell Gate six."

"Such as?"

Eva walked forth, "The vampires of this ward sir. Fangz and his children have control of this area along with the south. He possesses many human familiars in power and commands a large brood of vampires."

"Make him serve our cause, he might be most useful if properly motivated." The chairman commanded.

Asmodeus nodded, "Yes Mr. Chairman."

The chairman's eyebrow rose, "Any other complications."

"Anointed," Asmodeus said in a hiss.

"Ah yes I have heard rumblings that even after the success of operation Extinction there were a few that escaped The Changing Faces. What do we know of them, number two?"

Eva smiled, "Mr. Chairman they are children. All four of them are sixteen."

The Chairmen erupted into a fit of laughter. "Children yes indeed. "Number two I imagine you shall have no problems crushing these children. I imagine your power will magnify a great fold after acquiring each soul."

"I agree," Asmodeus said. "But I won't to bring to your attention that there is one among them, Jaden, the one who caused my early departure. He was the one who saved the child that will be undoing."

"Yes," The chairman said with his tone shifting significantly. "I'm afraid I have failed you, number two."

Asmodeus pressed further, "How so?"

"I instructed you to go topside ahead of this mission to find the child I saw vanquish you in the flame of light. But I believe that child not to be the infant, but the very boy that separated you from your host."

"Jaden," Asmodeus whispered.

"Yes," The Chairman asserted.

"I have looked into the child's eyes Mr. Chairman." Asmodeus stated, his jaw tightened, and his face lined with seriousness. "And I saw a great power. Raw power that I haven't seen in a long time since Solomon himself, but there was more."

"What else did you see number two?"

"I saw darkness." Asmodeus said with the word echoing around the cavern. "Now more so than ever the child is filled with a fury that can be useful. I believe with proper training he can fall for the darkness and become-"

"A warlock," The chairman finished.

Eva turned to him, "Do you believe it can be done?"

"Indeed it would be marvelous if so. We haven't had a capable warlock in our ranks for eons. There is none left to train him but I'm sure a devil with your ranking would be up to the task." The chairman applauded. "Do it number two, but don't let it distract you from the reaping. Remember the mission is imperative."

"Of course," Asmodeus agreed.

"And one thing before I return to the flame. There have been sightings of SMITE agents topside. Agent three has already encountered Raphael, while Legion believes Gabriel to be on his trail. There are rumblings that Michael will join the anointed topside. Have you heard word of this or seen any signs?"

"No."

"Very well."

A sudden boom exploded in the ceiling that made the demons stop talking. Huge chunks of the cavern rained down upon them, as twelve vampire riders descended on sleek black Ducati's.

"Fangz sends his best," Priyanka shouted as she leapt off the Ducati with her guns aimed. Priyanka sprayed the room with rock salt shrapnel, severing arteries, piercing eye sockets, and slashing throats. Blood misted the air crimson to mingle with the gurgling screams of the demonic hosts. Garrett brought his bike to a sudden stop, and he sprayed the demons with two semi-automatics as he flipped to the butt of the bike. Down the demons went, toppling and burning to ash.

Asmodeus rose his hands and an arc that appeared like glass rose to protect him and Eva, the bullets disintegrated to ash.

Mr. Chairman's flame visage grew taller to the point his head touched the ceiling. "You dare defy the Sons of Chaos?" He clasped his hands together and summoned a swirling ball of fire that shot across the cavern. It honed on each vampire like a beacon, burning vampires into ash. Priyanka ran alongside the wall and back flipped until the flame took out a chunk in the cavern. Priyanka hopped on her bike and exited with Garrett alongside her.

"Explain number two. What is the meaning of this?" The Chairman declared, his voice rolling like thunder.

"The vampires," Asmodeus bellowed as he watched the path of destruction left in Priyanka's wake.

*****

"Yesterday didn't go so well, but that's okay because today is a new day. So do whatever you got to do, take a deep breath, scream, shout or let it all out. Either way this training starts now."

Jaden filled his lungs with air. "I'm ready. Let's go!"

Thunder tore the air and mechanical clicking followed.

The room shifted, and Jaden woke in a white padded dojo. "Let's focus on fighting techniques using your telekinesis. There are three primary functions you want to use with, that is push, lift, and toss. When an enemy charges at you, you can easily use the spirit to push them away. Lift is when you levitate them in air, and suspend them, this requires more strength and focus, but it is a highly advantageous skill in gunfire. Some of the greatest anointed have been shown to have the skill to uncover their enemies without seeing them. The last function is toss, which you most likely use after levitating to defeat an enemy. It is important to know that levitating and tossing an opponent leads to death and you don't want to do that when dealing with anyone that is not a son of darkness. Do you understand?"

Jaden held his thumb up. "Sounds good to me. Bring it at me coach.

A demon landed in the room with a loud thump. Gingerly it rose and its jaw opened to reveal a long stinger.

"Listen Jaden I want to practice these three defenses. Begin with push, then levitate, and end with toss."

Jaden shouted upward. "I'm ready coach."

"Now," Coach Franklin's voice boomed.

Without hesitation the monster ran towards Jaden, with its jaws outstretched and hissing. The stinger lashed out of the demon's mouth like a whip, caught Jaden's neck, and he fell limp to the floor. A booming thunderclap echoed in the ring and Jaden re-appears in the room on his feet.

"What just happened?" Jaden asked.

Lay pressed the intercom. "You just died."

"But I wasn't ready!" Jaden shouted. He ran a hand across his feet and adjusted his stance. "Okay let's do it again."

"Let's do it again," Coach franklin said. He pressed the greenlight, "Action."

Jaden raised his hand, which glowed crimson, but the stinger latches dead center in his hand, and he fell limp to the floor. Another thunderclap and the room reset.

Jaden cursed under his breath. "This is ridiculous."

"It's okay son. You messed up but you are going to get it together, and you are going to do it now. Understand?"

Jaden nodded as sweat beaded his temple, and rolled off his back.

"Good. Just remember Push is like a snap reflex."

Survival instincts slammed into Jaden's head and when the demon took one step to advance towards him, he held up his hand, flatten his palm, and pummeled the monster.

"Good. Now levitate."

Jaden turned his hand palm side up and rose it gingerly, the monster levitated off the floor, kicking and flailing like a cockroach turned on its backside. "I'm doing it." Jaden said.

"Keep it up." Coach commanded.

Jaden swung his hand to the left and the monster glided. Sweat rolled off his forehead and mentally his body felt the same exertion as trying to bench press. "Woah this is a lot."

Lay said, "Your TK is like a muscle. The more you lift, the heavier the objects you can levitate. Try tossing it into the wall."

Jaden swung his hand to the opposite side, sending the monster crashing into the wall, smearing it with a green goo. "Ha ha this is lit!" Jaden exclaimed. The monster fell but he picked it up mentally again and swung him to the other side, and tossed him like a rag doll.

Lay turned to Coach, "I think he's ready to train with us.

"You think so?"

Lay shrugged. "Why not, I'd trust him to have my back in a fight!"

Coach Franklin pressed the intercom button. "Come out Jaden I want to train you all with this next simulation."

Jaden exited the room. When he came out in the observation deck, Coach Franklin had everyone in a huddle. His eyes met Imani's and lingered.

Imani nodded. "Saw you out there Hollywood. Looking good, hopefully you want need me to save your sweet ass next time."

Jaden chuckled. "Who knows I might be saving you."

Imani shrugged. "Possibly. I wouldn't bet on it though."

Coach Franklin cleared his throat. "As all of you may know, things are getting bananas out there. And I'm pretty sure it's going to get a helluva lot worse before it gets better."

"That's why we have decided to intensify your training," Ms. Day inserted. "I've talked it over with the Shepherd's Guild and they believe the Sons of Chaos are tripling their efforts globally." She adjusted her glasses. "Now we also have Romeo's latest revelations to add to that theory. With that being said, Coach, the Shepherd's Guild, and I all agree that you need to be ready to handle the worst. I will allow the coach to further explain."

Coach rolled his eyes from her to the huddle. "The name of the new simulation is to protect the innocent. Imani here is going to be your innocent and you have to protect her from powerful demonic assassins. They are a group well known amongst the Sons of Chaos called The Changing Faces. I call them changelings for short." He held the Book of the Anointed with a depiction of the demons.

Deshawn ran across the pages. "Don't look dangerous to me coach. Just look like people in masks."

"Tuh," Coach shrugged. "They have the ability to take any form of fear from our subconscious. Often times they appear as crazy people in masks we see from our favorite slasher movies. But that's one thing that makes them dangerous, people underestimate them. For the most part they appear to be average human like killers wielding knives, machetes, or blunt objects, but it's when they have you trapped that your ass is good as dead. When locked into the eyes of a changing face, they are immobile, which is useful, but you cannot blink. Because if you blink they move and multiply."

"Still coach this sounds like a cakewalk," Romeo said cockily. "I don't even think we need the whole team. I can do this by myself."

"But you're not by yourself." Coach Franklin corrected.

"In order to beat the tide of rising darkness that threatens to overtake civilization you will have to work together as a team." Ms. Day said as she shot a chilling glance towards Romeo. "And I suggest you start now."

Romeo lobbed his head nonchalantly. "Whatever. Is baby boy ready though?"

"He is," Lay answered.

Coach Franklin clapped his hands, "Okay it's settled. You boys head down to the ring. Once the simulation starts I will give you a brief moment to gather yourself together.

Together they all rose and walked down to the ring. Jaden's pits watered with an intense sweat and he wiped his forehead. He guessed he had exerted himself more than he thought during the first exercise.

Romeo turned to Jaden. "Look kid just do what we tell you and stay out of the way. I have some shawtys that was blowing up my line earlier, and I don't want to be all night with this."

"Do you have to act so butt hurt about everything?" Jaden spat back.

Deshawn's lips cackled dryly. "Damn Rome. Your gonna' let Jeremy crack on you like that?"

Romeo pushed him. "Shut up."

Lay held up a hand, "Guys can we just focus?"

Imani clapped her hands. "Please," she said. "Your acting like a bunch of wimps. Chill off Hollywood."

Romeo sucked his teeth. "Oh I wouldn't want to hurt

your lil boyfriend. You're so sweet on him."

Imani punched his shoulder.

Romeo flinched with a playful smile. "Ouch!"

Ms. Day pressed the intercom. "Can you please focus. This simulation is very dangerous and should be taken with caution in the most serious manner."

Coach Franklin put his hands on his back, "That's enough bip bop, let's begin the simulation."

The lights darkened and a bundle of nerves formed in Jaden's gut. "Here goes nothing," he murmured as he turned to Lay who smiled.

"It will be fine." Lay said.

Thunder tore the air, mechanical clicking followed, and Jaden's heart pounded immensely.

Chapter Twenty-One

The Changing Faces

Roaring engines rumbled around them as the ring reconfigured. After a deafening boom clap, they stood in a hospital room, surrounding a bed.

"Did I have to be pregnant tho?" Imani said as she touched her belly.

"We wanted to make sure you stayed put." Coach Franklin's voice boomed overhead. He chuckled softly.

The room was small and smelled dank like mold. It was easily one of the crummiest hospital rooms Jaden had ever seen. Brown stains covered the ceiling and dust swept over the equipment. Overhead the lights flickered casting a shadow over them.

"Creepy ass hospital. This should be fun," Deshawn said as he paced around the room.

Lay peeked through the blinds. "They're here."

"Who ?" Jaden asked as Romeo and Deshawn beat him to the window.

Romeo ripped the blinds apart, "The Changing Faces. Look." He ducked his head over.

Masked people gathered outside. Two of them sat on motor bikes with shotguns dangling from the side, silly faces painted on their masks. Standing between the men on bikes were three girls who waved butcher knives. All of them wore flowing white gowns with a smiling cheerleader's face painted on their mask. Planted in the center was a man wearing a mask made out of a potato sack, and lugging a red axe over his shoulder. Gingerly he rose his hand to wave at the boys who starred out of the window. Then in a blink of an eye, the whole group disappeared from the lawn. Fear stabbed all of their spines.

Lay shuddered. "That was very creepy."

"Hella creepy," Jaden added.

"What do we do?" Lay asked

"If this was a movie I would say run like hell." Deshawn quipped as he patted Lay on the shoulder. "But it ain't, so let's just blow everything up."

"Alright kid dynamite pipe down." Romeo asserted. "This is easy. We just go out and slay them all."

"Go out and slay them?" Jaden repeated. "The point of this simulation is to protect the innocent. If we all leave the room, then the innocent is vulnerable."

Imani raised a hand. "Listen to him! He is preaching."

Romeo huffed as he folded his arms. "Let me hear your plan then genius?"

Jaden was silent as he gathered his thoughts.

Romeo cuffed his hand around his ears. "What was that? I can't hear you?"

Jaden took a breath. "I say we spread out and we leave someone in the room with Imani. Lay you stay with Imani and hack into the hospital's security system. If you can hack into their security cameras, then you can be our eyes and ears. If you need to reach me then just think really loudly."

"Will do," Lay agreed.

"Then from there we just split up. Romeo, you and Deshawn can patrol the North hall and I'll go patrol the south."

"Sounds like a good plan to me," Deshawn said.

Romeo waited a beat. The blank expression on his face said he knew he was stomped. "I was going to say something similar anyway. Let's do it…. but give it everything you got, otherwise we'll be here all night."

"Let's do this." Jaden said as he led the way of the hospital room.

Imani clapped slowly. "Come through Hollywood." A sarcastic smile swept across her face. "Try not to get killed will ya?"

"I'll try," Jaden murmured.

Lay sat on the bed near Imani. "I guess it's just the two of us."

"Where are some Uno cards when you need them?" Imani said before smacking her head back against the pillow.

******

They walked out of the hospital room splitting off into two sections, with Romeo & Deshawn turning off to the left and Jaden trotting off to the right by himself. No more than two minutes down the hallway did Deshawn upset every ounce of Romeo's nerves.

Romeo curled his lip as he whipped his head over to Deshawn, "Will you shut up?"

"Bruh I'm sorry," Deshawn said. He crept his hand under the ruffles of his shirt and touched his belly. "I'm so hungry, I promise you I could eat two burrito bowls now. Hell, maybe even three."

Romeo nudged him with his elbow. "Shut up."

"Don't hate me bro. I have needs, a man needs to eat."

Romeo stopped dead in his tracks, and held his hand out to stop Deshawn. He felt a rumbling in his gut and a muffled buzz in his ear.

"What is it?" Deshawn asked.

A revelation snapped into Romeo's brain, delivering snippets of the future like quick cut scenes of a movie. Double doors of the elevator at the end of the hall peeled open, and two faces wearing pig masks, zoomed out towards them on motorbikes. They turn to run and two other faces attack them from opposite ends of the hall with machetes. Suddenly in a head jerking snap, Romeo came out of the revelation.

He turned to Deshawn with his blood pounding in his ears. "Get ready, because here they come."

Deshawn pulled out his axe. "Good because I'm

ready to get this over with."

Down the hall the elevator bell rang, and Romeo's dread stirred. The doors parted dramatically and the two changelings on bikes, revved the engines as they stood in the elevator.

"Get ready to spill your guts!" One of them said.

Romeo whispered to Deshawn. "When I tell you to slow down time, do it. Two of them are going to roll up behind us, attack them quickly, and remember don't look them in the eyes."

Both bikers revved the bikes again, as enthusiastic shouts came out of their mouths, and the smell of gas permeated the hall. Smoke filled the elevator and slowly filled the hall.

"We will bathe in your blood anointed," the rider on the right shouted. Then he kicked the clutch, both vehicles popped a wheelie, and came zooming down the hall on one wheel.

Romeo pulled out his twin daggers, hidden beneath his sleeves. "Now!"

Deshawn waved his left hand and a wide arc of energy went out in front of them. It glowed like a gleaming spider's web. The energy made the air around them seem like water being ripped by a small stone. Once the rider's entered this field, they moved at a snail's pace. As if time itself fought back every movement, every facial tick, and wrinkling of hair.

Romeo leaned back, angled his arms in front of him and put his fist together. Both fist burned bright like an overcharged light bulb, shining through the dim corridor of the hallway. He pulled back as if shooting a shotgun. With a precise aim he shot the rider on the left dead center on the chest, then he aimed over and shot the other on the right as well. Both riders fell back off their bikes slowly, arms slightly flailing, masks whipping, as the time field held them suspended mid-air, making their travel to the ground take an eternity.

"Nice," Deshawn complimented as they both ran back down the corridor.

Romeo sucked in a breath sharply, "Watch you're left, they will be coming at you."

Deshawn brought up his axe, "I'm ready to strike at anything that is about to pop out. Bring it on."

"Hi there. "A petite blonde in a cheerleaders' mask, and flowy dress sauntered up to him.

Deshawn's axe fell limp in his hands. "Damn," He murmured.

A loud grunt erupted from behind Romeo, and he dodged quickly, to deflect a butcher's knife. He pinned the butcher's hand under his Pitt and stabbed her into the chest. Instantly she vanished into wisps of grey smoke.

"Romeo!" Deshawn called.

Romeo glanced over his shoulder. "What?"

Deshawn backed up slowly, with his axe slightly raised. "I think I'm locked in big dog. She got me."

Romeo groaned as two cheerleaders, both wielding butchers' knives stalked Deshawn. "I told you not to look at them in the eye."

"I tried," he said. Then he twisted his jaw. "But I just

couldn't help it. They're hot."

Deshawn faced forward, closed his eyes, and in the smallest fraction of a second that he opened them, the cheerleaders vanish and reappear closer with another member. She jumped on Deshawn's back. "Help me!" He screamed to Romeo as butcher knife raises above his head.

Romeo aims, but the cheerleaders bring Deshawn down to the ground viciously. He wails in pain as their knives stab him. Then suddenly Deshawn vanishes.

"Deshawn!" Romeo shouted as he gaped incredulously at the floor. While cackling in a crazy hysteria, the cheerleaders lurched forward towards Romeo, he ran his hands across from each other, and a blinding wall of light rose between him, illuminating the whole hallway, and shining outside the walls of the hospital. As panic sets into his chest, he reaches for his dagger, and locks eyes of one cheerleader. His face twist in terror as he peers deep into her frozen blue pupils, and blinks. It happened so fast that Romeo didn't have time to think. In that split second when he opened his eyes again, three became five, and Romeo was stabbed from all over. A loud guttural moan escaped his lips, as his daggers was wrestled from his hand, his arms was pulled to the side to expose his chest, and three butcher's knives went into the center. Romeo vanished from the simulation.

******

Jaden became unsettled as he walked the south hall with no company, and no sign of the changing faces in sight.

"Here wookie, wookie" he called sarcastically.

He dragged his sword along as he strode through the hallway. It was eerily quiet on the hall except the sound of the lights overhead as they struggled to illuminate the hall.

Jaden, Lay's voice shouted in head like a ringing alarm

Jaden winced in pain and ringed his right ear. He cocked his head to the side as he responded to Lay. *Nice of you to pop in. What's going on?*

It's Deshawn and Romeo, Lay started, his voice continuously echoing in Jaden's head

Have they found snacks in the vending machine? Jaden thought

No they are dead.

"Oh no," Jaden said out loud.

You need to prepare yourself because they are heading right towards you.

Jaden brought up his sword. *Thanks for the heads up Lay.*

In the distance he heard a door shut and footsteps echo all the way down the hall. Fear made every muscle in his body tense as he mentally prepared himself to battle. A large grisly figure stood down the hallway. He could barely see it in the faint light. The figure inched forward and dragged something along with it.

Jaden strained his eyes ahead. It was a man in a butcher's apron and he was carrying a large chainsaw. He pulled the cord to crank the chainsaw but the engine fizzled out.

Vroom.

Jaden brought his sword up and suddenly realized something that almost turned his stomach sour.

Vroom.

The mask was made out of flesh. He was wearing a real human face.

Vroom.

When Jaden was close enough to see this clearly, the chainsaw roared with life, and the changeling came running at him, with a loud scream rumbling from his belly.

Chapter Twenty-Two

Blink and Die

Jaden's first instinct was to run. But he fought it by stone footing himself to the left side of the hall. His next instinct came from training. Jaden flattened his palm and hammered the changeling with a crimson cloud. It crashed back into the door, breaking off the exit sign, and shattering the wall. With a wave of his hand, Jaden sent the roaring chainsaw to the far end of the hallway.

The changeling struggled to his knees and Jaden tightened the grip on his sword. At the moment the changeling got up, Jaden charged, and brought his sword up in a swift arc. With a groan, the changeling fell over and vanished into the air.

Jaden reached out to Lay with his mind. *Lay can you hear me?*

Lay turned his head up to the window as he sat on the corner of the bed. *Yes. How is it looking?*

I just vanquished one of the changing faces. Are there any others coming my way?

Lay ran his hand along his arm and three translucent screens materialized in front of them. They were holograms of the hospital's data stream. He studied the monitor on the far left, which was a security cam of the south hall. Five changelings marched towards the room, they were led by a face who wore a sack cloth as a mask. He carried an axe and four maidens in flowy dresses followed behind him skipping along.

Lay turned to the door, almost as if Jaden was standing in front of him. *There is a large group heading your way and even more heading to the room.* Lay ran his hand across his arm again to summon a keyboard of light. *Don't worry I am sealing of access to the floor. That should keep them busy until you get back.*

Perfect. I'm on my way. Jaden dashed down the hallway.

Lay magnified the screen of the third monitor and his body froze in horror. The axe wielding changeling hacked his way through the door blocking the entrance to the room's hallway. *Hurry up Jaden,* he thought. With a flick of his wrist, he summoned his light staff.

A noise on the far side of the hall made Jaden stop. It was the sound of glass shattering. Coming through the glass came another tall face, in a janitor's outfit and wearing a hockey mask. A wave of fear wove itself around Jaden's spine. The Changeling towered over him easily by another foot, and his size reminded Jaden of a bear. Jaden gazed into the dark eyes of the monster as it stiffly walked towards him. Without thought he blinked and one janitor became two, and then two became three.

"It just got hella real," Jaden murmured as all three suddenly came stampeding towards him, with their machete's raised.

The first took swipe across Jaden's head. Jaden ducked very quickly, went under, and slashed him across the back. Another, on the right brought his machete down to Jaden's shoulder. Jaden side stepped and slashed the Changeling's hand off. From his left came another swipe. Jaden jerked back as the blade cut through air. It came so close that he touched his chest to check if blood had been drawn. Jaden reached out his hand, pushed and the monster toppled back. Then he raised his hand palm open and it rose. With a backhand wave, the face was slammed into the wall.

Lay and Imani watched the screen with intensifying dread. The changelings were almost through the door, the axe had managed to rip threw and shred it like a bird using talons.

Lay went over to the side of the bed. "Can you move? We have to get you out here."

"Barely," Imani said. She reached for him as he helped her up.

She struggled to swing her legs over, as Lay pulled her by her right arm. He put two fingers to his temple. *Jaden I'm going to move Imani. Meet me on the roof.*

Gotcha, Jaden responded telepathically as he sprinted down the hall. This section was darker than the first. Two little pigs on his left waved at him. Then they aimed their guns. Two red dots pinned Jaden's chest, and his heart thudded against his ribs. Jaden ducked around the corner as bullets raced past him, and shredded the adjacent wallet. There was something behind them that caught Jaden's eyes. He had to get another glance.

It was a soda machine. He dashed back around the corner quick enough to avoid getting hit. Beads of sweat were rolling down his forehead and icy droplets accumulated on his back. Jaden took one huge breath to subside the panic he felt inside, then he knelt down and reached out both with his hand and mind. The soda machine rocked side to side, and jostled to life, it came bulldozing the three little pigs like a train, tossing them to the side, and making them all vanish.

Jaden searched for a way up to the roof. There was an exit down the hall and to the left. A chill went up his spine, once he detected movement behind him. A face had appear wearing a white ghost face mask and dressed in tattered black robes. It reached into the folds of its black robe and retrieved something that shined in the faint light.

"Don't look," Jaden thought as he peeled ahead towards the door.

Lay was hauling Imani up the stairwell, gasping for air, when she suddenly collapsed. Water spilled on the floor and he at her uncertain. "What just happened?"

Imani's face soured. "I think my water broke. Why did they have to include that?"

Lay rubbed between his eyes. "Can't you just hold it in until this is all over."

Imani's face curled in anger. "I can't hold in a whole

baby that's trying to rip through my body."

"Oh God," he murmured.

Abruptly a door flew open below them. The changeling wearing the sack mask poked his head out and waved. Lay's skin prickled to gooseflesh.

"Hold on we're coming to get you!" One of the maiden's shouted from below.

Lay tugged on Imani's shoulder. "Come on we have to keep moving."

Imani trembled uncontrollably. "Thank god I'm already dead because this pain would've killed me." She pushed Lay further. "Just keep moving. I'm right behind you."

Lay climbed the stairs, inching Imani along. The changing faces were gaining on them. The joy on their plastic faces was brought to life in the way they skipped and hopped up the stairs, as if there was not a care in the world. This behavior terrified Lay more than any other vampire or monster.

After two flights of stairs, he found the exit. "It's right here come on."

Imani gasped desperately for air as she struggled to get her body to move. Normally she didn't mind getting dirty, but the excruciating pain she felt overwhelmed every sense in her body. They pushed back the rusty door and cool night air hit them. Changelings were so close that Lay knew he could no longer avoid them.

"Just run Imani," he shouted. Lay pulled out his light staff,

The doors to the roof blew open, and the sack face charged with his axe raised. In a lithe motion, Lay sliced the axe in half with a backhand swing of his staff. Both maidens charged at him from each side, he flipped in front of them, landed, and slashed both maidens across the chest. The axe man rose to his knees. Lay blinked. Suddenly two axe men stood before him. Both raised their axes overhead and rushed towards them. Lay rolled underneath in the space between them. Lay exchanged blows with both axe man, each striking at him after the other.

A maiden skipped towards Imani. "I'm going to kill the baby," She sung as she skipped along.

Lay's stomach nearly emptied itself on his shoe. "Imani watch out."

Something shiny glistened over to Imani's left. It was a butcher's knife left behind one of the vanquished faces. She wrestled it out of the gravel, and held it out defiantly in front of her. "Back away from me." She demanded.

The maiden changeling placed her hand on her hips. "No need for all that. I just want to be your friend."

"Lay get your ass over her." Imani shouted.

Lay ducked as the axe man swung at his neck. "I'm trying."

An elbow crashed into the right side of Lay's head, causing him to drop the staff. It bounces with a metal clink, and rolls on the ground. Then the axe man delivered a kick to Lay's chin that knocks him out on his back. Head spinning with the world a blur around him, Lay struggled to get up. An axe came down quickly towards his head and he grabbed at the hilt. The changeling applied pressure, forcing the blade of the axe further down until it dangled over Lay's nose.

Lay closed his eyes, almost convinced to himself that was over. Suddenly the changeling was thrown over his head. Jaden hoovered over him with his hand held out.

"Praise the Creator, your just in time." Lay says as Jaden lifts him up off the ground.

Jaden grabbed his shoulder. "Where is Imani."

"Over there." Lay pointed

Cold hands yanked Lay around and he matched eyes of one of the Ghost faces.

"Lay!" Jaden called as he stood over his shoulder. "Don't move," Jaden instructed with a hand on his back.

Lay froze right where he stood. He trembled under the dark gaze of the ghost face. The ghost face stood arm's length from him, with his knife raised in air, and robes outstretched. The ghost became a living statue, unable to move while caught in the gaze of a human being.

"They can't hurt us if we are staring them in the eyes, if we are looking beyond their masks. Just back out of the way." Jaden said slowly.

Lay took two steps backward at the pace of a turtle.

"I don't know how long I can hold this." Lay said, reaching back.

"Just long enough for me to strike him." Jaden said as he brought up his sword. "Whatever you do don't bl–."

Lay sneezes and blinks. Another ghost face appeared

on his left and buried a blade between Lay's neck and shoulder. A scream didn't come out of Jaden's mouth until Lay disappeared into thin air. For a moment he stood there focused on the spot where Lay stood before vanishing. Screams for help on the far side of the roof brought him out of the trance.

"Hollywood get your butt over here!" Imani shouted as the maidens surrounded her. Two maidens held her back as the other stabbed at her belly.

Jaden moved to run towards her but it was too late. Suddenly he was yanked by the neck. Cold steel pressed against his throat. And the knife glistened under the moonlight as it rose in the air. It came down and thunder tore the air.

Chapter Twenty-Three

How to kill a Devil

"What in the hell was that?" Coach Franklin shouted as he strode out into the middle of the ring.

Jaden almost collapsed he was so out of breath. They were back in the ring surrounded by white padding walls, standing all together in the center. Jaden struggled to catch his breath just like the rest of them, he hunched over with hands on knees and chest heaving.

"I guess if anything above a vampire pops out that Hell gate then the whole city is done for. That was pitiful." Coach said with distaste.

Ms. Day walked out behind him, carrying a clipboard. "Please coach I don't think becoming belligerent is going to help the situation. It was a tough training." She forced a sweet southern smile. "Are you boys okay?"

"She is right coach," Deshawn said in between short breaths. "That training was cray cray."

Coach Franklin's face showed no sense of mercy.

"Well I got some bad news for you sweetheart, it's only going to get tougher. A few weeks ago we had locusts creeping out of the Hell gate. Those creatures are not something that goes bump in the night. They devour and destroy. I can only imagine what will happen if any intelligent upper level demon hits the town." Coach Franklin threw up his hands. "If we leave it to the Anointed then we'd be better off running and hiding."

Ms. Day reached out to stroke him. "They simply were not ready. We should've given them more information and not put them against a danger like the changing faces."

"How are we supposed to slay those things?" Romeo asked.

"They were practically unstoppable," Lay added.

"I was hoping one of you would be smart enough to figure it out. That is the way of the Anointed especially being close to a Hell gate. The book has over one thousand demons chronicled within it, but I'm sure they are still churning out something new down there every day. As an anointed it is a gift and instinct to follow the wisdom of the spirit and let it lead you."

Jaden stepped forward. "All my spirit told me was to run like the wind."

"Mine too," Deshawn said.

Coach Franklin turned around and set his jaw hard. "Two ways to slay a face. You kill them quick without looking at all, take them out without showing mercy or taking a second thought. Another is to get them to look into a reflection or get them to look at each other. Once a changeling has locked eyes with another changeling, then it will blink out of existence."

There was a collective groan let out all over the room.

Lay tapped his foot. "I don't understand why nothing like this won't be on the internet. While everyone was patrolling I was trying to come up with a way to destroy these things."

Coach Franklin looked at him with a lazy shrug. "Sorry son but everything ain't online. That's why these trainings are so important. Upper level demons are nothing to play with. Not only did all of you die but your teamwork was half ass and you lost the innocent."

"Blame the newbie," Romeo shouted as he pointed. "It was all of his idea."

Anger made Jaden step towards him defensively. "It wasn't my fault you were too stupid not to get yourself killed. I held my own."

Imani turned to him, "Yea but you let me down."

Jaden's face softened as he grabbed her forearm. "I'm sorry. Really I am." He took a breath as he fought back the emotion. "Everything happened so fast. It should've been me that stayed behind."

Coach Franklin hit the wall. The sound echoed through the Ring. "No you all should've stayed together."

Ms. Day jumped back. "Coach that's enough." Her voice coated with warm authority. She folded her arms and stone footed herself in front of him. "I think we should send the boys home for the night."

Coach Franklin looked back at her and nodded along. "You're right." He looked over and said, "Everybody go home."

Everyone started walking out of the ring, and then Jaden spoke up. "Coach how do we slay upper level demons. Like for good. Not send them back to hell."

Coach Franklin kept his pace forward and leaned near Jaden's shoulder. "Depends on the demon. An exorcism from the host might destroy mid class demons but upper level demons...devils and princes are a bit trickier. Some of the stuff that works on the average wouldn't work on them. Hell I didn't know you could deport a devil until you did it miraculously."

"May I add that there are certain weapons used to destroy upper level demons," Ms. Day stated.

Romeo strolled over. "Like what?"

"The sword of an archangel or any weapon forged in heavenly fire. Based on ancient texts we also know of weapons made by demons to kill demons, as well as weapons enchanted by powerful spells. Many of these weapons have been documented throughout history, but their whereabouts are unknown. Some say Lucifer himself has hidden them from the outside world. The Shepherd Guild has spent decades in pursuit of them, like the legendary Colt gun, Excalibur, the screaming reaper, the battle axe of Belcalis, and a slayer's scythe. The existence of some of these weapons we believe to be true, while others just might be-" She adjusted her glasses. "They might be just planned ole myths."

Deshawn elbowed Imani. "Ayo Imani do you have

any connects at SMITE who can hook us up with the good demon fighting gear."

"That would be awesome!" Lay shouted. "I've heard...Well I read online about a sword that can make vampires turn to dust just from seeing it."

Deshawn wrapped his arm around Lay, "If we had that, then we'd have more time for Chipotle runs."

Imani rolled her eyes, "If I had any pull at SMITE, then I would be an archangel by now. Instead I'm stuck with you losers."

Lay giggled. "Ha ha very funny."

Coach turned to Jaden, suspiciously. "Yes there are many myths and fantastical ways to kill an upper level demon. Why are you asking? Is there something we should know?"

Jaden thought for a moment. "No." He responded.

Coach Franklin leaned his head to the side. "Are you sure?"

Jaden sighed. "Like I said before. If he ever came back, then I want to be the one to finish him off for good."

"That's understandable." Coach Franklin raked his gaze over the group. "Be ready around 10:30 tomorrow night. We will be hunting on the field, taking the graveyard shift."

"The graveyard shift," Jaden repeated.

"Looking for early risers," Imani said.

All together they walked out of the ring and took the L for the night.

****

Georgia cicadas enchanted Rest Haven with their beautiful call. A fog swept over the muddy waters of the lake, then in a shaded corner, winds gathered and stirred the misty clouds. Eva materialized right in front of the crypt door. She tossed her hair, readjusted her form fitting red dress, and knocked three times.

A peephole slides over and dead eyes stalked back at her. "What's the password?"

"Big money." She said seductively, parting her blood red lips.

The door opened and she stepped inside a crypt that was packed from wall to wall. Eva looked over at Mo and winked. The goblin's knees buckled. Larry shuffled past her and handed out goblets of blood. Over in the left corner, a vampire rolled dice at a craps table. Near the door, a crowd of well-dressed ghouls went up in cheers as the roulette ball landed on twenty-one black. A casket lined the counter, behind which stood a pink hair girl in all black, nimbly counting out change to a stocky demon in a flannel shirt. On stage a green demon with petite horns sang an 80's classic. Various creatures packed the crypt with fistfuls of money in their hands, and the desire to gamble in their eyes. Gilbert sat at the main table, in the center of the room. Tonight he sported a sleek black tuxedo with his thin white hair styled into a pompadour.

"Read em and weep fellas." Bones said as he laid out his hand across the table.

Eva strolled over to the bar seductively and all the creatures stared at her.

Bones turned to Gilbert, "Who is the dame?"

"Be careful, Gilbert warned. "That right there is a succubus. Those are the type to use you up and suck you dry."

"You don't say," Bones responded. "But I'm already nothing but bones," He said.

He and Gilbert erupted into a fit of laughter.

Eva prowled through the room slowly. Heads all over gaped at her curves as she glided across the room, the dark lights of the crypt somehow casting a magnificent glow on her sun kissed brown skin. A sudden quickening occurred in her chest. She could sense a human man amongst all of the demons. Following her instincts, she strolled to the bar. There he stood, middle-aged, average height, grey streaked hair and a lean body. Her belly rumbled. Eva pressed her elbows on the bar and glanced at him over the shoulder.

The man strolled over with a drink in his hand. "Excuse me miss. I just wanted to say that you look amazing." He said with a suggestive grin.

Eva purred. "I taste even better."

"Can I buy you a drink?"

She pulled him in by his gingham tie. "I'll do you one better. How about a kiss?"

The man chuckled and raised his eyebrows. "Sure."

A guttural moan escaped Eva's lips as she caressed his soft white cheek. She pressed her lips against his, and glorious life surged into her body. The man shuddered as his knees buckled. He tried to pull himself away but she clenched the back of his head, her nails transforming into red talons. Like a cobra she drew back from him, her head swaying, and his soul came streaming out of his mouth in magenta swirls. When the man's body fell to the floor in a clang, it disintegrated into dishes.

Eva wiped her mouth. "Delicious." Once Eva spotted Gilbert, she made her way through the room, leaving a path of lusty eyes in her wake.

Gilbert nudged Bones in the shoulder, "Hush, she's coming."

Eva raised her eyebrow. "Gilbert my love. How are you?"

Gilbert took a sip out of his mug. "To what do I owe the pleasure?"

She whipped her hair and sat on the edge of the table. "Filthy bloodsuckers attacked us. I need to know where Fangz and his crew are hold up."

Gilbert held up his hands. "Listen doll face, Fangz and his crew have been taking care of me and—"

Eva snapped her fingers and two full grown Egyptian Mau cats appeared. She placed them down, and the spotted cats slinked like cheetahs as they pawed across the table.

Gilbert's snake like tongue fell out of his mouth as he salivated. "Sheesh I'll tell you everything."

Eva's grin was shark like when she leaned to his ear. Gilbert took his glowing finger and pressed it against her forehead. She closed her eyes as the ghoul's magical touch made her shudder.

Eva kissed him on the side of his face, right on the

spot bone stuck out from his skin. "Thanks," She said. Then she purred. "Why don't you come on down and see me sometime?"

"No thanks. I have lots of business up here," He said as he straightened his tuxedo.

Gilbert stood. "If you will excuse me doll face. I have a show to run."

Eva adjusted his bow tie. She pressed her dark red lips to her palm and blew him a kiss.

"How do I look?" Gilbert asked.

"Terrible," she said.

The ghoul smiled. "Thanks."

Gilbert walked onto the stage and took the microphone. Applause filled the crypt "Coming next to the stage is the underworld's most famous girl groups... The Dead Girls." Three goblins in blonde wigs and bright pink lipstick took the stage, as Eva sauntered out of the crypt.

****

Swirling bursts of purple energy flickered in the darkness as Eva materialized on the doorstep of quiet suburban home. It was nicely proportioned, painted grey like the others, and almost all the lights were off except a few. Anyone looking from the outside in would think that it was just another ordinary house on Cherry ln with a lovely family on the inside dreaming sweet dreams. But that was the farthest from the truth, this family was actually in the middle of a nightmare, a horrible nightmare.

    Eva forced the door open with the frigid stare of her emerald eyes. A tumultuous scream welcomed her as she scrolled in. Eva slammed the door behind her. Eva was looking for him all night and finally she was led to him by his insatiable taste for destruction. She could feel he was getting stronger. Her corrupted spirit was almost drawn to the bloody path of bodies and tortured souls he left behind tonight. The demonic diva began ruffling the short red dress she had on that clung to her body tightly. She made her way up the stairs, running her hands delicately across the long drawn out scratches on the walls, taking every step leisurely while enjoying the corruption of what was once a warm loving home. She caressed her neck, because the chaos was beautiful and intoxicating to demons.

    Eva walked in the bathroom and his head popped up. The small confines of a regular bathroom that would be seen on this plane, shifted into a dark dungeon that could only be seen with a spiritual eye. Displayed behind several glass display boxes were the souls of his previous victims. Each looked like horrific porcelain dolls twirling through the air hanging from meat hooks. Preserved on their faces were the last screams that could escape before losing their heads to the electrifying powers of the demon. While other victims remained into their perspectives boxes, each displaying their own scene of death, Asmodeus worked in an open display that was an exact replica of a classic fifties style bathroom. Eva sashayed further into the darkness of the dungeon and stepped into a new display. Murky waters splashed over the edge of a stained bathtub filled with a current victim.

Asmodeus glanced over his shoulder, "Eva," he whispered as he devoted his attention to the tub that was filled by a woman bathing in crimson water. Long and deep cuts carved down her body. She writhed in the tub silently mouthing for help as life drained out of her body.

Eva ran her hands around the woman's husband who stared at his wife in agony. He hung off the wall by two hooks that pierced each of his shoulder blade. "I've missed you. Are you playing dear?"

Asmodeus turned to her with his face covered in a devilish grin, "Yes dear," he said in a high pitched voice that mimicked hers. Asmodeus was still possessing Tyler. The sheer evilness and power of the demon had transformed Tyler's appearance, to something more insidious and not human.

Rich crimson waters splashed out of the tub as the woman continued to struggle in pain, her body submerged with her jaws spread wide open by the hooks that impaled them and was anchored to the wall. Asmodeus gently caressed her hair as she continued weeping, "Shh shh.... you should be thankful for all the pleasures I have given to you and your dear husband. No more tears just...pure pleasure."

The demon's proficiency was patience, and he wielded it like a scalpel, only striking with delicate precision. Gently Asmodeus took his knife and caressed her exposed and severely cut chest. He then submerged it in the tub to make more incisions on her thigh. As he cut her with long drawn out slices, the woman reacted with loud yelps and tears.

Eva sauntered over and messaged his shoulders. "I found the ring," she spoke softly.

Asmodeus paused. And dropped the knife in the tub. "Where?"

She ran her hands delicately along her face, "It's confined in a statue that will be shipped to a museum within the city in the next four days."

Asmodeus withdrew his knife from the tub. Looking into the eyes of the tortured woman he reached to the bottom of tub and released sparks from his hands that made her seized until she was no longer crying but silent and cold. Asmodeus grabbed the temple of the woman and her soul flowed into him, feeding him. Asmodeus shivered from the sensation, he head fell back and his lips pursed in delight.

"With the ring I'll get back the powers Solomon stole from me," Asmodeus said as he hopped to his feet.

Eva seductively licked her lips, "Exactly. You will rise more powerful than before."

"Right," Asmodeus commented as he made his way over to the husband who was struggling with the hooks in his shoulder. Dominantly Asmodeus wrapped his fingers around the man's throat.

"Please," the man begged with fear in his eyes.

A surge of electricity slowly wrapped around Asmodeus' arm and then swirled to the man's head. The surge of energy continued to flow causing the man's head to violently shake and eventually combust. A soul flowed into Asmodeus feeding him further.

Asmodeus wiped the filth into his face. Staring at Eva his eyes shifted from the normal hazel color of Tyler's to a monstrous black. Quickly he pounced on her knocking her down to the floor. Eva was partly startled and turned on at the same time. Slowly he swirled his body on top of hers. He ran his tongue long and slow on the side of her face. "The only question I have is why exactly are you doing this? Why did you bring me back?" he asked forcefully, his voice gritty and aggressive.

Eva nervously began to shake, "Since the beginning I have always aligned myself with powerful demons."

Asmodeus cocked his head and began delicately running the blade of his knife along her thigh.

Eva quivered under the dominance of this powerful demon. "The seals are breaking. The horsemen have ridden out and the antichrist is here on earth. With the apocalypse looming... I felt this was the time to make a move to claim innocent souls for myself. I couldn't do it by myself, that's why I brought you back from the pit. I needed the proclaimed King of Demons. I needed a Devil level demon. You once took over Solomon's kingdom and I know together we can rule."

Asmodeus stuck the blade of his knife right along Eva's throat. "You better not betray me or I will drag you back to hell with me in pieces."

Eva shook her head, "No believe me I just want to serve you king. I just want to be at your side."

Asmodeus yanked Eva to her feet, "Very well then. I'll get the ring then I get my back powers and again blood will flow freely throughout the land when I rule."

Eva smiled. "That's not the only thing I found."

Asmodeus cocked his head, "What is that?"

"The vampires," She said. "I know where to find Fangz."

Asmodeus stood. "Come we shall deal with them swiftly. The chairman declares that they should be brought under the heel of the Sons of Chaos. That is exactly what I shall do."

Chapter Twenty-Four

Wings

Jaden laid in bed with his body oiled in sweat, and his mind drowning in a river of horrible images. He stirred in the bed, hands clasping the sheets in a bunch. Deep in his sleep he sensed a presence near him and he shot up, then looked over.

"It's you," Jaden breathed as he sat up, he touched her face, half convinced she had to be a dream, but no she was real. "What are you doing here?" Jaden asked as he sat up, his state of panic, startled her.

Imani withdrew her hands, "I'm sorry I didn't mean to scare you I just—I just couldn't take it any longer, I had to come see you, it was hurting me."

Jaden looked at her wide eyed and crazy, "Couldn't take what any longer?"

"Your pain, I couldn't take feeling your pain. These nightmares you've been having. I feel them too As your guardian angel your heart is connected to mine, and I feel when you're in danger." She scouted closer to him. "Whatever kind of nightmares you've been having they are so real to you that I feel that pain. I feel you late at night, and it hurts."

She ran her hand across his chest. "I wish I could heal your heart but I can't."

Jaden looked into her pretty almond eyes, "I wish it was that easy. But I don't know if I'll ever be able to let go. I just keep reliving that night over and over again. It's like a broken record that never stops, even when you want it too. It feels like happiness is a million miles away. I just wish it will all end." He sat up in the bed and rubbed his dry eyes. "I don't know what to do."

"It's always the darkest before dawn. And weeping may endure during the night. But joy comes in the morning." She grabbed his hand. "Jaden I see you as you are. You have an amazing, caring, and courageous heart." Then she stood up. Do you want to see something beautiful?"

Jaden peeled back the covers, "What?" he asked hanging on to her words.

Imani turned her back to him and peered over her shoulder. She took a deep sudden breath, and then she clasped her hands as she arched her shoulders. Suddenly her back sizzled. Etches on her back seared through her clothes, and out came magnificent wings. They were made of a beautiful, glorious light that spanned across the entire room, shining glory everywhere. Shades of gold adorned the outer trace of her wings, as hues of pink floral, and ivory made up the center. Her brown skin radiated with a tinge of sparkling light as the joy and love of the Creator swept into his spirit.

There was a park where he often went to as a kid, Lake Balboa. It was where his first shepherd started to train him, and it was where his mother took him to feed the ducks. It was peaceful place. To him it was spectacular. But the beauty of Lake Balboa paled next to the magnificence of Imani's wings.

Jaden admired her in awe, believing she would disappear like a mirage, she was too beautiful to be real. With hesitation he reached out with his right hand and stroked the back of her shimmering wings. Though they looked translucent like light, they felt like goose feathers.

He marveled again at the luxurious texture, then he stroked with the other hand satin smooth, cool as stone. Imani glanced over the shoulder, her hair perfectly framing her face as she watched him. It was in the face of an angel that he saw joy. And in that joy was strength to make it through the night.

"You are the most beautiful thing I've ever seen," Jaden murmured as he grabbed at her hand. There was a tingling sensation at the touch, he could feel her grace, the center of which her joy emitted from.

Imani turned around and faced him. She drew in a shuddering breath. "I never told you this but you remind me of someone special to me from my past life." Imani caressed his cocoa brown skin with the back of her hand. "He was a gentle soul like you."

Jaden grabbed her hand and held it against his face. His eyes closed and he lingered in the warmth of her touch. "When my mom died I thought she had taken everything that was good and pure in this world with her. All of my life she was the only one that accepted me, that could see me as someone who wasn't a freak. Then I met you. Imani you are my light."

Jaden pulled Imani in for a kiss. It was a kiss that took both of their breaths away and made them gasp for a moment as she pulled away.

"We can't do this," Imani said as a tear walloped in her eyes. "This isn't allowed. It's forbidden. They have destroyed many angels for less."

Jaden nodded his head, crushed. "True," he responded. He sat back on the bed, his head hung low. "I'm sorry If-"

"I should leave," she said in a whisper. Then she peered over her shoulder to look at him one more time. "But know this Jaden. I care for you, deeply and truly."

Jaden watched as bright lights faded away and she beamed back to Sanctuary.

One thing that he knew to be true was that he was unconditionally and undeniably in love with Imani.

****

Romeo laid in his bed, sleeping on his right side. His eyelids fluttered rapidly as the revelation unfolded in his mind. Instinctively his legs swung off the bed, and lifted the covers. His eyes were blinded and grey the whole time as he sat up and walked over to his white desk. On the desk was pin and paper waiting for him to sketch.

In this revelation he stood in the middle of an outstretching field that faced the city. Out in the distance the sky rumbled and he turned his head upward. In one large swarming cloud, the Locusts attacked the city. They shredded through buildings like paper. They snatched people off the ground like buzzards. And they devoured like lions with their outstretching jaws. Three girls cried out on his right. All of their mouths moved rapidly but nothing came out until finally.

They come to devour

Beware of the coming hour

Night of the reaping.

When Romeo's eyes snapped open and his eyesight returned to normal he looked down at the picture. He drew a locust with a face of a woman, tail of a scorpion, and was the size of a bus. The Queen.

Chapter Twenty-Five

Butterflies

As soon as Jaden walked through the double doors of North Central, he searched for Imani. His mind was in an array of emotions, some of them being happy yet fearful if their kiss would make their relationship awkward. *Where was she*? He thought as he surveyed the hallway. Lay passed by him with a stack of books, almost tall as his neck.

Jaden rushed after him. "Lay wait up. You got a minute?"

"Sure but make it quick. I have to get to calculus." Lay said as he struggled to keep balance.

"Have you seen Imani?" Jaden asked.

Lay stopped by his locker. "No I haven't. Have you?"

Jaden sighed in frustration. "No."

"Do you mind giving me a hand," Lay said as he handed his books over.

"Sure," Jaden said while Lay opened his locker and Jaden threw out a question. "Lay, have you ever been in love?"

Lay smiled. He had the type of smile that could light

up a room. "Only once but it was the most beautiful experience in the whole wide world."

"How did you know it was love?"

"You just know," he said as he stuffed the books in his locker. "You get warm fluttering butterflies in your stomach. And all day long you just think about them and how they make you feel."

Jaden nodded. "Wow that's hella deep. I think I'm in love." He said. Lay closed his locker and together they strolled along the hall. "So how did you tell her?"

Lay giggled. "I took fluffy home with me and I adorned her with kisses and treats."

"Like a dinner date? Should I learn how to cook? I don't think she would like all of that. I'm sure she would be fine with a waffle from the Waffle House." Then Jaden paused. "Wait, what kind of name is Fluffy?"

"She was my puppy," Lay said innocently.

Jaden shook his head. "C'mon man I'm talking about girls."

Lay chuckled. "Sorry Jaden. If you're talking about girls, I wouldn't know a thing about love if it hit me."

Suddenly a towering figure nudges past Lay's shoulder.

"Ow!"

"Watch it Jin-Soo," Lori shouted as she turned around.

Jaden rubbed Lay's shoulder. "Are you okay?"

Lay nodded. "I'm fine."

Dr. Ball rounded the corner and pulled both Lay and Jaden to her side from behind. "How are my two sophisticated sophomores doing today?"

Lay pushed his glasses back up his nose. "Just fine Dr. Ball."

"Wonderful," She said. Then she released them from

247

her grip. "Science fair is coming up Mr. Lee and I know you got something that's going to knock my socks off."

Lay giggled. "Yes. I do."

Dr. Ball smiled and hugged Lay again. "That's what I want to hear. And Mr. Davis, so far I have heard nothing but good things about you. Let's keep it that way."

Jaden forced a smile. "Sure, no problem."

"Okay I'll let you boys go. Just remember Jaden I got my good eye on you. And if you step out of line," She said as she side stepped. "I'm going to catch you. That's all. Carry on."

Jaden groaned as Dr. Ball walked away. Out of the corner of his eye he spotted Imani. Long dark black hair sweeping over the side of her soft face. She wore a pink hoodie, a black t-shirt, and some loose fitting jeans. Her whole vibe was casual but her whole swag was still alluring. It was an incredible mystery to Jaden, how someone could be so effortlessly beautiful.

"Lay I'll catch you later." Jaden said as he strolled over.

"What up," Imani greeted in a dry tone. As she always did.

He didn't look over. "Nothing. Just another day," He said as he continued walking.

"Did you get any sleep last night."

Jaden sighed, "A little bit. After you left I just watched some old episodes of Martin until I drifted off."

Imani snickered and nose wrinkled in the weirdest way. Jaden had noticed that whenever she laughed. It made him join in with her laughter.

"What episode did you watch?" She asked.

"The one where he pulls out the sandblaster to give Myra a pedicure."

Imani threw her head back. "That's the funniest one," She said in between fits of laughter. It took her moment to stop laughing and form a sentence. "Another good episode is when he fights–"

"The puppy." They said in unison before erupting into laughter.

A digital bell drowned their laughter. Jaden looked over at her and lost his train of thought. Jaden wondered *how something that came so natural could be wrong.*

Imani tugged at the straps of her bag. "Are you ready to go hunting tonight?"

"Ready as I'll ever be," He answered. Then he stopped in the hall and faced her as everyone roamed by. "It's going to be nice to train outside of the ring. I think that last simulation was hella stressful for all of us."

"Dude you can't complain. You weren't pregnant." Imani stated.

Jaden nodded "True."

"I keep telling coach that even though I am a guide I can still help on the field. It's like damn everyone is trying to stop me from being great. How else am I going to become an Ark and join SMITE."

Jaden threw up his hands. "Don't know what to tell you." Then he paused for a moment and cleared his throat. "Imani I just wanted to let you know, even though it was simulation, I let you down. And I don't know...I guess what I just want to say that in real life or any situation–I will never let anything hurt you."

Imani blushed as her skin warmed all over. She gave him a love tap on the arm. "Hollywood chill with all the soft stuff."

"Oh you calling me soft now. I was trying to apologize for letting you get killed but I guess I'll take that back."

Imani's jaw dropped. "You've been hanging out with Romeo too much. Now you're a savage?"

Romeo walked behind the two and grabbed them by the shoulders. "Good I was just looking for the two of you. We have to talk. Ms. Day's office now."

"What's going on?" Imani asked.

"Just had a revelation last night, and I feel like something big is about to go down."

Jaden looked at him with his face wrinkled. " Sounds serious."

Romeo looked at him, "It was one of the scariest revelations I've ever received" Then he glanced over his shoulder to see if someone was listening. "I'll tell you both about it once we get off the hall."

The urgency of Romeo's tone made them both walk in haste. Moments later they all stood in Ms. Day's office, everyone except Coach Franklin, who Romeo insisted was important to bring him up on facetime.

Ms. Day flattened her dress as she sat down. "What was so important that you called us together for this emergency meeting?"

"Yes I have Calculus and an organic chemistry quiz coming up." Lay declared. "I'd appreciate we can do this as quickly as possible please. I don't want to be rude. I'm sorry."

"This," Romeo said as he unfolded the paper he carried in his hand.

"The hell is that?" Deshawn shouted.

Ms. Day took the paper and grimaced. "What is this?"

"The Locusts," Romeo declared as he fold his arms. "Lots of them. I saw them coming out of the ground and swarming the city."

"Let me see!" Coach Franklin shouted from the

screen.

Lay took the phone and held it to the paper. "Here you go coach."

Coach Franklin's old eyes widened as he looked the image. Full grown locust flying in formation, red eyes gleaming, and fangs bearing. "Just like I remember her. That's the queen."

Ms. Day touched the temples of his head. "What else did you see?"

Romeo frowned. "There where these girls whispering–"

Deshawn learned over. "But where they hot girls tho?"

Romeo turned to him. "No I think they were dead."

"Focus. Can you please let him finish," Imani snapped.

Romeo took a breath. "There where these girls whispering and the one thing they kept whispering about was something called the reaping?"

"The reaping?" Coach Franklin repeated as he mulled it over. "What did they say about it?"

"They said it's coming soon, so I took that as we should get ready for it."

Imani leaned on Ms. Day's table. "Is that all that they said?"

"That's all that I got," Romeo snapped back. There was a hint of anger in his voice.

"From off the top of your head Ms. Day what does that sound like?" Coach Franklin asked.

"Like a ritual." She said as she wiped off her tablet. "I'll alert the Shepherd Guild at once and see if they know anything about this."

Ms. Day folded her arms. "Very well we must prepare ourselves. I will have the Shepherd's Guild to look into this and see what they can find. In the meantime, don't neglect your training." She paused to look at them all. "We are going to need you all to fall in line and be sharp" She stood up. "Now it's best if all of you head to class."

Lay bolted for the door. "Thanks. I will see you guys later before we go hunting." He reached for the door and whirled around. "Waffle house right?"

Deshawn nodded, "We will be in there."

Jaden turned to Romeo, "Waffle house?"

"We always go before or after a hunt."

Ms. Day clapped her hands. "To class. Now"

"Bye Ms. Bae–I mean Ms. Day." Deshawn said as he grabbed the door.

All in a single file they head out of the office and went to their classes, a ball of nerves in their gut.

"Mr. Davis," Ms. Day called.

Jaden stood aside at the door. "What's up?"

"Close the door and have a seat." Jaden did as told and took a seat in front of her.

She reached into her desk and pulled out a pad. "We haven't had a session in a while. I wanted to know how you are doing." Ms. Day asked.

Jaden shifted uncomfortably in the chair. "We still see each other at Sanctuary. I'm good."

Ms. Day nodded. "You seem to be fitting in quite nicely within the group."

"Yea the guys are okay." Jaden said.

She crossed her legs. "We never got the chance to fully discuss your big blow up after your match with Romeo."

Jaden threw up his hands. "What's there to discuss? He went below the belt and pissed me off?"

"I see." Ms. Day said. "Based on your prior records

and well," She adjusted her glasses. "You're after-school activities, it seems you are no stranger when it comes to violence. Are you mad? Would you say you have an anger issue?"

"No, I don't think so," Jaden answered.

Ms. Day intensified her gaze.

"Well um…. I guess fighting makes me feel better."

Ms. Day tilted her head. "Better how?"

Jaden leaned back. "I don't know just better."

Ms. Day smiled slightly. "You know Jaden you are a very peculiar young man. At school I see you come in, head down, sulking your way through the halls. Then at Sanctuary, I see a different young man. A quiet leader who is brave. Unfortunately, you have gone through a lot at such a young age. As most Anointed do. These traumas change us. So my question is who are you?"

"I don't know anymore. I'm just trying to get by," He answered.

"Just trying to get by," she repeated with a smile. Ms. Day put her head down and wrote a note on a bright pink sticky. She ripped it off and handed it to him. "Here, that is all for now. You may go."

"Thanks," Jaden said as he grabbed the note.

She tugged back. "Remember our sessions aren't over with. And I look forward to our conversation. If you want just feel free to come to me anytime."

Jaden took the note. "I'll do that." Then he walked out.

Chapter Twenty-Six

In the Lion's den

A bitter wind prowled the cemetery, raking skeletal tree branches across a frosty sky. The sky was a dull, sullen gray and it made everything below seem forlorn. Asmodeus blended with the shadows as he watched the anointed fight against a small clan of vampires with Coach Franklin monitored alongside. Patience was one of the values demons were taught in the pit, and Asmodeus was care strikingly patient, it was one of the qualities that made him the most effective Son of Chaos. The tree provided him cover as he stood stiff as a statue, concealed amongst a thicket of branches. He wanted the boy alone. A malicious smile swept across his face as he slinked behind a tall pine tree, his grimy curved nails clutching its bark. Even though he wanted revenge, it was the methodical side, the patient side, that could see the usefulness of turning Jaden.

"Keep your guard up Romeo. Stop rushing in so aggressive son and think." Coach Franklin yelled as a female vamp landed a kick to Romeo's chin that sent him crashing into a tombstone. She stood in front of him, snarling, claws out, fangs extended to a deadly seven inches, with her hunting face on.

Lay pulled Romeo off the ground, "Are you alright?" he asked.

"Pay attention son! Don't drop your guard! "Coach Franklin screamed.

A male vampire with short dreadlocks kicked the staff out of Lay's hands and hit him with an uppercut that knocked him off his feet.

Coach Franklin threw up his hands as he paced back and forth with his shotgun hanging off his shoulder, "I swear I'm so tired of this. Yawl gone have to do better. Because this is just pitiful right here"

Deshawn rippled time around the short dread head vampire. As the air rippled like water, the vampire looked incredulously at his limbs, as they moved sluggishly. Deshawn casually walked in front of him, "We got this coach. Stop tripping," Deshawn said as he swiped the vampire's head clean off with his old-fashioned battle ax.

Ashes blew in the air and just as Deshawn paused to admire his handy work, two growling vampires pounced on his back. He fell to the ground quickly. "Save me, Jacob!"

With a backhand Jaden tossed the two vampires into the air with his power, a crimson energy lifted them into the air and sent them cascading away. Landing in a bone crackling thud, the vampires still quickly flipped back on to their feet. Jaden spotted his sword on the ground. In one swift motion, he rolled over, beckoned his sword which was few inches away to his hand, and slashed one of the vampire's head off. Ashes covered his clothes. Outnumbered the lone vampire started running away.

"I'll go get it!" Jaden shouted as he glanced back.

Deshawn gave Romeo a hand getting up. "Tell me again why we don't just use the guns with the silver bullets?" Romeo asked as he squirmed in pain.

Lay turned the light off his staff. "Or the hellfire shooter I spent two months putting together."

"That's because I'm trying to teach you something," Coach Franklin barked back as he pulled his Bible from his coat pocket. "You kids are always trying to take the easy way out. I'm trying to teach you how to hunt vampires like real anointed." Coach Franklin made a cross in the air with his bible. "Ashes to Ashes. Dust to Dust. We smite in your name. Amen."

Jaden sprinted after the vampire who ran leaps and bounds ahead. He reached behind his back and pulled out a dark wooden stake. Jaden flung it towards the vampire. It whooshed a few feet ahead until it connected with the vampire's heart. Flames consumed the creature and the stake dropped into a pile of dust.

Jaden pumped his fist, "Yes."

There was a crackling in his head like a radio brought back to life. *Glad to see you are taking this seriously. He has risen.*

Jaden recognized the voice in his head, as the Creator. He cocked his head to the side as he responded to it. "Nice of you to pop in. I haven't heard from you in the last few weeks. Where have you been?"

I've been watching. Now I've come to warn you that the beast has arisen.

Jaden stopped in his tracks. "The demon with frozen eyes?" He asked.

Yes, the voice replied.

Fear made every muscle in his body tense as he allowed the thought to settle in. On one hand, he was eager to finish the job, and the other he was still petrified. "So what do I do?" he asked. There was a long stretch of silence afterward.

Jaden threw up his hands. "Great now you're gone again."

Jaden took his time walking back towards the group. A rustle from his left stopped him dead in his tracks. Fear coated him like a chilling breeze. Looking into the thicket of trees, Jaden connected eyes with another. Something whizzed behind him and the wind whipped his face when he turned around.

Jaden brought up his sword defensively. Again in a motion that was so quick, it could barely be seen by eye, something went past him on his left. Then it came back across from behind on his right. It dodged from tree to tree back and forth encircling Jaden all around.

Jaden pointed his sword. "You can stop running now. You're just going to make me mad. Come out and face me." He shouted out to the trees

Footsteps shuffled behind Jaden, and he sensed a powerful evil presence within his midst. It made every hair on the back of his neck stand up. And this feeling was exactly what Coach Franklin had been trying to describe for the longest time, it was a shift in the spirit that alerted the anointed of evil.

Asmodeus towered over him easily by a foot, and Jaden felt the warmth of the demon's breath burning on his neck. Swiftly Jaden brought his sword up in a wide arc and it landed between the demon's hands. His breath caught in his chest, as the shock washed over him. No matter the different meat suit, Jaden recognized him as his mother's killer. Asmodeus yanked the sword out of Jaden's hands and tossed it to the side. Rage coursed into Jaden's veins, and he curled his fist. He swung his fist and connected with the right jaw of the demon. Asmodeus took the attack on the chin, with a chuckle.

Jaden took slow steps backward. Fear replaced the rage in his spirit. Both sized each other up. He could sense the demon's power. The body Asmodeus occupied did not look the same. His skin a chalky ash white, tribal marks covered his right eye, what was once fingers were now thick black talons. There was no hair on his head and his teeth were jagged like an animal that shreds flesh.

Asmodeus cocked his head to the side, "You know who I am don't you?" he asked with his razor-sharp teeth gleaming.

Jaden's eyes narrowed, "You killed my mom,"

"Good. Very good Jaden. I didn't forget you," Asmodeus said as he ran his talons across his teeth. "As a matter of fact, I've come for you."

"Is that right?" Jaden asked in a cocky tone.

Asmodeus cackled low, "Yes."

"Well I'm not going nowhere without a fight," Jaden bellowed as he waved his hand trying to pummel the demon with his telekinetic power.

Asmodeus merely turned his cheek. Jaden tried again and nothing happened. He tried desperately to push him, move him, and throw him or anything with his mind. Still, the demon remained unmoved. Jaden's dread intensified as he stood there, bound by his fear, and shock by his inability to fight back. The fear was real, and it was a child's fear that made him want to cry out for help.

Asmodeus closed his eyes and stuck his nose in the air. "I can smell your fear. So delicious and intoxicating." The demon's eyes snapped open. "You're just ripe for the picking."

Jaden's chest heaved up and down, as he struggled to hold air in his lungs. Why weren't his powers working? He defeated this demon before why couldn't he do it now? Jaden threw a right jab at Asmodeus. The demon blocked it. Jaden swung one punch after the other. The demon deflected all his blows, and delivered a powerful kick to Jaden's chest, that knocked him back into the bark of a tree which shattered on impact.

The pain knocked all off the wind out of his body. Jaden struggled to his feet. He looked around and the demon was gone. A chilling breeze rocked tree branches in the demon's path. Asmodeus spun into the shadows and impaled Jaden with his favorite blade. Jaden gasped as the sharp pain ran through his chest.

Jaden screamed for help as red-coated his lips. The demon wrapped his claws around Jaden's neck. He brought his lips closer to Jaden's ear. "Almost poetic eh? This was the same way I had a poor mommy."

Blood trickled past Jaden's lips, "Creator help me," Jaden cried out.

"No Creator!" The demon shouted. "There is no Creator here. There was no Creator when I ran my blade across your mother's neck. And there was no Creator with us at Whatley Reid," he said in a mocking tone.

Tears rolled down Jaden's face. The blade was deep in his back. Memories of that night returned to his head. Feelings of despair and abandonment came back to him.

Asmodeus nibbled on Jaden's ear with his teeth, "Yes that's right Jaden. I was there with you. Only an evil spirit of course, but I was there. Just like I'm here now. I am your God. You belong to me," The demon whispered in his gritty voice as he snatched the blade out of Jaden's side and dropped him to the ground.

Jaden rolled over in pain. His hand quivered as he covered the wound that spewed out like water.

"You know I didn't lie when I said I wanted you." Asmodeus stated as he towered over Jaden and clutched his face. "You will be my new pet. There are so many pleasures I have to show you. And your powers shall be magnified in the light of the flame."

Asmodeus snatched Jaden by his jacket and shot out of the cover of the trees like a bullet. The demon sped through the woods with Jaden in tow, dragging him along the ground. Skin from Jaden's back scraped across grass, dirt, and branches. Dirt and dust mixed with the blood in his mouth. Jaden kicked and clawed at the demon to no avail.

"Let me go," he shouted in a faint voice. His chest throbbing in pain as he spoke.

They came to a sudden stop. Someone stood in the demon's path. A radiant light shined in front of them both. Imani unleashed her wings in a snap, and the light harkened upon them. Asmodeus squealed with fury.

"By the blood of Jesus, let him go now!" Imani commanded.

Asmodeus tossed Jaden in the air to his right. "Soon not even your kind can stop me." The demon declared before spinning into the shadows.

Imani rushed over to Jaden. His eyes were barely open. Blood and dirt coated his clothes. Imani laid her healing hands on him. "Jaden are you alright?"

Jaden fought to keep his eyes open. When he did he was comforted by the sight of his angel and bright lights. "Man you are forever saving me," he murmured, breathing heavily, he closed them as his beautiful angel Imani healed him.

Chapter Twenty-Seven

The Takeover

Eva materialized in Fangz penthouse, and a dozen or so vampire heads lobbed over. His children were sprinkled in the crowd, mingled in between human guests. But once they smelled the demon in their midst, one by one they all shifted into their hunting faces. Eva laid eyes on Fangz and strutted towards him indifferent to the different that surrounded.

Fangz stood on the balcony overlooking his pool. He turned his head, nonchalantly. "Who are you?"

Eva raised a brow. "You should know who I am. You sent your children to attack me."

A smirk swept across Fangz face. "Your one of the demons." He finished his drink and swallowed it down hard. "This is my territory and no one comes to Atlanta without me knowing. It's disrespectful. So I wanted to welcome you in a disrespectful way."

Eva smiled. "We are willing to forgive your treachery." She looked around the room, gazing into the eyes of the surrounding vampires, seemingly in the middle of a pride of Lions. "And we will only kill a few of you. The only condition is you will fall under the heel of the Sons of Chaos." Then she faced Fangz. "I have been told there is a place for you in the new dawn. Aid our efforts in opening the Hell Gate. We aware of the presence of the anointed and the threat Michael or Smite should they interfere. The option I am giving you is simple. Join us or die."

Fangz waved his hand and four vampires in covert attire with assault rifles surrounded Eva. They stood tall, firm, and ready to shoot silver bullets. Fangz leaned against the rail and took a long savoring sip.

"Anybody teach you any manners?" He said with a snarky grin. Fangz lowered his shades. "You don't roll up to anybody's crib making threats. I don't take orders from nobody ya heard me?"

Eva softened her demeanor. "My apologies." She took a step closer and all four guns clicked around her.

Fangz chuckled. "It's alright, stand down boys."

Eva ran her hands across his chest which spilled out from his half buttoned shirt. "Maybe my approach was a little too harsh. But it is urgent. The time of the reaping draws near. We just need you and your boys to oversee a transaction. We are going to the airport to pick up a package and we want everything to go smoothly," She said with her voice soft and diplomatic.

Fangz sucked his teeth, "So what do you got for me?" he asked with a wrinkled brow. "What are the True

Bloods getting out of this deal."

Eva raked her hands through his dreads, "A seat of power in our new regime and all the humans you can drink."

Fangz laughed, "All the humans I can drink? I got that now. If I want a virgin from Italy, all I have to do is snap my fingers and she's on the next plane." He stood and walked away from the balcony. "None of this concerns me." The pleasant look on his face went away and turned stern. "I'm a vampire. All I want is blood and money. Blood and money that's it." He said as he clapped at her. "So I'm sorry baby girl, I can't help you."

Suddenly the lights in the room flickered and the floor of the penthouse trembled underneath them. All of the vampires sensed the presence of something diabolical enter the room. Asmodeus spun from out of the Shadows.

Every vampire in the room dropped fang at the faint glimpse of the demon.

"Stop cowering to him it's pathetic. We don't need the bloodsuckers." Asmodeus said.

Eva turned around, "A pack of Locust hatchlings and a few demons is not going to help us against anointed warriors. Three of them at that! I don't know about you but I like my vessel. I do not want to go back to Hell."

Fangz looked at Asmodeus in disgust, "Who is this clown anyway? I'm not going to tolerate the disrespect around here!" Fangz shouted.

Asmodeus darted across the room. The guards rushed to defend their master but their speed was inferior to a devil. The demon snatched the heart of one of the vampires, and ripped the head off another with his talons. One of them aimed their rifle at Asmodeus. Before he could fire the demon threw a shock ball his direction and sliced the other guard in half. Ashes rained all over the balcony.

Priyanka and Garrett shot bullets into the demon's back, which bounced off and had no effect.

"You," Asmodeus hissed as his eyes narrowed on Priyanka.

Priyanka dropped her guns and stumbled back. Asmodeus spun into the shadows. He spun out beside them, tossing Garrett to the side like a rag doll.

"You have disrespected the Sons of Chaos." Asmodeus said as he held Priyanka in his cold grasp. The he turned to Fangz. "For that I shall take your general." He tightened his grip around Priyanka and lightening reduced her to dust.

"Priyanka!" Fangz shouted as he lurched into the air.

Asmodeus backhanded him square across the face and sent him soaring across the room, landing on top of his marble desk. Asmodeus pinned the master vampire to the desk. He gripped the side of the vampire's head tightly, and dug his right finger into Fangz eye. The master vampire cried out as he struggled in the iron clad grasp of the demon.

Asmodeus ran his nose across the side of Fangz face, delighting in the fear that dripped off of him. "Remember your place. We are the true beast. You are merely hybrids. There can only be one boss. One leader. One

King. That is me. You and your brood will be on guard at the airport as I retrieve my package." Asmodeus commanded.

Eva stared at the demon in awe. She caressed her neck as she delighted in the scene.

"And when I return to glory....be glad I don't wipe you off this plane. Let's go." The demon said as he spun back into the shadows.

Fangz touched his eye and roared.

"Boss are you good?" someone said from the back.

"No I'm not good," he shouted. "I should turn all of yawl to ashes." He reached into his pocket and put on his shades. "That's alright because we still got some moves to make." He turned to Garrett. "This ring. Is it the one you heard about from the ghoul. Do you think that's what they want us to secure?"

"I think so," Garrett answered.

Fangz grabbed him by the collar. "You make sure that as soon as you find that ring, you're bring it to me first."

"Got it," Garrett said as he straightened his shirt.

Fangz went to the window and tossed his desk in fury.

*****

Romeo tossed and turning violently in his bed. Sweat coated him as a fever spread across his body like wildfire. He kicked his blue comforter off and continued tossing back and forth over his white sheets as they rustled underneath. It was the violent images slamming into his head that was disturbing him so much. In a series of flashes, he saw the airport buzzing with people and workers. Then there were vampires slaughtering a group of workers who unloaded a cargo airplane. The screams of the workers filled his ear as he saw the delights of the vampire's faces as they tossed the workers about like rag dolls and ripped out chunks of flesh with their teeth. He could feel their pain. He could feel the fangs of each vampire bite into his own flesh.

Caught in the rapture of this fleeting vision Romeo continued to wrestle with his sheets as he tossed all over the bed. The final image was that of the terrifying grisly bat-like wings that stretched across the moon. He watched them blot out the moonlight and reign down over him. One image that stood out in the revelation was a ring. It was a ring unlike any he had ever seen before, it was small golden, and had several anointed sigils inscribed on the front. Suddenly everything all around him shook as lightning crashed. Romeo leapt out of his bed. He was breathing hard. Sweat continued dripping from his head. "Just a nightmare. Just a nightmare. I'm alright. I'm good." Romeo whispered.

The only sound in the room was his own breathing. Romeo turned the TV on. There was no way he was going to sleep after that. He'd just watch sports broadcasting until he passed out.

CHAPTER TWENTY-EIGHT

Touched by an Angel

It was around third period when Imani noticed Jaden was missing. She was sitting in their Spanish class when she noticed his desk unoccupied. He barely said anything after she healed him, and ran home without talking to anyone. Thinking the worst, she closed her eyes and reached out with her mind. She could still feel him. He was alive but his spirit was broken into shambles. To her right, she saw Romeo who was too busy drawing to notice her trying to discreetly grab his attention.

Romeo looked up and finally caught Imani's gaze. "Does this look familiar to you?" He held up a pencil drawing of a ring.

Imani shook her head, "No." She faced forward to see if the teacher spotted her, and once she noticed she didn't, she turned back to Romeo. "Have you seen Jaden today?"

Romeo thought about it for a moment then he

answered. "No."

Imani rolled her eyes and sighed as she slammed back into her chair. Once the period was over she sought after Lay in the hallway. He strolled past her with his tablet in hand, trying to balance four or so large books.

She stopped him, almost making him fall over. "Lay have you seen Jaden?"

Lay leaned his ear to the side. "Excuse me?"

"Have you seen Jaden," she asked again. This time her voice shook with anger.

Lay nodded, "Oh yes, Jaden."

Imani threw up her hands. "Yes, Jaden. Have you seen him?"

"I'm sorry I haven't, he was supposed to meet me today after school. I texted him this morning with no response. Do you want me to text him again and see if I can reach him?"

Imani patted him. "Do that."

When she spotted Deshawn he was talking to some girl.

"You know I'm trying to get to know you," He whispered into the girl's ear.

Imani pulled him away. "Deshawn, have you seen Jaden?"

"Way to go Imani!" He threw up his hands as the girl walked away. "Nice way to cock block. What do you want?"

Imani huffed and leaned in closer to Deshawn's face. "I'm looking for Jaden. Have you seen him?"

"No, I haven't seen Jerry. But I'm sure Romeo or Lay might have. I don't see you bothering them or destroying their love life."

Imani closed her eyes and searched for Jaden. He was home.

Lay saw her and rushed over. "I got him. He is home.

Imani rolled her eyes. "I know. I am going to see him this afternoon."

"Do you want me to come with you?" Lay asked.

Imani shook her head. "I'm his guide and it's my duty to help him."

Once the last period bell rang, she set off to see Jaden at home.

*****

Jazz music played throughout the living room, John sat on the couch silently weeping as old distant memories swirled about through his head. His lab coat was tossed over the coffee table and his tie hanging on the edge of a chair. The glass of cognac in his hand half empty. He took slow sips as his eyes were fixated on the picture of him and his wife. It felt like it was yesterday they were at their wedding reception dancing the night away to this very song. He rubbed at the pain stabbing him at the temple of his forehead.

His mind drifted back to a simpler time. When he wasn't John but just Jaden, a kid from Detroit attending Howard University. That's when he met Diana, the love of his life, his future wife, and mother of his child. He impressed her with his horrible Michael Jackson impression. That impression that was corny and humiliating to him became a staple in their marriage. Whenever things went wrong in their marriage he could always count on getting a smile out of his wife with his stiff moonwalk.

Now there was no more dancing. She was gone. Taken away from the both of them. John was a rational man and after five months the murder of his wife still made no sense to him. Death is natural. If she died of cancer maybe, he wouldn't feel so bad. At least he would be able to expect it. Maybe if she was in a tragic car accident he would be able to move on. But it was just impossible to imagine that life of his wife was taken away in front of his son. But he had to stay strong at the very least for his son.

Footsteps pounded down the stairs, John quickly wiped his tears away and turned off the music. Jaden paused mid-step when the music stopped. He already knew what his father was doing. He didn't even need to read his mind.

John sat his glass on the coffee table, "Son, what are you doing?" he asked

Jaden looked at his father with a blank expression, "Just going to get a snack from the fridge."

"Oh okay," John said quietly as he turned back to face a blank TV screen.

"Yea," Jaden replied as he went into the kitchen.

John glanced over his shoulder, "You know I was thinking we should go back to L.A this weekend and visit your mother. She could use some fresh flowers," he shouted from the living room.

Jaden slammed the refrigerator door. A brief moment of pain passed him by like a breeze. He shook it off and walked back into the living room. "Umm, I can't. I have something to do with my friends.... somebody is doing something. I think there is a basketball game" Jaden mumbled.

John saw through his lie, "I thought the basketball game is on Friday night."

"Yeah that's right it is on Friday. But you know Romeo is playing and since he has been at practice so much he hasn't had time to do this chemistry project. So I promised to help him on Saturday."

John stood up from the couch, "I'm sure Romeo will do just fine without you."

"Yeah but I promised," Jaden argued.

"Son we have to get over this sooner or later. You haven't visited your mother's grave yet. You need to do this. I know it's hard but you need closure." John protested in a low baritone.

"I can't. Just let me be with my friends," Jaden said with his voice cracking. The doorbell rang. Jaden ended the conversation as he answered the door. On the other side stood Imani.

"Can I come in," She asked.

"Come on," Jaden responded with a nonchalant nod.

Jaden closed the door behind Imani as she entered. "Dad, you remember Imani right?"

"Yes, I do. How you doing sweetheart?" John

greeted with a wave.

"I'm good," Imani said.

Jaden grabbed his board and pointed towards the door. He turned to his father, "We are supposed to be working together on this group project. Mind if we go to my room?"

"Go right ahead." John said as Jaden and Imani started to climb the stairs, "Just remember we are not finished with this conversation."

Jaden glanced over his shoulder. He realized that this was something his father would not easily let go. The problem went to the back of his head as they continued towards his room.

"So we missed you at school today," Imani said as she followed Jaden to his room. Jaden remained silent as he shuffled passed his door. He tossed a game controller to the side before falling back onto his bed. "Why didn't you come?" She pressed further.

"I didn't feel like it. I was too tired" Jaden groaned as Imani took a seat at his desk. "I didn't sleep at all last night, especially after what happened. I knew the demon that attacked me, it was the same one that killed my mother."

"Are you serious?" Imani asked, slightly speechless.

Then he looked out at the wall. "I can't believe he was right there and I couldn't do it. All this time I've waited for my revenge"

Imani cast a sidelong glance towards him. "But do you think that will finally make you happy. Will that ease your pain?"

"Yes," Jaden responded. Twisting his head to the side, he thought about it for a moment. "I don't know maybe. She's never coming back, so I'll be angry forever."

Imani touched his shoulder. "Don't say that," she said. Her touch was gentle and comforting.

"Crazy huh? I'll never forget those eyes. Those blue eyes have been haunting me every night since that night." Jaden peered down. He sighed, his gaze now riveted to her. Tears swelled in his eyes and he tried desperately to fight them back. "It told me it was there with me when I was in Whatley Reid. During the day I would be fine but when night came, when night came I could definitely feel it almost haunting me."

Imani got up from the chair and sat on the bed beside Jaden. She grabbed his hand, "Go ahead and tell me. Don't be afraid," she insisted.

Imani's touch was warm and compassionate. The silky touch of her cinnamon-kissed skin almost ignited his. Her pull was greater than he'd imagined, as she made him look at her again.

"The first month there was the most difficult. They had me heavily sedated and restrained. But that helped with the voices. When the second month came I got better. I learned how to tune the voices out. The third month was when everything hit me. I just couldn't help but to feel responsible for the death of my mom and Sam. So much so I tried to commit suicide."

"Wow that's deep," she gasped trying to soak it all

in.

"I know I just keep hearing these voices that made me feel…I don't know. Hopeless."

"How did you try to commit suicide."

Jaden shook his head. "It doesn't matter, because it didn't work. Funny enough when it didn't, I was mad about that for a long time. It felt like I was made to stay and suffer."

Jaden directed his smoldering gaze towards Imani. "I want to know why me?" Jaden asked with his eyes burning red with a question and a regret. "If I was supposedly chosen by God or the Creator as you call him. Why the hell would he put me through this?"

Imani caressed his face, "I'm sorry. I am....truly. For some reason the people he gives great power...he also gives great pain. It keeps them from arrogance. It ensures that they know who the source of their strength really is. I know what you're feeling must feel unbearable but know this. The Creator of the Universe will never put more on you than you can bear."

Jaden jumped up from the bed, "But I can't bear this. I am not that strong." he shouted with his voice muttered by his emotions.

"You think you aren't but you are," Imani argued, her words both harsh and true. "Think about it Jaden. God hasn't left you.... he was there the whole time. That demon was supposed to kill you that night five months ago. You were supposed to stay locked up in that mental institution. You were supposed to be eaten by a swarm of demons. All these things were supposed to kill you but they didn't. They made you stronger! Can't you see that?"

Jaden raked his fingers through his wooly hair or massaged his temples. "And look at you now. You are stronger. All these things were meant to destroy you and here you are still standing."

Jaden took a seat back on the bedside, allowing the truth of her message to resonate with him. Imani scouted closer to his side. Their hands slowly inched across the bed until they found each other. Jaden peered down. Compassion, love, and her strength was there. He smiled at the sight of their hands. She gazed into his eyes. The pain began floating away, almost as if she was healing the broken pieces of his heart.

"If you really want to avenge your mother. You have to be strong. Help us. Come with me back to sanctuary and help us identify the demon. Romeo had a dream last night and he thinks something is about to go down real soon. You can stop it Jaden, and you can save someone. You can also save yourself."

Their conversation was cut short by a loud knock on the door that made them both jump. Jaden went to the door and opened it.

"Come outside," his father said with anger in his eyes.

Jaden walked out of the room and shut the door behind him. "Why were you banging so hard on my door for?"

John held up his cell phone. "I just got a call from Dr. Ball. What the hell are you doing skipping school?

She told me you didn't come in today. You made me believe you did." He folded his arms. "What's going on?"

Jaden buried his face in his hands. "Ugh, I can explain. I just wasn't feeling good today and–"

"No," John blurted. "That's not it. You did it so you can hang with your new friends again."

"This has nothing to do with them!" Jaden shouted.

"The hell it is," John spat back. He walked away from Jaden and strolled back. "I didn't give up everything so you can do the same bullshit again." He said with his voice becoming a tumultuous scream. He went over and opened the bedroom door. "Imani sweetheart, Jaden will have to talk to you another time. He is in trouble sweetheart and I'm afraid you have to go home."

Imani stood up and shuffled to the door. "Is everything fine?"

"Everything is fine," John said as he ushered her out.

Imani started down the stairs and glanced back. "Jaden is everything cool."

"Yeah. I'll see you soon." He said as he watches her leave.

Once Imani walked out of the house, John continued. "Let me tell you what is going to happen. You're grounded. Don't expect to be going anywhere or doing nothing for a while, especially with your new friends. And we will be paying a visit to the doctors this weekend."

Jaden gasped. "Are you serious? Why are you tripping?"

"Tripping," John repeated with a frown. "Who do you think you're talking to? I'm not one of your little friends. I'm your father and I am trying to keep you from going down this path of destruction. So get out of my face and go to your room."

Jaden marched back in his room and slammed the door. The anger he felt brewed inside him fiercely. He ran his fist through the wall and felt nothing. Jaden knew he couldn't stay in his room all day. The other's needed him. He packed some clothes in his book bag and grabbed his skateboard. Then he opened the window and left for Sanctuary.

****

Coach Franklin paced back and forth, "Son do you know its name?"

Jaden shook his head, "No I don't know its name."

Coach Franklin cursed under his breath, "We need to know its name. Anytime you have the name of a demon, you have power over it. That's exorcism 101. I know one thing though.... this definitely smells like some upper-level type of hell bat."

"True," Deshawn added. Then he went over and sat on the edge of the table. "You okay, big dog?"

Jaden shook his head. "I'm fine. Thanks."

"What are we going to do? I need my sleep. I can't go another night like this." Romeo stated. "It seems like we searched every book and still nothing." Then he looked over to his right where Lay stood searching through holographic screens in air. "Anything Lay.

Anything at all?"

"Not as of yet," he said without taking his eyes off the screen. "I mean you haven't given me much to work with."

"Are you sure?" Jaden asked. "We couldn't have searched everything, there has to be something we can use."

Deshawn sat at the edge of the table, completely mesmerized. *Lay looks so cute in his little Harry Potter glasses*, He thought.

Jaden tilted his head and glared over.

Burritos...Burritos...Burritos, Deshawn thought as he got up and walked over to the far side of the room.

Imani paced the room. "Listen guys don't stress yourself. We have to believe the Creator will us his spirit to reveal us what we need to know in time."

Out of the nowhere the Book of the Anointed flew off the shelf, and sled across the table. Everyone flinched. The book flung itself open and flipped pages until it came to the story of Solomon.

Deshawn jumped back. "That's it, we need to put a lock on this thing or better yet a chain."

"It's only done this three times since I've had it," Coach Franklin replied. "Go ahead and read it son. It might have to do with our demon."

Deshawn picked it up and said, "I'm not messing with it. Here you go Lay." He tossed the book off the balcony, and it soared into Lay's hands.

Lay barely caught the book in his arms. He tilted it to

the left as he straightened his glasses.

The words in the book began highlighting themselves as Lay started to read them out loud. "Well it mentions what you said about Solomon. He was Anointed and he used a lot of demons to build his kingdom. The angels taught him how to trap and control demons. He was pretty successful until he came across this demon named Asmodeus."

Imani took a seat at the table. "Keep reading Lay."

"Listen to this," Lay continued. "Asmodeus is the demon of lust. He lusts for flesh and likes to possess men and compel them to do unspeakable acts to women. Asmodeus has the ability to channel lightening into his hands. It even says that the few men he did kill...he electrocuted them until their heads popped off."

Deshawn wrapped his hands around his head. "That doesn't sound like fun." Out of the corner of his eye he took a quick glance at evil Elroy in his case. He was sticking his middle finger up at Deshawn.

"Get back to the story. How do we kill it," Romeo questioned.

Deshawn tapped Romeo. "Look," he whispered as he pointed.

Elroy sat dormant with a smile on his face. His orange nose pointed and bright, his black eyes glossy, and his pinstripe bow tie fixed perfect.

"Stop playing," Romeo said with a frown.

Lay focused back towards the pages of the book, "It says Solomon was given a ring by an angel that allowed him domination over demons. Asmodeus managed to get this ring and when he did he took over the kingdom. After he got rid of Solomon, the demon threw away the ring in a river because he thought he didn't need it anymore. Somehow a few years later Solomon found the ring in a fish and he banished the demon back to hell. The ring since then has been known as Solomon's seal.

Jaden looked over to Romeo, "I think that's the ring you've been seeing in your dreams."

Lay placed the book on the table. "So my guess is we get Solomon's Seal and we get rid of the demon." He said with a hint of uncertainty.

Deshawn threw his hands up, "Oh great. How are we going to do that?"

Romeo staggered back as he was smacked by some invisible force. His eyes rolled to the back of his head. A smirk swept across his face. "It's coming tonight at the airport on a FedEx plane. We can go get it, but we won't be alone."

Lay continued reading and his eyes grew large. "Oh no this is not good. We can't let him get that ring before us!" he shouted loudly.

"Why not?" Coach Franklin asked.

Lay turned the book upside down, "The book warns he will turn into this."

They all gasped.

"Sweet black Jesus," Coach Franklin gasped.

"Sweet Jesus indeed Coach." Ms. Day as she strutted into the room, with a folder in her hand. "I just heard from the Shepherds Guild and they sent me everything they knew about the reaping." She threw the file on the table, and looked up at coach. "It's a ceremony to open the Hell gate."

Coach Franklin looked at her as if all the life had been sucked out of his face. "Well this just keeps getting better and better."

Ms. Day pointed a finger. "And wait there's more. There are already five activated. This would be the sixth."

"It would explain all the strange phenomenon that have been going on lately." Lay asserted.

Romeo sat up, "What are you talking about?"

Lay paced back and forth. "I talk to computers and I can see the internet. There has been some strange stuff going on lately. Death plagues, demon dogs, terrorist attacks, an increase in hauntings."

Deshawn swung his legs over. "The whole world has gone to hell."

Jaden shrugged. "What else is new?"

"Very well but it seems we are headed for rough waters," Ms. Day declared. "Imani have you heard anything from SMITE."

Imani swallowed hard. "SMITE believes that the Sons of Chaos are planning something big. There are three devils topside. One of them being Asmodeus, and the others Balthazar and Legion. I hear Balthazar is attempting to open the Hell gate in Berlin. They have sent Raphael after him and I believe it must be up to us to hold the line and prevent Asmodeus from opening the gate here."

Coach Franklin slammed his fist on the table. "I can't believe it." He sighed and waited a beat before he spoke again. "Well I hope you are ready gentleman, because Hell is knocking on the front door."

"Literally," Jaden added.

Deshawn clapped his hands. "But what are we going to do about it?"

"We need to get that ring," Romeo spoke up.

"I agree Jaden added. We can't let Asmodeus get juiced up." And there was a bone-chilling shudder that went down Jaden's spine as he said the demon's name for the first time.

Coach Franklin looked over to Lay, "Can you look up-"

"Found it," Lay interjected.

Imani stood up. "Let's go get it. I'm coming with you."

Everyone started putting on coats when Ms. Day spoke again. "Lay can you stay behind and help us research? Now that we know who this demon is and his plan. We have to use everything we can to figure out how to destroy it."

Lay nodded, "Sure."

"Rest of you roll out and stay safe out there." Coach Franklin said.

"We'll be straight Coach. Let's bail guys," Jaden declared.

J. MOON

CHAPTER TWENTY-NINE

Express Delivery

The arrival of another cargo aircraft roared outside and made the management office tremble. Jaden searched through the office computer looking for clues, while Romeo, Deshawn, and Imani ransacked the drawers of the office.

Jaden adjusted the volume on his headphones. "I'm not seeing a thing Lay."

Lay pulled up the shipment records in front of him at the Sanctuary. In his right hand a revolving arc of blue and white lights that controlled the holographic screen in front of him. "It's called the Ode to Solomon. I'm sending it over to you now."

"This is it," Jaden shouted as he clicked and scrolled down.

Romeo gaped at the computer screen. "Nice." He paused to read the description of the shipped item. "Ode to King Solomon. It's a 16th-century statue recovered from Spain." A sudden flash in his head showed Romeo the marvelous golden ring. "The ring is hidden inside the statue."

"But where is the statue?" Deshawn asked as he slammed a file cabin.

Imani walked over to Jaden's side. "It might be in temporary storage or a sorting facility."

Jaden searched further in the computer database. "Yeah that's what it says on the list. It has been stored but the question is where." Jaden lifted his headphone closer to his ear. "Anything Lay."

Lay scrolled through the hologram screens in front of him several times. Sweat beaded in the space between his glasses and eyes. "Not sure. The storage location information is blank." He brought his left hand up and a holographic keyboard rose. "Searching the layout of the airport's facility."

Imani hoovered over Jaden's shoulder. "Does he know where it is?"

He swirled his head to the left. Imani pressed against his cheek. "No, he's looking it up now." Jaden lingered in her gaze.

Deshawn slapped his hand on the desk nearby. "Stop with all that lovey dovey mess." Then he popped his head between the two of them. "Listen Johnny, if I can't date her then neither can you."

Imani hit him in the arm. "Shut up."

"Ouch! You're the most violent angel I've ever met." He said as he grabbed his arm.

"Got it," Lay's voice said through the phone. "Based on the layout of the airport hangar, the statue will either be in the warehouse you are currently in or the one on the other side."

Jaden nodded, "Great." He pulled his headphone away from his mouth as he spoke to the others. "It's either in this warehouse or the other one. We should split up into pairs and search each warehouse."

"That sounds good to me," Romeo commented.

Imani folded her arms, "Well me and Jaden can search this one, while you two search the other one."

Deshawn shot her a nasty look, "What?"

Jaden smirked, "You heard the lady."

"Weapons?" He asked.

Deshawn tossed two Nike book bags on the desk. Inside were flashlights, crosses, wooden stakes and water guns filled with holy water. Romeo grabbed a large double pump water gun that was leaking all over. "Again why couldn't we bring the guns and the wooden core bullets. Hell, I would be even glad to have some steel, a large knife, a pair of daggers .....anything better than these wooden stakes. It's going to take us forever to dust these vamps."

"How do you expect to sneak into an airport with guns and weapons?" Jaden asked candidly.

"I don't know but we could've tried," Romeo added as he shoved a stake in the pocket of his leather jacket.

Deshawn pumped his water gun. "I feel you. This makes me feel like a kid. But then again imagine if we were caught with real weapons. Homeland security would throw us under a jail cell, or in some government prison with some guy called Big Larry whose underwear we would have to iron every day. I'm not about that life."

They all raised an eye at Deshawn. Imani opened the door, "Okay let's go boys. Good luck and remember this is an extraction mission. All we want is the ring."

Deshawn saluted, "Sir Yes sir! Oh, I mean Mam… yes Mam. Soldier out." he shouted as he shuffled out of the office with Romeo following behind.

As the two strolled away, Jaden turned to Imani with a Cheshire cat smile on his face. "Now it's just the two of us."

She laughed and even though her eyes were tough as usual, she still couldn't hide the blush of her cheeks, and joy in her smile. "Calm down Hollywood. I don't want you to be too far. You might pass out again and I would have to heal you for the hundredth time."

"That's true," Jaden agreed as he stood up from the computer desk.

*****

Deshawn and Romeo stepped out of the warehouse, and were met by multiple blood curdling screams. Wails loud enough to match the roars of another plane landing. Looking at each other, Romeo and Deshawn could recognize those cries of pain anywhere.

Bloodthirsty vampires fed on Workers of a nearby aircraft. Like a pack of wild dogs, the vampires all dressed in black, violently fed on the workers as they ripped limbs and body parts apart. Rich red nectar covered their chins as they chomped and chewed at necks.

Deshawn turned to Romeo, "True bloods. Do you

think that our package came from the plane over there?"

"I don't know. But let's go see!" Romeo blurted as he immediately charged over to the blood fest.

"Wait a minute... Romeo, I thought this was an extraction mission. I could've sworn Imani said we were just here to get the ring and not fight if we don't have to. Aww man here it goes," Deshawn sighed as he reluctantly followed behind.

The delicious scent of anointed blood danced up the nose of one vampire as he incessantly munched the neck of a worker slumped over a lift. "Something smells good," he declared as he wiped blood off his chin. The others immediately stuck their nose in the air as they picked up the scent.

With their fangs drenched in blood, the vampires tossed their current meals to the side and prepared for battle. One of them hopped over the crane and attacked Romeo. He shot him a mouthful of holy water. The vampire spew blood as he fell to the ground thrashing, smoke wafting from his body, until he turned into ashes. His fellow brethren roared like starving lions and they sprung into battle.

Soaring down from the sky came two vamps male and female, down upon Deshawn. He tucked and rolled. Pumping the water gun, he splashed the male on the forehead and shot at the female who dodged the stream of water. The male retreated as he smoked and sizzled. She kicked the water gun out of Deshawn's hands. Immediately she met the back of his fist as he then tossed her over his shoulder and down to the ground, he reached underneath his shirt to grab silver, and plunged it into her heart.

Romeo attacked the vampires with his water gun like a trained seal holding an assault rifle. Flipping over various cargo handling equipment the vampires relentlessly attacked Romeo, who turned them into ashes headshot after headshot of holy water. One of them managed to catch Romeo off guard as it pounced on his back. Romeo spun around as he fought to keep the salivating fangs from the vampire off his neck, then he backed into the side of the abandoned cargo plane. The vamp fell to the pavement in a heap. Romeo took its head off with a precise beam of light from his fingertips.

"You boys better run if you know what's good for you." He boasted cockily, watching the ashes swirl into the air.

Suddenly he was lifted up high and tossed over head by a freakishly large vampire. "Bruce smells something good," the overgrown vampire exclaimed with his mouth watering.

Deshawn dusted another vampire. Looking ahead he saw Romeo cowering beneath the mutant size vampire. "Hold on Rome, I got big boy," he shouted as he ran to dropkick the vampire in its chest.

Looking more annoyed than hurt, the vampire staggered back almost unfazed. "Lively little boys huh? That's okay I like my fish squirming."

"Fry this!" Deshawn spat back as he charged energy in his hand and then tossed. The charged particles blew a hole into the vampire's chest the size of a basketball. With a shocked look on his face, the large vampire burned into a large pile of dust.

Romeo rose to his feet and wiped himself down. "Good looks," Romeo said before he gave a celebratory fist bump.

Deshawn looked around at the cargo that would've been properly stored before the vampire's attack. "So do you think the statue might be in one of these crates or on the plane?"

Romeo quickly scanned around, "No let's just go to the other warehouse."

"Wait how do you know?"

"I see the future remember. And also the computer in the office said it was already stored. This plane looked like it just landed."

"You've got a point," Deshawn agreed with a wagging finger as he followed Romeo to other cargo holding warehouse.

Twenty minutes in and twelve dusted vampires later, the two were still empty handed as they searched the warehouse up and down. Romeo used his fist as a flashlight as they continued their search. Stacked up to the ceiling were shelves upon shelves of cargo.

Deshawn wiped sweat and someone's blood off his forehead. "Man some psychic you are. Where is the statue Romeo? We should've went right to it, you know with your visions and all," he sneered.

"Shut up!" Romeo replied as he shined on another

large crate overhead.

"Whatever." Deshawn rolled his eyes. "Just know I wouldn't pay you a dime to tell me my future."

"Wait," Romeo said with a restraining hand. Eyes rolling back, he saw dark wings slowly descend upon Jaden as Imani laid slumped in a corner. "We have to go. Jaden and Imani are in trouble. This is the wrong warehouse."

Deshawn threw up his hands, "I told you."

They sprinted down a long aisle towards the door, with the light emitting from Romeo's fist cutting through the darkness of the warehouse. Again Romeo paused to stop.

"Another vision?" Deshawn asked, concerned.

"Move!" Romeo shouted as he shoved Deshawn out of the way, while he himself rolled backwards.

Fangz came crashing down upon them roaring, his fangs fully extended to a deadly nine inches as air ran through his long dreads. "What's happening boys. We meet again," he barked in his heavy southern accent.

Deshawn stuck out a cross into the vampire's face. Fangz growled before quickly knocking the cross out of Deshawn's hand. Romeo bent light into a ball before he hurled it at the vampire. In a blink of an eye, the master vampire dodged the attack and tossed Romeo high up into crates stacked close to the ceiling.

"One down," Fangz gritted with his eyes ignited by the lust for blood.

Deshawn backed up as the vampire slowly confronted him. Without thought he tried to throw a charged particle towards Fangz, but in a motion too quick to be seen, the vampire dodged it.

Deshawn cursed under his breath, then he used his power to ripple time around the master. In jerky fast and slow movements, the vampire resisted.

"Uh oh. Well I didn't expect that." Deshawn said as he cautiously kept his distance.

"Cute trick kid. But I'm a master. It takes more than some hocus pocus to slow me down" Fangz cockily boasted with a hearty laugh.

"I didn't take you to be lackey Fangz. What's good?"

Fangz roared, the sound rolled around the warehouse like thunder. "I'm not a lackey."

"Then why are you helping Asmodeus."

Fangz cackled, "Who said I was doing that? I want the ring for myself. It does grant user dominion over demons." Then he straightened himself, "And that could become very useful, especially if the Hell Gate reopens. Imagine me being the first vampire with legions of demons at my command. I could be-" Fangz thought about for a moment, and a smile appeared on his face. "I could be king of the world."

Deshawn shook his head in agreement. "I could see that."

"You know it's too bad," Fangz said in a sympathetic tone. "You could've been one of my children. But you and your little friends have been ruining my operation for a while. So I'm going to have to kill you. Don't worry it will only hurt for a few minutes." He opened his mouth wide and his fangs extended further down to ten inches.

Deshawn took off his jacket. "Alright then. Boom bye bye batty boy. I'm going to show you how a real rasta throws down. You bombaclot!" Deshawn replied in the worst attempt at a Jamaican accent possible.

Fangz lunged at him with his fist, and Deshawn blocked each attack with the ease of a boxer, once he spotted an opening in Fangz defense, he knocked the vampire off his feet with a front kick. Scrambling to regain his balance the vampire whizzed to Deshawn's left to land a sucker punch that caught Deshawn off guard. He shrugged it off and returned with two quick right jabs and a left hook of his own.

Pissed, the vampire flung his arm and caught Deshawn with an invisible fist. Deshawn made a strangled cry as he crashed into the wall, and toppled to the floor. Deshawn shook it off and stood on his feet. He charged towards Fangz, and the vampire spun out of the way, quick as the wind. Deshawn wrestled a stake from his back and ran it into the chest of the master vampire.

Fangz wobbled back as he held on to the piece of wood. He snatched it out of his chest and snapped it like a twig. "You missed. This is my chest not my heart." The vampire said with a snarl as he prepared to attack Deshawn again.

Deshawn clasped his fingers and released his explosive power near Fangz' chest. The Master vampire peered down at the wound with his black stagnant heart exposed. Fangz released a guttural growl as he examined the open wound with his hands covered in the black fluid that flowed from his chest. "We'll do this again!" Fangz declared as he crumbled into a dozen or so bats, that flew out into the night's sky.

Deshawn waved at the vampire as he flew away. "Boom bye bye batty boy."

Romeo struggled to climb down off of the shelf where he landed. DeShawn gave him a hand. "Let's move it Cleo, we have to go save the others," He said as they limped their way out of the warehouse and back across to the main one.

Chapter Thirty

Spreading of Wings

"Come on!" Jaden shouted as he grabbed Imani's hand, and they dashed down the aisle, bullets flew overhead as they narrowly turned the corner. Security guards possessed by demons thundered after them. With his heart about to pound out of his chest, Jaden frantically looked for a way out.

Footsteps pounded down the aisle. "There! Don't let them escape!"

Down another aisle they went as flashlights followed behind. "Wait here. I'll take them out one by one." Jaden commanded. Imani agreed without protest.

He sprinted back down the aisle. A guard aimed his pistol at Jaden's head. Jaden used his power to send him crashing into the wall, crumbling with several packages to the floor. Jaden stepped over the unconscious guard to kick away the gun.

Around the corner, a small group of guards sprinted his way. "There he is. Don't let him escape!"

Jaden connected eyes with one of the guards leading

the pack. "Attack." He commanded with his inner voice. The command echoed in the guard's head, and his pupils dilated. The guard turned around to the three others that followed him and opened fire. When all that was left of the group was the guard under his mind control, Jaden pummeled him to the ceiling by telekinetic force.

Just as he was about to catch a breath, Jaden heard more footsteps creeping his way from behind. Quickly he spun around, ready to attack.

"Wait it's just me!" Imani shouted with her hands in the air.

Jaden sighed, "I thought I told you to wait for me."

"I thought they might have shot you. But I guess you really can handle yourself," Imani said as she observed the bodies lain out over the floor.

"I can," Jaden returned.

A loud shatter erupted in the darkness. They both jumped. The source of the noise came from the next aisle over. Shining his flashlight, Jaden took slow steps towards the adjacent aisle.

Imani followed behind, her eyes trying to cut through darkness. "What was that?"

"It came from the next aisle," Jaden whispered as he walked around the corner, his flashlight leading the way.

As he made his way down the aisle it felt like he was stepping on rocks. Jaden aimed the flashlight down at his feet. Bits of stone scattered the floor. He pointed the flashlight further down. A sudden realization almost made Jaden want to collapse. They had spent the whole night searching for the statue and there it was in front of him, slashed in half.

Asmodeus wrestled Solomon's seal out of the center of the statue. Then the demon slipped the ring on his finger.

"Oh my god!" Imani muttered.

Thunder cracked in the sky, and the floor underneath them jittered. As the building shook, crates fell off the top shelves and rained around them. Jaden and Imani braced themselves. Asmodeus spun back into the darkness.

Jaden watched as the demon disappeared. "I can't believe this is happening. He is turning." Jaden yelled as the warehouse continued to tremble.

Imani anchored herself on a column, "Don't lose faith on me now. We can still stop him. Believe!"

The warehouse stopped shaking and Asmodeus leapt into the air.

Asmodeus floated above them with his body shifting into something more sinister and evil. Thick black horns twisted out of his skull. His skin hardened and cracked like cement. The talons on his hands and feet grew thicker and clenched. Massive dark wings clouded the moonlight as they grew from the demon's back. The shadows casted on the walls of the warehouse revealed a demonic hell bat.

Asmodeus grabbed Imani's shoulders with his clenched feet and tossed her across the warehouse.

"Imani!" Jaden shouted as he watched her being flung into the darkness.

The powerful flaps of the demon's wings echoed

against the walls of the warehouse. Asmodeus circled around Jaden like a vulture waiting to dive and feed. Jaden sprinted down the aisle. The demon flew furiously behind him, narrowing its wings and increasing its speed. Glancing over his shoulder, Jaden launched crate after crate towards the demon with his mind. Cunning and agile the demon easily navigated pass each object aimed at him. Asmodeus grinned in excitement. He could sense the fear and despair in Jaden's spirit and it made him enjoy the hunt so much more.

In a lithe move, Asmodeus dove to snatch Jaden. As if lead by the creator himself, Jaden ducked soon as Asmodeus tried to swoop in for him. The demon soared pass, and the wind that trailed behind knocked more crates and items off the shelves.

Jaden stood to his feet and lined the demon in his aim of fire. Waving his hand, he knocked the demon out of the air with a crate stacked on the ceiling. Asmodeus fell to the floor, with his wings flapping in a frenzy.

Jaden attacked him without second thought. Anointed warrior instincts took him over as they locked in for battle. Initially they fought blow for blow with neither gaining the upper hand. The tide of the battle changed when Jaden allowed a right jab to go unblocked. Knocked off balance, the demon swiftly took advantage by chucking an orb of electricity into Jaden's chest. Jaden sled across the floor before crashing into a wall.

Asmodeus sneered. "And now you can go be with mommy," the demon slurred as he prepared another shock ball in his claws.

"And you can go to hell homeboy," Romeo shouted as he blasted the demon with a beaming ball of light. Sparks lit up the warehouse as the demon flew ahead.

Deshawn went to Jaden's side as he got up. "You straight?"

Jaden shook his head, "He's got the ring. We have to stop him."

Asmodeus levitated off the ground. His horns were ready to ram into flesh. "You can't stop me!" He yelled with a grit.

Asmodeus raised his hands towards the sky in a devout manner. The demon was summoning a powerful force to his aid. Sounds of thunder filled the night sky as the building shook. A brilliant light shined above the warehouse. "Feel the wrath of my fury," Asmodeus bellowed. Crashing down the ceiling came a thunder bolt that shook the building, shattered the ceiling, and struck them all. Each one of the anointed laid out across the floor.

A faint voice called out to Jaden and made his eyes flutter. He looked incredulously at his hands and feet, as an ungodly smell of burning flesh wafted into his nose. He was smoking. They all were. He was the only one attempting to stand. Romeo and Deshawn laid beside him seemingly dead.

"Jaden you have to get him!" Imani commanded as she kneeled over Jaden with her voice coming in and out.

Jaden rubbed his eyes and squinted into the dust. The echoes of the fight muffled in his ears, and his knees struggled to support his body as he attempted to stand up. What he was able to make out were the large wings of the demon. He focused upon that and levitated the shards of broken glass around him. In a sweeping motion the shards rose up all around him, dancing and swirling in crimson energy, and like a python awaiting to strike, they all rose viciously and one swoop. Then when he whisked his hand, they shards all shot forward like a cannon, and ripped apart Asmodeus' right wing. And the cry the demon made in agonizing pain, was so loud and dreadful, that it made him cover his ears, and fall back down to his knees.

Deeply wounded, Asmodeus screamed and shattered the remaining windows. He squatted down to the floor, and shot up into the night's sky.

Jaden collapsed as he felt all of his strength leave his body. He peered over at Romeo and Deshawn who were sprawled out beside him. Sadly, he glances at Imani, "Are they dead?"

Imani knelt beside Romeo. "Almost. But I can heal them."

Jaden sighed in relief, "Good. Just imagine what we would do if you weren't here," he said.

Asmodeus swooped in and snatched Imani off the ground.

Jaden rolled over to his knees. "Imani!" He shouted.

Chapter Thirty-One

Seeing the Light

Jaden watched as the last bit of hope for saving his friends flew away. Asmodeus clenched Imani's shoulders tightly within his talons as he flew up and out of the gaping hole. Jaden fell back out on the floor as he watched the demon flap away into the night. Every ounce of strength he had seemed to fade farther and farther away. Jaden tried to force himself to stand but every muscle in his body ached, including his legs which felt like spaghetti.

Romeo and Deshawn remained still beside him. Neither of them moved an inch. He dragged himself over to Romeo whose ears filled with red. "Romeo get up," he murmured as he shook him.

Nothing.

Romeo didn't flinch.

Jaden rolled over. "Deshawn are you good?" he called. Deshawn's head remained tucked between his arm. "Deshawn…. it's Jerry. Say something!"

Jaden closed his eyes. "Please don't let it end like this. Please Creator—" He was brought to silence at the clamoring of footsteps near. One low moaning snarl in the darkness triggered many others to join in. Jaden's blood became ice with the sudden terror that loomed around him.

He rolled over and saw various shapes in the pitch blackness of the warehouse, slink towards him. He didn't have an ounce of strength to fend them off.

"What do we do now, without Fangz?" One uncertain voice asked in the darkness.

There was a guttural moan that echoed on Jaden's right and he turned to it.

"I don't know about you but I could go for some anointed right about now."

A female spoke from the other side. "I heard they taste like the most tender piece of steak. Like Ruth Chris or Outback or something."

"Umm I love steak," another voice said from the right.

Another growl sounded in the middle. "Alrighty then let's eat."

Inwardly Jaden hoped death would come swift and quick. The vamps took one step out of the darkness, and suddenly the light from the night sky grew incredible. One lone beam shined above them all, as wide and far reaching as the sun.

Shining light filled the cargo warehouse, and the vampires hissed and sizzled, as the light etched out their shapes in the darkness. Jaden looked up while trying to shield his eyes that an incredible light. He saw wings, the most beautiful set of wings he had ever seen, the hinges were gold, while the middle looked made out of a wrought armor. The ground trembled, as whatever flew above them dropped and landed with a powerful thud that knocked everyone off their feet,

Jaden rolled over as the light faded. A mountain of a man, adorned in gold and made of pure muscle, stood.

And the spirit of truth revealed his identity to Jaden. "Michael," he breathed incredulously.

The Archangel looked up from his kneeling position and all of the vampires, dropped fang and hissed like angry cats. Michael reached behind his back and brought up his sword, which pulsated a radiant light that reduced all of the vampires to dust instantly.

This was all Jaden saw before darkness descended upon him, his eyes struggled to stay open, and everything turned to black.

******

"I can't believe it," Ms. Day said. "An archangel here in front of me. I thought I would never see the day, just wait until I tell the Shepherd's Guild. We have so many questions to ask you about heaven and about SMITE."

"All will be revealed due time. I have come because I am needed. The Sons of Chaos have declared war against all who make up the Sons of Light. As I speak to you the demons are attempting to shatter the gates of heaven." Michael declared in his regal baritone.

"How in the hell can they do that?" Coach Franklin

muttered.

"I'm not sure, I've heard this news only through chimes as I descended to Earth. It is too late for me to turn back now, fore I am needed and here. So I trust the creator to enable my brothers and fellow agents of SMITE to hold the line. One thing I know for sure is if SMITE were too fall, and Asmodeus allowed the other Sons of Chaos entry to this world, then we will truly be in the era of a new dawn."

Jaden struggled to force his eyes open. He heard the voice of the creator and he stirred. When laid eyes on the archangel who he had to admit to himself, looked like a God among men with his incredible physique, another truth was revealed to him.

"It's you!" Jaden cried out. The two words were sharp enough to send agony in his throat which was still dry and raw.

"Jaden!" Lay cried out. "Drink this," he commanded as he presented water to Jaden.

Jaden drank fast and coughed as the water went down the wrong pipe. He wiped his lips. "It's you," Jaden shouted again.

Deshawn stood to the left. "I said the same thing to myself Jerry, a real life freaking archangel. Can you believe it?"

Jaden shook his head. "No." Then he struggled over to Michael. "It's you. You're the voice in my head. You called yourself the Creator. But you're not. You're just an angel."

"Yes it is me," Michael admitted.

"What?" Ms. Day gasped.

Jaden turned to her. "The day I confronted Asmodeus. I heard a voice in my head that lead me to him. You claimed to be the maker of heavens and Earth. And I believed you. Why did you lie?" Jaden stood. "Huh? Answer me." His voice shook with searing rage.

Michael held out a defensive hand. "Descendant of David, please calm down. If weren't for me, the three of you would be dead," he replied bluntly. The archangel paused as he allowed that truth to sit in. "Secondly, did you really think your meager human existence could comprehend the splendor of the Creator's voice?"

Romeo sat up from the cot he laid on. "Hey dumbass watch your mouth. You don't have to talk to him like that."

Michael glanced over at him and shot him a look. "The true voice of God would destroy him. This is the same voice that spoke life and light into existence. It would burn him inside and out to hear the glory of the Creator's voice. So I spoke from heaven as other angels have done before me."

Jaden cocked his head from the side, "How did you know so much about me?"

"Like every anointed warrior, you had a file."

Jaden took a breath as his head dropped to the floor. "So what about the baby? I risked my life for it and lost my mom to save it. Where is the baby now? And why have you been guiding me this whole time."

Michael took a step towards him. "The child is

insignificant. He was just an innocent that needed to be saved. Even though I have deceived you, I have never lied to you. The Creator has called your name and you are the one the oil flows out for. I needed you to be strong for this battle, and I needed you to be ready to lead this group. And I also had to conceal my movements. The Sons of Chaos would've focus all of their resources if they knew for sure I would land here."

Michael glanced back at Coach Franklin and Ms. Day. "Raphael has vanquished Balthazar in Berlin, but he was unable to stop the fifth Hell gate from opening. With all six Hell gates open, the Sons of Chaos can make their way into Earth."

Michael paced the room, "The Sons are the most powerful demons in hell. Most of them are fallen angels and the others are dangerously cunning enough to gain ranks. Either way if they are allowed entry topside, they will plot to seize control of the land, and raise their own legions."

Lay walked from around the corner of Jaden's cot. "Oh no that's not good. Not good at all."

"Apologies about what happen to your mother. But now you have to put that aside because I have come to warn you. You have a mission." Michael declared with authority. "We have to go find the Hell gate and shut it down."

"No!" Jaden replied back. "I'm not going on another one of your missions. I lost my mother trying to complete one of your missions. I refuse to go through that again,"

Jaden said as he hopped up out of the chair and headed for the door.

Romeo stopped him, "Wait bro. We need to hear whatever he has to say. Asmodeus has Imani." Romeo shouted, his eyes large and intense.

Once that realization settled into Jaden's head, he knew what had to be done. "I'm going to go get her." Then he turned his head and shot an icy glance towards the archangel. "Not because some angel told me too, but because that's my girl."

Deshawn stood up, "Wait a minute. Our girl."

Coach held his hands up. "Just hold on for a second. I don't think you boys know what you're getting yourselves into." He took a deep aching breath, as fear swept over his face. "I've been to an abyss before once in my lifetime, and it wasn't pretty. I saw true horrors down there. Monsters you could only have nightmares about. More than the locusts, changing faces, or vampires. I'm talking human centipedes, Black Cobras, Nephilim the size of giants, and just a whole bunch of nasties. There was seven us when I went down there and I was the only one that made it back out. That night I lost Romeo's father, Orlando and I promised him I would raise and protect his son. I'll be damned if you die on my watch."

"You can't stop me," Romeo declared. Then he glanced over to Jaden, "If you go down there, then I'm going with you."

A big smile swept across Deshawn's face as looked over to Lay. "Are you in?"

Lay folded his glasses. "I got left behind last time but

not this time."

"That's my boy. Ride or die." Deshawn dapped him up.

"Gentlemen please," Ms. Day said with trepidation in her voice. "This is a very serious matter, and I think you have to realize how much danger such a mission, should be." She raked her gaze towards Michael. "Can you please tell us why he would want Imani in the first place."

"He needs her as a sacrifice," Michael answered. "The blood of the lamb is needed to open the Hell gate."

A quizzical look came across Lay's face. "Correct me if I'm wrong, but I don't think Imani is a lamb."

Ms. Day nodded as she thought it through her head. "Not literally Lay. A lamb just means an innocent soul."

"And there is nothing more innocent than an angel," Romeo finished.

"That's not all." Michael stated.

Jaden raked a hand through his wooly hair. "What do you mean that's not all?"

Coach Franklin sat with his elbows on his knees. "Hell gate is going to need more blood once it's open, and the demons are going to need hosts when they come out."

Michael circled the table, "As we speak Asmodeus is probably capturing innocent people and dragging them to abyss. He intends on sacrificing them and opening a Hell gate here in the city. He needs seventy-two sacrifices for his seventy-two legion of demons he wants to bring onto this plane from hell."

"Sweet Jesus," Coach Franklin uttered with a grim look on his face.

Romeo cocked his head, "Seventy-two legions? How many is that?"

"Thousands upon Thousands. It's a lot," Lay said turning towards Romeo.

"Yes it is," Michael continued. "Demons like Angels just can't simply make their way physically onto this plane since we are divine spirits. Demons need cracked souls to possess a human. We angels require devout souls."

Jaden folded his arms, "So right now you're possessing someone."

"Not exactly," Michael declared. "His soul is in heaven. We angels tend to inhabit fallen soldiers and heroes. Men and women of honor once they die. And we can hold onto these vessels for centuries."

Michael stood up in Jaden's face, "I want you to stop it. You are the chosen ones. The only anointed in this generation. You were born to do this. Once upon there were hundreds of anointed, now there are only a handful."

"Why didn't you just stop all of this yourself. Aren't you supposed to be an all-powerful archangel? Why put us up to it?" Jaden spat angrily.

"Because we can't," Michael barked back as he stepped closer to Jaden's face. The two stared each other down. "We can't interfere. We can only influence. Trust me I know what a burden this is." Michael said with his tone softening.

Michael stepped aside, "Trust me you can do this. With the Holy Spirit as your power you can do anything. You're not alone. We fight the spiritual war while you fight the physical one."

"Well that is a big help," Jaden said sarcastically.

Michael placed a hand on Jaden 's shoulder. Jaden looked at it with mixed emotions. "I meant everything I said that day five months ago. You will be a king among men. But it won't be easy." He turned to look at everyone in the room. "For all of you it won't be easy. King, prophet, priest, and peacemaker. The power of your destinies come with a price. I don't know why you worry though. Tomorrow you will face Asmodeus and you will win for he the creator is with you and has already said so. It is up to you to accept him. You will fight hard with faith or will you fall from being succumb with fear. The choice is yours."

Michael's words touched each one of them. They were all silent. Looking at each other. Trying to find the courage to overcome fear and except destiny. Michael started to walk out of the room, then he stopped and turned back around.

"Did you get the package?" He asked.

Confusion swept them all.

Deshawn looked around, "Package. What package?"

"The package that should've been sent here yesterday by Shipquick.com." Michael replied.

Immediately Coach Franklin went to the adjacent

office in the study and brought out a large brown box. "I was wondering what the hell this was. I thought it was some boxing equipment or something."

"Open it.... all of you" Michael commanded.

Coach Franklin ripped the tape off the box with Deshawn's help. Green cushion peanuts fell out as Coach Franklin dug into the box and pulled out a long slim battle axe with a royal blue metallic ending, a long silver handle and jagged sharp tip. The weapon glistened in the light as Coach Franklin held it up.

"It's a battle-ax called Grace. A weapon forged in holy heaven fire and blessed by warrior angels called the powers. It's for you Deshawn. There are more weapons in the box. They are the only things on Earth that can permanently kill demonic agents or people who are possessed."

Deshawn's eyes lit up as he quickly snatched the weapon out of Coach Franklin's hands. "For me? And it's not even my birthday." Deshawn swung and slashed the air with the axe. The sharp blade whooshed as it cut air. "Oh Coach can I go kill something now?"

Coach Franklin raised a brow at Deshawn before digging in the box. He pulled out three more weapons. One a long sword with a marvelous golden handle and lion encrusted hilt. The other appeared to be a large throwing weapon with twin intricately cut steel blades in the shape of a semicircle. And the last a stick that was a hand sized stick.

"The Wings of Mercy goes to you Romeo, The Sword of the Holy spirit is yours Jaden, and the Spear of destiny belongs to you Lay. Use them well. Fight with faith tonight as the full moon set."

Michael handed him the blade, and Jaden saw light sparkle off the hilt of the weapon. It was beautifully crafted, the blade was a gorgeous metal, the hilt made of glittering fold.

They grabbed the weapons and looked them over in awe. Lay took hold of the stick, with a tight grip from his hand, both sides extended to full length.

Lay whirled the staff in his hands. "Impressive. It doesn't glow but I can upgrade it."

"Thanks but how do we reach you," Romeo said looking for Michael. But the Angel was gone.

Chapter Thirty-Two

There will be Blood

The abyss buzzed with activity as all prepared for the reaping. Vampires directed gagged innocents in large clusters towards the makeshift holding cell that already contained over three dozen victims.

Asmodeus stood overhead on a balcony overlooking everything. Candles lit the altar of the gothic cathedral erected within the abyss. The possessed walked below repeating prayers.

Eva sashayed to his side. "Are we pleased?" She asked in a low sensual tone, running her hand across his chest.

Asmodeus smiled. "Very. Once this gate opens, all of my brothers will be free." He said.

The demon looked onward to Imani who dangled from across suspended from the adjacent balcony. In all white, she had her eyes closed tightly as she murmured desperate prayers. They were not for her but for the paragons she vowed to protect, Jaden, Deshawn, Romeo and Lay. She cared not what happened to her. They were important. They needed protection. And they needed all the help they can get to defeat the darkness that was about to spill out of the abyss.

Asmodeus laughed at her. He floated off the balcony and stood before her. "Soon it will be time to bleed this lamb," Asmodeus bellowed as he pointed towards Imani. She narrowed her eyes at him. "This sacrifice will be the start of it all. A new beginning and a new dawn." The demon shouted with all the evil creatures below looking up to him in the rafters. "Tonight we will destroy one of his beautiful creations and the Earth shall tremble. He will know we are to be feared. And he will watch just like they all will watch as the Sons of chaos trample over his greatest creation. In the end the Creator will have nothing." Asmodeus roared to all the demonic entities below. Multiple sneers and shrieks of laughter rumbled along the walls of the abyss.

Imani tugged on her ropes, "I'm not afraid. When this body is destroyed, I know I'm going home. You on the hand are going on hot ticket back to hell. The Creator is still in control. His spirit strengthens me and the anointed. His hand will strike you down. I can guarantee that. They are coming and his will shall be done."

Asmodeus cackled, "Let them come. Either way there will be blood. We will strike against our oppressors and I will bring freedom to my brothers."

Imani frowned. "Oppressors?"

The demon dove to her ear. "Oppressors," he repeated. "For eons the angels and the Creator have kept us trapped in the Hell dimension. Long before the Creator came, we existed as creatures of emotion. Creatures who fed off of joy, lust, love, or anything felt like a living being. He brought forth the light and pushed us out of our home to make us own. He chained us like dogs. We were starved. But the only one emotion we could feed on is fear. And now we will rise and spread fear across the land, growing stronger than he could ever imagine."

"You can miss me with the sympathy for the devil crap." Imani said with frown.

Asmodeus strangled her. "I don't need your sympathy. I only require your blood." He ran his hand down her chest. "As I speak plans are in motion to break down the gates of SMITE. We will strike at the center of his fortress. The Sons of Chaos will reign over Earth and together we will usher in a new night."

Asmodeus strolled over to Fangz, who was still licking his wounds from the last battle. "I have decided to make some changes."

Fangz curled his lip. "Changes?"

Garrett walked over and stood beside Asmodeus. "For now on Garrett will give command over the True Bloods."

"But they're my children." Fangz declared.

Asmodeus choked the air and Fangz levitated off the ground, with crackles of electricity sparking off of his feet. "Do not take the mercy I've shown you for granted."

Fangz battle bulked. "I don't want your mercy." He spun in the air and kicked the demon square across the chin.

Asmodeus reeled back and when he stood up, a swarm of bats flew away into the abyss. Several of the possessed lurched forward. "Let him go," Asmodeus commanded. Then he turned to Garrett. "I need you to go and bring me sacrifices. Gather your brood and bring back hundreds of victims."

Garrett snarled. "You got it boss. I know just the place."

He turned to the crowd of vampires. "Saddle up boys. Tonight we ride."

******

Seven black Ducati's pulled up to Safari. The line to get in wrapped around the building, and as usual the bouncers held the line to build anticipation. The vampires strolled up to them casually in a large group, as If they were VIP guests.

Tiny walked over. "What are you doing you can't park there."

Garret slashed Tiny's throat, and the towering brute of a man crumbled to the ground with his hands clutched around his neck.

"Tiny!" Marvin shouted.

Two other vampires snatched him from the side and pulled him away from the door.

*****

Tamiyah turned to Jessica and sighed. "It is super dry tonight."

"Yes god," Jessica responded. Then she scrolled down her timeline. "I heard there was a party at

Devante's house. That might be the move."

Tamiyah nodded, "That's true. But you know he and Romeo are friends. I'm not trying to see him."

Jessica cackled, "Even better. You look cute tonight. Why not? Girl, make him jealous."

A smile came across Tamiyah's face okay let's do it. As the two girls got up, the music cut off and a dozen heads looked over to the DJ booth.

"May I have your attention ladies and gentleman," Garrett said in the darkness. "Please follow my comrades and do what we say…. or die." He bellowed.

When the spotlight fell on him, the crowd released a collective gasp. Tamiyah turned to run but it was too late as she was greeted with fangs.

****

"Right here Coach," Deshawn said as he pointed.

Coach Franklin pulled the Suburban alongside one of the inner gates of Rest Haven cemetery.

Lay leaned forward from the back seat. "Do you think the way to the Hell gate is in a cemetery?"

Deshawn looked over his shoulder. "No but this is where my connect likes to hang out."

Jaden twisted up his eyebrow. "Your connect?"

Deshawn shook his head, "Yes. The residential bone carrier from hell."

Gilbert rolled two large red suitcases out of the crypt. "Hurry up fellas. Pack it all up so we can get out of here." He shouted. Mo pulled a dolly with furniture, while Larry shuffled over with a box in his hand.

Gilbert turned his head. "Oh no not the anointed

too," he grumbled under his breath.

Deshawn threw his hands in the air. "What's up big dog?"

Gilbert rolled his eyes. "Deshawn my boy. What can I do for you?"

"I need your help." Deshawn stated. He glanced over his shoulder as he introduced his companions. "These are my boys Romeo, Lay, and Jerome-"

Jaden nudged him. "Jaden."

A small bag in Gilbert's hand fell out, and rolled off on top of Deshawn's foot. "Are you going somewhere?" He asked.

Gilbert pulled off his cap and scratched at his dry scalp. "I'm about to get the hell out of this town. And you should too. Once the Hell Gate is open, the demons are going to run this joint. Trust me kid, it ain't gone be too pretty. There a lot of guys I owe souls to and I'm not looking forward to seeing them." He snapped his fingers. "Grab the rest of our stuff Larry."

Larry picked up the box, but his left arm fell off like a broken twig. "Ouch," Larry winced as the box dropped on his feet.

Lay bent over and picked up the arm. "Hi, I think you drop this."

Drool feel from Larry's mouth as he stared at Lay, making both he and Jaden frown. "Thank you."

Gilbert's scalp reminded Deshawn of a desert with one or two patches of white hair. It burned him not to make a joke about it. "Don't leave, we will stop them

319

from opening the hell gate. We just need to find out where it is."

Gilbert laughed. "Good luck with that kid. You got better chance of sneaking Hitler into heaven."

"Please if you know where it is, tell us." Jaden pleaded.

Mo stepped in front of him. "Beat it kids, he doesn't want to talk right now. Just do yourselves a favor and get out of the way.

Romeo snapped and light appeared at his fingertips. "We're not going anywhere until we get answers. So get to talking or let's get to fighting."

"Woah," Gilbert said. "There is no need for all of that." Then he turned to Deshawn. "Where did you find this fella?"

Deshawn opened the box. "Look man I didn't come empty handed."

Gilbert looked into the box and saw four innocent kittens meowed at him. He picked one up and a tear swelled in his heart. "Nope I can't do it. I'm minding my own business this time."

"And I got something else," Deshawn said as he reached behind his back. It was a large glass bottle of Hennessy cognac. "This is for your tea."

"Really Deshawn?" Jaden said as he side-eyed him.

Gilbert looked up at him, with a distraught look in his face. "Kid you drive a hard bargain." He grabbed the bottle and handed it over to Mo. "Tell me if it's the good stuff."

Mo cracked the top, and took a long savory swig.

Then he looked at the bottle again. "That's the good stuff."

Gilbert huffed. "Lean over kid."

Deshawn did as told and the ghoul touched his head. He jerked up and looked back to the crew. "We should've known. The Hell Gate is over in the woods where the locusts were. I know how to get there."

Romeo clapped his hands. "Perfect let's go."

Lay waved at the undead trio. "Thanks guys for help."

"Bye bye," Larry moaned as he waved back.

Gilbert petted one of the kittens. "Good luck kids and try not to die will ya. Do this one favor for your Uncle Gilly." Once he watched them walk away he opened his mouth wide and tossed the kitten inside.

CHAPTER THIRTY-THREE

Now Behold the Lamb

"And now behold the lamb," Asmodeus slurred as he ran his thick black talons along Imani's neck. He curled his lips in joyous delight. There were few things that brought Asmodeus as much satisfaction as a perfectly executed plan, and as he stroked Imani while pacing the pulpit of the abyss, he delighted himself in the mastery of his stratagem. The sixth Hell gate will open and SMITE will fall, leaving the Sons of Chaos a chance to usher in the new dawn.

"You can go ahead and kill me," Imani said as she tugged against the rope that bound her. "I'm not afraid to die again."

Hundreds of candles floated in the air above them, shining like diamonds, casting light and warmth upon them on the altar beneath

Imani's silky white gown caressed her curves and made her appear like a lamb. The demon caressed the gown with the back of his hands.

"Such a pretty little angel. You should be afraid."

Imani curled her fist, she wanted to punch him in the nose so bad. "Afraid of what? I've been into heaven and seen the most beautiful light there is and I felt the greatest love of all. You won't win demon. My faith and grace is in the Creator. It's all the same. We will win."

Asmodeus curled his lip. "We will see." Then he drew his hand back and swiped through Imani's stomach so quickly that it couldn't be seen by eye. "Let it began!" He shouted and his voice rolled like thunder in the abyss.

A searing pain came across Imani's stomach as red stained her gown. Her blood fell like rain on the iron seal below, it glowed, and activated with life, twisting and folding, cranking like an engine being powered. Imani did not fear evil. But in the abyss, the space between a Hell Gate and Earth, she witnessed evil in its true essence. It was violent, lustful, angry, and bloody. She was surrounded by vampires, a few demons, spirits so far gone from humanity that they became something else entirely. Nevertheless, her faith remained in the will of the Creator, and her heart awaited a love that would come fighting for her.

Imani lifted her chin and grimaced from the pain. "Stay strong the Creator's will be done and I am covered by the blood of Jesus."

Asmodeus clicked his talons. "Time to play."

The demon carved into Imani with his talons, and her cries of pain echoed along the dark walls of the abyss.

****

Coach Franklin watched through binoculars as vampires wrangled in another group of innocents, "Well it's definitely a whole hell family reunion in there. Just spotted more vampires, along with men possessed by demons."

"I know I can't be the only one geeked here. We've got whole new weapons. We are all dressed in black. And we got a mission. Just look at me I feel like shaft," Deshawn gushed.

Jaden leaned forward from the back, "Romeo did you get anything on this place?"

Romeo nodded with a smile, "I had a vision before we even parked. Coach is right, there is a whole hell variety in there. From what I saw most of the vampires are on the west side of the tunnels guarding a cavern where they are keeping the innocents. They have a few demons that are circling the perimeter. Asmodeus is on a lower level with Imani."

"Is she all right?" Jaden asked.

"For now," Romeo replied.

Lay ran his hand along his arm, and holographic screens appeared before him. "Running the data from previous cave explorers and maps available online, I was able to put together a 3D map." An arc light twisted in Lay's hand as he expanded the 3d map. "Based on Romeo's revelations and my rendering of these caves, they should be keeping the innocent's here." He said as a red spot glowed on the western side of caves. "And if the innocents are being kept here that means Asmodeus will protect the Hell gate all the way over here in a chamber far deeper into the caves."

Coach Franklin dropped his binoculars, and peered over his shoulder. "Is there a central location to the matrix of caves?"

Lay thought about it for a moment, "It would have to be here," he said as he rotated the map. "This point is in the middle is sensitive to disturbance."

"Good," Coach Franklin said as he faced front. "Because I'm going to blow it up."

Jaden gasped. "You're going to blow it up?"

Coach stared at him as if he was crazy. "You heard me. I ain't stutter."

Deshawn twirled his battle-ax grace in his lap. "So what's the plan?"

Coach Franklin loaded a 9mm with silver bullets. "Simple. We go in there to face Asmodeus and we get whoever is left alive out."

Ms. Day opened her mouth and a small "Uh," escaped. She quickly shut her mouth. "Coach there will be many people that could die if we wait that long."

Lay sat up. "Yes I agree. We just saw them take a group of innocents. There is no reason we are even waiting now. If I may recall Coach, you once said before that the Anointed exist to save innocent souls."

Coach Franklin nodded, "Yes that's true. But we are dealing with an upper level demon who is about to unleash hell on earth. Those are different circumstances. You have to look at the bigger picture."

"That's the first time I ever heard you say that," Romeo said.

"We should split up," Jaden proposed as he pointed to Lay's holographic map. "Half of us will plant the bomb and the others will rescue the innocents. Then we can rendezvous in this main cavern and head down to take on Asmodeus together."

"That's a stupid plan," Coach Franklin spat.

"Sounds good to me," Romeo replied.

Lay removed his glasses, "Me too."

Coach Franklin rubbed his head, before he nodded in agreement. "We have to stick together down there. It is no telling what we will see in there."

Ms. Day turned around and said, "I'm sorry Coach, I have to agree with the boys on this one."

Coach Franklin secured his gun in the holster on the side. "Okay don't say I didn't warn you. Let's do this then. Ms. Day you, me, and Romeo will find the innocents. If the vampires are guarding them then we will need Romeo's light."

"I'm shocked Coach that you picked me to be on your team." Ms. Day said.

Coach Franklin leaned forward, "That's because I don't need the Shepherd's Guild up my ass if something happens to you."

Ms. Day frowned. "Thanks Coach."

"Jaden, Lay, and Deshawn will plant the bomb." Coach Franklin hopped out of the car.

Coach Franklin pulled the bomb out the car and for a moment, considered handing it to Deshawn but once he thought about it, he handed over to Lay. "Please don't mess this up will you. God forbid we fail, there will be an army of demons and hungry vampires waiting to attack the city. When we leave this cave needs to be collapsed. Set the timer for at least twenty minutes when you arm it. If we don't kill him by then, most likely we would already be dead."

Jaden cringed at the comment. "Nice way to think positive coach."

"Yeah...yeah," Coach mocked. "Just make sure you get that ring off the demon's finger. It's the source of his power. You take that then we stand a good chance at vanquishing this demon for good."

Jaden pushed his shoulders back, "I'm going to do more than get the ring. I'm sending him back to hell."

Coach Franklin smiled as nodded, "That's what I like to hear." He glanced back at the others. "Everyone we have our mission. Now let's get out there and stop this demon."

At Coach Franklin's command they all got out of the Hummer, and followed him to the back. Coach Franklin opened the trunk revealing a large variety of firearms. "Take your pick gentlemen. We got the best of the best. All packed with silver bullets with a wooden core."

Romeo snatched two dual pistols, "See this is what I've been saying from the beginning. Nothing wrong with old school but the modern way is so much better."

"So much!" Jaden added as he stuffed holy water bombs in the pockets by his leg. He tossed a black quick pump shotgun at Deshawn.

Deshawn smiled as he cocked the weapon. "Just like me. Long black and deadly!" he exclaimed.

Coach Franklin shoved an ammo belt against Deshawn's chest. "Hell fire shooter for those locusts."

Deshawn strapped the soaker across his shoulder.

Lay raised a finger. "In that case Coach I think we should all take hellfire shooters. The locusts are like the insects and don't like fire very much."

"I agree," Coach Franklin said.

Once Ms. Day grabbed her weapon, Coach said, "Okay everyone lock up, its prayer time." Everyone formed a chain link circle behind the hummer. "Close your eyes," Coach Franklin started and he waited a moment for eyes to close. Deshawn peeked through his right eye. "I said close em," Coach growled.

Coach Franklin took a deep breath. "Dear Lord it is your word that says if my mother or father shall forsake me then you will lift me up. It is your word that says you will place us on a mighty rock and we shall not be moved. It is you word that says you will protect us like a shepherd even in the valley of death. We come to you as your anointed who already claim victory. Let us move by the spirit. Let your will be done. And keep our minds guarded. Amen."

They crept with painstaking caution towards the cave. Each one had their weapon out and ready. As they stood at the foot of the cave, everyone shook their heads after taking one glance inside the darkness that twisted forward. It gaped like open jaws, waiting to devour.

Coach curled his lip. "What are you waiting for? It's too late to be scared now."

Jaden pulled his sword out of the sheath and lead the way in.

"That's what I'm talking about," he said with a chuckle.

The hard and rugged walls protruded into a sea of gloom. Pieces of rock scattered the ground, and made walking the path difficult. Lay placed a beaming light near the entrance. He handed over the bomb to Deshawn and he wrestled something out of his bag. "Can you hold this." He freed his hands, and reached in the bag and pulled out a palm sized tablet. Then he handed the tablet over to Coach Franklin. "Here Coach."

"What is this," Coach Franklin asked.

Lay smiled. "It's a tracer. It should help us find our way back"

Coach Franklin took one look down at the device, and then back to Lay. "I'm sure you've heard this before, but you're a genius."

"Thanks Coach," Lay said as his smile grew wider.

A few yards in, and the walls narrowed until they could only walk one at a time. It was ghost-quit inside except for the bubbling drip of water from the ceiling. Even though it was quit, Coach could still sense the demons near, the scent of pungent Sulphur hung in the air.

About fifty yards deep, the cave widened. A dense fog grew so thick it rendered the flashlights useless, and they had to pick up torches off the walls. Together they strode through the damp space, ducking in low spots, squeezing in tight, and trying their best to avoid the rodents that crawled underneath. There was no breeze or ventilation blowing through the caverns, and around one hundred yards in, an insufferable heat rose. Sweat and dread coated their skin, as they marched forward into the endless gloom that eroded hope with each step.

By now they had expected, or hoped to have run into demonic activity. Any other sound of life would've been better, than the incessant drip of water that echoed along the walls. Almost two hundred yards in, a sudden loud crash made everyone freeze in their tracks.

Deshawn dropped his axe. "I can't do this," he said, wiping thick beads of sweat from his forehead. "I'm hot and I'm scared, plus we're not one hundred percent sure we know where we are going. It feels like we are marching straight to hell. I can't do it."

Romeo cocked his head to the side, "Pick up your axe and stop playing."

"No I'm serious," Deshawn said. "It's way too dark in here and I'm hot." Deshawn shook his head. "I don't want to do this no more. Just let me guard the truck or the entrance. Send the innocents my way and I'll lead them out."

Jaden walked past Romeo and waved, "Come on. Pick up your gear and let's move." he said.

"I can't," Deshawn shouted.

Jaden turned away in disgust. He placed a finger on his lips, "Shh!"

Deshawn huffed, "I can't" he mouthed again.

Coach Franklin shooed him away. "Let him go. An anointed warrior crippled by fear is useless on the battlefield."

"Coach," Ms. Day said.

The sound of movement from above, made ice tingle down their spines. Deshawn leaned forward. Then Jaden leaned forward. And they all leaned forward.

"What was that," asked Ms. Day

Romeo held his hand up as something flashed before his eyes. Locusts gathered on the ceiling, rubbing their claws together, as their red eyes burned like dark embers.

As this vision came to Romeo, a flurry of thoughts trickled into Jaden's head, all saying the same thing.

Swarm

Swarm

Swarm

"Pull out the hellfire shooters now!" Romeo shouted as he peeled open his eyes.

They looked up to a huge cavernous ceiling to see twelve low crouched locusts readying to attack. All of them rubbed their jaws and a rattling noise filled the cave. With their jaws stretched open wide, over a dozens of them came crawling down from the ceiling in each way.

Jaden shot hellfire in the air. It came out in a blazing stream of liquid that turned to fire mid-air and licked at the locusts. Each locust released an ear shattering scream as the flames hit them.

Lay felt a wave of panic sweep over him. "We have

to get out of here. That sound is calling the others."

Terror seized them as they thundered down the cave, clearing hundreds of feet in mere seconds. Another long corridor stretched out in front of them, with multiple other caverns to take.

Behind them, the locusts cracked their jaws, scraped against rocks, and screeched their calls to others. Dozens of locusts pursued them. A deafening crack boomed through the darkness. Everyone screamed and the abyss shifted.

Chapter Thirty-Four

Descent

Everything became a blur of motion in the darkness. At one moment Jaden could see Coach and Ms. Day in front of him, then suddenly they disappeared, swallowed by darkness. Lay ran close behind him.

Blood drained from Lay's face. "Where did everyone else go?"

Jaden placed hands on his knees as he struggled to breathe. "I don't know. Both Coach and Ms. Day were in front of me and now they're gone."

"Great," Lay said with a shrug. He searched behind them for any clue of the others. "Do you hear any locusts coming?"

Jaden listened. "No."

"Oh good," Lay breathed out.

"We can still go plant the bomb." Jaden looked down at Lay's hands. "The bomb. Where is it?"

Lay smacked his head. "I gave it to Deshawn."

Jaden groaned. "Come on let's go find him."

Lay pushed him ahead. "Lead the way."

Jaden shot him a sarcastic smile. "Thanks best

friend. I'll die first for you."

Lay chuckled, "Don't worry, I'll watch your back."

Together they trekked forward in a labyrinth of shadows, until the narrowing walls of the cave opened out to a larger room. A streak of light glistened off of a small pool water. A foul odor hit their noses like a smack upside the head.

Lay examined the bones and blood in the water. "This looks like a feeding ground.

"Look," Jaden pointed. Just across the pool of water was a hallway with gothic archways illuminated by emerald fire.

"We have to be getting close," Lay concluded.

"Let's go then," Jaden said as he took a step forward. Lay held him back. A splash sounded in the water. Then another. A small tailed kicked at the surface. Bones from a human carcass floated to the top. Life was in the pool and it stirred within. Three or four figures went back and forth in the water.

Lay crouched to his knees. "I believe they are hatchlings. If we make too much noise they might swarm."

"How are we going to get across?" Jaden asked.

Lay rubbed his chin. "Good question. I don't know."

Jaden surveyed the cavern until he saw a long flat piece of wood that looked like a covering. He reached out with his hand, and the board lifted in a cloud of crimson, he pulled his hand to his chest, and the board jolted forward.

"Stand on the board, we will surf our way there.

"Jaden rested his hand, palm side down, and the board fell on the ground. Together they stepped on the board. "I've only done this once or twice so don't mind me if I break a sweat"

"No I don't mind," Lay responded. "I don't want to get into that water and die anyway. I'm sure the bacteria and viruses alone would be enough to kill us.

Jaden relaxed his shoulders. He pointed his hand downward, palm outstretched, and pulled. In a jerky lurch the board trembled, before lifting off. Cautiously he directed them across the waters, and they both peered down, daring not to breathe, and not to allow their nerves to take over. The water continued to stir, but as they hovered over at the pace of an escalator at the mall, nothing came out.

Lay smiled, "Almost there."

Suddenly a green head rippled the water. It squealed and made two other heads pop out of the water.

"Umm Jaden I don't want to rush but—"

Panic made Jaden twitch, and the board was swept from under their feet. They both shouted at the same time. Before their feet could hit water, Jaden brought his hand to his chest, and an invisible force slammed them into the opposite wall.

"Ouch that hurts!" Lay said as a sudden pain shot up his shoulder.

Jaden rubbed his shoulder as well. "You good?"

"Fine," Lay replied.

While they laid on the ground, the hatchlings looked

at them, unsure if it was okay to get out of the water or not. Jaden pulled Lay's shoulder. "Let's go."

They both grabbed torches hung from opposite sides of the wall and trekked forward. It was quiet as they walked along, and the silence made Jaden more nervous. Dead bodies littered the ground, and the rotten smell that hung in the air was strong enough to make them hold their breath.

Two naked bodies, covered in lacerations, slumped in the corner. One body twitched. "Is that what I think it is?" Jaden asked.

Lay shined the light from the torch over the crumbled bodies, and the body jerked to life. In the corner the boy looked lifeless and dead, until he sat up, twisted at a 180 degree and something groaned within his belly. He dropped its head, arched back, twisting out from his side came two sets of arms on each side. Rising through the space between the stomach and chest popped two hairy eyes. Antennas poked out of the ears. The monster gave a roar and skittered up the walls.

Both Jaden and Lay darted back, raising their shooters in the air. Like a roach, the human centipede skittered into the shadows and along the ceiling, leaving a smudge red trail from its extra human parts.

"Stop," Jaden declared. "We can't waist all of our hellfire."

Lay tossed his shooter at him. Then he whipped the bag from over his shoulder and pulled out the lance of destiny.

"Hurry up and kill it before it gets away!"

Lay twisted and clicked the staff until it elongated to its full deadly length. "Light," he shouted as he pointed the staff to the corner of the room.

Jaden shined towards the exit way heading back. A chilling terror swept over him once he got a full look of the monster. Two human bodies stitched together, with smaller slimy hands, and hairy eyes that bulged out of the stomach.

Lay lined up his spear like a javelin, he took a few steps forward, and threw. The spear cried out as it cut through air and caught the centipede right in the center, just below where the waist and head met.

"Nice shot," Jaden exclaimed.

"I got lucky," Lay said as he yanked the spear out of the demon, which collapsed to the floor.

Gunfire echoed throughout the caverns somewhere in the distance.

"That must be the others," Jaden declared. "Let's go."

Lay ran his finger over the green goo that covered the middle of his staff. "I hope they are having better luck than we do.

******

"How did we lose them?" Ms. Day asked as she followed Coach Franklin's shadow.

Coach Franklin reached out blindly. "It's the evil magic protecting the Hell gate. It can disorient reality, twist the mind, and create some of the darkest terrors you've ever seen." He looked behind her on instinct to talk face to face, though he could not see. "Why did you think I said we need to stay together?"

"I thought you were just telling exaggerated war stories. Now I believe you, sugar. I don't think this is anything like I ever read in my studies."

"Is that so?" Coach Franklin said sarcastically. "You know for this to be your first outing, you're not too bad."

"Thanks coach...now can we please do something about the lighting. I think there is a rat that has been running back and forth on my foot, and it's creeping me out."

Coach Franklin sighed. He pulled out flare from his pack, popped it open and glaring light pierced the darkness. His heart skipped a beat.

"What?" Ms. Day asked. "Is it a rat?"

Coach Franklin shook his head. "Listen to me...don't move."

Every hair on Ms. Day's body stood at attention. Her breath caught in her chest. "What do you mean don't move? What is it…. a rat?"

"Just trust me," he said as he inched towards her. "Don't move—"

"Is it a bug?"

Coach Franklin took another step forward. "Don't move."

Something cold slithered over Ms. Day's shoulder. "Please God just don't let it be a snake." A hiss near her right ear made her want to leap out of body.

Coach Franklin's raised the flare. In one lithe move he grabbed the snake and presented it to her. "Come on look at this fella it's just a garden snake."

Ms. Day clutched her chest. "Darn it. Get that thing out of my face." She said with her gun pointed.

Coach Franklin wrapped the snake around his wrist. "This little guy is harmless.

"Throw that thing away!" Ms. Day shouted.

Coach Franklin chuckled, and then he cradled the snake to the ground.

Terror scraped Ms. Day's throat raw. She gasped as her gaze whisked past Coach to something far larger that lowered behind him in the darkness. She pointed. "It's a big snake behind you."

Coach Franklin side-eyed her. "Yeah okay. I'm sorry for scaring you."

Ms. Day shook her head. "No it's a giant snake behind you."

It uncoiled from the ceiling in a slow menacing drop, with its black-green scales glistening, and fangs dripping venom as it hissed. Coach Franklin could feel it stalk him from behind. He outstretched his arm and drew his shotgun

Slowly Coach Franklin craned his head and the demon opened its jaws wider. It had the body of a cobra and the arms of a man. It towered him easily by two feet with its body coiled. The creature rattled as it uncoiled itself in the shadows, growing larger in size.

Coach franklin's breath left his lungs in a hissing rush as he called the monster by its name. "Black Cobra!" Coach Franklin shouted before blasting away with his shotgun. The Black Cobra cried out in a high pitch squeal as it reeled. "The other way, now go!" Coach Franklin said as he shot at the demon's head.

Ms. Day led the way into a spacious cavern lit with flickering torches. She spun, fired, and sunk a bullet in the Black Cobra's right eye.

"Nice shot!" Coach Franklin said as he reloaded.

Ms. Day continued firing, "I told you I was a crack shot."

Coach Franklin scanned around the room. A shift in the spirit drew his eye upwards. There was a rock formation in the ceiling shaped like a sickle. "Keep it busy."

Ms. Day nodded, "You got it." She took three steps back and to the right. "Over here you big guttersnipe."

With a hiss the Black Cobra snapped, and narrowed its eyes on Ms. Day from across the cavern. It dropped lower to the ground as it slithered her way, and she unloaded into it. Gunfire echoed along the walls as the bullets ricochet off rock.

Ms. Day kept focus on both the Coach and the Black Cobra.

Coach Franklin took off his leather jacket. "C'mon big god," he chanted as he concentrated.

Coach reached up toward the ceiling, hands outstretched, grunting. A wave of heat and Sulphur hit Ms. Day as the Black Cobra came near. It coiled and drew back, preparing to strike.

"Hurry up coach!" She shouted, her voice shaking.

Sweat poured off the top of Coach's head as he

pulled with all of his might. From the ceiling came the sound of a deafening crack as rock broke, and the surrounding walls trembled.

Ms. Day continued shooting and back stepping until…. click.

"Coach!"

The pupils of the Black Cobra glowed as it bared fangs, reared its head, then struck. Ms. Day threw herself to the left. The Black Cobra struck the wall. It strikes again and Ms. Day throws her body to the right. She looked over and saw two dents in the cave where the Black Cobra struck. It paused and slithered closer, then drew back to strike again.

Ms. Day's blood froze in her veins as the Black Cobra reared its head back. "Coach!"

Just before it could sink its fangs into Ms. Day, Coach Franklin brought the sickle crashing down. Loose gravel rains upon them as the walls in the cavern tremble. The sickle slices through the Black Cobra like a warm knife through butter. And the impact makes the ground shudder underneath them. The Black Cobra went down slowly, whining and hissing as blood gushed at the site of the sickle struck.

Ms. Day squealed. "What took you so long?"

Coach Franklin wiped his brow. "That took a lot out of me."

Behind them came the sound of gunfire and guttural moans.

"Bloodsuckers," Coach Franklin concluded. "Let's

move out," he ordered.

Chapter Thirty-Five

Horrors of the Abyss

Fear ran rampant throughout the holding cells. Every minute the vampires brought another group. Some retreated to the corners to cry, others tried to comfort their loved ones, and a few brave souls tried to fight back. It was pure chaos and noise with everyone screaming and begging for freedom. Tamiyah joined the choir in cries for help.

Five vampires guarded the cell full of human sacrifices. Three paced back and forth, one guarded the door, and the other sat across on the other side.

A demon who appeared as man dressed in a modern tailored suit walked over. "Another one is needed."

"Take your pick?" One guard suggested.

His cold black eyes raked across the holding cell. "That one," he pointed.

Terror seized Tamiyah's heart and she gagged. He pointed towards Jessica.

Jessica fell to her knees and cried. "What? Not me" She cried out as she tried to sink to the back of the cell.

"Alright come on," the guard said as he opened the cell.

"No!" Jessica screamed.

"Run!" Tamiyah yelled.

Her foot lurched to the right and the vampire griped the air, then he pulled her back like a magnet. He cackled. "Why do you still continue to run, if you know we can do that?" Then he shook his head as if he was scolding a child. "I hope I wasn't that dumb when I was still human."

He tossed her over to the demon, who waved his hand, and made her fall to sleep.

"Jessica!'" Tamiyah cried as she stuck her face between the bars.

One lone vampire strolled in with Daquan and Quentin. "I brought some more for the reaping."

Quentin pushed off the guard. "Let me go homie. You got it all wrong. We're just like you." He said.

"Yeah, we want to be down with the True bloods." Daquan added.

The vampires looked amongst themselves and laughed. One larger vampire, a pale mass of blubber stood. "So you want to be a part of the True bloods, aye?"

Daquan nodded. "Yeah."

"You want to dance in the new night?" Another vampire added from the left.

"Drink blood, roam the night, and take crap from nobody?"

"Hell yeah," Quentin emphasized.

The vampire smacked Daquan on the shoulders hard.

"Well I got news for you buddy. We have an opening, but it will only be one of you." He reached in his pocket and pulled out a switch blade. "Which one of you will it be?" He dropped the knife.

Both Daquan and Quentin glanced at each other in uncertainty.

Daquan turned to the vampires, "No I can't—

Before he could finish his sentence, Quentin wrapped his hands around his neck and twisted swiftly. Daquan fell to the floor with the shock of death on his face.

"Ouch he didn't see that coming!" One of the vampires shouted before they all exploded into laughter.

Another one patted Quentin's shoulder. "Good job. You might just be one of us after all."

Quentin reached into his pocket, pulled out and put on his golden fang grills. "Gang gang the night calls my name." He rolled up the sleeve to his right arm. "I'm ready for the bite."

The large vampire snickered. "Fellas he said he's ready for the bite."

All of the vampires laughed until their fangs dropped. He turned back towards Quentin. "Kid let me tell you something."

Quentin poked out his chest. "What?"

The large vampire's fangs fell down. "Be careful what you wish far." Quicker than a lick of a flame he pulled Quentin into his arms and fed on him until turned stiff and blue.

Once Quentin was dead he tossed him to the side. "I'm still so freaking hungry," the vamp declared with his mouth covered in blood. He wiped his chin and strolled over to the cell. Tamiyah's neck caught his eye. Her pulse quickened and his fang extended another inch. He ripped open the cell doors and snatched Tamiyah by the back of her hair. "Ah she looks delicious!" The vamp shrieked, licking his lips.

A patrolling vampire, with slick hair, and thick sideburns placed a hand on his shoulder, "You've already drained two. The boss needs the sacrifices."

"Forget that! I'm hungry." the vampire said as he dragged her.

"Get the hell off of me," Tamiyah roared as she struggled within his grasp.

He smiled as he shook her. "Little firecracker aren't you? I like that, makes the blood taste better. C'mon"

Tamiyah whimpered as the vampire dragged her by her neck. "You don't want to eat me. I'm on the Hollywood master cleanse diet." The vampire paid no attention to her as he turned her around and yanked her head sideways. "I probably won't even taste that good. There are at least a dozens of fat chicks in there. Don't eat me! "Tamiyah cried in a cracked terrified voice.

Romeo crept near the holding cell just in time to spot the vampire bury his head between Tamiyah's shoulder. He threw the wings of mercy in the air. Whooshing all across the room, the wings of mercy collected three heads before returning to Romeo's hands. Dust blew all around.

"Oh my god I would've never thought I would be

glad to see you," Tamiyah gasped as she jumped on Romeo and wrapped her legs around his waist.

Growls sounded from the left as two vampires by the door took aim at their heads. Coach Franklin and Ms. Day stormed in and blew rounds in each of the vampire's chest with a shotgun.

"Okay people we are here to get you out. Let's move!" Coach Franklin ordered as he opened cell doors. People swarmed out of the makeshift cells. "Single file everyone we are exiting to the left."

"Ms. Day …. Coach. Where is everybody?" Romeo called.

Ms. Day hurried over. "Are you alright?"

Romeo nodded, "I'm fine. Have you heard from the others?"

"No but I'm sure they are okay."

Coach Franklin handed the tablet to Ms. Day. "Ms. Day do you think you can handle the innocents out of here."

Ms. Day flashed him a wry smile, "Of course. I am a shepherd." She turned to the crowd. "Follow me everyone."

Coach Franklin cocked his gun. "Romeo you're with me. Understand?"

Coach heard backup forces coming around the corner, and ran to meet them.

Tamiyah burrowed he head into Romeo's shoulder. "Come on you have to get out of here. Follow Ms. Day ." Romeo told Tamiyah as Coach Franklin continued freeing captives.

More vampires ran down toward the cells. Romeo placed the Wings at his side as he withdrew two duel pistols. He drew near Coach Franklin, "Get everyone out of here. I'll hold them off."

Coach Franklin nodded, "Come on people follow the lady."

Romeo pushed past the people following behind Ms. Day. Romeo raced to meet the line of vampires. Eyes filled with blood and lust, they came darting towards him with their fangs bearing. He turned the first one to rush him into dust when he shot him in the heart. Bullets whirled through the dust of the fallen back towards Romeo. He threw himself to the side and shot back. Wooden core bullets connected to the vamp's hearts and the fell back through the threshold of the door. Ash covered Romeo as he blew the smoke from the barrel of his guns.

Romeo walked passed the threshold of the cavern, and a revelation came to him. Death waited from them around the corner. Horrible images flashed in his head. A ball of electricity ripped Jaden apart. Asmodeus then broke Romeo's neck as he soared above air. Then the demon ran a sword through Deshawn's chest.

Coach Franklin shook Romeo. "Where the hell did you just go? Didn't I say you were with me?"

Romeo shook off the haze of his vision. "But there was this girl and—"

"I don't care about no girl." Coach Franklin interrupted. "Focus on completing this mission. Now let's go."

Coach Franklin strode away and Romeo followed.

******

"Jerry are you there?" Deshawn called to the darkness.

There was no answer and his fear increased by tenfold. Deshawn felt like he was walking around in circles. The dark paths seemed like a never-ending maze.

"If I find a way out, then they are all out of luck." Deshawn murmured out loud. His voice bounced off the walls and he had to laugh at himself, since he was used to performing for an audience. A strange feeling swept over him after he stopped laughing. Deshawn turned his shoulder

"Hello?"

There was nothing but endless shadows on the other side. He took two steps forward and stopped once he heard a footstep behind him. A footstep he couldn't tell if it was his own or another. Suddenly a noise rang throughout the cave, raising the hairs along his neck. Dread burned a hole in the pit of his gut. A few yards ahead a shape took form in the shadows. At first it appeared fuzzy to him, but as it crept closer it became clear. A male figure around six foot, dressed in hunters clothing, with a plastic red Elroy mask on.

Deshawn dropped the bomb to the side. "We meet again Elroy."

"Don't you want to tickle me?" The Elroy face asked

in a low, bone chilling voice. It had an axe that it kept slapping into its right hand.

"It's a real changing face." Deshawn said to himself. "I can handle this. I failed the homework but I can finesse the test," He said as he tossed the torch to his right. He retrieved the battle ax strapped on his back. In his right hand, he charged a particle to throw. "Okay Elroy, if you want to play then let's play."

The Elroy face kept cuffing the axe in his hand. It ran towards Deshawn. The sound of the axe chilled Deshawn's blood

Deshawn took a deep breath to subside the rising panic. "I can do this. Just don't blink." Then he reared his right hand back as he clung on to the axe. "Don't blink."

Elroy stood in front of him and stopped cuffing the axe.

They locked eyes, and Deshawn blinked.

"Jesus Christ! I did it again."

Elroy disappeared from in front of him and reappeared at the same spot. On Deshawn's left stood another. Quickly he threw the charged particle at Elroy's feet. It detonated and smashed the monster back into the wall. Elroy two swung his axe, and Deshawn spun just in time for the blade to miss by an inch. With his own axe, he swung back at Elroy two, aiming for the bright orange noise and he misses.

The original Elroy lurched towards him. Deshawn shoved a knee in the monster's stomach, and slammed it into the wall. With a guttural moan the other, tugged him from behind and Deshawn elbowed it in the face.

Constricted by the tightness on the caves, all three of them were practically on top of each other. If only he could slow time, but he had no room to waves his hand or fully swing his axe. He clung his axe to his chest, closed his eyes, as they both descended upon him, and a wave of energy sprouted from his chest outward. Deshawn looked up, and hands jerked towards him. He backed up.

"Silly Elroy...tricks are for the kid." Deshawn chuckled. He waved his hand and the flow of time went back to normal.

Both Elroy's looked into each other's eyes and screamed terribly as they blinked out of existence.

Deshawn dusted his shoulder. "That was easy." He went back over to pick up the bomb and torch.

He walked the few yards ahead to enter a manmade corridor. The area was brimming with locusts, hopping and flying over each other. It all looked like some sort mating ritual to Deshawn. They crawled along the walls like caged animals. Deshawn slowed time with a charge from his right hand. The emerald arc rippled right down his arm and swept pass the locusts in the room.

All around him, the ugly looking demons moved in slow jerky movements as they fought against time field slowing down their motion. Deshawn blasted his way through the pack of demons with a double barrel shotgun. Locusts erupted in flames as Deshawn shot each one dead center in the chest, ripping them apart with his shotgun.

Deshawn cocked his shotgun. "That's it?" He asked arrogantly.

Arms, legs, and other body parts glided through the air at a snail's pace. Nothing but awful smelling green goo remained from the decomposing locusts. Deshawn armed the bomb following the written instructions taped to the side.

"You know this was too easy," he whispered to himself.

A guttural roar echoed behind him. Fangz strolled in cool as cucumber, with his hunting face on. "Sup short-timer."

Deshawn smacked his head, "I shouldn't have said anything." Deshawn brought his axe up. "You better beat it, before I finish the job."

Fangz smiled and his diamond crusted fangs glistened. "If you think ya bad playboy…. then go ahead and swing."

Deshawn lunged at the master vampire and Fangz body collapsed into a swarm of bats. Fangz reformed behind Deshawn and snatched him into his cold grasp. Forcefully he pulled Deshawn's head to the side, dropped fang and bit into his neck.

A sharp pain burned on Deshawn's neck and made every vein in his body throb. He shouted out in horror and pulled himself from the vampire, but Fangz snatched him back, and held him down. Deshawn struggled against Fangz, like a rat caught between the crushing muscle of a python.

Life surged into Fangz and he felt his body heal itself. Anointed blood filled his veins and a burning fever swept over his cold body. The sensation grew so strong that he released Deshawn and threw him forward. Fangz snatched off his sunglasses and ran his hand on the right side of his face. His eye took form and rolled out like new in his socket. Fangz licked his lips, "I knew Anointed blood would be good but I didn't know it would be powerful."

Deshawn scooted backwards on the ground with a hand over the right side of his neck. "Back up!" he shouted in terror.

Fangz trekked forward. "Or what you gonna do?"

Deshawn charged a particle with his other hand and threw it towards the vampire. Fangz leaned to the side as the particle soars past him and detonates into the wall. "That's it?" Fangz cackled. "I wonder if I drain you…do you think I can walk in the sunlight? Let's see." Fangz lurched forward and his foot tripped across a massive object on the ground. He peered down to his feet. "What is this?"

Deshawn scurried backward, with blood spilling across his fingers. "It's a bomb."

Fangz wiped his mouth. "Is it enough to take out this whole system of caves?"

Deshawn scratched his braids. "Hell if I know. I hope so."

Fangz circled Deshawn and pondered. "Maybe I won't kill you after all short-timer."

Deshawn reached for his battle axe. "Yea, well how about I still turn you to dust?"

Fangz shrugged. "You can try playboy, but why

would you?"

"Because you just took a freaking chunk out of my neck. And your evil."

Fangz arched his brow. "Hardly. Just because I'm a vampire that doesn't make me evil. If you don't mess with my money, then your cool with me. Now you and your boys have been messing with my money. And that's not cool, at all. But Asmodeus is going to put me out of business. So I say that the enemy of my enemy is my friend."

"I neva' heard of that before. But it sounds like something someone evil would say. Especially if they're trying to protect their boss."

Fangz roared. "He's not my boss, hence why I'm trying to help you vanquish him."

"Where do we find him?"

"He's holding out over the seal. It's in the sunken altar. He's also got your little angel friend over there. She didn't look too hot last time I seen her."

Deshawn groaned. "Ugh I need to hurry up. I have to get down there but I don't know how and I keep getting lost."

"Because the Hell gate knows you're Anointed. It's protecting itself. I bet it's probably throwing all of your friends for a loop too. But I know how you can get down there and find your crew."

"How?" Deshawn asked.

Fangz squatted to the ground, dropped fang and bit into his wrists. "Drink."

Deshawn shook his head. " Are you crazy man? I'm

not doing that."

"You want to save your friends don't you? And if you hadn't noticed sunshine…you're losing a lot of blood."

Deshawn peered at his hand which was covered in blood. For once he was speechless.

Fangz grinned. "And I bet you didn't know that a mortal wound near the hell gate can kill your angel?"

"No I didn't know that." Deshawn propped himself against a wall. "What am I going to do?"

Fangz stretched out his hand. "Just drink, all it takes is one little drop and the Hell gate will stop working against you, it will heal your wound, and you'll be back on your feet before you know it."

Deshawn thought for a moment. "Just a drop?"

Fangz nodded, "Or two, but that's all it takes. C'mon."

Deshawn leaned over and took Fangz hand. "No funny business okay?"

"Cross my heart and hope to die…. then come back."

Deshawn opened his mouth and lifted his tongue. Fangz clenched his fist and three drops of blood rolled onto Deshawn's tongue. Deshawn's face soured when he closed his mouth.

"How do you feel?" Fangz asked.

Deshawn face twisted. Then he sucked in a sudden breath. "I don't know the same." He felt along his neck and the bite marks faded. There was no more bleeding.

Fangz pulled him up. "Take the tunnel to the left to

access the main caverns. From there move lower in the valley across the locust eggs. There you should be able to get to the altar from there."

"Thanks man."

"No doubt," Fangz responded as he turned.

"Can I say something?"

"What?"

"Don't tell my boys, but I loved your mixtape. Blood and gold was pure fiyah." Deshawn gushed.

Fangz pounded his chest. "If I had a heart that would hit me right here. Good luck." Fangz turned the corner and chuckled. "Idiot," he murmured in amusement as his body crumbled into a swarm of bats.

A surging pain slammed the right side of Deshawn's brain. Jaden's voice flooded into his head, like he was listening to a song on full blast. *If you any of you can hear me. You need to come now to the main cavern.*

Deshawn shook his head, "Hold on Jacob, I'm coming."

Chapter Thirty-Six

In the Valley of death

The humdrum sounds of locust buzzing and rattling grew near. Jaden knew they were getting closer to the Hell gate. They emerged into a large circular space with a tunnel that lead to a level lower. For once cool air stirred in the cavern.

"Do you think they heard you?" Lay asked.

"I'm not sure but I could feel them when I reached out with my mind."

"I see. Well hopefully they're close." Lay ran two fingers along his arm and a hologram map of the cave appeared in front of him. He pointed to the red dot. "This us and we are here at the main cavern. Only way to go is down. Do you want to wait for them?"

Jaden shook his head. "There is no time, Imani needs us."

Footsteps sounded from behind, and they both pulled out weapons.

"Stand down soldiers." Coach Franklin said.

Jaden breathed a sigh of relief. "Where is Ms. Day?"

Coach Franklin swallowed hard before he responded. "She is leading the hostages out of the cave."

Romeo crossed his arms. "Everyone good?"

"All good," Lay responded.

"Lay, did you plant the bomb?" Coach Franklin asked.

Lay frowned. "No Deshawn had it."

"I took care of it Coach!" Deshawn shouted as he ran over from the left.

Coach nodded, "My man." Then he raked his gaze over to the others. "Let's go shut this thing down boys."

"Let's go get my girl," Jaden added.

"Excuse me?" Coach Franklin said.

"I mean our girl." Jaden corrected.

"We have to go down this tunnel to reach the Hell gate." Lay said.

"Okay let's move," Coach Franklin ordered.

All together they trekked down the path on full alert, their eyes searching, and hands ready. The path down was a steep decline. Only a few steps downward and gravity took hold and pulled them tumbling down. Jaden braced his red sneakers against the dirt as they continued down.

As the group fell forward, the cave widened again. Romeo felt a shift in the spirit, then he stopped them. Sweat fell from his brow and his heart pounded in his throat. "Guys get ready."

Suddenly the air above them picked up significantly and rattling filled the cavern. Everyone held their breath while they watched in horror. A swarm raged towards them

Coach Franklin pulled his semi-automatic off his back. "Let's clear a path people!"

The locusts came at them like a raging storm. They clouded the air above them in a swarm too large to count, it would be easier to count the grains of sand that laid beneath their feet.

Shooters came off backs and streams of brilliant fire illuminated the cave. It casted a haze of smoke and sulfur as the locusts fell from the air in large heaps. More Locusts entered the fray, and Jaden felt a sharp pain strike the right side of his brain. One word echoed in his head.

Swarm

Swarm

Swarm

Deshawn stepped in front of the group and rippled time around them, slowing the onslaught of the swarm. As soon the charge rippled down his arm, he dropped to his knees and cried out in pain. All of the energy in his body seemingly left in one foul swoop.

"Deshawn!" Jaden shouted as he reached to help him up.

"Don't drain yourself," Coach Franklin stated. He yanked Deshawn up. "Remember gentlemen we prepared for this. Now blast those suckers out of the sky." Once the swarm got within range, Coach unleashed a hail of bullets, dropping burning locusts out of the sky and laughing like a mad man.

Romeo whirled over two locusts that swooped down

upon him, and burned them to ashes with a stream of hell fire. Another locust came at his head, and Lay was on it in a flash. He leapt over the locust with his staff raised, and nailed the creature to the ground.

Three shots later and the hell fire coming out of Romeo's shooter dimmed. "I'm out," he shouted as he tossed the gun.

"Me too," Jaden added.

Jaden dropped his shooter and slugged forward. Lay called out his name as he struggled to cover his back. Locusts flew in from a hole on the far side of where they entered. Jaden's guts twisted sickeningly once he realized the locust surrounded them in every direction.

All together the team drew in, back to back, with shooters and weapons raised. The Locusts were everywhere, flying around the cave, crawling towards the ceiling, and surrounding them with their jaws outstretched.

Lay stumbled back. "Coach they got us. What are we going to do?"

"No they don't. I'm not done yet," Coach Franklin said. He reached behind his waist and flung two Holy-bomb grenades in the space before the team. The grenades rolled a few feet forward, clicked, and detonated. Everyone shielded themselves back from the explosion and flames that erupted.

A thick bead of sweat rolled from Deshawn's braids to his chin. His head followed another swarm that entered into the cavern. "If there was anytime we needed a miracle it would be now."

"Pipe down we got this," Romeo boasted.

Lay looked over, "Honestly it can't get any worse than this."

A loud call erupted from around the corner and the locusts dropped from the ceiling.

Romeo pushed Lay, "You just had to say something dumbass."

"I'm sorry I didn't mean to," Lay said.

Another call went into the air and magnified their fears.

"Coach what was that?" Jaden asked.

Coach Franklin tightened his trigger finger. "The queen."

A creature stepped out of the far side of the cavern. It had the long shape of a locust with a crowned woman's face, lions' teeth, long wings, iron breastplates, and a tail with a scorpion's stinger.

Coach Franklin cocked his gun. "You look good darling. Time hasn't changed you at all."

Jaden raised his sword, "Coach how are we going to slay all of them?"

"Faith," he said with his voice dropping to a serious murmur. "We got to have faith."

Be still, the locust Queen commanded with her voice ringing in Jaden's head. All around the locust fell to the ground and circled them with their jaws outstretched and hissing. *Oh creator don't let this be it*, Jaden thought. He watched the locust as they stood still as statues, subservient and obedient. A sudden idea came to him.

"Lay are locusts like bees and ants? Do they have a hive mind?" Jaden asked.

"Not exactly."

"What makes them swarm then?"

The Locust Queen made her descent slow and menacing. With each step the Queen took, the ground shook underneath them and the walls quaked.

Romeo snorted loudly. "Will you two nerds stay focused. This is not the time for Biology."

"Romeo shut up. Lay, answer my question." Jaden said.

Lay thought for a moment. "It's the closeness. Being near each other triggers a signal in their brain."

Jaden shrugged. "Not the answer I was looking for but it will work."

The cavern shook as the Locust queen clawed forward. Her eyes narrowed on them and she filled the cavern with her bellowing roar.

"If you got a plan then by all means take your time." Coach Franklin said.

"On my cue, get ready to hit her with everything you got." Jaden said before he sucked in a big breath. He closed his eyes and said out loud. "Swarm.... Swarm...Swarm."

A few of the locusts twitched in the back. Others rubbed their snouts.

Deshawn looked over his shoulder. "Coach hit him with the holy water, he's possessed."

Jaden continued chanting. "Swarm...swarm...swarm."

The Locust Queen crept closer to them and all of the locusts cleared a path as she came, roaring and hissing."

Hot tears stung Lay's eyes and he buried his face in his hands. "Oh my god I can't look. I can't take this."

"Don't be afraid," Coach Franklin shouted. "We are the Anointed. We are the chosen. And we are covered by the blood."

Jaden continued chanting with his eyes clenched shut. "Swarm, Swarm, Swarm."

Just behind the Locust Queen, Romeo spotted a dozen locusts out of the many who stood up. Their eyes glowed with an eerie crimson cloud. "Wait a minute I get what your trying to do. Keep going!" Romeo shouted.

Jaden collapsed to his knees, focusing all of his energy on connecting to the locusts. "Swarm!" he shouted. His voice thundered around the cavern.

The locust Queen stopped in her tracks. She whipped her Hummer-sized head around. Her children stood against her in defiance. All of them circled her with red glowing eyes.

Jaden stood to his feet. He turned his hands palm side up. On his command all of the locust rose as one. He looked over his shoulder. "Ready?"

Coach Franklin changed his clip. "You better believe it."

"Swarm!" Jaden shouted.

The locusts flew into the air like a tornado that swirled in a cloud of death and clashed into the Locust Queen. She gave a mighty roar as the locusts tore into her, like a colony of ants devouring cake. Bullets and beams of light blasted the queen and she crumbled to the ground in defeat.

"Nice job Jaden," Lay shouted in excitement.

Jaden stumbled to his knees. His energy dips and then it replenishes. All of them gasped as new energy renewed them.

"We need to get to the altar," Romeo said.

"Only one problem big dog," Deshawn pointed. "Seems like it's guarded.

Stone Gargoyles swooped off the ledges of the iron gates bearing bone crushing fangs and razor sharp claws. Bursts of flames and swirls of light jetted towards them as demons materialized on the floor, carrying balls of fire, lightening, and acid in their hands.

The stone ceiling exploded above them, and a jet of light spotlighted Michael as he entered. With all might and glory, he arched his wings and raised his sword. Michael descended to the ground and stood before them.

He turned to Jaden, "Go save your angel and vanquish Asmodeus. I will hold them off you as you escape."

Jaden nodded then he waved a hand to the others, "Come on guys!"

Lay ran and noticed Coach Franklin did not follow. "Coach are you coming?"

"Go ahead. I'll stay with Michael." Coach Franklin said as he shot at a locust that flittered overhead.

"But Coach–" Lay protested.

Coach Franklin fired another round. "But nothing.

Carry on!"

****

Jaden opened the door and ghoulish bats flew out. Harrowing wails came from the center hall, and together they crept towards the altar. More of the bats soared overhead. Jaden ducked as they continued to flap and crash into the ceiling as they passed by. As he neared the opening to the main hall he knew one thing to be clear, he was walking in the shadow of death.

Lay whispered a small prayer to himself as he followed Jaden out onto the balcony of the main hall. Loud wails of pain surrounded him as emerald lights flickered in his brown eyes. Tortured souls swirled and twisted. The Hell Gate had been cracked open.

"We are too late," Romeo said.

Jaden remained silent. His blood froze at the sight of the evil spirits that clawed, kicked, and screamed as they drifted into the abyss of the Hell Gate. If there was any moment where he missed the comforting arms of his mother it was now as evil surrounded him.

Asmodeus tossed innocent people three and four at a time into the Hell Gate. They popped back out, marching in line. Though the people still looked the same and dressed the same, their eyes were a monstrous black. Jaden could sense the evil essence that replaced their souls. Asmodeus had turn the abyss into a mass production demon making factory.

Jaden spotted Imani Hidden behind the flickering

emerald lights of the Hell Gate. Imani's head slumped low. He could sense her slipping away. The demon prepared five more victims to throw into the Hell Gate.

Lay peaked out from behind a column. "What are we going to do?"

"Distract him while I grab her."

Romeo nodded an okay.

"Do you got a shot from here?" Deshawn asked.

"Only one way to find out," Romeo responded as he leaned back, and summoned light into a ball in his hands.

Jaden took off.

Asmodeus could sense the danger when the ball of light rocketed across the room. While the demon followed the ball of light, Jaden threw his sword from the other side. Asmodeus threw up his hands to deflect the ball of light, but the sword slashed across his shoulder. Jaden jumped down from the balcony and rushed over towards the cross. He glanced over to Asmodeus who was kneeling from the pain.

With a flick of his wrist Jaden released Imani from the confines of the cross. He caught her in his arms as she fell down to him. "Imani are you alright," Jaden asked as he shook her in fear that his guardian angel maybe gone for good.

She opened her eyes, "It's about time you got here."

Jaden helped her up, "I figured I'd save you for once. Will you be alright?"

She cracked a smile. "Yes. Just give me some time. Where are the others?"

Asmodeus threw a ball of electricity at their heads.

Jaden backhanded it into the wall. The force blew a hole leading to another cavern.

"Get of here. I have to end this, go with the others," Jaden shouted as he took a defensive stance in front of Imani.

She shook her head, "I won't leave you."

"Go get the others. I'll be fine. I'm not fighting this battle on my own."

Imani smiled and ran her hand across his face. She exited through the hole in the wall.

Asmodeus cracked the muscles in his neck, "Just me and you,"

Jaden reached for his sword and it soared into his hands. "No, you're forgetting Him," Jaden said with emphasis.

The demon sniveled at the sentiment. Flying out of the Hell Gate came ten newly possessed agents. Asmodeus turned to the demons, "Kill them!" he shouted with a grit.

Monstrous black eyes stalked Romeo, Deshawn and Lay. The demons charged towards them and the Anointed met them head on.

Asmodeus slammed his fist into the wall of the cavern. Fissures radiated from the spot and the walls quaked. Asmodeus ripped off his top and a broadsword materialized in his hands.

Asmodeus held up his sword, "I will take pleasure in taking your head with my sword."

Jaden brought up the sword of the spirit confidently.

"You can try!"

The two warriors dashed across the cavern and locked blades. With each clash their blades released small sparks. Passion and fury guided Jaden's hands as he blocked and swiped his sword in defense against the powerful demon. Jaden thrust, struck, and thrust again, driving the demon back. Something inexplicable yet holy flowed through his veins and allowed him to match the efforts of the demon.

Asmodeus rolled backwards and interrupted the flow of their deadly dance. He huffed with fury. With his razor sharp talons, he hurled a shock ball towards Jaiden's chest. Jaden dodged each attack, his breath thin in his chest, and his arms shielding his face from bits of rock that exploded from the shock balls hitting the wall. Asmodeus released his wings and took towards the ceiling. The air crackled around him and thunder rumbled. Asmodeus roared from the top of the cavern and called lightening down.

Jaden crossed his arms. The lightning came down in a sharp, brilliant bolt that filled the cavern. Jaden heard the rumble when it fell, and smelled the smoke when it filled the cavern. But when he opened his arms, and lifted his head, he was unharmed.

"Impossible!" Asmodeus shrieked as he circled up above and peered down at the young boy.

Asmodeus swooped low to the ground, sparks came from his feet as he slid into a sudden stop.

"Jaden look out!" Romeo shouted.

Jaden turned his head. Then in a lick of a flame, the

demon spun into darkness, and surprised him from behind. Electricity coiled into his hand and he chucked it dead center in Jaden's chest. Jaden crashed into the wall with a bone shattering thud and collapsed to the ground.

Asmodeus spun again, he snatched Romeo and flew into the air. Drifting far above the cavern, Asmodeus ran his hands arounds Romeo's neck until there was no longer a light in his hands nor his eyes. The demon dropped him like a bag of trash. And Romeo's body slumped to the ground.

Lay called out Romeo's name. The demon pointed with his claws and brought lightening down upon him. Lay fell over in a moan as Imani cried out.

Deshawn's eyes darted everywhere as he searched the skies for any sign of Asmodeus. To their left they could hear massive movement heading their way.

Imani yanked Deshawn's arm, "Look they're coming!"

Dozens of the possessed charged their way with weapons in hand. Deshawn rippled time. The crowd slowed their charge.

"What are we going to do?" Imani asked.

Deshawn grabbed her, "I got it. Let's run!"

Deshawn ran and the demon crept behind him. A broadsword materialized in the demon's hand and he buried it into Deshawn's back. Shock ran across Deshawn's face. He fell to his feet until his head crashed on a loose boulder. Imani ran to his aid. Before she could reach him, a shock ball struck her down.

Bodies laid all over the cavern. Jaden laid in the center, smoke billowing off his chest with his eyes glazed over. Romeo was not too far from him, face turned to the side and sprawled out on his stomach. Deshawn laid face first with a sword sticking out his back. Lay and Imani laid crumbled beside each other, covered in smoke. All of them dead.

Chapter Thirty-Seven

Miracles

Asmodeus licked clean the red off his hands. He stood amidst his carnival of destruction, with his face a cruel mask of smugness. The anointed were defeated. A legion of demons entered the world. Asmodeus descended to the cavern floor and trekked along the bodies.

When Deshawn opened his eyes, pain exploded through him, the first sign he was still alive. He crawled along the dust, sword still pierced through his chest. The demon cackled as he struggled in pain.

Deshawn crawled towards Imani. She laid limp and lifeless on top of jagged rocks. Still inch by inch Deshawn moved himself further. He glanced over his shoulder and saw the demon was behind. His breath caught in his chest and he desperately tried to get his body to move. Deshawn was a wounded tortoise stuck in the path of a devouring lion.

It couldn't end like this. Something clicked in

Deshawn's head. The archangel told them they would win if they believed. He lifted his head towards the sky, "Creator we need you. Help us," he cried out with his voice constricted with blood and emotion.

The Creator heard his plea and the spirit fell mighty upon him, granting him the ability to do a new thing. At that moment time reversed backwards to the previous minute. The Legion of demons returned to the Hell gate, and everyone fell back in step to their previous position exactly one minute ago. Everyone and everything around Deshawn froze. Blinding white light crackled in of the corner of the cavern, and another angel appeared. Deshawn drew near to her.

A vision of loveliness stood before him, bathed in white lights. "You have only three tries to get this right. You can only go back one minute. That's all the spirit will allow."

"Three?" Deshawn repeated. He thought for a moment and said, "But what if—"

"Only three." She repeated sternly. "Anymore and the spirit will drain your life energy then you will die."

Deshawn frowned. "Yikes."

The angel smiled. "Rejoice for the creator will use you all to do a new thing." All of the lights faded away and the angel vanished before him.

"Jaden look out!" Romeo shouted as Asmodeus spun out of darkness.

Then in a blink of an eye, the demon chucked a shock ball dead center in Jaden's chest. Both Deshawn and Romeo had a strong sense of Deja vu.

"Wait this just happened!" Deshawn shouted as he turned to Romeo.

Romeo felt the same strange feeling, "Your right," he replied.

In one quick swoop Asmodeus snatched Romeo into the sky before he could continue. Deshawn was shaking his head and freaking out, "Wait....wait I wasn't ready. We need to restart this again."

In the request Deshawn tapped into his power and again time reversed back to the moment Asmodeus spun into the darkness, "Tell me I'm not the only one who just experienced that?" he asked.

"Nope and personally I don't want to die for a third time," Jaden declared.

Once more the demon spun out of darkness to attack Jaden. Deshawn waved his hand and the air around him shimmered. Time moved slowly around the demon. Deshawn did this and a sudden pain constricted his chest and brought him to his knees. Blood trickled from his nose.

"What's happening?" Lay asked.

Imani went over to Deshawn. "He's using too much of the spirit."

"No, I'm good." Deshawn said as he painted.

"I have an idea," Romeo shouted as he went to climb a nearby ledge. He climbed along the wall and jumped up on the ledge. "Okay this time Jaden be ready to throw the shock ball back at him. I know how we can get him this time." Romeo yelled below to the others.

Jaden raised his hands and leaned forward. "Ready?" Lay tightened the grip on his spear.

Time became normal around the demon and he spun around the room like a tornado. Sparks came from his feet as he sled into a sudden stop on the ground. All of them stood ready. Asmodeus hurled the shock ball at Jaden's chest. Jaden sent it back towards the demon. Asmodeus stumbled back on impact. The demon shook the attack off and flew straight ahead towards Jaden, Deshawn, and Lay. Just as the demon passed the shadow of the ledge, Romeo jumped on his back.

Asmodeus soared up high as he tried to wrestle Romeo off his back. The demon bucked, twisted, and dove in air trying to through Romeo off of him. Persistent, Romeo rode the monster like a wild and angry bull. He ran his hands along the demon's horn and broke it off. He impaled the demon deep within his chest and the beast stopped mid-air.

Romeo pulled on Asmodeus' wings and gravity pulled them down. They were falling. Romeo shifted his weight on the demon whose wings laid limp as they continued to fall to the earth. Deshawn rippled time, Lay threw the spear of destiny and Jaden levitated Romeo to a safe landing.

"Man you are fool for that. Are you alright?" Deshawn asked as Romeo landed on his feet.

"I was scared for a moment but I'm straight." Romeo sighed.

Time around Asmodeus resumed and he formed a crater once he landed, with his monstrous wings wrapping around his body, and the spear of destiny poking out.

"Now Jaden! Pull the ring off his finger!" Imani beseeched as the demons marched from the Hell gate.

With his palm open, Jaden glanced towards the demon and Solomon's seal jumped into his hand. Suddenly the roar of many footsteps drew their attention back towards the gaping hole in the cavern. Asmodeus' army continued to flock out of the tunnels ready for battle. If that wasn't bad enough the demon's wings flapped again as the demon struggled back to his feet.

His heart pounded against his chest. There was so much happening around him at the same time. Jaden placed the ring on his finger. And a perfect silence surrounded him. Every demon in the abyss stopped in their tracks, almost in a daze. Jaden scanned around the darkness, and all the demons bowed down to him. All along the cavern, demons, vampires, and monsters bended knee and bowed head.

Deshawn gasped, "Now this is some crazy."

Romeo picked up Jaden's sword. "This is your shot man. Kill him. Kill the demon. Do it for your mother."

Jaden caught the sword and crept up to the demon who too was bowing down to him. Jaden prepared to swing.

"Wait," Asmodeus pleaded in a light rasp.

Jaden kept his sword drawn back.

Asmodeus clutched at his chest. "Think about this kid. You don't want to kill me. I can help you like I did

Solomon."

Jaden listened further, strangely intrigued by what the demon offered.

"I can give you the world. Me and my army. I helped Solomon build a kingdom. I can help you build a nation, or I can just give you what you want the most." The demon pointed to the left and an ethereal ghost image of Jaden's mother appeared. "I can reunite you with your mother."

"Don't listen to him!" Imani warned.

Again Jaden drew his sword back.

"I can bring her back," the demon slurred.

Jaden paused again. For a moment he wondered if it were true. Could it be done? Was it possible? He looked over at the swirling ghost image his mother's face. Jaden could smell her perfume, and almost feel her warm loving arms wrapped around him. Just seeing her made him want to collapse into tears.

Imani walked closer by his side, "Don't give into him."

Jaden looked at Imani. Again he drew back his sword.

Imani held his hand back, "And don't kill him. I know you might not care for the evil inside. But that's still a person Asmodeus is possessing. And you can save him. If you kill the demon, you could send the boys soul to hell with him. Exorcise the demon out."

"But what if he comes back?" Jaden questioned as he let his sword fall below his waist.

"Don't worry about that. You're covered by the

creator. Anointed and protected. Your duty as anointed warrior is to smite but not at the cost of saving a soul. Send the demon back to hell and let me save the boy's life while I can."

A sudden idea came to Jaden. Focusing on the evil spirit he blasted the demon with a mental projectile. The demon shook and roared as black serpents came slithering out of his mouth. Serpents coiled into a ball and formed a giant bat. Jaden remembered this as the true form of the demon. He lifted the sword and stabbed the creature. With a sharp cry, the bat sizzled and erupted into flames. He had vanquished the demon. Once the demon crumbled to dust, the hell gate went dark and grey, it snapped on itself and closed doors.

Romeo went over to Tyler's body. With the demon expelled, his body snapped back to its former appearance. Romeo ran a hand across Tyler's neck. His flesh was cold and rigid. "He's dead." Romeo said in disbelief.

Lay sighed. "At least his soul will be at peace."

Imani touched Jaden's shoulder. "You did it. You vanquished him."

He wrapped her arms around her.

"Mission accomplished." Lay said. Then he went over and wrapped his arms around the both of them. Romeo rolled his eyes and joined the group.

A sudden thought came to Deshawn as he glanced down at his watch. "Oh snap! Normally I'm down for the group but we might want to get out of here. I set the bomb to go off like thirty minutes ago."

"Do you know how much time we have left?" Lay asked.

Deshawn checked his watch, "Six minutes?"

"Let's get out of here!" Romeo shouted as he grabbed Tyler and Lay pulled out the tablet to lead the way.

"What about the other people? Can I save them? Can I exorcise all of the demons out of them?" Jaden asked as he glanced back to the demonic agents who was still trying to make their way out of the factory to attack them.

"No time," Imani squealed. "You did the best you can do by saving Tyler but you need to live to fight another day."

Jaden wrapped his arms around Imani.

Coach Franklin and Michael ran in.

"Coach I don't think we will have time to escape" Lay exclaimed.

Michael stretched out their wings and in a blast of light they materialized in front of the black Hummer, the caves collapsed within from the explosion.

Ms. Day ran towards the group. "Thank God I didn't think you were going to make it." She took Lay in her arms and cradled his head to her chest. "Is everyone all right."

She raked her gaze around the group and heads nodded behind her back.

"It depends what you mean by alright," Deshawn said. "I'm pretty sure I crapped my pants."

Imani nudged him by the shoulder. "Deshawn." Then she flinched and ran her hand near the stab wound.

Jaden cradled her hand. "Are you alright?"

Imani nodded. "I'll should be fine. I can heal now that I'm away from the hell gate."

Jaden took her into his arms and clung onto her like he didn't want to let go.

Coach Franklin touched Ms. Day's shoulder. "Did you get all of the innocents out?"

"Of course. I believe they directed all of their forces towards you. The caves were empty on our way out. They are people still making their way to the road."

"That's good." Coach franklin said as he sighed. A tear swelled in his eyes. "I can't believe we made it out alive. All of us." He slapped Romeo's shoulder. "Your father would be so proud of you. I'm proud of you all."

Michael strode forth. "As you should be. You were all brave and brought praise to the creator's name." Then he caressed Imani's shoulder. "Especially you Imani. You have shown a pure faith in the face of evil. I believe you will make an excellent member of SMITE and I will make it my duty to train you myself."

Imani let out of a squeal of joy. She started to jump but the pain in her side reminded her of the wound.

Jaden looked down at the ring. It glistened in his hand. He walked over to Michael. "You should take this back and make sure it never ends up down here again."

Michael turned his golden gaze to Jaden. "Thank you." He took the ring and it melted in the palm of his hands. Then his gaze softened towards Jaden. "I know you are still made at me. But I just want to say that I'm glad I saw before you got to saw yourself."

Jaden frowned. "What?"

Michael ascended back to the heavens in a swarm of golden light, leaving Jaden with the question on his tongue.

Chapter Thirty-Eight

Benediction

The Saturday sun shone down through Jaden's room and the world to them seemed like such a great place to be. They vanquished Asmodeus and his armies were blown back with him. Dozens of innocent people were saved and along with them the entire city, and maybe even the world. The saint squad celebrated their victory over the forces of evil just as any regular teenage boys would celebrate any victory, with cartoons and cereal on a Saturday morning.

"So what are you saying homie. You don't want to go to the mall and talk to some girls?" Deshawn asked as he stuffed his face with a spoonful of fruit loops.

Jaden shrugged, "I wish but I'm grounded, for life. My dad is still furious with me, but he's happy I'm home. Plus, I have to pack. I'm leaving for L.A tonight."

"So you're going to visit your mom after all?" Lay asked.

"Yep. I figure I'd put some fresh flowers on her grave and say a proper goodbye," Jaden said as he tossed two more pairs of jeans into his suitcase.

"That's good," Imani said as she watched the newscast coverage of the collapsed caves.

Deshawn laid back on the bed and tossed more chips in his mouth as he watched the T.V. "I can't believe we just blew up a cave full of demons. As if I don't have enough on my record."

"I know right." Jaden added. Romeo fidgeted on his phone. "The only bad thing is that I'm mad we missed you playing in last night's game."

Romeo sucked his teeth, "Yeah that sucks. It's okay though... the coach benched me but I know I'll be playing soon."

"Well look at it like this," Deshawn said. "If you get cut off the team. You will have more time to hunt demons with the homies," he said with his voice dripped in sarcasm.

Romeo cackled sarcastically. "And have a good ole time huh? After last night I don't want to see another vampire, demon, or anything else that wants to eat me in a while."

Deshawn swallowed two more big spoonful, "Well after that I doubt we will even see another demon for the next few months. Hell they probably know that the redeemers mean business and the Anointed are about to run this town."

"I hope so," Romeo said with a sigh.

Imani turned the tv off. "I'm about to use the

bathroom."

Everyone else nodded but Jaden followed behind her. He closed his bedroom door. "Imani," Jaden called.

Imani looked over. "What's up."

Jaden took a deep breath. "I wanted to talk about us."

"Jaden," She pleaded with a heavy breath. "I think we should just be friends. You know how much I care for you but I wouldn't want….it would just be completed."

Jaden crumbled on the inside. "I was just going to say the same thing." He lied. "Well can a friend get a hug?" He asked with his arms outstretched.

Imani smiled. Then she fell into his arms.

"Jaden…Imani come quick!" Lay's voice cried.

Jaden ran into the room. A massive force slammed Romeo against the bed, His arms and legs were pinned almost by an invisible might pressing against him.

Imani rushed over to Romeo, whose eyes were a milky white and were twitching. "Romeo….Romeo what's going on?" he cried.

Deshawn jumped up and the sudden movement sent the bowl of cereal on his lap on the floor. He started shaking Romeo, "Come on Romeo, speak to me big dog."

Romeo laid there, eyes milky white and twitching as he received revelation. He was having vision. A powerful vision. It was not of something that was going to happen but it was a vision of something happening right then and there as they sat safely in Jaden's room.

****

Caution tape covered the remains of the collapsed cave. The news reporters and camera crew were packing up and leaving after coverage of the accident. Stones and rubble was all that was left of the abyss. Smoke still covered the area even after firefighters put out all the embers of the fire late last night. Cutting through the smoke was a female figure dressed in a short fiery red cocktail dress. Eva sashayed through the stones, and into the depths of the abyss. Her eyes darted all around the rubble. She was looking for something. Smoke was still rising and falling everywhere making it almost impossible to see but she didn't need to see it because she could sense it. Her eyes turned milky white and in a vision she determined the location of the item she so desperately needed. Her treasure was buried under rubble. She scurried across the lot with her heels making loud clacks as she made her way over. With a whirl of her hand she moved the rubble with her power. -She bent down and picked up a bloody and broken horn. She smiled. Eva made her way back into the pulpit. The cross which Imani hanged from laid on the floor half burned. Blood was still on it. The demon had all she needed right then and there.

Eva gazed down at Asmodeus' broken horn as she held it in her hand. "Sorry love nothing personal. It had to be you. And it had to be like this." she said as is speaking to Asmodeus herself.

Eva positioned herself over the cross and started chanting. A thunderous clap erupted as the Hell gate reopened. Eva was pleased. Evil spirits clawed, kicked, and screamed as they helplessly drifted into the abyss of the Hell gate. Emerald lights flickered in the monstrous eyes of Eva as she watched it like a roaring fire. "And now I can bring all the big boys to the party."

Eva needed a more powerful demon to open the Hell gate. Once Asmodeus was gone she could still remotely access the gate to hell just as long as she had a piece of the powerful demon and blood of an angel. Now she had the power to bring a few of her friends back from hell and summon low level demons to make her own army.

In a burst of a flame, a man dressed in a magnificent blue suit appeared.

Eva nodded, "Mr. Chairman. What do you think?"

The chairman looked down at his human hands. "It will do for now."

She smiled as her horns twisted out. "And the Hell gate."

The chairman nodded. "We can rebuild."

The Anointed will return in

BOOK OF THE WEEPING PROPHET

Turn the page for an exclusive sneak peek from **SMITE** featuring Archangel Gabriel
The first book in J.Moon's Legend of the Archangel series

SMITE

Gabe placed a hand on the hilt of his sword, as the doors of the elevator parted. The archangel was on high alert, his whole body tight and vibrating. Gabe raised Lucy and parted the door as silently as he could. They all leaned out, staring. Together they walked out to the main floor of the factory. Graveyard silence all around. Within a few paces, the SMITE matrix sent Gabe warnings, each more frantic than the previous one.

Shanice looked out, "Where is everyone?"

"All the workers," Josephine added.

"It's like they all vanished," Langston finished.

White light crackled in front of them and the air shimmered all around. League cyborgs appeared in the main entrance and surrounded them. A man dressed in a magnificent cream suit strutted towards them. And they instantly knew they were about to be introduced to the mysterious benefactor Mr. Lynch.

Gabriel buttoned his jacket. "Mr. Lynch I presume," he said all proper.

"Don't be formal with me archangel. Call me Legion." Legion's cold eyes buried deep into the face of Gabe as he stood surrounded by grunts on the floor, and elite cyborgs in the rafters who aimed their sniper rifles to the archangel's chest.

Gabe grinned, "Look at you all back together again. Humpty Dumpty. Ain't that precious."

"Back and better," Legion declared. His voice a raspy melody of gloom. "We have been tracking you archangel. And now you are within the almighty grasp of the League."

Gabe took a step forward, confidently. "Yeah about that, me and my posse here just wanted to take a tour of the factory. Got to say we didn't like what we saw. Gift shop sucks, and it's way too expensive. I think we will leave now." Gabe chuckled. "And if you know what's good for you, then you will mosey on out of our way."

Legion set his jaw hard. "The League will not be threatened. You cannot destroy us."

Gabe raised a brow, "Did you forget about Jerusalem?"

"We do not forget. You were only able to scatter us. Now we have formed a hive of cybernetic minds. A League that is all powerful. I see no savior or no Anointed with you. You cannot banish us." Legion declared with his arms spread wide.

Gabe pulled out his fiery sword and whipped it around his head. The deadly glint of the blade reflected into the light. "But I can still harm you. Rip you all piece by piece." Gabe held Lucy so firmly that the blade quivered in hands.

Legion looked from the side of his head. "No. Archangel you will not risk the lives of the humans."

Gabe looked over his shoulder and was brought back

from his battle stance.

"And that is your weakness. Give us the girl before we annihilate the others." As soon as the threat left his lips, there was the click and sounds of weapons aimed at the group of humans.

"Trust me.... that's something you don't want to do," Gabe threatened. "While they are protected under the covenant of the Creator, you will not harm a single hair on their heads. If so...I will bring down his holy wrath upon you."

Legion snarled maliciously. He had the archangel right where he wanted him. If Gabe was alone, he would take on Legion and his cyborgs. But he couldn't. Not without risking the lives of the others. Their only chance was to escape. And if they were to escape, he had to think quick. He scanned around the room. There had to be a way to overcome this situation. His faith had always served him. Gabe had to keep talking to distract the demon. To buy time to escape.

"So why do you need her? Shanice that is?"

"She is required."

"Required for?" Gabe echoed with his hands flailing

"She is simply required."

Shanice took a step out of the pack. "Let's not play games tin man. Why do you need me? What do I have that you could possibly want? I'm just an around the way girl from Brooklyn."

Gabe cracked a smile. He spotted an exit to the tunnels just behind them. Still, he kept the conversation going. "C'mon Ms. Ebony don't say that. You're quite remarkable if I say so myself."

"The league has no need for remarkable or regular. Shanice Ebony is simply required."

Gabe's face became stone cold. "Assess," he murmured.

"There are six grunts on the floor, three Elite armed with sniper rifles in the rafters, and two enforcers. Probability of attack success without casualties.... ten percent." The SMITE matrix analyzed.

Gabe rolled his eyes. Thanks for nothing, he thought to himself. He looked back at Legion. "And what about the black men you've been kidnapping? Is this where you've been taking them. Is this how you built your army?"

"Yes."

Gabe was surprised at how candid the demon was. "Why them... Black men?" He strode forward, his forehead wrinkled. "Why travel all the way to 1926 to do this?"

"There is a power in the souls of the oppressed Archangel... that is stronger in this time. And that power is valuable to the League."

Gabriel rubbed his chin. "Well that is very interesting. I'm not sure what that means. But it is coming to a stop. So if you have any of them here... alive...they will be coming with me as well."

"Archangel we grow weary of your talk and banter. Hand over the girl or you will be annihilated." Legion stated with an emphasis on will.

A plan came together in the archangel's mind. Gabe thought if he could use the smartwatch to manipulate the lights, drop a smoke matrix to distract the snipers, then he just might be able to guide the group to safety. It would be close to impossible. But the angels don't believe in the impossible they believe in the strength of their creator. And if he was going to do it, then his timing had to be precise.

Gabe gnarled. "Like I said before. Harm one hair on her head and I will bring vengeance upon you in the name of the Lord."

"Grab her," Legion commanded.

As the grunts lurched into life, coming towards them, Gabe tapped his smartwatch. A cone of light shone up from the watch and the lights flickered off. There was no time to waste. With a flick of his risk he summoned his shield to block the shots of the elite snipers. The bullets reflected, and the sound was like pellets hitting tin. In his right hand he materialized his Halo and flung it high into the ceilings. It shattered the barrels of the sniper rifles above.

"Run!" Gabe shouted as he grabbed those behind him.

With a twitch the lights came back on and he was able to find the exit. "Head to the tunnels" Gabe shouted as he pointed to the right.

Bullets of light fired at them. Gabe rose his shield and protected the group from behind. Once the last person went out the door, he scurried behind. They ran at a furious pace, the archangel hauling the terrified

Josephine Baker in his arms through the dark tunnels of the factory, while Shanice and Langston sprinted ahead. He used the cone of light from his smartwatch as a torch.

Amidst the hissing and dripping of the pipes in the tunnels, the League grunts were waiting for them further down the long stretch. Bullets whizzed at their heads from the top of the pipeline. There was a cut in the pathway to the left. Gabe pushed them over as the grunts continued fire.

With his chest heaving, he leaned against the wall. He needed to know what he was dealing with so he took a quick look around the corner. The League were readying an attack with tight military precision. Various squads formed up in their battle order- first grunts took cover with assault rifles, then strikers were already moving in with Katana blades aimed, And the enforcers hung back. Getting out of the tunnel and to the Ark will be a hell of a battle.

Gabe looked over at Shanice. She still had the battle rifle in her hands.

"Give me that," Gabe commanded.

He checked the ammo. Once he saw there was only half a clip, he wanted to curse.

"Gabe what do you need us to do?" Langston asked in despair.

"We will make it. But to do that we need to be tight. I'm going to punch a hole through their battle line. Each time I do... you all need to find a place to cover. We need to keep a steady rhythm. From when I fire to when we move." He cocked the rifle, then looked over. "Got it?"

"Got it," Shanice parroted.

Leaning against the wall, the archangel paused for a moment. Under the cover of the wall, he measured inches and angles, as he thought of a strategy. First, he'll target the strikers. They will be on them in any moment. After taking them out he will push. Gabe knew he could easily dodge the energy bolts from the enforcers so he would eliminate the grunts next and smite the enforcers last. Excellent he thought to himself. The archangels train to be tougher than any soldier, spy, or mercenary. Gabriel had an entire millennium of battle experience. It was the archangel's nature as supreme warriors to control all battlefields.

With a grunt he rolled out of cover and unleashed the barrel onto the three strikers charging at him. The bullets flew across the tunnel and they fell like dominoes.

"Go!" Gabe shouted as he brought his shield up.

Together the humans shuffled behind the archangel as he raised his shield. Gunfire and screams echoed in the shadows as Gabe's shield was pummeled by bullets and bolts of dark energy. They made it a few inches and Gabe could hear the crackling of his shield. Luckily there was another cover spot to his left.

"To cover!" he commanded.

Amidst screaming and gunshots, the group dove to the left. And just as Josephine hopped over to cover, Gabriel's shield broke to pieces like shattered glass. Again he raised the assault rifle and unleashed. He managed to successful take out two grunts on the right.

Steam hissed from the weapon. It was overheated. No Bueno he thought to himself. Gabe pulled out his eagle eye hand gun and rolled into cover.

Gabe winced as he felt a searing pain on his right shoulder. He looked down and saw plumes of smoke. One of the enforcers got him with a shot on his right shoulder.

"Oh dear God," Josephine cried as she touched the archangel's scorched shoulder, with steam still wafting from the wound.

"Don't worry I'll heal." Gabe stammered.

Langston shook his head. "Gabe we have to stop this madness. Surely we won't be able to make it."

"Yes we will. Have a little faith." Shanice spoke. And in that moment she was inspired to do something either very clever or stupid. "We just need a distraction. To give Gabe the opportunity to take them all out."

Shanice looked over and saw another nook to the right. Without a second thought, she darted across and gunshots followed behind her. Both Josephine and Langston screamed loudly.

"Shanice are you alright?" Langston asked from cover.

"Fine!" She shouted back.

"You crazy girl... what are you doing?" Gabe roared from around the cover of the wall.

"I'm going to give you the perfect opportunity. Don't miss archangel." She called back.

From the nook she raised her hands. "Don't shoot!"

she cried out to the League collective.

And she came out of the cover with her hands raised. "We give up. I'm turning myself over to the League." Shanice said as she walked forward.

Josephine leaned around the corner. "Has she gone mad?"

Gabe smiled. "No, she is being clever." He leaned around corner and commanded the smartwatch to help. "Assess"

"Three armed grunts and two half charged enforcers remained. SMITE matrix estimates a forty-five second clearance with aid of sharp shooting matrix and remaining clip."

Gabe turned to Langston and Josephine. "I'm going to get us out of here. Don't move until they are all dead."

"Well good luck and God speed," Langston stammered.

With the sharp shooter matrix activated, Gabe's sight was acutely focused and his accuracy to complete a headshot was enhanced. "Shanice duck!" he shouted.

Shanice hit the floor and soon after bullets flew above her. From behind the cover the Archangel shot the grunt crouched in the left cover then he aimed, and sent a bullet through the skull of the enforcer who already had a charged energy bolt. Bullets came his away, to the floor he rolled, and a split second he popped back up. His eyes narrowed towards the head of the other enforcer, a bullet was sent through it. Bullets came at him, he sidestepped and took out the remaining grunts. The Archangel looked down at the bodies keeled over at his feet.

"Danger cleared." The SMITE matrix declared.

Gabe looked over his shoulder, "Everybody all right?"

Langston and Josephine peaked around the corner and nodded. Shanice patted herself for gunshot wounds. Once she found none she gave a thumbs up.

"Let's roll." The archangel commanded.

Acknowledgments

Thank you to everyone who bought and read this book. It has been a long journey for me. I have been writing forever. I want to give a big thanks to my parents for believing in me. My dad for teaching me his work ethic and my mom for always telling me to believe in magic. I want to send a big thanks to everyone in my family, especially all of my cousins who didn't make me feel like an only child. Special thanks to Bridget and Peaches for always being my biggest supporters. I have to thank my sister April Christina Cook for everything, I don't want to get too mushy but you know you're like my right hand. I also want to give thanks to my other pea in the pod, Dr. Teneshia McIntyre. Thank you for providing your insight on depression in teens.

Shout out to all my Howard University family. Shout out to all my WHI coworkers. Remember to racks those racks and scan those vials. I want to give another big shout out to my shady goat best friend Trey. Whenever I called to talk to him about foolishness, he reminded me I had a book to finish. I want to say what's up to DC3. Kelly and Michelle I love yawl and I absolutely could not be where I am without you guys. Last but not least, thank you to all my precious Moonies. Get excited because Smite will be out before you know it. Then hopefully Conjure, because I always wanted to write a story about bad witches. Then we'll have BOA part two which is tentatively titled Book of the Weeping Prophet.

CPSIA information can be obtained
at www.ICGtesting.com
Printed in the USA
LVHW091933110119
603456LV00001BA/142/P